Gimme Everything You Got

Iva-Marie Palmer

WITHDRAWN

BALZER + BRAY

An Imprint of HarperCollins*Publishers*

Balzer + Bray is an imprint of HarperCollins Publishers.

Gimme Everything You Got
Copyright © 2020 by Iva-Marie Palmer
All rights reserved. Printed in the United States of America.
No part of this book may be used or reproduced in any manner whatsoever
without written permission except in the case of brief quotations embodied in
critical articles and reviews. For information address HarperCollins Children's
Books, a division of HarperCollins Publishers, 195 Broadway, New York, NY
10007.
www.epicreads.com

ISBN 978-0-06-293725-4

Typography by Jenna Stempel-Lobell
20 21 22 23 24   PC/LSCH   10 9 8 7 6 5 4 3 2 1
❖
First Edition

*To me at 17, not sure of anything but trying anyway;
get a load of you now.**

*Possibly less sure, still trying anyway.

One

The first day I ever gave a shit about soccer was September 4, 1979—the day that Mr. McMann showed up at Powell Park High. You know those moments when everything changes almost at once, like some kind of wave rolls over a room and whatever you had been doing gets washed away as it dawns on everyone that something way bigger is taking place? It was like that.

It wasn't even like Bobby McMann turned the tide on a particularly boring day. It had been eventful as hell. There'd been tryouts for *The Sound of Music* in third period. Every girl I knew was bonkers for the movie—the Rialto had brought it back for a special engagement that summer. I'd gone to see it with my best friends, Tina Warner and Candace (sometimes Candy) Trillo, who'd loved it. I was bored. Everyone in it was too nice (except the Nazis, of course).

I hadn't tried out for the play, but Tina and I had gone to watch Candace give it a go. Candace wanted a part because she was forever on boyfriend lookout, and school plays always seemed to yield a few new couples. She'd told me I should have auditioned because I was almost seventeen and no one had ever touched my breasts. They were small and unevenly sized, though the slightly bigger right one had a Farrah Fawcett quality to it. I wasn't opposed to them being touched, but I'd never gone to even one school play starring a guy I'd be eager to have doing the honors. Anyway, despite Candace's spirited performance, Tina and I had our money on Peggy Darnell getting to be Maria because during the auditions, while she was spinning, Julie Andrews–style, her giant, braless, totally symmetrical boobs had busted out of her top, to the delight of our drama teacher.

"Julie Andrews was totally flat in the movie," someone at the end of our cafeteria table was saying. I couldn't see who through the mess of smushed paper bags and trays and girls leaning forward so other girls could help them with their hair. We messed with our hair at lunch a lot, in ways our mothers would say was unsanitary. But our cafeteria was a large gymnasium with long tables rolled out in the center for lunch periods, and the room smelled like sweat and feet, so what was a little hairstyling?

"Doesn't matter—Mr. Doberton is a total perv," I said knowingly, and took a sip of my Yoo-hoo. I practiced my knowing looks in the mirror sometimes, because I liked hiding how little I actually knew. "He's probably writing 'Peggy's jiggly tits' on the cast sheet next to 'Maria' right now."

Our table became a laugh chamber. And it was precisely in the middle of that laughter that Bobby McMann opened the double doors to the cafeteria.

At 12:07 p.m., all concerns about who'd been overshadowed by D-cups became moot.

You know those Coke commercials where you see the bubbles pouring mesmerizingly over ice and the liquid ripples like it's dancing and your mouth gets dry and all you want is a Coke? Even if you've never had a Coke, or you've just had one?

In a way, I'd just had one. Sort of.

Before I tell you any more about Bobby McMann, whose name I didn't even know yet, I should explain. See, sometimes, something will stir me up. On that day, it was the back of Alex Noti's head in fourth-period physics. His neck looked really nice: strong but not too ropy, with his light hair cut in a clean line just below his earlobes. And since he didn't turn around (Alex Noti's face would ruin everything), I imagined his neck was Paul Newman's. *The Long, Hot Summer* Paul Newman. My weird urge was to lick that line of hair. Fantasy Paul Newman did not think I was weird. His skin was warm and he shuddered as he turned around to see me. Then Paul Newman's lips were near mine, not even kissing, just breathing into my mouth like he *wanted* to kiss me, and wanted to get it exactly right. That idea of Paul Newman created this not-bad . . . stirring at my fulcrum (it's a physics word for the thing a lever sits on, but I think it sounds like a nice way to say "crotch"). I crossed my legs and had to fight off getting too carried away. I know from past at-school daydreams that taking it too far means walking around all day feeling like I have an itch I can't scratch.

Boys would call it being horny. Girls would call it the same thing, I think, but not out loud.

It's not something I'd put on a job application or anything, but I don't want to lie: I'm good at getting myself off. When I got my first period—this was back when my parents were still together—my mom told my dad we were going out, just us girls, and she took me for pizza. And at the pizza parlor, she didn't just show me how to use a maxi pad—she also let me have some of her red wine and drew a picture on her napkin of the vagina and told me that I was a woman now and she really wanted me to understand the clitoris, so she circled that part and she even wrote it there in pen. C-L-I-T-O-R-I-S. She told me, "Susan, the men in your life sure aren't going to care about it, so you'd better," and I hadn't realized it but I guess it was an early sign that she and Dad were done. Then she just left it on the table at Vito and Ray's, a vagina napkin. Which, as first periods go, was slightly less embarrassing than bleeding through my pants.

When we got home, she gave me a book called *Our Bodies, Ourselves*, and "clitoris" was right there in the index. So was "masturbation." Not step-by-step instructions, but enough to clarify that those feelings in my fulcrum—feelings I'd felt before, riding a bike or sliding down the banister of my grandma's house in Wisconsin—could lead to something good. So I read between the lines.

And came up with elaborate footnotes.

It's not that my thoughts are that dirty. I daydream about being undressed like one of the heroines in a Rosemary Rogers book, or about Han Solo pushing my hair out of my eyes, or Roy Scheider from *Jaws* squeezing me a fresh lemonade and watching me drink it. The fantasies can be brought on by small aspects of boys I know—like Alex Noti's neck—but whose other aspects take them out of contention as fantasy material. Candace always tells me I need to give more boys in school a chance, get to know them, but honestly, I feel like I know enough about the boys we know: Most of them stink. And even the okay ones are no Han Solo.

If I wasn't so proficient at masturbating, maybe behind-the-scenes groping with some bumbling stagehand would sound more appealing to me. And if I were a boy, I probably wouldn't be so secretive about it. Masturbation and boys went, well, hand in hand. At school, boys had nicknamed stalls in their restrooms the Spankin' Station (first floor), the Beat-Off Box (second floor), and the Jerkin' for Jerkins (a stall in the third-floor bathroom next to the teachers' lounge that got its name because visits there were often inspired by the curvy geometry teacher, Ms. Jerkins). I'd actually tried to masturbate between second and third period once, but I couldn't do it standing up, and lying on the bathroom tile was out of the question. It seemed unfair, in a way, that guys not only could yank their things in almost any position but also had almost-official places to do it right at school. But I guess it's not that different from how boys can just pee against a wall in an alley if they have to, while girls are expected to hold it until the proper time and place.

Anyway. That day, I'd come to lunch fresh off my Alex Noti/ Paul Newman daydream when—*BAM*—this guy, this *man*, this vision in tight nylon shorts appears. I'm not even going to describe him in detail just yet, because I won't do him justice. If I say he was a white guy who had day-old stubble along a cut jaw and hairy, muscular calves, I could just as easily be talking about our plumber, Mr. Mariano. But there he was, in the cafeteria, collapsing the tower of my disparate thoughts—school play, geometry homework, the weekend's parties, the zit I felt growing right under my lip—into one compact and focused mass:

Who is this man?

I downed the rest of my Yoo-hoo in one slug, not knowingly this time. I definitely knew nothing.

"Wow," said Tina. Next to her, Candace said, "Wow," too, but no sound came out of her mouth.

"Who is that?" I watched him stride past tables of girls now agog. Our eyes had to be bugging out of our heads like in a cartoon, because McMann's shorts pressed along the hard line of his inner thigh, leading my gaze—and everyone else's—up, up, up to this hypnotic . . . instrument at *his* fulcrum. With every other step he took, you could see the whole shape of *it*, even if you were nearsighted and your glasses were broken. I crossed my legs, tight.

"I don't know," Franchesa Rotini choked out over a forkful of the, yes, rotini her mom put in her Thermos every Tuesday.

"Maybe a hands-on sex education teacher?" Arlene Swann suggested, a little on the loud side. "If we're lucky."

Walking behind him was the school principal, Mr. Dollard. Compared to the man we were all ogling—whose physique finally helped me understand what "sinew" was, as the tautening of his mesmerized me—Mr. Dollard appeared to be composed of parts this other fellow had cast off for being too average.

But it was Mr. Dollard who stood in the center of the rows of tables and waved his hands so we would all settle down. "Good afternoon, students," he said, and stiffly pointed to the statuesque figure next to him. "This is Robert McMann. He'll be taking on coaching duties for our brand-new girls' soccer team."

Robert McMann nodded and smiled at Mr. Dollard, then at all of us. It wasn't only the girls who were watching him—guys were staring, too, but in a different way, like he was a lesson in something they'd never understand.

"I'll keep this brief," he said.

A female voice said, "I'd love to see your briefs," and a nervous titter of laughter vibrated across the gym.

"I love soccer," he continued. "I love coaching. And I'm looking forward to putting together a team to make the school proud as we join the Powell Park High athletic legacy." When he said "legacy," I couldn't help but glance at the gym ceiling. It was lined with banners for all the boys' sports teams, announcing the last year any of them had had any real glory. Not one of the dates was after 1970.

"Also, you can call me Bobby, or Coach McMann." *Bobby*, I thought, as his name sighed over the length of my body.

"Soccer sucks," a guy cough-muttered.

Once again, if Bobby heard it, it didn't faze him; his mouth ticked up in a half smile that only made him hotter. "We're going to have tryouts tomorrow for any interested young women, and I'll post a sign-up sheet here in the cafeteria. If you show up, I'll have much more to share." He gave a little wave and headed down the rest of the aisle toward the bulletin board.

"Sign. Me. UP," Tina hissed to me and Candace, and we nodded.

"He's a dreamboat," Candace said as Bobby tacked his sign-up sheet between flyers for the Future Business Leaders Club and the Home Economics Bake-Off. "I wonder how long his eyelashes are up close." Leave it to Candace to think about how long his eyelashes were when the whole cafeteria had seen that he was *plenty endowed* elsewhere.

I've known Candace since kindergarten. Since seventh grade, she's been on some kind of diet, and even if she could lose the ten extra pounds she wants to, I think she looks better with them. She hates how she looks in Jordaches (or the copies of Jordaches we can actually afford), but when she wears her older brother Frank's work pants, I think her ass looks really good and I tell her so. She is also totally stacked. Each of her boobs is the size of a softball and has about the same feel as one of those after a few games: firm but with a little give. (Yes, I've felt them. When you've known someone since you were five and one day you notice that, out of nowhere, her backpack straps are framing what can only be called jugs, you ask her if you can touch one.)

"I bet he loves to eat," Candace said, still looking at Bobby McMann, with the same expression she'd give a Nutter Butter after she'd promised herself she'd stop eating them.

"Jesus, Candace, you want to cook for him? I can think of four hundred better ideas."

That was Tina. She transferred to our district from a suburb outside Milwaukee at the end of junior high, not long after her mom remarried. We became friends when we got paired up to dissect a frog in freshman-year bio. She told me later I was the first person she'd met at Powell who didn't kiss her ass or treat her like garbage, which was the most common Powell Park High reaction to someone whose nicer clothes set them apart as having more money than the rest of us. She also told me that she thought I'd be a weirdo because of my red corduroy pants, because Tina can be a snob. (The pants were fine, by the way.) Clothing aside, it turned out that we had a lot in common. We bonded over the ways we'd found to navigate parental divorce, our shared disdain for *Happy Days*, and the fact that she—unlike Candace—agreed with me that most of the boys at our school had a good three years to go before one could even consider them dating material. (Of course, Tina had a long-distance boyfriend in Milwaukee to unfavorably compare them all to, and I had Han Solo.)

"What are the four hundred better ideas?" I asked her, because I loved when Tina got into list-making mode. She'd tick things off on her fingers, all businesslike, and shut you down with a look if you didn't agree with her.

"Drop my books on the ground and wait for him to pick them up. Make him pose like Michelangelo's *David*. Watch him mow the lawn. What do you got, Susan?" Tina raised an eyebrow and flicked my empty Yoo-hoo bottle closer to me with one of her shiny fuchsia nails. (Her nails are always done, because her mom owns a salon, and she says Tina's impeccably neat appearance is like free advertising.)

I probably had four *thousand* ideas, but I was saving them for my poor Holly Hobbie sheets, which had witnessed some very un-Holly-like activity over the years. "Well, after Candace cooks him a nice lasagna—"

"Shut up, men love food!" Candace said.

"—I'd put on a record. Maybe Earth, Wind and Fire, or Peaches and Herb."

"Peter Frampton," Candace said.

Tina shushed her. "He ate your lasagna. This is Susan's turn! She gets to pick the music."

"And then I'd say, 'Do you want to take off your shoes . . . ?'" In my head, I came up with some good stuff, but out loud, my fantasies emerged gangly and awkward. Sort of like how I'd made out extensively with fantasy Eddie Van Halen, but in real life, I'd kissed exactly two boys and both times had been disasters. One of them had moved away the next day, and I'd been relieved.

"What are soccer shoes called, anyway?" Candace asked.

"Who cares? Susan was about to get to the sensual foot rub," Tina said.

"They're cleats."

Without turning around, I knew it was Mr. McMann.

He was standing right behind me. And had probably heard about the foot rub.

"Whuu . . . why? Hi! Hello."

I'm sad to report those were my first words to Bobby. Every girl at the lunch table looked up at him like he was Jesus at the Last Supper, complete with the fact that we were going to be eating him.

"Cleats. You'll need them if you make the team." He looked right at me. "And I'll work you so hard, you'll need all the foot rubs you can get." He sort of saluted us and grinned, with teeth. They were perfect, even this close up. Not stained or crooked or too little for his face. His dark eyes were deep set and ever so slightly hooded beneath his eyelids, which did have the long lashes Candace imagined. His chiseled jaw was balanced by full, almost pretty lips, and his nose was just a bit crooked with the slightest bump in its bridge—it suggested Han Solo danger and adventure, even if I knew he might have broken it just walking into a wall. United, his features told me he was thoughtful and that he knew how to do important things, like read a thick book, change a tire, or kiss prolongedly. He was the first real-life guy who had no visible flaws to disqualify his positive attributes, which didn't stop when he turned around. As he walked off, his shorts hugged his butt like it was a package wrapped by an over-achieving Christmas elf.

"Susan's wriggling in her shorts," Tina said, making me even redder in the face. I picked up one of my greasy cafeteria fries and ate it, trying to look thoughtful about something else besides Mr. McMann's sex walk through the cafeteria. "You should have asked him if you could try out right now. You're dressed for it."

"Oh my God, she is!" Candace said. "It's like you're soul mates!"

"What are you talking about?" I asked them, even though the phrase "soul mate" fizzed in my chest. If Bobby and I were soul mates, that meant we could also have sex, right?

"Your shorts," Candace said. "Aren't those sort of what soccer players wear?"

I looked down at my bare legs. It was the Tuesday after Labor Day, but in Chicago, you clung to summer, which meant wearing as little as possible for as long as possible. My shorts were the same elastic-band nylon shorts that I'd worn every other day since the eighth grade. Not the same exact pair; I had three pairs from Sportmart—one red, one blue, one green—each with white piping around the legs. I didn't wear them because I played sports. I first bought them because they were cheap and I could pull them on over my swimsuit to ride to the Powell Park pool.

Then, this summer, I realized maybe the shorts meant something bigger. Like that I was a feminist. Not one who didn't shave her armpits, but a sexy one. In this other book my mom gave me, *Fear of Flying*, the main character talks about a "zipless fuck." (I didn't read the whole book, and I wondered if my mom had before she gave it to me.) It was supposed to be a sexual encounter with no strings attached. It sounded simple compared to how Candace was always upset about a guy who ditched her, or how Tina pined for her long-distance boyfriend. Simple, like the shorts. Not that I'd know what to do if some guy suggested we try some no-strings sex, but it was easier for me to imagine the sex part of being with a boy than the part where you felt some kind of deep soul connection, or whatever happened when people talked about falling in love.

(Also, not for nothing, but early this summer, I was wheeling my bike down our alley 'cause the chain had fallen off, and I heard Jeff Sipowitz, who has the best hair in the eleventh grade but terrible acne, say to my neighbor Dave Kazlov, "Boing!" I didn't know what he meant, but later Dave told me that Jeff thought I had a nice ass and "boing!" was what I did to his dick. And I sort of liked hearing that, even if Jeff is gross. So, okay, feminism is more complicated than my elastic-band shorts.)

But after three years at a high school where every boy—even the ones who seemed worth a crush for a minute—proved to be a letdown, maybe I could allow myself a crush on Bobby McMann, teacher or not. I'd have to allow it, since my mind was already picturing us grabbing one another by our matching waistbands. More realistically, I wondered when and how I'd see Bobby again.

And that's how this whole thing started.

Two

I'd read a horror story once in some weird magazine one of my older sister's boyfriends had left at our house about this town where a mysterious orb showed up and all the women became bold and sex-crazed. I think about that story a lot because it seemed to be saying that all my fantasies were weird somehow, like they needed to be connected to some demonic orb. But I didn't care—Bobby McMann was my orb.

But, within a few hours, I realized he was having the same effect on every girl at Powell Park. The last time there'd been this much commotion over a guy was freshman year, when someone brought in an issue of *Cosmo* from, like, five years before in which Burt Reynolds was lying completely naked on a bearskin rug, with his arm casually draped between his legs, over his fulcrum. But Bobby wasn't a photo, available to anyone who got their hands on that issue of *Cosmo*. He was Powell Park's own resident hunk, like a gift specially for the girls at our school, maybe to make up for all the things we didn't have, like attractive guys, flattering restroom lighting, and gym uniforms that didn't give you a rash. Even the maxi pad dispensers in the bathroom still sold the ancient "sanitary napkins" that you had to wear with a belt.

We were in last-period Kitchen Arts, which was like extra home ec for people who wanted to focus on eating cake batter. Our teacher was Miss Cuddleton, a sweet-faced round lady with a squeaky cartoonish voice. We called her Miss Cuddle and abused her very limited authority so we could gossip in class.

We were supposed to be making lemon pie. We only had to make the curd filling. Because it was the start of the school year and we were still kitchen losers, not artists, Miss Cuddle had made all the crusts. "If you really love the people you're feeding, you don't buy store-bought crust," Miss Cuddle had said. Candace had nodded the same way she did when a priest said, "And Christ died for your sins."

I was standing at one of the Formica counters next to a pile of lemons Miss Cuddle had made into a neat pyramid. Dana Miller and I were doing a sloppy job grating lemon peel while Candace waited to add it to the curd mixture she had on the stove. Tina was measuring out sugar.

Dana was this kiss-up sophomore who said she wanted to be a school principal even though no one started out actually wanting to be a principal. She worked as a student aide to Assistant Principal Lawler, who she sometimes called by her first name, Theresa. Dana's family and mine intersected. My uncle's brother-in-law was her uncle, and even though this meant nothing—it wasn't like she showed up at my family functions or vice versa—she always acted like it did. Thus, she'd immediately paired up with me in Kitchen Arts. At least today it was turning out to be useful. She'd dug through a few files and found out that Mr. McMann had graduated from Southern Illinois University, where he'd been a soccer player, and that he would be teaching freshman algebra.

"I heard one of the office managers call him a 'Title IX hire'—you know, that legal thing where they have to have sports teams for girls—and I bet he's only coaching girls' soccer because he couldn't get a boys' sport," Dana was saying, loud enough that people a few stations over could hear her. She was on the tall side, but she always bent forward at the waist when she talked to people, like she wanted to be shorter. Meanwhile, I was short and always had to draw myself up taller when I talked. Maybe the only way to be happy with how you looked was to never look at anyone else.

"If he was a soccer player, maybe he really wanted to start a team," Tina interrupted her. "We don't know what's inside his head."

"I just want to know what's inside his pants," a sophomore at the next cooking station interjected.

"We all saw THAT," Candace said, holding a rolling pin in front of her pelvis and waving it suggestively.

"And thank God it's not shaped like a rolling pin." I corrected her penis shape comparison by picking up a banana from one of the fruit bowls arranged by a previous class.

Dana cleared her throat and I tried not to roll my eyes.

"Anyway, he was a last-minute hire," she told us. "If you remember, we were supposed to have a girls' basketball team. But resources didn't permit it." She even sounded like a principal. I wondered if she practiced.

"Oh yeah, because of the gym," Tina said, referring to the

spare gymnasium at the back of the school that had been closed off at the end of last school year when a huge chunk of the ceiling had fallen in.

"Why soccer? Who would a team even play?" I asked, more out of concern that Coach McMann would be taken from us before we even got to know him. I didn't pay much attention to sports—I'd only go to football or basketball games when Candace dragged me—but I still knew none of the other high schools around here had a girls' soccer team. Even boys' soccer was limited to the private schools. Guys at our high school acted like it was girly to play soccer, and the joke was that the guys who played it only did because they hadn't made the football team.

Of course, Dana looked ready to answer my question, but Candace cut her off.

"Who cares?" she said, swiping her finger near her lip, where a dot of powdered sugar clung. "Tell us more personal details."

Dana continued authoritatively, like she was already in charge of Bobby's fan club. "His birthday's November seventh. Scorpio." You could tell by the way she said it, she was compatible with Scorpios. But so was I, as an Aries. "He drives a 1973 Datsun," she continued, "the blue-gray one in parking spot twenty-seven. This is his first teaching job."

"Oh my God, are you guys going to camp out by his car or something?" Tina shook her head. "The poor guy. He only wanted to shape minds."

"He is shaping minds," I told her. "Dirty ones."

Dana pursed her lips tight, like my impertinence was the same as if I'd suggested peeing in the lemon curd. "He's never been married. And he lives on Mansfield, probably in one of the duplexes near Rocket Slide Park."

"And what are his turn-ons and turn-offs?" I said, getting a laugh from Tina and Candace and another look from Dana. I gave my lemon one last run across the grater and filed away all the information Dana had offered like it was answers for a test I'd be having soon.

"Do you think you're going to try out?" Tina said, mostly to me and Candace.

"I don't know," I said. I hadn't known I'd even been considering it before she asked, but I realized in that moment that I'd made a mental note of the place and time for tryouts the next day when I had passed the sign-up sheet on the way out of the cafeteria. "Are you?"

Tina nodded with certainty. "I want to," she said. "It might be fun." I could imagine Tina on a team. She was good at everything she tried, which we teased her about. She claimed she did well in school and joined extracurriculars because it made her parents happy—Tina's mom kept a stack of college brochures on the coffee table—but I knew she kind of loved that her house was a shrine to her accomplishments.

"I was thinking it could be good exercise," Candace said. "And maybe we'd bump into the boys' teams if we practice after school?"

"Yearbook doesn't really get going until winter, and I don't have a fall activity," Dana said.

"But none of us know anything about soccer," I said.

"Who does?" Candace waved the whisk, sending a spray of lemon curd toward me. "I'm sure no one."

"But why not tennis, or swimming? Why soccer?" I couldn't imagine a world where I'd make the team, much less one where I'd want to practice every day after school. But if my friends could see themselves doing it, did I want to be the one left behind? Plus, getting to look at Mr. McMann in his shorts every day might be worth faking an interest in a sport.

"You guys, the curd's going to burn," Candace said, now stirring furiously. The other teams of girls were already assembling their pies, while our curd smelled like toast on fire.

Miss Cuddle padded over to our station and tilted her head. She looked like Mrs. Claus's cousin with her short copper curls and soft gaze. "Good work, girls," she said, clearly not noticing or at least not caring that our work was anything but good.

When the bell rang, Tina offered me a ride home but I turned it down, saying I needed a couple books from the library. As the halls emptied, I made my way to the cafeteria.

I stood in front of the soccer tryout sheet Coach McMann had tacked up. There were a few names on it, but most of the lines were cluttered with guys' handwriting and rude fake names, including a couple for Coach McMann: *Booby McMann. Bobby McNads.*

My stomach growled noisily. Our team's lemon pie had been mostly inedible after the curd had turned brown and stuck to the bottom of the pan. I eyeballed the blank line where I could write my name.

No. I would sleep on it.

"Need a pen?"

I recognized his voice instantly. How had he snuck up on me twice today?

I spun around and was looking right at Coach McMann. *Bobby*.

I gulped. "Um, no," I said.

His grin faltered. He held up a palm, like he was apologizing for bumping into me, and said, "Oh, I'm sorry, I thought you might be thinking about trying out."

"I am," I stammered. "I mean, I'm going to."

This got a smile. A smile that made me sure I was going to try out.

"Oh, good," he said. He peered at the sheet. "Do you think Jimmy Carter's Balding Ballsack knows this is a girls' team?"

I laughed and involuntarily reached to flip my hair over my shoulder, a gesture I'd only ever been inspired to use in my daydreams. "Don't worry, I know a few girls showing up tomorrow who aren't on the list. I bet there will be a lot of us."

That smile again. "Good to know. Maybe the sign-up sheet is silly," he said. He pulled the paper from the bulletin board. "I'm looking forward to seeing you tomorrow . . . um . . ."

"Susan," I said. "Susan Klintock."

"Susan, I'll see you tomorrow."

On my walk home, I was able to make my stomach flip over and over just by thinking about my name spoken in Bobby's voice.

Susan, I'll see you tomorrow.

My mom's car was in the driveway, and I walked into the house with the same feeling I got when I broke curfew. Like my mom would smell the lust on me and be disappointed that I was so interested in a man. For all her concern about me knowing what the clitoris was, she mostly read self-help books with titles like *How to Be Your Own Best Friend* and said she wanted to find her whole self before she committed to anyone else again.

Even though Dad paid alimony and child support, Mom worked at a real estate title company as a file clerk in charge of all the documents or whatever from home sales. She wanted a job downtown as a title assistant for commercial real estate deals or something excruciatingly boring like that, and she was taking a bunch of dull classes at the community college to build her résumé. While Dad dated, Mom buried her head in textbooks. She almost never went out at night except if the college had a guest speaker she wanted to see. She had mostly stopped cooking except for casseroles she'd make on the weekend to last us through the week. She didn't even have time to watch *Charlie's Angels* with me these days.

She'd put men on the back burner, or on ice completely, and she almost never asked me about boys, either. It was like she thought our period talk and the anatomy lesson were all I needed. Not that I was complaining, necessarily. It's not like I would have much to say if she did ask.

I went into the kitchen and saw Mom's friend Jacqueline there, wearing a shiny gold blouse with a deep-cut neckline that showed off the big gold Capricorn medallion that hung to her breasts. Her hair was curled in glossy rolls away from her face, where her eyes were smothered beneath glistening purple eyeshadow. Mom's textbooks were open and scattered across the kitchen table, along with what looked like the contents of Jacqueline's makeup bag.

"Dierdre, I'm not saying you shouldn't go to school. I'm just saying you shouldn't go to school like *that*." On the word "that," Jacqueline gestured to what seemed like Mom's whole body and every life experience and choice she'd ever made while living inside it.

"Jackie, I'm not going to school to catch a man," Mom said. "I'm going to catch a better job and more self-sufficiency. I'm working on *me*." She said this like she had to remind herself of these things, not just Jacqueline.

Jacqueline looked up and saw me, and her face dropped before breaking into a fake smile. I'd once heard her say to my mom how she'd give anything to have been born later because the "young girls are going to get to have all the fun now that everything is changing." I wasn't so sure about that, because I didn't really know what things had been like before, or if I was having any fun, but regardless, she didn't seem to like me.

"Susan, tell your mom a little lipstick wouldn't kill her."

"If it's poisoned it could," I said, grabbing the can of Cheez Balls off the counter and popping three into my mouth at once, which seemed to disgust Jacqueline.

"What happened at school today?" Mom asked, looking up briefly from her math book.

"We're getting a soccer team. I'm going to try out." If she asked more, I decided, I'd tell her about Bobby. Not *all* about Bobby, but I'd say, "Coach McMann seems nice." Just so his name could float around our house.

Mom nodded. "Hmm, sounds interesting," she said, but nothing else. I thought she'd be impressed, since I never went out for things. Tina's mom had probably already started deciding where Tina's trophies would go.

"Soccer?" Jacqueline said, and poured white wine into one of my mom's Snoopy coffee mugs. (Mom had let Dad take the wineglasses.) The wine, Jacqueline had probably brought over. Mom didn't drink all that often. "I know someone who played once. Such a rough sport. But you're built for it."

I ignored what had to be an insult as Mom said, "You'll have to tell me how it goes, honey." She scratched some numbers out on a legal pad next to her and frowned, then looked up like she'd remembered something important. "You left your light on while you were at school. The power bill doesn't pay itself."

"Let Albert pay it," Jacqueline said, at the same time I said, "Doesn't Dad pay for that?" The tiniest flicker of irritation crossed my mom's face, and I wondered why she couldn't be maybe a *little bit* like Jacqueline. Mom's quest to prove she didn't need help from anyone meant that instead of me being the girl who got to live with a Fun Divorced Mom who took her out for manicures and clothes shopping, I got stuck with *my* mom, who wanted to be practical and intellectual.

Maybe she felt stuck with me, too. It would be easier for her to work on herself if she were *by* herself.

I was about to head to my room, Cheez Balls in hand, when my mom pointed a finger in the air, as if spearing a thought before it got away. "Oh, and your dad called. He said he'd love to have you over on Sunday."

"Will Polly be there?" I asked. Polly was my dad's girlfriend, the only person he'd dated whose name I had learned and whose age was at least midway between mine and my mother's instead of closer to mine.

"Yes, she's cooking. Probably something fabulous, knowing her." Mom never said much about Polly, not really, except that Polly was "everything I am not." She took off her reading glasses and gave me a rueful look. "I know you don't love the situation, but you can't avoid your father."

Jacqueline and I huffed out identical sighs. "Really, Dierdre, I don't know how you can be so calm about all of this. You're letting him win the divorce."

Mom shook her head. "Jackie, there's nothing to win. I asked for this, and honestly, I'm glad Albert has someone."

"You could easily be dating a gorgeous stud if you'd just let me take you to A Single Thing," Jacqueline said, naming the singles bar that had opened a few towns away. Jacqueline, who'd been divorced once, had met her new husband at the bar, if you could call him "new." He was so old that I figured he would die having sex with Jacqueline before I graduated high school.

All I wanted was to not be there anymore. I could see how soccer would be good for that.

"I'm going to go study," I said to Mom, who was back to reading her textbook, and Jacqueline, who was topping off her glass of wine.

I went upstairs, locked my door, and lay on my bed. I closed my eyes and thought of Bobby saying my name like he had, then took the thought a step further.

September fifth, a field somewhere. Bobby McMann sits on a bench, rolling a soccer ball between his strong fingers, looking across the empty expanse of grass. No one's showing up for soccer tryouts, he knows, and it feels like no one cares. Frustration sets his beautiful face into a frown. He shoves the ball into his duffel bag and stands up to leave. Then there's a tap on his shoulder. He turns, and it's her. The girl he told about cleats. He'd hoped she'd show up.

"Are you here for . . ." He trails off, staring into her determined eyes.

"You," she says.

He touches my hair and pulls my face to his, a little roughly, like he might explode if he can't get closer to me.

(My fantasy thoughts always started in the third person and switched to the first person once I got going. It wasn't like I was being graded.)

On my bed, my body tensed up and I inhaled a sharp, urgent breath as my right hand trailed down my body, the side of my palm pressing softly over the top of my shorts. I used my left hand to trace my mouth, imagining my fingertips were Bobby's lips, and tugging my lower lip as if Bobby's mouth was doing it. The nerve endings beneath my lips must have aligned with my pelvis, because bolts of what I called the Almost There shot straight to my crotch, where my hand was working faster, brushing up and down, still over my clothes. When I got to this point, like always, my breath grew ragged as my whole body quaked, my hips now pushing up against my hand.

I yelped and covered my mouth more tightly, and my body spasmed—my head lifting from my pillow—as I came.

If the way I did it wasn't pretty, it didn't matter, because it always felt pretty after.

I got up and looked at myself in the mirror. My cheeks were flushed and my light brown hair was messy and I thought I might look . . . sexy. Was I sexy? Could you be sexy if you'd never had sex?

If I wanted Bobby to notice me, I had to look as sexy and maybe experienced as possible at tryouts the next day. I had attributes I could play up. My dad had given me a curling iron last Christmas and I'd mastered getting the longer sections of my hair to flare out around my face, sort of like Jaclyn Smith on *Charlie's Angels*, but only sort of. Jeff Sipowitz had endorsed my butt, and I liked my legs. They were still a little tan from the summer, and there was a cute freckle next to my left knee.

Bobby was definitely sexy. Sexy like someone who could have sex with anyone, in real life, not in his head. He wouldn't have to masturbate. He could go up to a crowd of women and ask, "Who's next?" and someone would volunteer.

I turned on my radio and a Donna Summer song came on—"Love to Love You Baby." I adored the breathy way she sang it, and now it felt like a sign: I hadn't been writing off the boys at my school for no reason. I'd been waiting for someone I was excited about, in the same specific way Donna was for the guy she was singing to. I'd picked him, instead of hoping to be picked.

Okay, so picking our new adult teacher–slash–soccer coach wasn't ideal. But I thought Bobby was worth choosing.

I'd find out, starting with tryouts.

Three

What I'd told Bobby was right. There were so many girls at try-outs the next day, I wasn't even sure I went to school with them all. There had to be more than sixty girls there. Either everyone had discovered latent athletic ability overnight or, more likely, they also were fueled by their hots for Coach McMann, because way more girls had shown up for soccer tryouts than for *The Sound of Music* auditions.

It was an even bigger deal because the tryouts were inconvenient. We were supposed to get to use the north half of the practice football field across the street from school, and the freshman boys who normally played there would get the other half. But in seventh period, Assistant Principal Lawler came over the staticky intercom to announce that soccer tryouts had been moved to Oak Meadows Park, a mile and a half from school. The rumor was that one of the football coaches didn't want a bunch of girls distracting his players.

Some girls had walked over from the school. Tina had driven me and Candace in her Buick, which her mom had given her when she'd bought herself a new Cadillac. Now all of us were waiting for Coach McMann. There were chemical clouds in the fall air from the rampant spraying of Baby Soft perfume and Aqua Net hairspray and Secret deodorant. Everyone was grooming like we were getting yearbook photos taken.

I had put on my favorite Lip Smacker (Dr Pepper flavored) but I didn't want to go overboard. I thought I would stand out more to Bobby if I looked sort of athletic, like I could be his female counterpart. I wore my red shorts, but rolled them up at the top so they went even higher than usual and became what my sister would call asshuggers. Unfortunately, it wasn't that warm out. The goose bumps on my legs stood out beneath the layers of baby oil I'd massaged onto them.

"Susan, do you want Mr. McMann to feel you up or use your body as a Slip 'N Slide?" asked Wendy Kowalski, who seemed to have bleached her faint mustache for today's big event.

"At least Susan only had to shave the hair on her legs," Tina said snidely, strutting across the field in her gym uniform, which wasn't flattering on most girls but made her look like a taller Wonder Woman with caramel-colored hair. She linked arms with me as she shot Wendy a dirty look. They'd been clawing at each other ever since they both ran for class secretary last year (in the end, they'd been edged out by Jeremy Rokowski).

Tina doesn't like Wendy but says at least Wendy's a bitch to everyone and doesn't pretend to like her, the way a lot of girls do. Once I walked into the girls' bathroom on a day Tina had really dressed up, in a new emerald blouse and dark green bell-bottoms, and two girls who were always fawning over her in public were talking about her. "Who does Tina think she is? It's school, not a fashion show." "Well, she's not happy unless she's showing off." When I came out of my stall, they shut up, and I said, "You were saying?" and drew a line between them and me with the edge in my voice, even as I wished I could say something more cutting. Later, they came up to Tina in the cafeteria like a two-headed monster and said, "Love your outfit," in a really phony way. But Tina handles catty girls better than me. She'll say something like "Did you pick out that blouse yourself? Oh, interesting . . ." and it will sound like a compliment until you realize she didn't say anything positive. She's basically a genius.

We found Candace standing off to the side, retucking her white T-shirt into her denim cutoffs. She looked pinched and tense, and I realized her boobs looked different.

"Are you not wearing a bra?" I asked her.

"I taped them," she said. "My brothers said it would hurt if I had to run and I was only wearing a bra. I really hope we don't have to run."

"Taped them?" Tina asked. "And that's *less* painful?"

Candace put a palm over each of her boobs and shifted them. "I didn't ask for these," she said. "But they're my responsibility."

"For once, I'm happy to be flat," I said.

"No you're not," Candace said.

I flipped her off, because it was true.

"What is Lynn wearing?" Tina used her chin to subtly gesture to Lynn Bandis, who was so built that rumors had gone around school that she'd signed a contract with Hugh Hefner to be a centerfold in *Playboy* as soon as she turned eighteen. She had on some gold shorts that looked like they had been spray-painted onto her body, and a crop top that exposed most of her torso as she did graceful stretches. Compared to her and Tina, I probably looked like the squat round Kewpie doll my dad had won for me at a carnival once. I'd thrown it away because it gave me nightmares.

"More than she has to," Candace said. "Girl could walk around naked and no one would be upset about it."

"It seems unfair," I said, watching as Lynn touched her toes. Her best friend, Marie Quinn, who was wearing shorts similar to mine with a tight red T-shirt, mirrored her stretch. Marie wasn't as pretty as Lynn, but boys liked her almost equally. They seemed like a set, Lynn and Marie, but where Lynn could be aloof, even icy, Marie had a quick sense of humor and never seemed tongue-tied around guys. "I don't think Lynn ever went through an awkward stage. She was just born like that."

"That had to be weird for her mom," Tina joked.

"You look cute," Candace said, snapping the waistband of my shorts. "Your butt is as nice as hers, if that's how Mr. McMann is picking the team."

"Bobby wouldn't do that," I scolded her, in the same grave tone I used with Randy, a seven-year-old monster I babysat.

"So it's *Bobby* now?" Tina asked.

"Yes. And he's not like that." As I said it, I realized how much I wanted it to be true. Because if he *was* like that, what if the butts he picked didn't include mine?

For all I or anyone knew, Coach McMann could have been some kind of hyperattractive psychopath. But even though he'd made me think some really unwholesome thoughts, the more I thought about him, the more I believed he was wholesome, like a sexy Mister Rogers.

"Oh God, Susan, you're hot for a teacher," Tina said.

"Like you're not here for the same reason," I said.

"Sure, it doesn't hurt that he's hot, but I really think it'll be fun," Tina said. "Especially since I knew you'd end up here, too, the way you were undressing him with your eyes."

We were all so busy giving each other shit and sizing one another up that we almost didn't notice Coach McMann had arrived. Without saying anything to us, he set his equipment bag down on a bench and began walking across the field. His face was set in a puzzled frown; he seemed to be surveying the park as if he might be able to flip it over and find it was better on the other side, like an old mattress.

"He's so intense," a younger girl I didn't know said.

"Do you mean your panties are so intense?" her friend said.

Someone chuckled. But when Bobby broke into a jog down the length of the field, we all shut up and just watched him run. It was more mesmerizing than when the PBS nature show *Nova* filmed a lion chasing after an antelope in slow motion and you knew it would eventually snare the animal and tear part of its midsection away.

An involuntary, guttural half sigh, half purr came out of my mouth.

"Whoa," someone else muttered.

"Wow," a chorus of girls cooed.

"Holy shit."

That was Candace, who slapped a hand over her mouth.

He ran back around, and absolutely no one was looking at his face. Finally he stopped, stood before us, and clapped his hands together. "Wow, this is quite a turnout!" he said, and I thought he looked at me. "I had no idea so many girls would come."

"Happy to come . . . ," someone behind me murmur-coughed.

"So, I'm Bobby McMann. Coach McMann to you, if you make the team. How many of you girls have played soccer before?"

No one raised her hand.

The day before, if you'd suggested we play soccer, we would have laughed our asses off. At our school, girls mostly participated in sports support: cheerleading, dance team, pep club to buck up the Powell Park Pirates. But sports just for girls had only really started a few years before. At my freshman orientation, the athletic director, Mr. Burke—after talking forever about how "very proud" he was of the tradition of excellence our school's teams had—had stumbled his way through a paragraph he'd read right from a sheet of paper about how under Title IX, Powell Park was working "to offer females more equal opportunities to join teams." He had been as enthused as he'd be reading instructions for a topical ointment.

I remembered the moment because at the time, Candace, sitting between me and Tina, had said, "I think I'd rather be permanently on my period than join a sports team." Joining teams was something for other girls, like the handful of girls who played tennis or swam in the fall, or were on the softball or badminton teams in spring. Cynthia Weaver, who'd set school records for the

100-meter butterfly, was a real athlete, and we sometimes made mean jokes about her behind her big back. But it was fair to say most of us had ignored sports until now.

"Hmm." That glorious frown came over his face again. "Okay, well, how many of you play sports?"

"Does roller-skating count?" someone said.

Bobby didn't answer, just asked, "Anyone like to run?"

A few more people put up a hand. I did, too. I didn't run as a sport, but technically I'd run before. I used to be the fastest kid on my block, when I was six or seven and boys and girls just did everything in a pack and our moms all cut our hair the same bowl-shaped way so you couldn't even tell who was a boy and who was a girl.

"Okay, then," he said. "Well, I played soccer at Southern Illinois University and it's one of my passions. But what I really care about is getting the best out of my team. We're the new guys on the block, though—" He stopped himself. "Girls on the block. I wanted a field for us at the school, but this one will have to do." He gestured toward the spot where he'd just run and shrugged. "It slopes up a bit. Not great, but we can work with it."

He dumped about a dozen soccer balls from his bag onto the ground in front of us. "I don't have enough for everyone, so we'll have to go in phases," he said. "Looks like we have about sixty people. . . . Line up in twelve groups of five. Then let's see you dribble one of these down the field and back."

"Dribble like a basketball?" Marie asked, snapping her gum.

"Um, no, with your feet," Bobby said, deftly touching a ball with the tip of his shoe and kicking it in little bursts, passing it from foot to foot as he moved it toward us.

It looked easy enough. I put myself at the front of a group that included Tina, Candace, and a couple of sophomores.

"And *go!*" Bobby blew his whistle, and the first twelve of us approached the balls on the ground with uncertainty, like they were rabbits that might hop away.

I nudged mine, but I must have done it too hard because it jumped five feet in front of me. I ran toward it and almost tripped over it. When I got my bearings, I started toeing the ball more gingerly, realizing I could make it down the field if I went slowly. I felt like an old woman but at least I was staying upright; a few girls around me had fallen on their asses. But how did people do this and still see where they were going?

Bobby blew his whistle. "Wait, wait! We're going to start with something else!"

He ran toward us and stopped in front of me. He flipped my ball up from the ground with the top of his foot, catching it as he smiled at me. A special smile, I thought. "Starting slow like that's okay, a good way to get used to finding the ball," he said, just to me.

I felt dizzy with his attention. Tina poked me in the ribs when I returned to the line. "Need to catch your breath, Suzie Q?"

"Shh," I said, because Bobby was looking at all of us apologetically.

"I shouldn't have started you with dribbling. It's tough if you haven't played before," he said, and I could tell that in his world, dribbling wasn't tough. "We'll get to ball handling"—someone giggled—"but why don't we start out with some calisthenics instead? How about fifty jumping jacks?"

A chorus of incredulous voices answered back, "Fifty?"

"Did you say fifty or fifteen?" Candace asked.

"Fifty," he said, grinning, his whistle balanced at the corner of his mouth. With his bottom lip, he lifted it and blew.

Jumping jacks were easy for me, and I guess for Tina, who didn't even break a sweat. And Candace's tape must have been working because she kept going, too. But after a few minutes, some girls gave up—they didn't just stop jumping, they left the field. We were down to about fifty people now.

"Good!" Bobby said when we were done. "Now push-ups, at least fifteen. Feel free to put your knees on the ground if that makes it a little easier."

"It would be easier if you did them and we watched," I heard Joanie Fox, a sophomore, say under her breath.

"What was that?" Bobby asked.

"I said, you got it," Joanie said.

Push-ups were harder. Candace, next to me, was panting after doing three. I felt terrible for her. "Are you okay?"

"I'm fine. You should do extra, though," she huffed. "You . . . might . . . grow . . . some . . . tits." Her face was so red, she looked like the devil when she grinned.

After a few more, Candace sat back on her knees and adjusted her T-shirt, which had ridden up, before getting back into position to finish. Tina and I eked out our last push-ups—my arms felt like chewed gum by the end—then sat up. I was sweating, but I tried to look unfazed as I bent my legs up in front of me and looped my arms around them, like I was posing for *Seventeen*'s back-to-school issue. I wanted to be worthy of Bobby's admiration, but not look like I was angling for it.

Some of the other girls were murmuring complaints to each other, deciding whether to stick around, and others were silent and sullen. None of us had talked about what we expected from tryouts, but that was probably because none of us had tried out for a sport before.

It was clear Bobby was just getting started, too, as he waited for us finish and consulted a clipboard. He stood in front of us; our eyes were level with his shorts. I forced myself to watch some kids playing on the swings instead of staring at his crotch.

"Good work," he said. "We've got forty survivors, I see. Impressive. Okay. As your coach, I can teach you plays, but no one can teach you speed and endurance, which is what soccer is all about. Give me ten laps, from that tree to the fence to the bike path to the playground."

A collective groan went up among us. "I'm not Rocky. I'm out of here," Lynn Bandis said, getting to her feet and strutting away like she thought Bobby would beg her to stay. I was glad he didn't. "You coming, Marie?" She turned around to look at her friend, and Marie gave Lynn a long look, as if by not bailing on tryouts, too, she'd be severing something. But then Marie shook her head, saying, "I think I want to stay."

A flash of surprise crossed Lynn's face, but she recovered quickly, tossing off a chipper "Okay, then," before she sauntered off.

Though Marie stayed, a few other girls followed Lynn's lead

and left. Bobby did nothing to stop them, either. There were maybe thirty of us left now.

"Let's see those laps," Bobby said, and blew his whistle like nothing had happened.

I took an easy early lead, grateful that we didn't have to do more push-ups. Running with the longest strides I could, I was the sleek-limbed creature in the *Nova* special and I wanted Bobby to watch me, like a hungry tiger—or at least nod to himself, like, "*That's* who I'm looking for." To do what, I didn't care.

Behind me, some girls were chatting.

"Jesus, if he wasn't so hot, I'd be out of here."

"I know. I thought this was going to be kind of a joke."

"How do you play soccer, anyway? Is there this much running?"

"Maybe he'll stop us after one lap."

But after the last person rounded the playground, Bobby yelled, "Nice! Nine more!" The chatter fell away and was replaced by a chorus of huffed breaths as we churned into the second lap. Several girls gave up and went to gather their stuff. I kept going. I was surprised that nothing so far had been too hard for me to do. As I ran, I focused on keeping my chest out and not looking too sweaty. I wasn't even going as fast as I could, and I was at the front of the group.

Still, by the sixth lap, I felt a stitch in my side. I gritted my teeth and told myself I just had four more to go. Tina was a few paces behind me, and I could hear the footfalls of other girls farther back. Candace was so far behind that I was coming up on lapping her.

As I puffed by Bobby, he called out, "Looking good. Love the spirit!"

He loved my spirit. It gave me a fresh burst of energy, and I sprinted fast past him with my head thrown back.

The stitch went away, and Tina pulled up next to me. "Were you always this fast?" she said.

"I am now," I huffed, wondering what would happen if I were the only one to finish. "You scared?"

"No, just thinking we could go faster."

Playing anything with Tina was like a blood sport—we both liked to win. Still, I was surprised at how much I liked running out ahead of everyone like this. Each time I turned at the slides and saw Bobby waiting for us to make it back around, I liked it a little more.

Fifteen of us finished the laps without bailing. Well, Tina and I finished first, then a handful of other girls came in behind us, with Candace and Sharon Henderson at the end.

When they finally did, Bobby asked us all for our names, which he wrote down as we took turns waiting to take drinks from the park's crusty-looking water fountain.

"Hmm, fifteen girls. Great," he said.

"What do you mean, 'great'?" Dana Miller asked, wiping a dribble of water from her mouth.

Bobby threw his hands out to gesture at all of us. "I mean, it looks like we have our team."

Four

Practice wouldn't start until next Monday, but the day after try-outs, Bobby made us each sign a contract for the season stating that we'd be on time and dressed to play, and we'd keep our grades up and take care of our bodies.

"I know you might have a beer at a party. I was your age once, too," he said at the team meeting where he'd passed out the contracts. "But don't overdo it. And no smoking or drugs."

Normally, we'd have mocked a teacher for being so square. But it felt like Bobby really cared about us. Or maybe we just wanted to believe he did.

He also tacked up a sheet with all our names on the bulletin board in the lunchroom, and people actually looked at it. Paul Mahoney, who was the kind of guy who asked if you had your period for not saying hi to him, gathered a group of football players and lurched over to our lunch table. "Trillo, Klintock, Warner. You girls think you're athletes now? Do you even know how to handle balls?" Some of the other guys laughed.

"It's less about handling than kicking, which sounds okay to me," I said.

"Nice, Suze," Tina said. "What's it to you, Paul?"

"I'm sure nothing," Paul said. "Your pretty-boy coach doesn't have the stamina to keep this going."

"Funny, Arlene said the same thing about you," Candace shot back. Arlene Swann was Paul's recent ex, and had also made the team.

"Paul, you gonna take that?" asked his zitty sidekick jock whose name I didn't know.

"You let chicks think they can play sports and this is what happens," Paul said, shaking his head.

From down the table, Franchesa Rotini, who'd also survived tryouts, muttered, "Maybe we should tell Coach McMann how you feel."

"Like I care what some *soccer* coach thinks of me," he said, but he did walk away. I didn't care what Paul Mahoney thought about me, but I guess I was a bit surprised that our team and Coach McMann rankled him enough that he felt compelled to share his shitty opinions with us. It seemed like a waste of the energy he could have expended leering at freshmen girls.

As word got around that there now was a girls' soccer team at Powell Park, the news was mostly met with a shrug, but a few girls—like Peggy Darnell—told us we were lucky to have an excuse to see Mr. McMann every day.

She also told us there was going to be a party at Dan O'Keefe's house Saturday night. I felt conflicted, like I shouldn't be breaking the terms of Bobby's contract. I didn't want to treat him like a joke the way other people were, but I also knew I wasn't a jock like Cynthia Weaver. He'd said we could have a beer or two, after all.

"Hey, it's the ball-kicking lesbos."

Paul was the first person to see us, and he shouted over the noise when we walked into Dan's house. I had actually been daydreaming about Bobby as Candace and Tina talked about . . . I actually don't know what, when Paul's voice rattled me back into the moment. The house was vibrating with music from Savage Hunger, a band headed up by Rick Spellman, a senior who should have graduated two years ago. If his grades matched his band's abilities, it was no wonder he still hadn't gotten his diploma.

"Go to hell, Paul," I said.

"'Go to hell, Paul,'" he mimicked in a singsong voice that sounded nothing like me. Candace gave him the finger.

We made our way to the keg in the corner of Dan's basement, where Reggie Stanton was handing out red Solo cups. He was a second-string quarterback with a mustache that he was extremely proud of, and that currently had beer foam clinging to its dark hairs. Over the summer, Candace had decided he was cute, but I thought her interest was entirely based on the fact that he'd wolf-whistled and winked at her on his way out of Wojo's.

"Oh look, our new lady athletes," he sneered, making a show of handing us cups.

"Is McMann gonna teach you how to do headers? 'Cause if not, I can show you,'" said Keith Barnes as he gyrated his hips while pretending to be holding the back of, I guess, a woman's head.

"You wish, Keith," Candace said. But then she put her hand over her mouth and laughed, and her boobs jiggled. Reggie watched. "It's not like the team is this serious thing. It's just fun."

"I think it's cool," chimed in George Tomczak, who'd wandered over from a corner of the basement. "Soccer is a really athletic game. You must be in great shape to make the team." He directed his praise at all of us, but he gave Candace a special look. She covertly turned toward me and Tina and pinched her nose. We called George "Garbage Breath" because his was always foul, like he'd gargled with sour milk and tuna water.

"Thanks, George," Candace said, but she was looking at Reggie the whole time. Reggie sidled up to whisper something to her and she giggled again. I wanted to pull her away, but I knew Reggie was her bad decision to make.

At least George got the hint. He nodded to Tina and me and said, "Well, good luck, fellow Pirates," and slipped away before Tina and I could even offer a half-hearted thanks. But it was better not to encourage him.

Tina sighed as we took our first sips of watery beer. "I miss Todd," she said, and it took me a second to remember who Todd even was: her boyfriend, in Milwaukee. They met in seventh grade and still saw each other when Tina visited her dad. Tina says she loves him, but their relationship seems like so much work, not only with being long distance but also because it's a secret. Tina's afraid to tell her mom about Todd, because he's kind of artsy and wants to skip college to go save the environment or something, and Tina's mom had her fill of artistic do-gooders with Tina's dad, her first husband. But Tina's totally into Todd, and he does write her letters and gets her clothes from the store where he works. So that's something.

"Guys like this make me realize how good I have it," she continued, ignoring how every boy at the party seemed to be staring at her.

"Totally," I agreed, like I had a clue what having it good with a guy was like. We wove through the crush of people in the humid basement. A few of them were dancing, and on an armchair in the corner, most of Becky Logan's underwear was visible where her skirt had ridden up as she made out with some guy I didn't recognize. Two guys got up from a couch, and Tina and I plopped into their empty seats with our drinks.

Dan O'Keefe, our host, who was okay, came up to us. "Having fun, ladies?" He was already drunk, but in a Dan way, which just made him act like someone's dad. "Help yourself to some chips. My mom went to the Jewel earlier." He gestured to the table like a woman on *The Price Is Right* showing off a prize showcase, and I grabbed a handful of chips to show his generosity was appreciated. Dan pointed at me. "Oh, Susan, remember Michael from the summer? He asked about you. I told him he should say hi."

"Michael?" Tina said, elbowing me. "You mean Michael Webster?"

I'd seen Michael at a few parties of Dan's in the past. Over the summer, Michael had poured me a beer and we'd made some good eye contact, and I'd been interested enough to ask Dan if

Michael had a girlfriend. Dan had told me he'd find out, but then Michael had left with his friends before we even got a chance to talk. I looked past Dan to see Michael standing by a bookcase filled with Dan's dad's bowling trophies. Michael Webster was no Bobby McMann, but he was still cute. Cuter than anyone at Powell Park High, at least. He went to St. Mark's and had light, shaggy hair and dark brown eyes. He was wearing his black-and-gold jacket covered in varsity patches and holding a beer.

He looked over and saw Dan, who nodded some kind of signal and walked away. Then Michael came over, all six-foot-two of him.

"Hey," he said to me, sitting down on the arm of the couch so he kind of loomed over me and Tina. "Good party, right?"

"It's okay," Tina and I said at the same time.

"O'Keefe said another keg is coming. It'll get better." Michael moved to sit on the couch and I scooted over. His leg was touching mine.

"He's kind of hot," Tina whispered to me, pinching me lightly on the arm. I shot her a look.

"You two go to Powell Park?" he said.

"Yeah, we're juniors." As I said it, I realized his arm was already around me. It felt heavy, but kind of nice, and his fingertips touched lightly where my sleeve met my skin. I looked into his eyes and he smiled with one side of his mouth. If this had happened in the summer, I might have passed out, but now I could only think that he was Not Bobby. Michael was suddenly as exciting as the teddy bear I practiced kissing in my room, even if he had real boy parts.

"I'm at St. Mark's," he said. "I play football. Maybe you should come to a practice."

I liked the idea of him asking, but I also liked the reality of not being able to say yes. "I just made the soccer team," I said. "So I can't."

He settled his arm deeper into the nook between my shoulder and my neck and gently tugged me closer. "Soccer, huh?" he said, as he brushed his fingertips lightly over my collarbone. "That's kinda cute. But they don't make girls practice every day, right?" He didn't wait for an answer as he leaned in toward me, his face hovering in front of mine. He had Bobby-ish lips, full and soft. He wanted to kiss me. A real guy, a good-looking one, who might have been a little drunk, was about to kiss me.

"Yup. Every afternoon after school," I said, poking a small hole in the moment. I wasn't 100 percent sure why, but it had something to do with him calling soccer *cute*. It was okay if Tina and Candace and I were still figuring how serious this whole soccer thing was, but I was getting ticked off by guys acting like us playing a sport was some adorable joke.

Michael pulled back ever so slightly, but he was still smiling as he pushed a lock of hair away from my face. Even though I was annoyed, I wanted him to think I was pretty.

"Hmm, you'd look awfully good in the cheering section." He shrugged. "Maybe I can change your mind and make you wanna see the Webs in action. On the field." He started to close in on me again.

I involuntarily rolled my eyes and saw that a few feet away, leaning against Dan's fireplace, a guy was watching us. He had pale skin and short dark hair that stood up in little points, and he was looking over the top of his red cup at me. He smirked when I caught his eye.

I looked back at Michael, who was waiting expectantly.

"Wait, are *you* 'the Webs'?"

He nodded, like this should be obvious, as he edged even closer, angling for the kiss. His arrogant expression was the look of a guy who'd say, "Well, I didn't really study," if I beat him on a test. It was like a switch had flipped. He repelled me.

I put a hand on his chest and pushed him gently away. "Honestly, I don't think I want to make out with a guy who refers to himself by his own nickname," I said. Sometimes I couldn't think of comebacks until way after the moment for them had passed, but this one came out so fast, I wasn't even sure I wanted to say it.

On the other side of the couch, Tina was covering her mouth as she laughed. And Pointy Hair was observing our exchange like he wasn't even remotely embarrassed for eavesdropping. I glared at him, and he tipped his cup to me. Was I a joke to every guy at this party?

Michael retracted his arm and slid away from me fast, like I'd begun oozing pus. He scanned the party, looking for somewhere new to go. "Just because girls can play sports doesn't mean they should. It's not good for anyone."

What he said got to me, because it reminded me of something my dad had said to my mom when she was filing for divorce: "Dierdre, you could be happy if you'd accept how things are supposed to be. You can't have two suns shining or no one would get any sleep." She'd told him it was the most poetic he'd ever been.

"What does that even mean?" I asked as Michael stood up. I didn't like him and yet I hated that his arm wasn't around me anymore because I played soccer.

"It wouldn't make sense to a chick like you," he said, one foot already stepping toward a group of girls at the far end of the basement. "Don't mess up your face on the field. It's half decent."

"Fuck you," I said, but I don't know if he heard me. I looked toward the fireplace to see if the skinny guy was still watching, or laughing at me, but he was gone.

I grabbed another fistful of chips as Michael made his way toward a girl who beamed like he was handing her an oversize Publishers Clearing House check. Tina waited while I ate each chip methodically, then said, "You okay?"

"I'm guy-repellent, but I'll live," I said.

"He was so full of himself, he's probably a shitty kisser," Tina said. "Let's get Candace and go. This party's lame."

We never left Candace at a party, even if she tended to always leave us. We were used to her habits by now, and always ready for the fallout if and when a guy she disappeared with disappeared on her the next week. Unlike me, who could find something wrong with anyone, Candace could find something right about them.

"Do you know where Reggie and Candace went?" I asked when we found Dan. He had a freshman on his lap and looked like he was half asleep.

"Did you blow off Michael?" he asked. "What's your problem? I told him to talk to you."

I couldn't believe I'd appreciated his chips, the way he was

47

talking. "Just tell us where Candace is," I said. "We have to go."

He rolled his eyes. "Probably the guest room. Upstairs, down the hall next to the kitchen," he said, and got back to kissing the freshman's neck.

"Thanks," I said, and flipped him off.

Tina and I went upstairs and banged on a closed door near the kitchen. Reggie opened it, zipping his pants right in front of us, and I already knew what had been going on; Candace was a champion at hand jobs. If she gave them because she found it fun, that'd be fine, but she clearly thought it would get her a boyfriend, and had cried many times because it wasn't working. She was sitting on the daybed and, when she saw us, fixed her shirt.

"Come on, we're going," I said.

"Already?" She smoothed her hair and looked at Reggie, as if she was hoping he'd ask her to stay. "Is that okay with you?"

"Yeah, I'll call you," he said, like he wouldn't.

"Bye, Reggie," she said, and leaned toward him for a kiss. He barely brushed her lips with his gross mustache.

"See ya," he said, dazedly walking back into the party.

As we maneuvered our way out onto Dan's front porch, where a few people were sitting around smoking a joint, I said, "Seriously, Candace, you could do so much better."

She gave a little laugh. "He seemed to think I was pretty good at what I did."

"Gross," Tina said, but laughed. "That mustache needs to go."

"Do you even like him?" I asked Candace.

In the dark, I could see her scrunch up her face in annoyance. "If he asks me to homecoming, I'd like that," she said.

Tina pointed to Candace's blouse, which was buttoned up wrong. Candace giggled and started fixing it, saying, "I'd better say some Hail Marys tomorrow." She was serious. The Trillos were Catholic, but Candace made up her own penance because she worried an official confession would get back to her mom somehow.

"I'm sure Mary gave Joseph a few hand jobs and she still got picked to make Jesus," I said.

Candace's eyes widened. "Susan!"

"Okay, okay," I said as Tina snickered. And then, because I wanted to know, "Did he make *you* feel good?"

"Jesus?" Candace said.

"No! Reggie. It seems unfair if he got off and you didn't." I may not have had Candace's experience with actual boys, but I definitely had some authority on getting off.

Candace sighed. "God, Susan, at least I've done more than a couple sloppy kisses," she said, and I knew the answer was no. I hated that Candace acted like I was a complete idiot about guys, when it wasn't like she chose them so well. But after the scene with Michael, I worried she had a point.

We turned onto the sidewalk to make our way to Tina's car.

"I've had more than a couple sloppy kisses," I said, leaning across Tina to put the words right up in Candace's face. "I have experience." The beer must have gotten to me a little, because not only was this an exaggeration, but I was also talking too loud.

"You guys—" Tina put up her hands in front of us, as if to hold us back.

"Hey, it's my hero," someone said in the dark, shocking me sober.

We crossed under a street lamp and there was Pointy Hair Guy, leaning against a beat-up Chevy Nova, his cup still in hand. He smiled in the dark. For someone with such a messy haircut, his teeth were the whitest ones I'd ever seen. He had high cheekbones on a thin face, giving him a sharp look, but his eyes twinkled like everything was a joke. Or at least like *I* was a joke.

"I'm not in the mood," I said. The last thing I needed was some scrawny jerk teasing me about getting rejected by some not-scrawny jerk.

He lit a cigarette and held out the pack to us. We all shook our heads.

"What? I mean it," he said. "I thought the way you told off Webster kicked ass. I mean, 'the Webs'? He's practically begging for the verbal abuse."

I laughed, even though I didn't want to.

"I'm Joe, by the way. Joe Gianelli." He stepped away from the car and held out his hand for me to shake. I took it. It was cool and dry and refreshing after Dan's hot, sweaty basement. "I used to go by Joey, but I didn't want it to seem like I was copying Joey Ramone."

I'd heard of the Ramones, but there were so many of them, I didn't know who was who. "This is Candace, and Tina," I said, wondering if Joe had heard me arguing with Candace. "I'm Susan. I used to go by Susie, but that was because I was five and my parents didn't give me a choice."

He laughed. That was twice tonight I'd said something funny right in the moment, instead of thinking of it two days later.

"Well, I'll let you and your friends be on your way, Susan," he said, still holding on to my hand. "For real, that was impressive, the way you shut down Webster. Being witness to it was a quite an experience."

The way he said "experience," I knew he'd heard me telling Candace I had it.

"Thanks," I muttered, now flustered. I dropped his hand and hurried toward Tina's car, almost tripping when the toe of my sneaker got caught on a square of the sidewalk where a massive tree root had buckled the concrete.

"I'll see you around," he called after us as we walked away.

"I think he likes you," Candace said, when we were—I hoped—out of earshot.

"You're just trying to make up for being a bitch," I told her. "And I doubt it. Just a weirdo in the dark, messing with me."

He probably called out to every girl walking past his car. He seemed like the type, with his permanently amused face.

The whole way home, as Tina and Candace sang along to ABBA, it wasn't Joe I imagined watching me tell off Michael, but Bobby. Maybe he would have been impressed, too.

Five

On Sunday morning, part of me regretted not drinking more at the party on Saturday. Like, enough to be so messed up that I passed out in a drainage ditch like Renee Ozlowski had after prom last year. Because spending early Sunday only semiconscious and covered in mud on the side of Roberts Road would have been preferable to what I had to do: go visit with my dad and his girlfriend Polly.

Polly wasn't the first of my dad's post-divorce girlfriends, but she was the most serious. I knew because I hadn't met the others, just overheard my mom and Jacqueline, at times over the past year and a half, discussing "Albert's latest catch." My dad had started dating pretty soon after the divorce papers were signed, but he'd seemed to only go out with women for a couple of dates, maybe a few weeks at the most. I only knew this because sometimes my weekend visit would be pushed back by an hour or two, and that was when my mom got mad and accidentally badmouthed my dad. "He's not even serious with this . . . dancer . . . and he's rearranging your visit." Or "He's acting like a sex-crazed fifteen-year-old instead of a grown man with responsibilities."

But Polly was serious: she'd lasted for six months already. My dad had met her at Jeffries Auto, a used-car lot Polly's dad owned in Elm Ridge, where Polly answered phones and made coffee. He'd traded in his Oldsmobile for a white Chevelle Laguna and she'd gotten him a coffee, one sugar. Now they lived together. "From Mommy's bosom to a divorcé's condominium," Jacqueline had said when Mom told her the news. But Polly was thirty-five, not nearly as young as some of the women Dad had dated. And when Mom heard they'd moved in together, it was one of the few times since the divorce that she'd seemed a little sad about the whole thing, which she otherwise regarded rationally, like a business arrangement with agreed-upon terms that, when not honored, irritated her. When she told me, "Your father's seeing someone, and it's serious," she was drinking his favorite whiskey and staring at the ice cubes melting in the glass a little too long for me to believe she was entirely okay.

It was bizarre, my dad living with someone else. The last time I was at his condo—at the start of summer, a month before Polly moved in—there'd already been signs of Polly. A long blond hair on the brown couch, a second toothbrush in the cup with his. But what was even weirder were the things like the glass bowl of seashells next to the bathroom sink, the fake flowers on the kitchen table, and the pitcher of fresh orange juice in the fridge when my dad had only ever bought the store brand in the carton. If I hadn't known he had a girlfriend, I'd have thought he'd been replaced by some kind of homemaking impostor.

My mom drove me to his condo and rolled to a stop at the curb. "What, you're not coming in?" I asked her. I half wanted her to because she looked pretty today. Her hair was loose around her shoulders and curled to frame her face, and she had on an old Chicago Bears V-neck. She was going to a how-to seminar at the library, something about computing, and was excited, so her eyes looked bright, too. Kind of interested and ready, not the eyes of someone who'd grown tired of her life, which was how they'd looked when she was married to my dad.

It wasn't that I wanted my parents to get back together. I'd never looked at my mom and dad and thought they were some amazing love story that needed to be saved. They were just people who talked to the same kids every day and shared a television. But I did think my dad's leap into a new relationship was sort of his mild revenge on my mom and that my mom deserved some equally light retribution on my dad, in the form of looking good on a Sunday afternoon.

"Ha, ha," Mom said. "Just because I don't hate your father doesn't mean I want to pal around with him. But they invited you, and I don't want you pulling anything like not going inside. You owe him that."

"Well, I don't owe Polly anything," I said.

"She's obviously trying," Mom said. "She was very pleasant at our dinner." That was one of the divorce contingencies: that before either of my parents introduced me and my sister, Tonia—who had only had to hear about Polly over the phone since she calls herself Chartreuse now and lives with some guy in Venice Beach, California—to a new love interest, the other one be present. I had no idea how they'd come up with that rule, but based on the really awkward meal we'd all shared at a steakhouse in downtown Chicago, I'd thought it would be better if my parents could hate each other a little more post-split.

"Okay, Gandhi," I said and hopped out of the car to head up the walkway. The newish condo complex was called the Elm Tropics, which I found hilarious. There was nothing remotely tropical about Elm Ridge, or Powell Park, or any city in Illinois as far as I knew. But someone had put flimsy effort into the "tropical" vibe by placing potted palms—that would surely die by November—on each side of the glass door.

I pressed the buzzer for Klintock/Jeffries (Polly's last name) in 3A, and Polly's voice lilted over the staticky crackles of the intercom: "Susan, is that you?"

"Me" was all I said, and she let me into the vestibule, where I trudged up the stairs.

Polly already had the door open and had come to the landing, where she watched my progress. She had her arms out for a hug before I had even cleared the steps. "Oh, we're so happy you're here! We have NEWS!" She sprang at me for the waited-for hug and then pulled me into the condo by the arm. Her perfume was floral and not obnoxious. I would have liked it to be obnoxious, but I can't lie, it was nice.

Nice, like Polly. Polly, who put a dish of seashells in the bathroom. Polly, who squeezed orange juice. Polly, who probably never masturbated and would be appalled by the wave of feeling in my fulcrum when I thought about Coach McMann. *Bobby.*

The living room was the first thing you saw when you entered. Dad was there, sitting on the couch, watching a football game. "Hi, Dad," I said. He didn't get up, which was kind of annoying, but at least it made him feel like the same old dad.

"Hi, Susie," he said, tipping his beer can to his mouth and then yelling, "Come on!" at the screen.

Polly looked from him to me and back at him. "Albert? Can you take a break so we can share the news with Susan?"

"Share the news" sounded vaguely like they were now in a cult and were going to ask me to join.

"Yeah, okay," Dad said. He stood up, following Polly as she led us through the kitchen, where something in the oven smelled delicious. He was looking back at the TV the whole way.

The dining room had been empty last time I was here, but now it was filled by a new table that was ever so slightly too big for the space. Its surface was covered in vases of different flowers in varying shades of orange.

"Did someone . . . die?" I asked.

Polly's smile flickered then returned, like when the TV goes out for a split second and the picture comes back without you even having to mess with the antenna.

"Your dad and I are getting married!" she squealed and then clapped at her own announcement.

My dad sort of shrugged his shoulders like, *What can you do?*

I stared at them in shock. Couldn't they have suggested I sit down for this? They had enough chairs for it, even if you couldn't pull one out from the table without hitting the wall. "Does Mom know?" I asked Dad.

"Yeah, I told her that we wanted to tell you here. In person." Dad shifted his weight and smiled without his teeth.

"We wanted to tell you over dinner but I couldn't wait," Polly said. "The roast has another two hours."

She took my hands in hers as Dad continued to smile and nod, like this had all gone very well. Then he ambled back to the football game, the life-changing news taking less time to deliver than a first down. He was just leaving me there, clutching hands with his future wife, like this happened every day. Part of me was glad he left—I hated the look on his face, like he was confused by the whole thing. But the way Polly was looking at me was worse, like a desperate animal who'd followed me home and wanted me to keep her.

"I just want you to know that I am going to think of you as a daughter, even though I will never try to take the place of your mom, and I don't expect you to think of me as anything more than a stepmom," Polly said in a rush, as if she'd practiced the words in the mirror. A vision of Polly trying to read present-day me the Betsy-Tacy books my mom had read me as a kid flashed before my eyes.

Oh my God, I had to sit.

I pulled out a chair a smidge and then crammed my body between the seat and the table. Polly was my stepmom. Or was going to be. Did I want her for my stepmom? Did I want anyone for my stepmom? Before I had time to consider the answer, Polly turned as much as she could in a room mostly taken up by a hulking piece of furniture and plucked a leather album off the sideboard, then sat down next to me.

She opened the book to a page of drawings that a kid must have done. "This is my bridal wish book," she said, smoothing her hand over the pages. So *she'd* done the drawings. "I've been keeping ideas for my wedding in here since I was a little girl. Do you have a bridal wish book?" She blinked her blue eyes at me expectantly.

I gulped, thinking that I could fill a wish book with my masturbation fantasies. "Not . . . really," I said. Candace had an old issue of *Brides* under her bed, but even she didn't have something like this. I wanted to ask Polly if when she'd thought about her wedding as a little girl, she'd ever imagined it being to a fifty-two-year-old divorced dad with abundant ear hair and two adult (or practically adult, in my case) daughters.

"I guess I'm just silly that way," she said, and blushed. In her lilac blouse with its tied neck, smoothly tucked into her purple pants, she was so pretty and neat, just like everything in the book was so pretty and neat, and yet she didn't seem proud necessarily, or like she thought it was off-putting that I wasn't pretty and neat, sitting there in my fake Jordache jeans with the patch on the knee and my ratty Sunkist T-shirt. She flipped past pages of pictures, cut from magazines, of crystal and cakes and couples kissing on beaches and the whole thing seemed so *lonely*. Not marriage itself so much as spending all your time dreaming up a wedding with a cake that probably wasn't even chocolate on the inside and the kind of fancy wineglasses that never looked as sparkly after you'd used them one time. I decided to be nice to her, at least right now.

"It's not silly," I said.

"I'm so glad you said that. I don't have sisters, or even any great girlfriends, and . . . I was hoping you might be my maid of honor?" She put her thumbnail near her mouth like she was about to bite it and then stopped herself. She was nervous. I didn't know how someone so pretty and neat could be nervous.

"Um . . . suuuuuurrre," I heard myself say.

"I'm so happy!" Polly hugged me, again, and clapped, again. "I have my wish book, so you won't need to do any of the usual maid of honor duties."

I had no idea what maids of honor usually did, besides stand there, so I said, "Okay, thanks."

She squeezed my shoulders and held me at arm's length, taking in me and my Sunkist shirt. "And if you look that good in orange, wait until you try on the bridesmaid's gown. It will be dusty peach!"

"What's a dusty peach?"

She pointed to the flowers. "Our colors. We're doing this quickly, so imagine this. Fall nuptials with a harvest theme." She grinned as if the word "harvest" would mean something to me, but all I could imagine were those cornucopias we had to make every year in grammar school. "Pale peach is too summer. But dusty makes it autumn . . . al. I can never say that word! Autumn-al. Al. Autumn. Never mind. You'll see when I show you the fabric swatches."

As she continued, I made polite noises and thought about the gown I'd wear, imagining something off the shoulder, even though I wasn't sure that was autumnal. My hair would be curled like Jaclyn Smith's, and to go along with the impossibility of achieving that hair, my eyes were also bigger and darker and, for some reason, looking into Bobby's, as he held out a hand and asked me to dance. He'd hold my waist tight and say, "You're cold, come closer."

"Wow," I said, out loud by accident, and the dining room became even smaller.

"I know, I think it's gorgeous, too," she said, gazing at the flowers, which she'd been rearranging while I daydreamed. "I've always had a knack with flowers. I'm going to take a Polaroid and show the florist."

"Mmm," I said, willing the stirred sensation between my legs to leave, which was easier than at school because I noticed a baby picture of me on the sideboard. You couldn't be weaving impure scenarios in your imagination while looking into your own baby eyes.

"Thank you so much for being so great! I'm absolutely thrilled," Polly said, and squeezed my shoulder as she left the room. "I need to check on the roast!"

I sat there for a minute, unsure what to do. If I went to my room now—it was the condo's guest room, with a bed shoved against the wall and no other furniture—I'd seem like a sullen, angry teen who didn't want her dad to remarry. That wasn't really true. I could have happily gone without ever knowing what dusty peach was, but whereas the divorce had shed light on my mom and who she was, I hadn't learned anything new about my dad. He'd gone from Albert, guy left by his first wife, to Albert, guy about to get a second wife. I loved him, of course, but he could have been anybody. If my mom was one of the detailed pages in my old Barbie coloring books that made me excited to color in the intricate accessories, my dad was the page with Ken standing against a stark background that I skipped over.

I felt sorry for thinking that, so I wandered into the living room and took a seat next to him on the couch. A commercial for

Budweiser was on TV. "Polly told you about the harvest thing?" he said, without looking at me.

"Yup," I said, as the commercial ended and Soldier Field came back onscreen.

"I appreciate you not, you know, giving Polly a hard time," Dad said. "I told her you don't much go in for all the flowers and romance."

He said it like he was almost proud of me for it, but before I could decide whether it was actually a compliment, he added, "Your ma mentioned something about a soccer team?"

He packaged his comment as a question, like he was interested in talking about it. So Mom *had* told him about it. I couldn't remember the last time they'd both seemed tuned in to something I was doing.

"Yeah, I made the team," I said. "We have practice tomorrow."

Dad mulled this over with his eyes on the TV. "Huh. I always thought soccer was kind of a girly sport. Guess it makes sense they got a girls' team going."

It wasn't the exact sentiment Michael had expressed, but it was in the same family. "It's pretty tough, actually," I said, even though I'd only had the one tryout and assumed at the moment that that was as hard as soccer would get.

"Oh yeah, I'm sure it's just like the gridiron." Dad chuckled lightly and put down his beer. He leaned forward with his elbows on his knees. I looked at the TV, watching as the quarterback got mowed over. I didn't want to get mowed over. But was that because getting mowed over was something for guys to do and not girls? Or was not wanting to get mowed over universal?

"Our coach is a guy, and he's in really good shape," I said, thinking this fact would legitimize a girls' team. Justifying the existence of a girls' soccer team suddenly felt harder than the push-ups had been.

"Poor guy," my dad said. A set of wavy lines skittered over the screen. "Dammit," he said. "Reception's for shit in this condo."

His frustration was satisfying. I'd been nice about his stupid harvest wedding. He could be nice about soccer, even if he thought it was dumb.

Polly walked in and set a tray of cheese cubes and salami, a can of Pringles, and a bowl of what looked like lumpy cream cheese on the table. "The roast is going to take a little longer than I thought, and I don't want you to starve, so I whipped up some snacks. The Jewel had fresh clam dip today, so don't give me any credit!"

My dad and I both mumbled thank-yous and looked at the clam dip like it was a bowl of worms. Polly was humming as she sashayed out of the room, her blond curls bouncing. We reached for the same slice of salami and then pulled our hands back. "Go ahead," my dad said, like I was some random kid waiting in line at a buffet. I took it and chewed slowly and he did the same while we sat mostly silent as the Bears gave up a touchdown and Polly sang "Chapel of Love" softly in the kitchen.

Six

Exactly one good thing came out of the Polly-and-Dad wedding-to-be, and it wasn't that I learned there are several shades of peach. It was that after Polly and I had cleaned up the dishes from her enormous dinner and we'd eaten her homemade cream puffs and we'd all sat down to watch *Mary*—which was Mary Tyler Moore's variety show that wasn't as good as *The Mary Tyler Moore Show* and definitely not as good as *All in the Family* but that Polly seemed to like, and what could I say when it wasn't my condo or my TV—she saw me lifting the cover of an issue of *Cosmo* that was on the side table and she told me, "Oh, take it. I'm so busy with this." She held up a gargantuan *Today's Bride* magazine like it was a trophy.

So I took *Cosmo* home and couldn't even be all that mad at Mom when she asked if I was upset she didn't tip me off about the wedding, because I was desperate to read an article called "How You Can End Up Turning a Man Off When You're Trying to Turn Him On." The article started with stories about women who couldn't get second dates because they hadn't asked a guy enough questions or complimented his car, but a box next to it was titled "Seductive Moves He'll Find Irresistible." I stopped reading the main article. The moves sounded perfect, and I liked the introduction even more:

Waiting for that man to wake up and realize you'd like a date? It's the '70s, sexy! Ask him yourself! Or, if you're really wanting him to make the first move, give him a nudge in the right direction with these tricks that signal you're ready to say YES.

I knew Bobby wasn't actually going to ask me out . . . but couldn't these ideas translate to helping me get his attention at practice?

I called Candace. It was a little late and I worried Mr. Trillo wouldn't let me talk to her, but Candace picked up on the first ring. When I said, "Hey!" she answered with an "Oh, hi."

"Um, were you expecting someone else?"

"I thought you were Reggie. What's up?"

I couldn't go right from disappointing her with my not-Reggie-ness to asking about a guy, so I grabbed for whatever neutral topic I could. "I'm in my dad's wedding," I said.

"What?" Candace clucked her tongue. "I can't believe he's getting married already. What colors are they using?"

"Like, orange or something," I said.

"Oh boy," she said. "I'm sorry. Are you okay?"

"Yeah, I guess. Polly is nice enough," I said. She was, and in that sense, I was okay. It wasn't like my dad was giving me a stepmother like Jacqueline. I found I didn't have much to say about the wedding after all. I smoothed down the glossy page of *Cosmo*. "Are you ready for practice tomorrow?"

"Sure," she said. "It'll be nice to hang out with the girls."

"Yeah, I can hardly wait to spend more time with Wendy Kowalski," I said. "She's a gem."

"Did you see the way she leaned all over Coach McMann when she was spelling her name for his list?"

I had. I'd wanted to shove her out of the way. "Do you think everyone has a crush on him?" I asked, and my throat felt tight at the thought.

"He's a teacher," she said, like this explained something. "I doubt anyone's, like, *into him* into him, but who wouldn't like having a cute coach? And soccer's something to do."

"But so is pep club, or yearbook, or, like, badminton," I said.

"Pep club and yearbook are run by bitches," Candace said, reminding me that she'd gone to meetings for both of those things last year and quit right away. "And badminton is like tennis's weird cousin."

"I wish I were out of high school and met Bobby at the gas station or something." I wanted to talk about Bobby but I wasn't quite sure how to do it, even with Candace, who was my oldest friend. Of course she knew I thought Bobby was cute, but that I imagined meeting him outside of school was a new revelation that made my stomach rise up in my rib cage as I waited for what she would say.

"He's a *teacher*," she said again, but this time like it was a law I'd broken. My stomach dropped back down.

"I know," I said, the edge of a whine creeping into my voice.

"It's just weird, because my dad was twenty-three when he met my mom, and she was eighteen. I'm seventeen and Coach McMann is probably about twenty-two."

"I don't know, Susan," she said, sounding like her mom. "An older guy is different than a teacher, you know?"

"You're right," I sighed, because she was. "We don't know anyone that hot, though."

"Reggie is hot," Candace said. I held back the gagging noise I wanted to make.

"But Coach McMann is like a movie star," I said.

"That's your problem. You always get crushes on movie stars because you're afraid to confront a real-life penis," Candace said, clearly enjoying her expertise as someone with many penis confrontations to my zero.

"It's not fear. The penises in Powell Park are attached to the boys in Powell Park, is what it is," I said.

"I don't know. I think you should try to be more realistic and go out with someone at school."

Like you do, with every single boy we know, who all treat you like shit, I wanted to say. I'd rather squeeze my legs together through a million of my fantasies than have to put up with some guy who thought it was sexy to pretend a girl's nipples were radio dials. I bet Bobby wouldn't do that.

"Yeah, okay," I said, annoyed. "I'd better get some sleep."

We hung up and I went back to the magazine, alone. Candace was wrong. Maybe actually dating Coach McMann was unrealistic right now, but at least I had good taste. Every real-life guy I'd met before was a gutter ball, but Coach McMann had bowled me over. If anyone was unrealistic, it was Candace, for thinking that a football team neanderthal like Reggie was going turn into boyfriend material because of one hand job. It was more likely that his dick would start laying golden eggs.

I read through *Cosmo*'s tips carefully, but I was confused over which would work best. So I fell asleep after deciding to try each one until something clicked.

Tip #1: Skip the bra. Men love a woman who embraces freedom. If you catch him looking, smile.

So Monday Susan went to practice without a bra.

It was hard to find a shirt that wouldn't emphasize the unevenness of my breasts, but I finally settled on an old Lynyrd Skynyrd shirt of Tonia's that was soft from the wash and clung just right. But I hadn't counted on how brisk it was going to be at practice. It was one of those September days when the wind was just cold and fast enough to feel like a slap, so my nipples were pointy and hard within minutes of getting to the field.

Still, the magazine had suggested I throw my shoulders back and be daring, so I did.

"Is that one Hi, and that one How Are You?" Candace said, pointing at my breasts.

"More like Come, and Get It," Tina said. "Do you want to catch his eye or put his eyes out?"

"Shut up—Bobby's here," I said.

He came onto the field looking, momentarily, like someone who'd be described as pure of heart. It was most likely because the day was overcast and he was standing in the sole patch of sunlight, but I crossed my arms over my chest, thinking now was not the moment to make my bralessness known.

"It looks like everyone's here," Bobby said. "I hope you're all as excited as I am to get things going. This first week, we'll be focused on the basics. Foot-eye coordination, ball handling, overall conditioning. I know a lot of you haven't played before, but I have complete faith that you're each going to feel like you know what you're doing very soon. All I ask is that you don't get discouraged. Some of the best athletes are made, not born, so don't be afraid to get things wrong. I'm here to help."

Despite his encouragement—and the praise he peppered over everything we got even half right—we struggled through the basics, repeating things until they grew boring. Bobby must have noticed our attention waning, because toward the end of practice he said we could try kicking at the goal—which was just a section of the field marked off by some old cones he'd brought, since we didn't have a real goal.

Sadly, there was no way for Bobby to notice my boobs when our feet and their lack of cooperation were his only concern.

"Don't worry, kicking a soccer ball only looks simple if you've worked on it for years," he said, positioning himself in front of the ball and reeling back his right leg, then sending the ball on a fast forward trajectory toward the cones. "Once you get it, there's nothing more satisfying."

I could think of many more satisfying things.

We took our turns and not once did Bobby give me a special look. On Dana Miller's turn, he came over and helped her get into position, touching her shoulders. On my turn, I hoped for the same thing to happen. But instead I rocketed my ball sideways, sending it into a row of bushes, and I had to go fish it out. My shirt got snagged on a branch and I left practice with a scratch on my nipple.

Tip #2: Remember the power of good old-fashioned eyelash batting. Play up your peepers with dramatic makeup and lock stares with that handsome stranger.

Tuesday Susan lined her eyes.

I spent ten minutes after school applying turquoise liquid eye shadow until my eyes looked as big and bright as Bambi's, and then I had Candace help me glue on fake eyelashes so thick, I felt tired keeping my lids open. "You look really good," she said, and I started to forgive her for her lack of early support.

"You're all looking good," Bobby told us as we muddled our way through the same things we'd done the day before. He'd given another long and inspiring speech, but even though I acted like I was paying close attention, I never got the eye contact I wanted. Instead, Wendy faked a twisted ankle and Bobby stopped everything to hold her leg in his hand and check it.

"I bet you wish you'd thought of that," Tina said, as Wendy sat there with a smug grin. I did.

When we finally had to run laps, I sprinted ahead of everyone just to be alone for a minute, even though it made my eye makeup melt and trickle into my eyes. I felt like an idiot and wanted to cry.

Tip #3: Don't be afraid to get wet. A woman's skin beaded with water fresh from a shower or a swim is an earthy, natural enticement. Try it at the beach, or when you greet your favorite delivery man!

Wednesday Susan brought a milk jug filled with water from home.

I wasn't sure how much water I'd need. Bobby had us do more of the same drills we'd run the last two days. He staked three sets of short colored flags in circles into the ground and broke us into three groups. Then he called out a color for us to kick our balls to.

"This again?" Wendy asked.

"When do we get uniforms?" Dana inquired.

I shifted my weight from foot to foot. I needed to at least crack a light sweat so I could douse myself with the water, but we were just standing there.

"Can we be done early today? I'm helping the pep club bring cookies to the football team." That was Candace.

"You're not in the pep club," Tina chided her.

"I know. But I made cookies and I'm getting mine to the field before they do," Candace replied. "If they think they get to decide how I show school spirit, they thought wrong."

"Maybe we need to start a new club for people with vendettas against the pep club," I said. Candace and Tina laughed.

"The sooner you focus, the sooner you'll get out of here," Bobby said, looking right at the three of us.

"This flag thing is so boring, though," said Lisa Orlawski, as Lisa Kowolski and Lisa Jaworski nodded behind her.

"I get it, but this is a very basic drill and you need to master it before we move on to anything harder," Bobby said. He smiled tightly.

"What about the uniforms?" Dana asked again.

"Yeah, are they cute?" asked Sharon Henderson.

"Let's stay focused," Bobby said, blowing his whistle. "To red!"

"Someone's cranky," Candace said to me as we plodded toward the red flag in our circle. "What's the water for, anyway?"

"Just wait," I told her. I wondered if Bobby being cranky would make him more or less receptive to being seduced.

"More practicing, less chatting, ladies," Bobby said to us. "To red, Sharon, not orange!"

But we weren't the only ones talking. Everyone was. Besides Coach McMann's lousy mood, there was other gossip, like how Peggy Darnell had gotten caught backstage with a guy from St. Ignatius after rehearsals the other day.

"Okay, you're a mess out there," Coach McMann said, blowing his whistle so loud it startled me. He had his hands on his hips now. "You all need to shake out whatever's keeping you from having your head in the game. Five laps around the park. Go!" He blew the whistle again.

Everyone groaned—everyone except me. If I finished first, I'd have time alone with Bobby. I could splash my face and enticingly glance up at him with glistening beads of water dappled across my cheekbones. One long look from Bobby would make all this crap worth it.

So I took off, the cadence of my footfalls a drumbeat in my ears. Halfway through the first lap, Tina caught up with me, breathless. "Wait up," she said.

"Can't," I huffed, and charged forward.

By lap three, everything hurt, but I was way ahead of everyone, and as I passed him, I saw Bobby give me a thumbs-up. "Keep it up," he said.

I finished at the bench, well ahead of the team but completely out of breath. "You okay?" Bobby asked as I grabbed the bench and reached for my water.

"Yeah," I said, struggling to untwist the cap. "Just . . . hot." I didn't know if my voice sounded breathy and intriguing, or medically unsafe.

Bobby was smiling at me. "You're fast," he said. "Great stride."

I took this to mean he'd been looking at my legs and I smiled at him, still unable to speak properly. As I tried to tilt the jug to pour some water into my free hand, my grip slipped, sending a stream of water down the front of my shorts. My crotch was soaked. "Oh my God," I said.

Bobby had turned back to watch the other girls and barely looked as he threw me a towel from inside the equipment bag. "Dry off—there's more to do," he said. Then he turned and pointed at my milk jug. "Smart idea, though. I'll bring water for everyone tomorrow." He clapped for the girls headed into their last laps. "Looking good, ladies."

So he just complimented everyone like that.

I was dabbing at the water as the other girls started to come back. Wendy yelled, "Oh my God, Susan, did you wet yourself?"

Since Bobby had turned away from me, I mouthed *Fuck you*, but she was too busy laughing to care.

Thursday Susan didn't even get a chance to employ *Cosmo*'s fourth tip, because I made him mad. Well, we all did.

It started when Bobby showed up to practice that day. Most of the girls were looking at their cuticles or checking their hair for split ends instead of warming up, like we knew at this point he wanted us to.

"We're missing some people," Bobby said, looking around. A few girls had ditched, and he sighed as he dumped the soccer balls out on the field. "You guys should be stretching if you get here before me." He seemed annoyed, even more than he'd been the day before. In the same tone, he told us, "By next week we'll have a soccer goal at either end of this field. I've been pressing the school for a more permanent practice space on school grounds; they can't make it happen right now, but I did get them to work with the park district to put in some nets here, so it's a step in the right direction."

None of us were really paying attention, and then Dawn Murphy raised her hand and said, "I need to leave early today." Dawn was one of the few girls on the team who wasn't outwardly interested in Bobby—she seemed to genuinely like playing soccer—but she was a mystery in other ways, too. After her sophomore year, she'd disappeared, and everyone had assumed she'd left because she'd gotten pregnant. When she'd returned this year—as a senior—whispers followed her around, as people wondered if she'd given the baby away or if her mom was raising it. No one ever asked her outright and Dawn didn't volunteer anything. These last few practice days, she had been in a hurry to leave, and some of the team had gossiped that she had to get home to her baby.

"Look," Bobby said, "I don't think you all realize how hard it is to get a school board and a park district to cooperate on outfitting this space as a soccer field. Real nets are going to give our practices more purpose, right?"

We mumbled "yesses" and "sures" from our spots on the grass, where our stretches were as lackluster as our enthusiasm for goals. No one cared about the school and park districts cooperating, and our apathy only made Bobby crabbier.

"Dawn, go ahead and leave if you have to." He blew his whistle and said, "The rest of you, a hundred jumping jacks. Go."

"Not fifty?" Candace said, with her arms folded over her chest as though to protect her boobs from further discomfort.

"A hundred," he replied. "You can do it."

I wasn't proud of it, but by that point I was frustrated with him for barely having noticed me once that week, after all the ways I'd worked for it. And maybe everyone had some grudge against him, because we half-heartedly clapped our hands overhead, putting little effort into the jumping part of the jacks.

"More energy, team," Bobby said, as he pumped up one of the soccer balls. "Now, twenty push-ups."

"What?" Joanie Fox asked. "It's soccer, not football."

"We can make it fifty if you'd rather." Bobby's tone was icy. I was pissed at the other girls for putting him in such a foul mood, but I was more pissed at him. It's not like any of us knew what we were doing. We'd all told him we hadn't played soccer before. Why was he being so *serious*? Were we supposed to make him a crown because he'd gotten us some goals?

We started the push-ups, but everyone was sort of faking them. While we were doing that, Bobby took out a stack of cones and made four rows of four halfway down the field. No one got up off the grass when we finished.

Bobby said, "Stand up. Take a ball. Dribble down your row, around each cone, then back. Take it slow if you have to. I want to see you keeping the ball close the entire time. When the person in front of you passes the first cone, next one goes."

There was none of his usual smiling or encouragement, and as we slowly got to our feet, he said, "Let's move. This isn't optional."

"What about the flag thing?" Candace asked, looking with dread at the cones. "I thought we had to be good at that first."

"I changed my mind," Bobby said. He blew his whistle and put his hands on his hips. We set off. I was in line after Tina, who was doing pretty good until she knocked over the second cone. I took off behind her, but I peeked back at Bobby to see if he was watching me—even though I was mad at him, if I saw him smile at me, all would be forgiven—and I lost my ball.

"This is getting old," someone behind me said, and it seemed like everyone felt that way. No one had the energy we'd had earlier in the week.

"Speed it up," Bobby said. His face was stony and he'd folded his arms over his chest, like he wanted to build a wall between us and him.

"You said to go slow," Arlene whined.

"Slow like you care, not like you died." It was as stern as Bobby had ever sounded.

When we all returned, he said, "Grab some water, and we'll do it again. This time with a little speed."

"Someone's testy today," Candace said, taking one of the small paper cups set out next to the cooler of water Bobby had brought.

"For real," Dana said, pushing a sweaty lock of hair off her face.

"I didn't know he could be such a prick," Marie Quinn said.

"Yeah, he can bite me," Joanie moaned.

"You'd like that, wouldn't you?" Tina retorted.

"No, that's Susan," Candace said.

"Shut up, Candace." I looked over my shoulder to see if Bobby was listening, but he was straightening the cones.

"I didn't know this was going to be so hard," Wendy said.

"Or pointless. Like, we don't even have a game," Sarah Foster said.

"This is so boring," Arlene said. "I thought he'd be more flirty."

"He's gonna hear you, Arlene," Dana said. "Besides, isn't hanging all over Tom Meyer enough for you?"

"I don't hang all over Tom," Arlene shot back.

"I heard your ex Paul is going out with Jessica Simich," Joanie said. "He got over you fast."

Arlene tossed a cup of water at her. Joanie tossed one back at her, and then Dana shot a cup at water at me.

"What'd you do that for?" I said to her.

"Because you're showing off, trying to outrun us all so you get time with Bobby."

I looked from Dana to the other girls on the team, who were all nodding.

"Is there such a thing as 'coach's pet'?" Marie asked.

"Yeah, I thought *I* tried to be a showoff," Wendy said. "But at least I wear a bra."

"It's kind of twisted," Dana said, her voice going full prude.

"It's not like that. Shut. UP," I said. I had a cup of water in each hand and tossed both at her. But Dana stepped out of the way, and two streams of water sailed through the air and—

Hit Bobby, who'd been standing right behind her.

"That's it!" he said, and blew his whistle again. His eyes were sharp, and his nostrils flared. He directed his angry face at me for a second before moving on to the rest of the girls.

None of us spoke.

"All week. All week, *I've* shown up. All week, I've tried. And here and there, I see it in you—that you can *do* this. But just as one of you starts to show potential, another one decides to slow down, or complain, or fuck around. I've shown up. But you haven't. SHOWN. UP."

He kicked a soccer ball so hard, it coursed through the air, hit a nearby tree, and ricocheted back at us. He had his hands on his hips, framing his perfect pelvis, as he said, "Know what suicides are?"

"Like, someone killing themselves?" Franchesa Rotini, who rarely spoke, asked with a quiver in her voice.

"Yeah, that. But on the field. They're what my coaches had us do when no one was taking practice seriously and they were sick of our shit." He turned and pointed. "Run as fast as you can to the middle of the field and back, then as fast as you can to the playground and back. Touch the ground at the middle and at the playground."

He blew his whistle, but we all stayed where we were, looking at each other.

"Now!" he growled.

With that, we started running toward the middle of the field and back. When we touched the ground near Bobby, he yelled, "Pick it up!" I sprinted toward the playground, way ahead of everyone, but when I got back, I stopped and bent over, panting.

Bobby looked at me and shook his head. "You stop when I tell you to stop." Then he yelled, "All of you, keep running until I say you're done." He blew his whistle three times rapidly and watched us, his hands in fists at his sides.

"Fuck," someone behind me said.

I was out in front, with Tina and Wendy not far behind me. On the third round, the three of us slowed down when we reached Bobby again, and he said, "Speed it up. Set the pace." When we'd made it halfway to the playground, we could see some of the other girls just getting to the middle of the field for the third time.

"Keep going," Bobby yelled at the stragglers.

I kept running because I was angry at him. It was the only explanation because really, with each suicide, I thought, *Why are we even doing this?* I had joined the team for him, didn't he get that? But all he did was ignore me, and now he was treating me and everyone else like garbage because he wanted us to take this seriously. Nobody at school took us seriously, and probably no one did at the park district. He was lucky to even have a team, to have us.

He was lucky to have *me*.

Candace stopped in the middle of the field, clutching her side. She was breathing heavily, and she looked like she was going to puke. Gritting her teeth, she glared at Bobby.

"We can't do this," she hollered at him. "We're just girls!"

Bobby started walking toward her. The three Lisas stopped running, and the rest of us started to slow down, like Candace was a car crash and we wanted a better look.

"What did you say?" Bobby asked her. He narrowed his eyes.

"I said, we can't do this."

Bobby blew his whistle and held up a hand for us to stop, even though most of us already had. If his expression hadn't been so angry, I'd have been jealous at how Candace had his full attention. "No. The second part."

Candace paused, like she knew this was bad but had no other choice. She took a deep breath in and let it out. "I said, we're just girls," Candace repeated, in a whisper.

Bobby bent his chin to his chest and rubbed his forehead. It was completely quiet.

We all looked at Candace like she'd saved us. But then Bobby shook his head and raised his gaze to her and then to all of us. His lips were set in a hard line as he breathed through his nose.

He spoke softly, but each of his words was injected with fury. "I don't want to hear you're *just* anything. You're *athletes*. Do you hear me?"

I couldn't see Michael Webster or my dad thinking soccer was cute if they could have seen how scary Bobby was right then. We were all standing petrified like we were in a game of freeze tag with nobody "it," but each of us managed to nod.

He blew his whistle again. "Now run."

No one left practice right then, but only because we were too terrified. We ran.

Every time we got back to the start, he told us to go again.

Me, Tina, and Wendy were in front most of the way, but my side ached and I pinched it as I ran. Behind us, Sharon and Candace and the rest of the team were hobbling. Finally, some of the girls quit. Candace collapsed onto the ground. Dana made an awful death-gag sound and staggered off the field. Even Tina grabbed for a bench on one of our returns and put her head down, breathing deep, before starting again.

I kept running. After a few more sprints, with Bobby yelling, "Again!" I glanced back and saw only Wendy and Tina still running, while everyone else looked like bodies on a battlefield. But if Bobby didn't tell me to stop, then I was going to keep going. I didn't know if I ever wanted to see him again after today, but I wasn't about to give him the satisfaction of knowing that he beat me.

Finally, the only footsteps I heard were my own. The inside of my chest felt like it had been scorched and I was having trouble pumping my arms. It was going to be dark soon. Bobby held up his hands and said, "You're done."

Tina extended her arm for me to grab and I almost missed it. We flopped down in the grass. Wendy, I noticed, was sprawled on the ground like she'd jumped from a high building.

Bobby didn't explain himself or apologize. "Get some water if you need it."

We formed a line behind the jug, silent except for our panting, as if we all knew better than to speak.

When we each had a paper cup and were gulping thirstily, Bobby said, "Well, you all survived. 'Just girls.'" He shook his head. "And I'm sure some of you will go home tonight and think,

'Screw Coach McMann, I'm not running like that again, he's not going to treat me like that.'"

He passed his eyes over each one of us, and I thought his look stopped on me for longer. Two days ago, that would have made me happy, and I might have even tried to glance away coyly, like *Cosmo*'s sixth tip advised, but today, I just glared at him.

"Sure. That was a tough practice. And let me tell you this: We're going to have more of them, because I'm treating you like *I* would want to be treated. Like an athlete. So if any of you want to put in the effort, if any of you want to claim what's yours— the right to say you gave it your all, instead of acting like this is some kind of joke and I'm the punch line—then I'll see you here tomorrow. Otherwise, this isn't the team for you. And I'm not the coach for you."

He didn't give anyone a chance to protest, just reached for the bag of balls and slung it over his shoulder. Then he turned and strode away, like he couldn't care less what we did.

Seven

Friday Susan decided to quit.

Well, I decided Thursday.

I got home from practice ravenous. I made and ate two boxes of mac and cheese and what was left of the Cheez Balls and a scoop of leftover hamburger casserole Mom had made on Monday for us to eat during the week because she had night classes. Then I flopped on the couch and felt every inch of every muscle I didn't know the name of screaming at me.

For the first time in a while, I was too worn out to go to my room and get off. I wasn't motivated to, either. I tried, for a second or two, to imagine finding Bobby alone, and how I would apologize to him, but Bobby's anger was too radiant in my mind. And then I remembered I was angry at him, too.

I flipped on the TV, and a commercial for *Charlie's Angels* was on. The Angels were so pretty when they ran. None of them looked as bad as the team did after suicides. None of them looked like they were going to puke, that was for sure. Would Coach McMann make the Angels feel like they weren't good enough, too?

I was more than angry. I felt stupid. When I'd first seen Coach McMann, I'd felt some kind of spark, like if I could just be around him, he'd see I wasn't a typical high school girl. Attention from him—a special kind of person—would transfer some of the same specialness to me.

I was mad, too, that I'd been so obvious in my quest for his desire that the whole team had noticed. Except him. He wasn't going to notice me. He could barely stand me. Even though he'd made it obvious he didn't particularly like any of us at the moment, I thought it was possible—for no exact reason other than I wanted to wallow in how differently things had gone than I'd hoped—he disliked me the most out of everyone.

My mom walked in the door, laden with her book bag and her purse, looking drained. "Did I miss the Angels?" she asked.

I perked up despite myself. "Yes and no, because it was on last night," I said, and then, because she looked disappointed, added, "It wasn't that good." It had been really good.

She sat down next to me on the couch. "Are those your soccer clothes?" she asked, pointing to my sweaty T-shirt. "You don't have a uniform?"

"No," I said dully. "And I won't. I'm quitting."

A frown twitched at the corner of Mom's lips but she corrected it before she thought I saw. "Oh, I thought you were excited about the team," she said. "So it's not what you imagined?"

I shrugged. "It was worth trying. But I don't think it's for me."

Mom slung her arm around me. "Well, as someone who's

tried to be a few new people over the last couple years, I think it's great you attempted to branch out." She sounded genuinely proud. Belated or not, I'd take it.

The next morning, as people gathered in the halls to start talking about the weekend, I found Tina and Candace. We were standing at my locker when I told them, "I'm going to quit soccer."

Candace paused. "I lost two pounds this week," she said. "But my boobs hurt and I don't ever want to run like we did yesterday again. I don't want to go back, either."

Tina wouldn't meet my eyes for a moment, but then she sucked in a breath and drew herself up. She shook her head. "I hate quitting," she said. "Are you guys sure you want to give up already? I thought we were having fun."

"I'm not cut out for it," Candace said, which Tina seemed to accept. That Candace wasn't made for sprinting and push-ups was no surprise. But Tina gave me an unswerving stare, like my motive for quitting had spelled itself out on my T-shirt.

"We could join something else," I offered. "Soccer's a drag, isn't it?"

"This is because Coach McMann was an asshole, isn't it?" Tina said. "You should do what you want, but I think you're making a mistake. He's a coach—he's probably going to yell sometimes."

Her comments only made me want to quit more. If I was just another player for Bobby to yell at, then there was no reason for me to be there. Candace felt like she could just stop showing up and it would be no big deal. I wanted Bobby to *know* that I was out of there. And for him to feel terrible about it. So I decided to be late for lunch and went to the athletics office.

A few of the assistant football coaches—how a team so bad needed so many coaches was a mystery to me—were bent over a desk. They looked up as I walked in. "What do you need, honey?" one said, as though I was lost.

"Sorry," I said, apologizing reflexively only because I could tell they didn't want me there. "I need to talk to my coach. I mean, Mr. McMann." He wasn't my coach anymore.

I wove through the room, crowded with baskets of kickballs and footballs and jump ropes dangling from an old coatrack. The office smelled like stale sweat and something medicinal.

"Oh, heh," the coach said, lifting his shirt a bit to scratch his hairy stomach. "We'll watch our language with a lady present."

"Okay," I said, only because I didn't think I could say "fuck off" to a teacher.

Bobby was sitting alone at a small desk in the corner of the office, and when he looked up and saw me, he beamed. My insides went into overdrive.

"Susan," he said. "What brings you here?"

He was so happy compared to yesterday, the speech I'd memorized left my brain. "Um, hi," I said, tilting my head to one side. "I . . ." Alone with him, but not alone, I didn't know what to do. I looked at his lunch—two sandwiches on some sort of unpleasant-looking brown bread. I crushed my lunch bag in my sweaty palm.

He stood up and reached for something behind me, his wrist lightly brushing my bare arm. Then he backed into his seat and put an overturned bucket next to his desk. "Sorry, I don't have another chair, but have a seat."

I sat, trying to remember the exact words I wanted to use as I scanned the room, with its old calendars and schedules, the Green Bay Packers poster that served as a dartboard. I was turning up a blank. "Um, so, I . . ."

"I think I know what this is about," Bobby said, and his voice was deep but soft. He leaned across the desk toward me, and I was so startled, I drew in a sharp breath. "Can I tell you a story?"

I nodded, relieved he was going to talk since I couldn't remember how.

"When I was a kid—not in high school, younger—I was pretty small for my age, and kind of uncoordinated. My brothers played football, just like my dad, and they never let me join in because I was the runt. Every now and then, they'd let me be kicker."

He looked somewhere over my shoulder, like he was trying to see the memory clearly. "And that's how you started playing soccer?" I said.

He shook his head. "No, I hated being kicker. Mostly because my dad would be yelling at my brothers to run faster or take a harder hit or whatever and then he'd pat me on the head and say 'good job' even if I hadn't done one. Like I wasn't even worth the trouble to yell at."

"So you yell because you care?" I said. God, did he hear how dumb that sounded?

He nodded. "I'm not proud of it," he said, "but, yes, I was being hard on you guys because if I say 'good job' when I know you can do better, that's like lying to you. And to me, that's worse. Do you see what I mean?"

He was looking right into my eyes, like I was the most beautiful woman he'd ever seen. Or like he really cared what I thought, which was almost better. Maybe it wasn't so dumb after all.

"Anyway, you didn't tell me why you stopped by," he said, as I was trying to pull my stare away from the faint stubble along his jaw. He was so foxy.

"I, uh . . . ," I stammered. I forgave him. Not only because he looked so gorgeous, like he was a prince trying to convince me to come down from my tower. It was because he'd apologized, and he'd also *explained*. And his explanation wasn't to blame something else, like his freshman algebra class had been shitty that day. He'd given me a real reason. Something personal. He'd told *me*. How could I not forgive him?

"Will we get uniforms?" I finished.

"I wanted us to have goals first. But I'm working on uniforms," Bobby said. He looked at the piles of football uniforms on the shelf across from his desk. "I know, it seems like the boys' teams have more than enough equipment, but that's how pioneers like us have to operate. You might want to consider getting a pair of cleats in the meantime."

"Oh, okay," I said, getting up, because I had no other reason to be there. "That's a good idea. Thank you."

I turned to go, but my heart caught when he said, "Susan, can I say one more thing?"

I've been noticing you and I can't stop thinking about you.

I don't know if I can be your coach for much longer, because these thoughts I have are inappropriate.

You have an amazing ass and I dream of it at night.

I know you're special, but we can't be together—at least, not now.

"Sure," I said, only turning halfway toward him so I didn't look too eager.

"I thought you were going to quit the team just now," he said, standing up and putting one hand on my shoulder as he looked into my eyes. My whole body got warm. "I know it's a lot to learn, but I'm so glad you're sticking with it."

His voice was soft and . . . significant. It was important to him that I believed him, I could tell.

"I'm going to stick with it . . . ," I said, trying to load my voice with as much meaning as I could. It was like speaking in code, my words saying a simple thing while the way I said them had to convey something much more complex.

"Do you think anyone is taking it seriously? I don't know if I'm getting through." His eyes looked hopeful, not unlike Polly's when she'd asked me to be her maid of honor. "It's new territory for me, and I want to be a good coach."

What could I say? *No, we're mostly hopeless jerks who think you're hot* likely wouldn't be the right response. And he was asking *me* what I thought. It was somehow way better than if he'd asked me for a date. "I think . . . I'm very happy to be on your team."

"I'm very happy you're on my team, too," he said. "You have amazing potential."

Eight

I told Candace and Tina at lunch that I'd changed my mind and decided not to quit. Tina tried to hide her grin as she said, "That's cool."

I hoped Candace might reconsider, but she seemed bewildered. "I thought you said soccer was a drag."

"I don't know," I said. "I started to feel like maybe I have some potential, and I don't want to give up so fast." I wasn't going to mention the one-on-one meeting with Bobby, but I liked putting his word—"potential"—in the air, like it linked us somehow.

"Um, okay," Candace said. We were used to being on the same wavelength, and my sudden shift from leaving the team to staying on it clearly didn't make sense to her.

"Maybe you don't want to quit, either?" Tina suggested.

"No," Candace said, putting a straw in her Tab. "I've been so happy all morning knowing I don't have to go back today."

Tina caught my eye across the table and gave a slight shrug.

That afternoon, we had a short practice. Bobby was obviously trying to be a touch gentler after the way things went yesterday, but we were all trying harder, too. We didn't dwell on the day before, but when he sent us home for the weekend, he said, "I'm glad to see most of you back. Keep showing up and I promise it will be worth it." We all managed not to giggle at the many ways we could interpret that. But I also took it to mean he'd noticed Candace hadn't returned, and also that we'd lost Sharon Henderson and two of the three Lisas, Lisa J. and Lisa K. (which probably at least made things less confusing for both Bobby and Lisa Orlawski). I also noticed that he hadn't told the entire team he saw potential in them. That he'd chosen that word specially for me made me even happier I'd decided not to quit.

I kept turning the whole conversation in Bobby's office over and over in my mind. When Tina dropped me off at home, I saw a pine cone on the sidewalk and tapped it from my left foot to my right, then dribbled it back and forth as I headed to my front steps. I felt competent, even if it was a pine cone and not a soccer ball, and I'd only dribbled it about twenty feet.

Though the sun was starting to set, I went inside, washed my face, and went back out, walking the few blocks to Ninety-Fifth Street and crossing to Sportmart, where I'd bought my soccer shorts. I had babysitting money in my pocket. It was a perfect time to buy cleats.

"Can I help you with something?" A guy with a lot of chin acne whose name tag read "Greg" came up to me. "Shopping for your boyfriend?"

I play soccer, asshole, I was tempted to say. But in all honesty, I'd never *really* played soccer. I'd run across a field a bunch of times, and kicked a ball around, and tried to get my coach to look at my tits and ass for a week. But I hadn't actually *played*. Not yet.

"No. I need soccer cleats. For me," I said.

"Oh. Girls' cleats. They don't make those," Greg said, and just stood there, like I'd led him to a dead end and he didn't know where to go.

"Well, where are the men's cleats? I'm sure there are some small sizes."

"We don't have a lot of soccer stuff. Soccer cleats are down aisle fourteen. Assorted gear and clearance." Greg pointed toward the back of the store.

The aisle had several racks of raglan-sleeved baseball shirts that were on sale for the end of the summer, and some really random stuff, like Greg had promised: Ping-Pong paddles, a few marked-down beach towels, a pair of flippers, and several shelves of cleats. There was dust on top of most of the boxes. I knew Powell Park Sporting Goods would have a better selection, because they sold jackets and jerseys to all the high schools, including the Catholic schools with soccer teams. But everyone said Powell Park Sporting Goods was really overpriced.

I was holding up one of my Keds to a cleat in a men's size six when a voice behind me said, "Hey, killer. I knew I'd see you around."

I dropped the shoe onto the shelf and turned around to see Joe, the spiky-haired kid from Dan's party. His mouth was turned up at the side, like he had a joke he could tell me but was trying to decide if I'd get it.

"Hi," I said, turning back to the shoes. I'd been buzzed the night of the party but now that I was sober, I had a strong feeling that what I'd thought might have been flirting was just his personality.

"Whatcha buying?" He stuck his nose between me and the aisle and reached for one of the shoes I'd put back for being too expensive.

"Cleats, in, I guess, a men's size six," I said. I reached past him for the cheapest pair in my size and sat down on an empty shelf to try them on. When my mom took me to Carson's for new shoes, someone fetched them out of the stockroom. I was kind of relieved that I could do it myself here.

"For soccer," Joe said. "You must be good."

I shrugged. "Not really." He didn't need to know about my amazing potential.

"Hmm," he said, and went about pulling an armful of baseball T-shirts from the shelf a few feet away.

I started to slip on the shoes and lace them up. "You play baseball? You don't seem the type."

"Not very open-minded for someone trying on men's cleats," Joe said, but he smiled. "But you're right, I don't play baseball. I'm going to make these into band T-shirts. I hate capitalism, but I love the idea of someone wearing my band's name on a T-shirt."

"What are you called?" I asked.

"The Lady Soccer Players," he said, his eyes twinkling as he waited for me to react.

"Screw you," I said, but I laughed.

"I'm kidding. We're the Watergate Tapes," Joe said, coming

closer. He put a finger under the lid of my shoebox. "But really, soccer, your own cleats . . . It's very punk rock of you."

"Punk rock?"

"You know, The Clash, the Stooges, the Buzzcocks. I love the stuff." With his finger still beneath the box lid, he looked right into my eyes.

"Yeah, I know what punk rock is," I said. "I was questioning your use of it as an adjective."

He grabbed his heart like he was wounded. "Ouch, grammar police," he said. "Punk rock *is* an adjective, because it's a way of being."

"Whatever you say," I told him and, satisfied that the shoes I'd tried would be good enough, put them back in the box and stood up to go pay.

"Don't get those," Joe said. He pointed at the box I was carrying. "Never skimp when it comes to shoes. Your feet will thank you." He pulled the more expensive ones off the shelf.

"What do you know about cleats?"

"Enough. I used to be a goalie for St. Mark's. I can play forward, too, if called upon."

"You? Played soccer?" I took in his black jeans and ratty black T-shirt.

"So into appearances, aren't we?" he shot back. "But yeah, I played for two years. Hamstring injury took me out for a while, and seeing myself act like a single-minded jock who didn't know what to do with himself when he couldn't play soccer took me out permanently."

"Oh," I said, wishing I knew how to reply to that. I picked up the pricier cleats. "These are only five bucks more, I guess." Two extra hours of babysitting Randy the Terrible down the block, but I could swing it.

"Good luck," Joe said.

"Thanks," I said, turning to go. I wanted him to say "See you around" again but he was examining the shirts.

"Joey, they didn't have my gum at Walgreens," came a female voice behind me. I turned to see a slim girl with dark blond hair slouching against the end of the aisle. Her bored expression looked like a permanent condition, but it almost made her glamorous, like Jerry Hall. "Hi," she said to me, clearly not bothered I was talking to Joe. Maybe it was his sister.

"We'll try somewhere else, babe," Joe said. *Babe.* So she was not his sister but his . . . babe. And he clearly wasn't worried about being found talking to me.

"Did they have the shirts?" the babe asked. She didn't have to put any effort into not looking at me. It was like I wasn't even there.

"Got 'em." Joe slung his arm loosely around the babe's neck and steered her down the aisle.

"We need to get to Jeff's," she said, a little whiny, as she leaned her head on his shoulder. "And I'm hungry."

But he turned back and looked at me. "Enjoy the cleats, punk rocker."

As he rounded the corner, I waited in the aisle a minute. I didn't want to be standing in line at the register next to Joe and his girlfriend.

I finally picked up the shoes and left the aisle to go pay, but almost crashed into Joe. "I just thought of something," he said, grinning at me. "If you wanted, we could, you know, train together. At soccer. I don't do the team thing anymore, but I wouldn't mind kicking a ball around. Here . . ." He fished a Wendy's receipt and a pen out of his pocket and scrawled his name and a phone number on it. As he thrust the paper into my hand, I opened my mouth to say something. But he spoke first. "I'm pretty good, so if you're serious about getting better, think about it." He closed my hand around his number. "Ball's on your pitch, killer."

He spun around and jogged to the front of the store as I looked down at his scribbled number, wondering what the hell a pitch was.

Nine

The following week, Coach McMann started off by running the same drills we'd done before. I wasn't sure any of us had improved, but halfway through practice that Wednesday, he said we were ready to try a scrimmage, where we'd face off five on five with one sub in a kind of mock game on a short field. He explained what all the different positions did—there was a jumble of terms, fullback and striker and sweeper and forward—and though we all tried to follow along, I'd bet no one would have aced a pop quiz right after. In the first scrimmages that week, Bobby had me play as a forward—his position—a few times, but later he switched me to a midfielder, which was sort of a combination defensive-and-offensive position that Bobby said required a strong runner.

Even if that was true, I wanted to be a strong *scorer*. But any chance I got to shoot at the goal—in drills or scrimmages—I flubbed. The transition from running with the ball to kicking it into the goal felt like when Candace and Tina had learned the Bus Stop dance and I couldn't get it. Bobby kept emphasizing that every position on the field had a purpose, but by now I knew that was just how Bobby talked. I sensed forward was his secret favorite position.

At first, it wasn't a big deal. No one was a super scrimmage standout. But as we racked up more practice, some of the team started to improve. Dana scored a goal on Monday and Tuesday, and Tina had three for the week. Joanie had even gotten one, and she'd been playing defense. By Friday, I was frustrated. I sweated buckets running up and down the field, and was half relieved and half jealous when Tina scored a goal on Dawn Murphy to end the scrimmage. While I was congratulating her—I was glad it was her and not Dana—Coach McMann said the worst thing he could possibly say.

"Great job out there today, ladies," Bobby told us as we walked off the field. "I'm seeing so much amazing potential from you!"

"Amazing potential" . . . the exact words he'd said to me the day I'd almost quit. I wondered if he still saw more potential in me, or just someone who couldn't be a forward.

So there was that, plus Candace. Our friendship felt strange. It wasn't like we never did anything without one another, but I think doing something with just Tina—something that wasn't us waiting for Candace at parties—made Candace anxious. Since she'd quit, she hadn't once asked us how soccer was going, and showed next to no interest in what she was missing. And in Kitchen Arts, Candace had mentioned that Reggie Stanton was going out with Karen Baker, but like it was funny and didn't bother her at all. When Tina had teased her, asking who'd replaced Reggie, Candace had said "no one" and gone back to slicing peppers for our

Denver omelet, but I could tell she was lying and I wondered what was up.

So I was in bad mood, or at least a blah one.

My mom noticed as soon as I walked into the kitchen after practice on Friday. She was scrubbing the sink in her big yellow gloves. They were the same ones Polly had at her and Dad's condo. Yellow dishwashing gloves seemed like something you didn't put in a bridal wish book but got anyway.

"You look like you had a rough practice," she said.

"Not really," I replied. Unless you counted the rude awakening that Bobby thought amazing potential was everywhere.

"Your shirt is filthy," she said. "And you stink."

I looked down at the grass-stained blue scrimmage jersey I'd forgotten to give back to Bobby as I skulked off the field. It was a castoff from the football team. Great—all I needed was to make the whole house smell like some freshman football player of seasons past.

"It's not mine," I said. "It's, like, communal."

"The community has not been kind," she said, smirking. "I'm glad you changed your mind about quitting."

"Me too," I said, not sure I meant it. The confident, walking-on-air feeling I'd had when Bobby told me I had amazing potential had been replaced by the sense that I was missing something that everyone else had. But if I told my mom that, she'd probably have advice for me from one of her self-help books, or tell me it didn't matter what everyone else did as long as I was doing my best. Ugh.

I opened the fridge to find that she must have gone shopping before coming home and putting on the yellow gloves, because there were two new packs of lunch meat, lettuce, mustard, and cheese from the deli. I pulled everything out to make myself a sandwich.

"Don't you have class?" It was only five thirty, and she usually wasn't home until seven or so on Fridays.

"Oh, it was a goof-off," Mom said, now attacking one of the crusty casserole pans with a brush. "The instructor was sick so the fill-in told us to think about where we see ourselves in five years. And then pretty much sent us home." She turned from the sink and looked at me as I took out three slices of bread to make a double-decker sandwich. "Can you imagine?"

"You mean, where I see myself in five years?" I asked, peeling several round circles of salami away from one another. Did *all* the salami slices have amazing potential, or only one?

"Sure, but the idea that someone is even *asking* me that question and there being more than one reasonable option," my mom said. "When I was your age, if you'd asked me, I would have said, 'I guess married and maybe with a baby.' And I would have been right, since I was twenty when I had your sister." She put the casserole dish in the drying rack and turned to me. "I hope I don't need to tell you that I don't regret that path for a second, since it got me you and your sister. I guess I just think it's nice that your worlds can be bigger."

"I wonder what Tonia's five-year plan is," I said. The last time I'd talked to my sister, she told me she was on her way to an aura-cleansing disco.

"You mean Chartreuse?" My mom laughed. I supposed it was

good that she was taking my sister's new identity in stride. "Well, I told her your dad would really like if she could make the wedding. It would be nice to see her."

I had assumed my sister would be required to come to town for Dad's wedding. In fact, I was counting on it. Wasn't the point of having a sibling that you had to endure your parents together? I bit into my giant sandwich and caught the fuzzy look in my mom's eyes as she swiped beneath them with the knuckle of her glove. Okay, maybe Tonia's faraway life bothered her more than she let on.

"So where do you see yourself in five years?" I asked her.

"Management," she said decisively. "And maybe attending your college graduation."

College wasn't something I'd necessarily planned on. Even my mom had never talked about me going to college until after the divorce, and I really couldn't imagine it as something I'd do. If you asked me to look five years down the road, from my seventeen-year-old vantage point, my first thought was that I'd be twenty-two, and Bobby would be twenty-seven and not my coach anymore. But I couldn't picture marriage or a white dress or, jeez, a kid. I also couldn't picture management, whatever that meant. The surroundings in my future were a blur, but I could still see me. The same me who was standing at the counter, finishing her sandwich.

Then that me was on a soccer field. The wavy vision cleared up and there I was, playing forward, kicking that goddamn goal with Bobby looking on approvingly. I didn't have five years to wait.

"You should think about your future," my mom said gently as she picked up the next nasty casserole dish. "The possibilities are so much bigger for you than I ever thought they could be."

Those possibilities scared me. It would be so easy to pick the wrong thing, wouldn't it? "I know," I told her, instead of coming up with something better.

My mom smiled faintly. In the kitchen light, the dark circles under her eyes stood out.

"Give me the gloves," I said. "I'll do this."

She didn't protest, just passed me the gloves, then put her arm around my shoulder and squeezed. I hoped she saw my offer as a way of saying thank you.

I washed the rest of the dishes and scrubbed the sink again until it shone. Then I went to my room and found the Wendy's receipt with Joe's number on it and called him.

When I turned the corner to Oak Meadows at eight a.m. the next day, I was jolted with surprise to see Joe already there. I would never have taken him for a morning person. He had a stack of cones next to him—did he and Coach McMann shop at the same cone store?—and was bouncing a ball off the top of his foot, with the quick repetition of one of those paddleball games.

Shit, he *was* good. I hoped I wouldn't embarrass myself.

"Hey," I said, and he turned around. He was wearing warm-up pants, but he still looked punk, with his spiked hair and a black T-shirt with holes that appeared strategically cut from the chest and shoulders. I felt nearly naked in my shorts. And cold.

"Hey," he said. "I didn't know there were goals here now."

"They're new," I said. "Our coach got them."

"Nice," Joe said, gesturing to his cones. "I brought cones to make one. They might still come in handy if we practice footwork stuff." Then, noticing my shorts, he added, "You need to get some track pants. Next time we practice, I'll bring you a pair."

Was he this easy around everyone? Bringing cones and offering pants? Maybe that was how he'd landed the "babe" from Sportmart. "You don't have to but, um, thanks," I said, not knowing what to say to him already mentioning a "next time." He seemed too *eager*, I guess, to be a punk. Or at least what I thought a punk was. "And thanks for meeting me."

"No problem, champ," he said. "I'm a little rusty but I remember the basics." At that moment, with me standing about ten feet away from him, he flipped the ball off the top of his foot and, nimbly tapping the ball with the inside edge of his Puma, sent a pass my way. Instinctively, I kicked it, but too hard. The ball flew over his head and landed on the playground.

"Good reflexes," he said. "We just need to work on that control. What position are you?"

"I don't exactly know yet?" I said. "Not goalie, though. That's what you played, right?"

"Yep," he said, clicking his tongue and tilting his head as he sized me up. "You look quick. Maybe a midfielder, or forward?"

"I'm fast, yeah, but I don't have a great shot. I haven't scored yet," I said. "But I really want to. Score."

Joe clapped his hands and winked. "Well, you're gonna score today. We're not leaving this park until it happens."

I rolled my eyes but smiled. It was the first time I'd said it out loud like that, that I wanted so badly to score a goal, but it felt good, it felt right. And I wasn't even embarrassed about the double meaning, that "scoring" was another word for having sex. It's not like it mattered, with Joe. He was cute and all, and it was nice he was here to help me, but I could already tell he was the type of guy who was way too cool to take anything seriously.

I could hear Candace in my head, telling me that I found something wrong with everyone. And she wasn't wrong—but that didn't mean I was. There *was* something wrong with everyone. Michael Webster was too full of himself. Jeff Sipowitz was a gross, lechy pig. Joe seemed fun and funny, but these sorts of irreverent, flirty dudes rarely turn out to be boyfriend material (not that I had a lot of experience with boyfriend material), and besides, he already had a "babe." Was it really some great mystery why I was fixated on Bobby?

Joe told me we'd run a passing drill and I'd work on scoring in the empty goal first; then later he'd let me try to shoot on him. "Don't let me being a skinny dude fool you. I'm all legs and arms. You kick it at me and it's a mess. For you."

"We'll see about that." I grinned, even though I was already worried this would take all day and he'd regret offering to help me.

Joe passed me the ball again and we dribbled alongside each other, trading passes until we approached the net. Then he'd kick it sidelong to me and I'd have to kick it at the net. The transition from running to shooting messed me up immediately, just like at practice. Several times, I kicked the ball way too high, or too wide, or too lightly, so it stopped just short of the goal. A few times, I misplaced my kick and my leg sliced air.

"Maybe I'm not cut out for this," I said. "You'd think one would go in by accident."

Joe waved me off. "You know what it is? You're rushing."

"I only have a few seconds to kick it, though. Or less, if someone steals it."

"Seconds are long, man." Joe came up behind me. I tensed a little, sensing his body right behind mine.

"May I?" he asked. His tall frame cast a shadow on the grass next to mine. I came up to his shoulder.

"May you what?" I turned my head back to look at him.

"Like, put you in a good position? I don't want to just grab you." He put his hands up like he wanted to show me what he'd be using to touch me.

"Yeah," I said. I thought of some of the romance novels I read, like *Captive Bride*, where the hero grabbed the woman all the time. I liked those parts, but it was nice to be asked, too. Especially because for Joe and me, it clarified that we were friends, even if he was a constant flirt.

He put a hand on each side of my waist and gently nudged me so I was at a slight angle. Then he got on the ground and moved my nonkicking foot so it was even with the ball and about a foot away from it. I was glad I'd shaved my legs.

"That's your place foot," he said, looking up at me. "Your body points toward the goal, not away. Then look up for a split second, see the goal and where you want to go. Do you see it?"

I nodded.

"Now, give the ball your full attention as you pull back and nail it. Use the inside edge of your foot—that'll give you the most control." He was still on the ground as he said this, and I was pretty sure Bobby had demonstrated something similar and I'd been focused on his butt and not the lesson. How much better I'd be at soccer if my coach wasn't hot wasn't even a question I could answer.

Joe sprang up from his crouch and nodded his head toward the goal. "Wanna try?"

I was already in position, so I let out a breath and said, "Yeah."

"Okay, think about where you want to go and go there."

I looked at the net and thought how Wendy and Dawn had both let by kicks into the bottom corners. I had a feeling those goals were as much about Wendy and Dawn being inexperienced goalies as about anyone on our field calling her shots, but if I could call a shot, how cool would that be?

I drew back and gave the ball a nice solid kick with the inside of my cleat. It cleared the grass, hurtling fast, and hit the back of the net—not the corner, but close.

"Yes!" I screamed. Even though I'd made goals standing still before, this felt different, as if being more intentional made the result more exciting. I wished the goal had made a noise like a pinball machine.

"Nice one, champ. So if you've got it"—he moved to stand in the goal—"now try to get one by me."

"Already?"

"You're ready."

I did everything the same way, bringing the ball down the field toward the goal. But even though my kicks were better when I got into position, it was obvious I wasn't going to get the ball past Joe. He moved way too fast, seeming to anticipate where the ball would go before I even kicked. He shot out a leg here, or an arm there, knocking away anything that came close.

"You weren't kidding about the long arms and legs. But also, do you have, like, Spidey senses? How do you always know where I'm going to kick it?"

"Goalie secret." He smirked.

"I don't think I'm going to get one by you," I told him.

"Not today, anyway," he agreed. I pouted, but I had to admit I liked the fact that Joe wasn't going to *give* me a goal. Other boys might have, and in a way that would let me know they were doing it to be nice because it was "cute" that I played. I thought about Bobby, and what he'd said about his dad and brothers after he was so rough on us at practice.

I really wanted another lesson. Fortunately, as Joe hefted his cones and tossed me the ball to carry, he said, "I have my car, so I can drive you back—and I can pick you up next time, if you want."

"Next time?" I was relieved he'd said it again and I didn't have to ask.

"Yeah, you're not yet wise in the ways of the Force," he said. ". . . Sorry, have you seen *Star Wars*?"

"Sure, but what, you're Obi-Wan now, and I'm Luke?"

"I retain my claim to higher-ranking Jedi until you get a ball past me," he said, stopping at the curb next to his car. "But anyway, the big thing you need to learn is, every goalie has his weakness. Like, Ken the Lame, this guy at St. Mark's who took over my position? Fucker practically lays out a red carpet to the top-right corner of the goal for everyone who wants to take a shot on him."

"Why didn't you go back, after your leg got better?" I asked. I'd been thinking about it all morning, since it was so obvious that he loved to play. "You're really good."

He shrugged and pursed his lips for a second. I could tell immediately he didn't want to talk about this but also didn't want to admit he didn't want to talk about it.

"Started my band, didn't like the whole jock thing," he said after a moment. "Especially at St. Mark's. All that 'Strength, Honor, Courage' crap, but the best athletes are all the worst people. Being on a team mostly means blindly following whatever the shittiest guys want to do. Like the Webs, the guy you shot down. He's a turd. The teams are mostly turds."

He loaded the cones into the trunk of his old Nova and I threw the soccer ball in beside them. For the first time that day, he seemed unsettled, and I felt bad for making him talk about his ex-team.

"So what's *your* weakness?" I asked as I opened the passenger door and dropped onto the ripped seat next to Joe's.

He looked over and smirked. "Nice legs," he said.

I slugged him in the arm. I'd called it. He took nothing seriously. "You're lucky you're a decent teacher."

Ten

After Joe dropped me off, I walked to Sportmart again, this time to buy my own soccer ball. At the rate I was spending money, I'd be babysitting Randy the Terrible forever.

Later, I was practicing positioning myself on the shag carpet in the den while I watched *The Love Boat* when the phone rang. It was Candace.

"It's Lasagna Night tomorrow—are you coming?" she said. I could picture her on the phone in her kitchen, which was nearly identical to the phone in our kitchen except hers was a pukey shade of green and ours was more a baby poop shade of yellow.

Picking up the phone to hear Candace on the other end was as familiar as the rumble the radiator made when our house's heat kicked on, or as reliable as the drawer next to our stove being filled with the rubber bands and twist ties my mom saved from bags of produce and bread. But as soon as her voice came over the line, I realized I'd been nervous about us ever since she'd quit the team and I hadn't. I knew she wasn't angry, but I was worried she was hurt. I didn't want our separate decisions to be a sore spot—more a clarification that we were who we were, the same as the tacit agreement that she would always wear a mud mask at our sleepovers and I would not. (They made me claustrophobic.)

When I said, "What time?" and she brightly answered, "The usual," I knew I was worrying over nothing. Our friendship was solid. I could almost smell her mom's spaghetti sauce and feel the scratchy fabric of their couch.

"Okay, I'll be there," I said. I didn't ask if Tina was coming, for two reasons. One, Tina usually had to eat Sunday-night dinner at her house; and two, from the way Candace had been acting the last week, I knew she wanted to feel like it didn't matter to me if Tina came, too.

Lasagna Night happened once a month at the Trillos. When we were younger and our dads worked together, my whole family went. Mr. Trillo and my dad had met working for the phone company out of high school. Now Mr. Trillo managed a team at a steel mill in Chicago and my dad still worked for the phone company, but no longer had to climb telephone poles. They were still friends, but the days of my whole family attending Lasagna Night had faded toward the end of elementary school.

As I headed out the door the next evening, I called goodbye to my mom, who had a textbook open next to one elbow and a pile of bills and her checkbook next to the other. If someone wanted to paint her portrait, that would be the pose she'd be in.

"Lasagna Night?" she said, as she flipped back through the check register and then looked at a bill again, like the amount might change.

"Yes," I said, and then, because she looked so small behind

the books and the bills, added, "Is that okay?" I knew better than to ask to use the car, too, since gas was so expensive.

"Sure, lord knows I don't have a plan for us."

The Trillos lived a mile away, in a redbrick house on a street two blocks past the high school, in the direction of a McDonald's on Ninety-Fifth Street that students would walk to after school. When we were younger, Candace and I would sit on her porch and crane our necks to see girls in groups sharing french fries or couples with their hands in each other's back pockets walk by. We'd imagine that high school was going to be the beginning of our real life. If you could decide when you got to eat McDonald's and had someone who liked to squeeze your butt, wasn't that all you needed?

I showed up at five, because even though supper wouldn't be until six, I always helped Candace make a salad and lay out plates and utensils. The big treat for Lasagna Night was that we all ate on tray tables in the TV room, and by the time the ABC Sunday Night Movie started, Mrs. Trillo would have dessert ready. My family had never had these kind of rituals, and now I wondered if that was why my parents had split up, or if we'd never had the rituals because they were people who didn't belong together.

The front door was unlocked for me. The smell of Candace's mom's sauce—a simmering mixture of garlic and tomatoes that made me feel as warm as it did hungry—created its own weather. I followed the aroma into the kitchen, where Candace was slicing a loaf of Italian bread and her mom was laying a final wavy lasagna noodle atop a layer of cheese and sauce.

"Susan!" Mrs. Trillo said. "Can you fetch me the ladle, sweetie?"

I grabbed the ladle from a ceramic jar on the counter and handed it to her.

"We'll do the salad and get the plates out and then we're going to go to my room, okay, Ma?" Candace said. I could tell that she wanted to talk, so we worked fast, me slicing a cucumber and Candace tearing the lettuce. We layered it all in an oversize orange bowl. Candace dotted it with red cherry tomatoes before we left it on the table with the rest of the stuff for dinner.

We crossed through the TV room on the way to Candace's room, and her brothers, Frank Jr. and Marty, offered up a lazy "Hey, Suze" as we walked by.

"Where's your dad?" I asked.

"In the garage. They're going to be laying people off at his job, and he's the one who has to do it. The Folgers can is almost full," she said, referring to the coffee can Mr. Trillo ashed into when he was stressed and smoking in their garage.

In Candace's room, I picked up a copy of *Seventeen* with Phoebe Cates on the cover. "What's the Sunday-night movie this week?"

"*The Sting,*" Candace said. "Paul Newman. Your favorite. Unless you only have eyes for Coach McMann now?"

I tossed a pillow at her. "It's not like that," I said, even if it was a little like that. "He's my coach. I'm not throwing myself at him."

"You did wear fake eyelashes to soccer practice," Candace said, grinning mischievously.

"Look at this," I said. In the magazine, there was a two-page photo spread of girls playing soccer. Their shirts were tucked neatly into belted shorts, and none of them were sweating. An inset box contained totally basic soccer facts, and I felt as if I were reading a profile of a celebrity who I knew personally. It was wildly self-satisfying to be ahead of the average *Seventeen* reader on something. "Would you ever want to rejoin the team?"

"I don't think so," she said, without even thinking about it. "I went to the football game last night. With some of the pep club."

It sort of bugged me that she was skipping right over a chance to ask me about soccer to throw the pep club in my face. I had been planning to tell her about Joe, just for something to talk about, but I knew she'd barely ask about our soccer practice and only want to talk about his boyfriend potential. And since there wasn't any, I kept my mouth shut.

The doorbell rang, and Candace's head swiveled to look at me. "It's George!" she said.

"Wait, who?" The news hit me in the stomach, especially the way she announced it, like I should have figured this George person would be there. "What George?"

"Tomczak," she said. "I was about to tell you—he drove me home from his practice the other day and Mom invited him to stay for dinner, then yesterday I saw him again at the game." Candace practically skipped toward her dresser. She lifted the top from her Coty powder and patted the puff against her nose and cheeks and checked her angles in the mirror that hung on her wall.

"You had George Tomczak over for dinner and you didn't say

anything? Garbage Breath George?"

"He ate three plates. Mom was in heaven." Turning away from the mirror, she said, "I know I sometimes pick guys who aren't the greatest, so I wanted to wait to tell you anything until I knew he wasn't a jerk."

He might not have been a jerk, but no one would *pick* George Tomczak so much as get stuck with him. He had one of those "aw, shucks" personalities that drove me nuts and a haircut that you just knew his mom gave him. Plus, his breath. Had Candace forgotten she'd blown him off for Reggie Stanton at Dan O'Keefe's party a few weeks ago? The only thing George had that Candace said she wanted in a boyfriend was a spot on the football team. But even I knew the names of the football players who were supposed to be good, and he wasn't one of them.

"Do I have to mention again that we call him Garbage Breath?" I said. "For good reason?"

Candace frowned. "He's really sweet," she said. "And I can work on fixing his breath."

"'Work on'?" My tone was meaner than I wanted it to be, but I was kind of shocked. "Is he your boyfriend or something?"

Candace blushed. "I think so. Maybe . . ."

"Are you sure you really like him, though?" I asked. I could hear the way my words sounded, but I wasn't sure I cared. Was I supposed to be happy for her? "I thought you were into Reggie."

"Reggie is a jerk," she said with finality. She wasn't wrong. But I was still dumbfounded. George Tomczak?

"Come on, he's waiting." I followed Candace as she traipsed downstairs toward George, who was already being greeted by her brothers like they were old friends.

"Hi, Susan, how are you today?" George couldn't even say hello like a normal person.

"So-so," I said, subtly touching my nose as if to block his bad breath from entering my nostrils. He was chewing minty gum, but he'd definitely eaten onions recently, too.

While the lasagna finished baking, Candace suggested we hang out in the TV room. *One Day at a Time* was on. "What I wouldn't give for Valerie Bertinelli to show up in my bedroom some night," Frank Jr. said to George and Marty.

"Only way that'll happen is in your dreams," Marty said. "And even then, she'd probably have somewhere better to be."

"She's really funny in this show," George said, cutting off Frank and Marty before they went any further in their Valerie fantasies. George smiled at Candace and me as if we should be grateful for this intervention, but it wasn't like we hadn't heard Frank and Marty talk that way before. I'd once had the unfortunate experience of hearing Frank describe to Marty what he thought feeling up Carol Burnett would be like. Instead of being thankful for George stepping in, I was more ticked off by the fact that they had zero problems talking about women with me and Candace in the room. If I'd detailed my specific Bobby thoughts out loud, none of them would think that was okay.

Frank said something about the game on Friday, which Powell Park had lost by only three points, and George started talking about their defense. Candace grinned at me, looking victorious, as if the conversation was proof that George was all the great things she claimed. I turned my attention to the TV.

"Susan, how's soccer going?" George asked me, interrupting my favorite Hamburger Helper commercial. (I loved the talking glove.)

"Pretty good," I said. And then I added, more to Candace than to him, "We got goals at the park, and everyone on the team really gets along."

"That's neat," George said. "Some of the guys on the football team say the only reason anyone signed up is because everyone has a crush on Mr. McMann, but I—"

"No," I said, straightening up on the couch. "Bobby's a really good coach. We respect him."

George looked as embarrassed as if I'd walked in on him peeing. "Oh, I know you do. The guys say that, but they're wrong. Mr. McMann seems like a great coach."

The fact that George thought I was going to appreciate his support of my team only made me more irritated with him. The show came back on and I gave him the cold shoulder. Maybe it would freeze his stupid, smelly mouth.

"I'm starving," Frank said, to no one in particular.

"I'm really excited to try your mom's lasagna," George said to Candace as he slung his arm around her.

Poking him affectionately in the ribs, she said, "I hope there's enough, if you eat three plates again."

I rolled my eyes and vowed to eat more than George.

Mrs. Trillo came in with a bowl of chips and some cold cuts. "George, it's so nice to see you," she said, beaming at him. He still had his meaty hand on Candace's arm like she was a big fish he'd caught. "Now, I know you have a good appetite, but don't fill up too quick. I made an extra-big lasagna."

"Can't wait, Mrs. Trillo," George said, with a charming smile. I hated people who expertly sucked up to parents.

"Hey, does anyone want a pop?" Candace said.

"That would be great," George said. Her brothers nodded.

Candace stood up. "Susan, can you help?"

"Sure," I said. Maybe George's girthy arm on her neck was too much and she had come to her senses.

I followed her to the basement, where the Trillos had a small second fridge for drinks and the cuts of meat Mrs. Trillo bought on sale and kept frozen until she needed them.

"Did you want something, too?" she asked me.

"No thanks," I said. Then, whispering even though there was no way George could hear, I added, "So did you have to get away from his breath?"

Candace poked her head out of the fridge and said, "What's your problem with George?"

She held out a bottle of 7Up for me, which I waved off. It looked delicious, with the condensation beading on the bottle, but I didn't want to be distracted. "I don't have a problem—I just don't get it," I said. "Remember when you read *Love Story* and said you wanted a guy like that? You really think that's George?"

"That was just a book, and also the girl dies at the end," she said.

"I'd rather die than kiss George."

"Good thing you don't have to," Candace huffed. She looked toward the stairs, like she was anxious to get back to him. "All

I'm saying is, the only boys you ever talk about are guys like Paul Newman and Mr. McMann. You pick people who aren't even real choices. Prince Charming isn't real."

"I hated *Cinderella*," I said, toeing a dust bunny from under the laundry machine with my shoe. "And *Snow White*."

"I just mean no one is ever going to meet your unrealistic expectations."

"You don't know what you're talking about," I said. I wasn't angry, but I didn't like the way she was looking at me, like she felt sorry for me.

"Just give George a chance," she said, eyes pleading.

I wanted to ask her, Why? He'd probably ditch her like every other guy. Instead, I said, "It's not like I called him Garbage Breath to his face."

Candace gave me the same look I gave Randy when he tried to lie about his bedtime. "George is waiting," she said. "And the movie is starting soon."

She went up the stairs, leaving me at the bottom. Why was it always so easy for her to leave when there was a guy around? I stood there for a few minutes, until the fridge kicked on and I remembered how creeped out basements made me.

I had no choice but to go upstairs. But instead of going back into the TV room, where I could now hear Mr. Trillo and George talking football, I went into the kitchen.

"Oh, Susan, just the set of pretty hands I need," Mrs. Trillo said. "Can you put the salt and pepper out on the table? And slice a little more cucumber for the salad?"

I did what she asked and then, when she finally looked up from garnishing the lasagna—its top layer of cheese molten in the center and browned at the edges, where the corner noodles would be just the right amount of crispy—I gave her a hug and said, "Can you tell everyone I'm not feeling so great? I think I need to go home."

Mrs. Trillo cocked her head to one side, and I was sure she could see through my lame excuse. "Are you sure, sweetie? Do you want me to wrap you a plate to take?"

I shook my head, even though my mouth was watering. "No, thank you, I really don't feel well." Carrying a foil-wrapped plate out the door and walking the mile home with it seemed more pathetic than listening to my stomach grumble. Besides, then I'd have to explain to my mom why I wasn't eating it at Candace's.

I snuck out the front door and started walking as quickly as possible. I could smell the hot fries at McDonald's and my stomach rumbled doubly, but I had no money.

Twenty minutes later, I slipped into my house to find my mom still at the table, the crusts of a peanut butter sandwich on a plate next to her. She looked up. "You're back early. Isn't *The Sting* on?"

I shrugged. "Yeah, but I remembered I have an English test tomorrow and I have to finish the book." That was comical, as I was so far behind reading the Faulkner novel Ms. Halliday had assigned that I would have to ditch school for a week to read it all.

I thought Candace might call me to ask why I'd left, but she didn't. I fell asleep with my stomach empty and no idea what William Faulkner was talking about.

Eleven

When I got to school on Monday, I worried about what Candace had thought of me bailing the night before, and I was trying to decide whether to play up how "sick" I'd felt. But if Candace had been angry, she didn't show it. When she stopped by my locker before first period, there was a hickey the size of a half dollar on her neck. She'd put enough cover-up on the mottled purple circle to make it clear she was trying to hide it while not actually hiding it.

"What's with your neck? Did George not get enough lasagna?" I asked.

Candace ignored my joke. "Do you feel better?" I could tell she knew I'd lied but was letting it slide thanks to her good mood.

"Yeah, thanks," I said.

"You should have stayed," she said. "Mom made a carrot cake."

Mrs. Trillo's carrot cake was my favorite. Candace definitely wanted me to feel bad for leaving.

Practice that afternoon was hard, not to mention frustrating. I was trying the tricks Joe had taught me, but I felt like I was always out of position. At one point, I was making good progress toward the goal when Marie crashed into me to get the ball and sent me sprawling to the ground. To make up for my missed shots and clumsiness, I turned on my speed during our suicides, doing more of them than anyone else before Bobby called time.

I hobbled over to Tina afterward, since she'd been driving me home after practice most days. She gave me an apologetic look as I bent to scrape a chunk of mud off my kneecap left from when Marie took me out.

"My mom and stepdad are doing the family dinner thing, and I'm already running late," she said. I knew what this meant. Every so often, Tina's mom would invite another family that they knew from church or from her stepdad's office to dinner. The families almost always had a son around Tina's age. Every time, it was apparently two excruciating hours of making polite conversation with a perfectly nice guy and then coming up with some excuse not to make any further plans with him.

"That sucks," I said. She was still changing her shoes, so I asked, "What does Todd think of these dinners?"

Tina smiled. "You know, that's like the first time you've ever asked me about Todd."

"I've asked you about him," I protested.

She shook her head. "Maybe if I bring him up, but otherwise, no."

I knew she was right. As much as Candace and I talked about

boys, it had always been hard to ask Tina about this guy we'd never met, and a relationship that seemed like such a pain to maintain.

Or maybe that was just what I'd told myself, and I was a selfish friend.

"Well, I'm sorry, but maybe I'll get to meet him someday," I said. He had to be better than George.

Tina's smile widened. "You might, Suzie Q," she said. She got into the car and checked her face in the rearview mirror, swiping beneath her eye to clear away the mascara she'd sweated off. "I'm sorry about the ride, but I need to clean up. Like, I one hundred percent don't want to do this but I'd still like to make a good impression."

"Good luck," I told her. "Call me later if you want."

I started down Oak Center Drive toward home. I'd gone about a block when a car horn honked not far behind me. I started to raise my middle finger like I always did at catcallers (even if I sometimes secretly tallied how many complete strangers told me I had a nice ass) when I saw that the car that pulled up next to me was a Datsun.

Bobby's Datsun.

I turned halfway toward him, trying to pose in a way that was both casual and devastating. I smoothed my hair and a dried leaf came out in my hand.

He stopped and got out on his side, looking over the top of the roof at me. "I thought you usually went home with Tina," he said. "Do you need a ride?"

Did I want a ride home? From Bobby?

"That would be great," I said.

"What's your address?" he asked as I hopped into the car.

I told him and he thought for a second. "You know, one thing, do you mind if I make a quick stop on the way? I'm trying to conserve gas."

"Of course," I said, wishing I had something intelligent to say about whoever was responsible for gas being so expensive this year—maybe something insightful and political would make me seem older. But how could I remember what OPEC stood for when I was in *Bobby McMann's car*?

"Good practice today, huh?" he asked, pulling onto the street. "I think we'll be ready once we get a game."

"Me too," I said, unable to find a comfortable way to sit in his passenger seat. If I leaned back too much, my thigh would touch his hand on the gearshift. You couldn't throw your thigh at a person who'd never touched it before, right? "I've been practicing a little on weekends, actually." Okay, so I'd only practiced one extra time, but he didn't have to know that.

We were at a stoplight and Bobby looked over at me. "Wow," he said with an approving nod. "That's real commitment." I was waiting—or hoping—for him to add, "That extra work really shows," or "I should have known—you're my best player," or to at least look longingly at me. He didn't, and the light changed.

I'd finally settled on folding my hands in my lap when Bobby pulled to a stop in front of Happy Seeds, a health food store.

"Come on in," he said as he hopped out of the car and waited at the curb for me. I had the thrilling idea that someone might see me with him. *Is that Susan Klintock with Coach McMann?* the person would think, and I'd have to fend off inquiries at school the next day.

I'd been in Happy Seeds once or twice with Mom, who every now and then would go in search of a new vitamin. The sharp mineral smell of the place hit you right away, like dusty pepper. Bobby grabbed a small basket and we made our way to the bread aisle. An older black man with gray hair and muscular arms greeted Bobby with a back slap. "Hey, Coach, what's happening?"

"Hey, Earl. Picking up some supplies." Bobby gestured to me. "This is Susan Klintock, one of my star players."

"Star, huh? Coach doesn't say that kind of thing lightly. Nice to meet you, Susan." Earl wiped his hand on his apron and stuck it out for me to shake.

I shook his hand and he told me he was excited to see us play a game, then excused himself to get back to work as Bobby surveyed the breads. They were laid out on a table, and all of them were brown or coated in seeds. They looked like harder work to eat than running fifty suicides.

Another employee waved and smiled at Bobby, a woman about my height with pale skin that could have really been helped by a little lipstick under the grim lighting in here. I doubted the grim lighting was doing me any favors, either, and thought better of trying to catch my reflection.

"Hi, Bobby," she said. He was Bobby to her and not Coach like he was to Earl. I bristled.

"Charlene, hi," he said. Once again he gestured to me and

made introductions, and this time I reached out first to shake Charlene's hand, which felt limp in my grip. No way could she handle Bobby's practices.

I followed Bobby toward a cluster of barrels filled with grains and seeds that you could scoop yourself. He pulled a bag off a roll and poured in a scoop of granola, holding it up to see how filled it was. Satisfied, he twisted the top and tied it into a knot.

"There's a lot more seeds than I realized," I said. Had I really made an observation about the many kinds of edible seeds? Was I possessed by George Tomczak?

"Don't worry, I like a nice burger, too." Bobby grinned. "All things in moderation, even seeds. I need to pick up wheat germ; then I'll get you home so you can finish your homework and whatever else you need to get to."

I thought of how, after riding next to him in his car, the first thing I'd be doing likely wouldn't be homework. I flushed, as if my intention to masturbate had scrawled itself across my forehead.

Lucky for me, he'd already turned to the wheat germ.

"Got it," he said, looking victorious, and we headed to the checkout. Earl rang him up, gave Bobby another back slap, and told me to listen to my coach.

"He knows what he's doing," Earl said.

I'll bet, I thought.

Near the exit, Bobby paused at a bulletin board covered in flyers advertising babysitters for hire and bikes for sale. In the center was a flyer with the words "Personal Best Training" across the top, and beneath that, a photo of Bobby that must have been cut from a larger image. He had his leg up on a weight bench.

Someone had drawn a large penis extending out from his shorts.

In haste, he tore it down, but not before I saw that almost none of the row of flaps where he'd printed his phone number had been torn from the bottom.

The sad look on his face as we walked to the car made me desperate to say something.

"I think having goals at the park has really helped out," I said. "It's cool you got them."

Bobby faintly smiled. "You know, the school gave me an account for Powell Park Sporting Goods. For jerseys. I ordered them last week."

"That's good, right?" I said, so chipper I could hear the pity in my voice. "Like they're excited about the team?"

"The account was for twenty-five dollars," he said, unlocking the door. I didn't know how much jerseys cost, but I knew that there was no way he'd get nearly a dozen of them at Powell Park Sports for that amount. "But I know how uniforms make you feel like a team in a way not much else does. So I got them." He tossed his now balled-up flyer into the back seat. "I'm hoping my personal training business picks up. Teacher pay . . ."He shrugged. "You know."

I didn't, but I could see Bobby carefully considering jerseys for us the same way he compared wheat germs. I wanted to think of the right words to say thank you. He'd spent his own money.

"Don't say anything to the team yet," he said, as I started to open my mouth. "I want it to be a surprise. But you asked me before, so I figure it can be our little secret."

The words "our little secret" uttered as Bobby looked into my eyes were as exciting as if I'd put a scoop into one of the barrels of seeds and lifted out diamonds.

"I won't tell anyone," I said. "I can't wait to see them."

"They weren't my first pick of colors, but there's always next year," he started saying with excitement. "I hope they'll be ready next week."

I didn't care about the jerseys. He'd spent his own money on us. He was making plans for the next year, for us.

He deserved a team that was worthy of him, and if he was going to call me his star player, I had to try to live up to the title.

Twelve

Joe picked me up on Saturday morning for our next practice at the park. His Nova had ripped brown seats that were taped in places and the glove box door was missing, but you could tell he took care of the car. One of those pine-scented trees dangled from the rearview mirror.

"Um, what is that?" I asked, pointing at the tape sticking out of the 8-track player. "You like the *Doobie Brothers*?" My dad liked the Doobie Brothers.

Joe grimaced. "It's been stuck there since I bought the car from my uncle," he said. "I thought you saw it last time and were too nice to say anything. So we can either listen to the radio or 'Takin' It to the Streets.'"

"Whatever's good."

He put on the rock station and a Boston song poured out. "Ugh. Someday, I'll play you some real music." He spun the radio dial, dissatisfied with everything.

"Here." I pushed the button for the 8-track. "The Doobies would want it this way."

Joe's appreciative laugh made me laugh, and we listened to part of the song before he asked, "So how did practice go this week? Any goals?"

"Still no," I said.

"Don't be upset," he said as he slowed for a stop sign. "It'll happen."

"Easy for you to say," I told him.

"True."

I made a gesture toward the radio. "So what's *your* band like?"

"The Watergate Tapes? We're sort of awful but we make it work for us," he said. "Our drummer got a serious girlfriend, though, so we've barely been practicing."

"Oh," I said, thinking of Candace and George. "Do you think they'll last?"

"I hope not. She's super critical of everything Ben does. But you can't explain why people like who they like."

"So your girlfriend isn't like that?" I said.

"Who?"

"The girl you were with at Sportmart?"

"Oh, that . . . didn't really work out," Joe said.

I wasn't sure if I should ask about the break-up; I didn't want to give him the idea that I might be interested or anything like that. But it didn't matter, because we were pulling up at the park. Joe turned to me and said, "Has your coach shown you chops yet?"

I squinted at him.

"That's a no," he said. "Come on, we have work to do." For someone who seemed so unserious, Joe was taking our practice really seriously. He jogged out to the field, looking happy to be there, then waved me over. "I think there's a peewee football game here today, so we need to get going!"

Learning the chop was fun—it was a way to trick a defender by kicking the ball sideways from you to get around her.

But even though Joe declared me a natural at that, I hadn't improved when it came to scoring on him. He was a walking, talking wall at the goal. He sort of loved how good he was, I could tell, from the way he flung himself in front of every one of my shots.

"Maybe I'm not meant to be a forward," I said with a sigh after he easily fended off what I'd thought was a genius kick.

Joe shook his head and lobbed the ball over me to the center of the field, where I'd been starting from. "I think you have to use the power of attention," he said.

"I'm paying attention!"

"No, no, I mean my attention. Say you're coming up from the left," he explained, as I dribbled the ball around a cone and toward him. "You're going to want to aim for the opposite corner of the net, since I'd be looking at you and the ball."

"Yeah, but that's not going to work now," I said. "I'm the only player out here—you'll see me coming. It's not like in a game, where you might get distracted."

Joe puffed himself up, "Me? No freaking way. I'm always ready. Like, this one game, against St. Rita's—"

And as he began to talk about how great he was, I lined up a shot and kicked, angling my body directly toward him. Joe, who normally saw shots coming from a mile away, looked stunned as the ball clipped by his ear and into the net.

"Fuck!" he said, at the same time I leaped into the air and screamed, "Hell yes!"

He was staring at the ball like it had betrayed him somehow.

"You knew I was going to make one someday," I said, jogging up to him with my shoulders back. I picked up the ball with propriety and patted it like it was a loyal pet.

"You're pretty proud of yourself, aren't you?" he said, bending down to retie his cleat.

"You know it. Now I'll be ready for my first game."

Joe looked up, raised an eyebrow. "You got a game?"

"Not yet," I told him. "But soon."

The peewee football coaches had shown up, and they shot Joe and me dirty looks, like they'd caught us having sex on the field. I started to gather the cones Joe had set up for me to weave around during warm-ups.

"Till then, you want to keep practicing? With me?"

"Yeah, definitely," I said as we carried the stuff to his car. Standing behind him, I waited for him to unlock the trunk. "I mean, if it's okay with you?"

"Of course." He chucked his gear into the car and took the cones I handed him. Light passed over his face, and his mouth pulled into the grin that meant he was about to say something flirtatious. "You didn't really think you were done after one score, did you?"

"No," I said. "I haven't made you cry yet."

"I wouldn't say that," he said. He pointed at my T-shirt, Tonia's old Styx one. "I just want to be alone when I cry over your tragic celebration of Styx."

I would have flipped him off if I hadn't been laughing.

My lessons with Joe began to pay off during the next couple of scrimmages. At one point on Tuesday, Marie confronted me as I dribbled toward the goal and I knocked the ball left with the outside of my foot—a chop—then took possession again. I drove toward the goal and took a kick, getting my shot by Dawn.

Bobby clapped from the sideline, and said, "Whatever you're doing in your own time, keep doing it."

Tina shot me a look. "What does he mean, what you've been doing in your own time?"

"I don't know," I said. I'd mentioned my ride home with Bobby, but I hadn't told her about the lessons with Joe yet. I felt bad for lying, but I'd been hesitant to tell her because talking about a boy with your friends—even if you said the guy was just a friend—meant they'd start pointing out signs he liked you.

But when Tina called Wednesday morning to offer me a ride to school (it was raining), I thought I'd use the ride to tell her about practicing with Joe. Then, Tonia called.

"Hey, Suze," she said. "Mom around?"

"No, work. What are you doing up? Isn't it, like, five a.m. there?"

"I just got home from a crazy party, but I needed to talk to Mom about the wedding thing."

"You mean Dad's wedding?"

"Yeah, how fucking weird, right?" Tonia said, impatient.

She hadn't talked to me in months; could she at least try to see what was going on in my life? "Can you tell them I can't make it? There's a maybe thing going on in Joshua Tree, and it's too expensive to fly out there anyway."

"I think Mom said she and Dad would pay for your ticket," I told her. Dad would definitely want Tonia there, but I was more angry she was bailing on *me*. "Won't there be other maybe things in Joshua Tree? Dad probably won't get married again, again."

"Ha, there are guys out here on their third wives; you never know." Someone in the background called Tonia's name. "Look, I have to go."

"But—"

"You're a big girl, Suze. You'll be fine." She hung up.

I was so worked up by the whole thing, I spent the rainy car ride bitching about my sister to Tina, who agreed that she was being selfish. After that, she reminded me how we'd caught Ms. Lopez hunched over a Harlequin romance the day before, when we'd had a test on Faulkner, and I knew she was trying to cheer me up. It was working, until we saw Candace getting out of George's car wearing his letter jacket.

My face must have registered my disgust, because Tina said, "I know he's a doofus, but she seems happy."

"We should get out of the rain," I said, and we ran through the doors of the school with our backpacks over our heads. As we shook ourselves off and turned down the hall to my locker, we saw some of the team gathered in the hallway.

"Coach wants us to meet in his classroom," Dana said before either of us could even say good morning.

"What for?" I asked.

"Probably to tell us practice is canceled," Dawn said. "Sucks."

She was right. I was genuinely disappointed, and not just because it meant no Bobby. After talking to Tonia and seeing Candace with Garbage Breath George, I really would have liked to be on the field kicking something rather than going home to sulk after school.

"He said he has a special announcement, too," Dana said, loading her voice with extra officiousness.

I looked at Tina. I'd let the jerseys secret drop to her after describing all the details of my ride home with Bobby, wanting her to be impressed with his generosity.

"Well, let's find out what he wants," Tina said.

When we got to room 133, Bobby was standing behind his desk in a button-down shirt and tan slacks. I must have given him a strange look, because he glanced down and said to the room, "I can't wear shorts to teach algebra. At least, not anymore."

"I wonder why," Tina whispered to me. We took seats at the desks as Bobby stood up, hefting a large box onto his desk.

"I'm sorry, we'll have to cancel practice today—the field is just too muddy," Bobby said. "But I'm hoping I can brighten the day anyway."

"The shorts would have helped with that," Joanie muttered behind me.

Bobby patted the box and cleared his throat. "You've been playing like a real team," he said. "And it's time you looked like one."

He reached into the box and pulled out shirts with "Powell

Park" written across the chests in powder blue. The powder blue color was nice, if the words hadn't been printed across a shirt that was the same yellow that the armpits of white T-shirts turn after you sweat in them a lot. But Bobby held one up proudly and tossed it toward us.

No one reached out to catch it, but it half landed on the edge of Franchesa Rotini's desk. She pulled it toward her and politely said, "Thank you."

"I hope you like them," Bobby said, as he passed out the rest.

The word "hope" was weighted with an apology. He reminded me of Fred Farris, a boy with a skin condition who'd been my square dancing partner in PE last year. "I'm not contagious," Fred had said about the warts on his hands, which had prompted me to hold his hands tighter, so he wouldn't feel bad.

"There are a few different sizes in there, and some extras, in case anyone forgets hers on game day," he continued. "You can trade each other for the ones you want."

"They're definitely attention-getting," Tina said, using her genius way of phrasing things to bring a smile to Bobby's face.

"We love them," I added, clutching my number 15 and trying to compensate for the team's bland thank-yous.

"Well, good," he said, standing in what I'd come to think of as his coach pose: hands on hips and his feet planted shoulder-width apart. In shorts, coach pose made every one of his muscles, every angle and slope of his body, available for careful study. But it still worked even in long pants. "You're going to need them . . ." He paused dramatically as he looked from player to player. "Because I also got us a game."

A cheer went up from everyone at once. We jumped from the desk chairs, shrieking like we'd already won the game we'd just found out about. The team's collective excitement surprised me, almost as much as my own did.

"We're official," Tina said, waving her jersey over me and Dawn Murphy, who actually was smiling, too.

"Who do we play?" Marie asked.

"Is it a school around here?" Arlene chimed in.

"It's another high school girls' team, the Wauwatosa Warriors. They're just outside of Milwaukee," Bobby said. "The only problem is, we have to play early morning, so I think it'll be an overnight."

"Yes!" Marie Quinn said. "Freedom!" Her somehow-not-rained-on blond hair swished as she grabbed Joanie's and Arlene's hands and spun them around.

Bobby held up a hand. "That is . . . if we can raise enough money for a bus and some of our lodging. We're going to need to have a fundraiser. Any ideas?"

"I hate to say it, but candy bars?" Tina offered.

"Everyone is sick of candy bars," Wendy countered. "The tennis team ruined them."

"Homework help?" Dana suggested. She looked at everyone like this was a great idea.

"No one wants my help with their homework, believe me," Arlene said.

"We could have a bake sale, or the boosters offered us the chance to work the next football concession and take a share, but I don't know if either of those things will be profitable enough," Bobby said.

"Well," I said, "the cheerleaders hold a spring car wash to raise money for the next football season. But no one does a car wash in the fall. Why not us?"

"That's brilliant," Bobby said, drawing a frown from Dana that I enjoyed a little bit. "Who's in?"

"I am!"

"Me too!"

"We don't know how to wash cars," Dana said.

"Soap, water, sponges," Tina said. "How hard can it be?"

"Wisconsin, here we come," I said.

Thirteen

Powell Park Girls' Soccer Car Wash
Saturday, October 6
Doesn't Matter If It's a Boss Ride or a Beater,
If It's Got Wheels, We'll Wash It!!

When the day of the car wash arrived, we showed up looking less like a girls' soccer team and more like we were working a kissing booth that sold a lot more than kisses. It was mostly the result of Marie's advice the day before. "We need girl-next-door . . . meets lady of the night . . . but during the day."

So even though the morning was pretty chilly, Arlene and Joanie had on suntan pantyhose under their short shorts and Wendy's red bikini top looked dangerously close to popping open. When Tina pointed this out, Wendy said, "And if it does, we'll charge extra." She winked a blue eye, looking annoyingly like Suzanne Somers.

Dana had even departed from her usual button-up blouses to wear a tight tank top and Daisy Dukes. I noticed with some irritation that her boobs were bigger than mine, which I'd never realized. "Perky headlights, Dana," Marie said. "Good work!"

Franchesa, who always struck me as somewhat mousy, had removed her thick glasses and let her hair down from its ponytail. She had on a short yellow cheerleading-style skirt and a halter top that looked good against her naturally tan skin.

"Wow, Franchesa, where'd you find the sexpot clothes?" Marie asked. "And the bod?"

Franchesa grimaced. "They're my mom's. As I was leaving, I heard my dad say, 'You're lending her the outfit?' This thing had better be a success, because I think I'm wearing my mom's sex clothes."

We all shuddered. I had a thin white shirt on over my bikini top because I hardly needed some guy to point out my mosquito bites. But I wore a pair of denim cutoffs even shorter than my Sportmart shorts and had tested the outfit in the shower to make sure it looked good wet.

We'd gotten permission to use the school's overflow parking lot for the wash, the same spot the cheerleaders used in the spring. There was a three-way intersection in front of the high school, and we were positioned in view of all the traffic lights, giving a lot of drivers plenty of time to spot us.

At ten a.m., we officially cut the ribbon for our car wash, and Dawn—who'd actually put on makeup and was showing her curves in basic cutoffs and a T-shirt—said, "Here goes nothing."

After all the plastering of flyers and reminding our families, I think we all expected a line of cars to be waiting for us when we opened up shop, but that wasn't the case. Instead, we were greeted by the roar of traffic as it passed us by. My hope started to evaporate as I stood there freezing with my shorts riding up my butt.

"What do the cheerleaders do to get customers?" Joanie moaned. She adjusted one of her auburn pigtails.

"Wear cheerleading outfits," Tina said. She had on a jumpsuit that hit high on her thighs with the zipper pulled halfway down. "And probably cheer and shit."

"And raise money for a team people actually care about," Dawn said, her tone sour. We all knew what she meant—a *boys'* team.

We tried yelling at cars stopped at the red lights. We jumped and waved the two signs Joanie had made with her perfect bubble letters, and we shot a stream of water from the hose into the air. If people looked our way at all, they pretended they hadn't seen us.

"Cheap-asses," I muttered.

"Are we deformed or something?" Joanie asked, checking her reflection in Tina's windshield.

Just as we all seemed ready to call it quits, several cars filled with guys pulled up. Some of them were the more unsavory players on the football team. My disgust at seeing them mixed with relief that we finally had some customers.

"Three cars, guys!" Dawn said.

"That's nine dollars!" Franchesa said.

"At least nine dollars!" Arlene chimed in. "Push the Turtle Wax."

Keith Barnes hopped out of a Buick, which had to be his dad's. "You, you, and you," he said, pointing at Marie, Franchesa, and Wendy. "If you do a good job on mine, then my buddies will get a wash, too."

"It's a fundraiser, Keith," I said. "We're not looking to start an official business."

"Klintock, the customer is always right," he said, casting a glance at my chest that made me feel self-conscious. "Now, I want to see how these girls stroke my ride."

Wendy looked like she wanted to kick him in the nuts, but we needed his stupid three dollars.

The girls started working on Keith's car, and the other guys in his car got out to watch. The guys in the second car also got out. Michael, the St. Mark's guy who I'd blown off, was standing there, sneering at me. Tina gave him a sarcastic, waggle-fingered wave. "Guess he's not used to being rejected," she said to me.

"Definitely don't let those chicks wash your ride, Stan," he said to one of the other guys, pointing out me and Tina. "If they do it for free, you overpaid."

"Lean into to it, sweetheart," one of Keith's buddies was saying to Franchesa. "I want to see those hands working."

"Hey, Marie, feel free to use your tongue if you want," Keith said. Marie gritted her teeth but didn't lob one of her usual insults at him. We were at their mercy until we had their money.

"Are we seriously going to have to deal with this kind of shit all day?" Dawn asked me. "These fucking guys are assholes."

"I know," I said. "But if we want to go to Wisconsin . . ."

"All I know is, if they hold a car wash, I'm getting payback," Tina said.

"Ugh, I do not want to see them in short shorts," I said.

When the girls finished, Keith shoved three balled-up dollar bills at Marie. "What do you say, fellas? Get some grub?"

"What about the other cars?" Marie asked.

"Got places to be, sunshine," Keith's friend said.

"Fuck you," Marie said. She kicked Keith's tire.

He waved a scolding finger in her face. "Cute girls like you shouldn't be so angry. This is why chicks shouldn't play sports."

They drove away, and we put the three bills with the bit of cash our parents had chipped in that morning. We had twenty-six dollars. "The rest of the customers might not be so shitty," I offered.

"What customers?" Marie asked, gesturing to our lack of a line.

The next hour passed too slowly. A few more cars pulled in. One was an old couple who needed directions to the expressway. Franchesa's brothers each came by in a muscle car, and while they were much nicer than the football players, they managed the entire process, giving us tips for how we could do a better job. Tom Meyer came by to flirt with Arlene, who practically rolled her body over the hood of his car and gave him a discount in exchange for his promise to take her out that night. Fortunately, Joanie coaxed Sal Mondello to pay extra for his wash to make up for their date the night before, when he'd dragged her to a horror movie after she'd thought they were going to see *10*.

"Where's Bobby?" Tina said. "Shouldn't he be helping us?"

He'd told us he'd be a little late, and I'd hoped it was for a Personal Best customer, not a date who he had to make breakfast.

With two hours to go, we had $66. Even if we made that much each of the next two hours, it wouldn't be enough.

A car pulled up next to me. It was coated in bird poop and the inside was loaded with greasy fast-food bags and random junk. The man inside rolled down his window. His face was oily and he smelled awful. "Are you cheerleaders?"

"No. Soccer players," I said.

"Never mind," he said, rolling up his window and driving away.

I let out a long sigh. We had to make this money. Bobby would be so disappointed if we couldn't go.

Three p.m. Southwest Highway. Susan counts the money from the car wash one last time . . . yep, it's all there, $750, more than enough for their trip to Wisconsin. She's sent the rest of the team home—they worked hard—and waits for Bobby to come pick up the metal box of cash. When he arrives, he's astounded. "How did you do this?" I smile. "I knew how important it was . . . for us." "You sure did," he says, taking me in his arms. "Now, let's get you out of these wet clothes."

"You look like you're trying to think of a way to end world hunger."

Joe's voice shook me back to reality, and as I mentally filed away my grammatically unsound fantasy to use for later, I gave him a smile, surprised he'd shown. When I'd told him about our game and the car wash at last week's practice session, he'd been excited for me. I'd teased him that we'd probably have to charge extra to wash his beast of an old Nova, and he'd contested that I owed him a discount, if anything. But I hadn't called to remind him about the car wash, figuring he was helping me out enough already with the practices.

"Hey!" I spun around and saw several of the girls already tackling his Nova. I also saw that he was with a girl, someone I hadn't seen before. So he must have been officially over the babe from Sportmart. This one had shorter black hair, like Janet on *Three's Company*. Together, she and Joe looked like a matching set: Punks Who Are Cooler Than You.

My surprise caused the smile to slip from my face, but I tossed out an upbeat "Thanks for coming!"

"A promise is a promise," he said, even though he hadn't promised to come. His left eyebrow and the corner of his mouth raised in equal degrees as he smirked at my outfit, like he knew how many I'd tried on to get the right look. He nodded sideways to the girl. "This is Lizzy. We're going to go see *Rock 'n' Roll High School*."

"Yeah, even though he's seen it about forty times. The Ramones are in it." Lizzy raised her eyebrows at Joe as she nudged him in the ribs. He blushed. Their familiarity made me feel like I'd been caught eavesdropping.

"I'm Susan," I said to her. "Joe's friend." I don't know why I needed to clarify this, and Lizzy didn't seem to care.

"How's it going?" Joe asked me, as he slung his arm around Lizzy's shoulder.

I shook my head.

"It'll pick up," he said, as if he could know such a thing. I was embarrassed that he had to feel sorry for us. "You've got more people than the Watergate Tapes gets at a lot of our gigs."

"I should help with your car," I said. "You got interior and exterior?"

"And the Turtle Wax. Plus, I tip." He squeezed Lizzy's arm as he looked at her. "We'll still have time to get some food before the movie, right?"

"I think so," she said. "Otherwise we can double up on popcorn."

I wondered if I should ask how long they'd been going out, or some other question to show Lizzy I would definitely not be trying to steal her boyfriend, if that's what Joe was. But I couldn't think of a graceful way to do that. So instead I said to Joe, "At least someone supports us. Thanks."

"Wisconsin's your destiny," Joe said. "Now get to work."

I got into his Nova, vowing to spend extra time Turtle Waxing Joe's now-familiar car, when I heard the rattle of Bobby's Datsun as he pulled up.

"Finally," Wendy said, using a clean rag on Joe's steering wheel. "Coach is here."

"Yeah, maybe he can help with this massive line of cars we've got," Dawn commented sarcastically as she Windexed Joe's rear-view mirror.

Bobby hopped out of his car and rubbed his hands together eagerly. He was wearing a track jacket over his usual shorts and had a towel slung over his shoulder. We all stopped working on Joe's car for a second to drink in the sight of him.

Joe stepped away from Lizzy to peek in at me in his car. *"That's* your coach?"

"Yeah, that's Bobby," I said. A giggle slipped out of my mouth, like I was introducing Joe to my adorable new kitten. "I mean, that's Coach McMann."

Lizzy was making no effort to hide that she, too, was

devouring Bobby with her eyes. "Shit, I hate organized anything, but he could get me to play soccer."

Joe glanced at her. "Hmm," he said, with a wry smile, first at Lizzy, then me. "Interesting."

"What's that supposed to mean?" I asked, giving his dashboard a final wipe. It looked brand-new.

"Nothing," Joe said, turning away from Bobby.

"Voilà." I flung the rag over Joe's shoulder into a bucket as I struggled to get out of his car in my tight shorts. I headed toward the team, who'd gathered around Bobby.

"All right, ladies, how are we doing here?" Bobby asked, taking in the pile of extra supplies that we still hadn't touched.

"Great," Dana lied, ever the authority-pleaser.

I shook my head, with a look at her. "We're not on track to make what we need for Wisconsin."

Bobby surveyed our setup and said, "Maybe one of the signs needs to be closer to the curb." He looked up. "Sun's coming out." He unzipped his track jacket and tossed it on the hood of his car, then picked up the bigger sign and jogged toward the light on Ninety-Fifth. He leaned the sign against the traffic pole just as the light turned green.

A woman in a Chevelle who'd been doing her best not to look directly at us during the red light suddenly swung her wheel right and pulled in. "I was just thinking that I needed a good car wash," she said to Bobby.

Meanwhile, the traffic on Central had stopped as a woman in a Firebird swung out to make a U-turn and entered the parking lot from the other direction.

"Hey, two customers," Bobby said, looking from the brunette who'd emerged from the Chevelle to the redhead scrambling out of her Firebird. He flashed them both a radiant smile.

Franchesa started to hose off the Chevelle, but Bobby stepped in. "No, no, I showed up late. I'll do them both."

"I'll bet he will," Franchesa mumbled.

He started to hose off the Chevelle, and the Firebird woman gave the Chevelle lady the evil eye. My teammates and I looked at each other, not in astonishment, but maybe confirmation. We'd talked here and there, theorizing whether Bobby knew how hot he was. But now it was clear.

He *knew*. And he was going to make it work for him. Or, really, the team.

The girls had finished with Joe's car and Joanie asked me, "Where'd the cute weird guy go? I've got his keys."

I looked over to where we'd been talking and didn't see him. "He's at the pay phones," Lizzy told me. She still hadn't taken her eyes off Bobby.

I brought the keys to Joe as he hung up the phone. "Hey, champ, I called some of the guys in my band and told them to get out here." He pointed toward the line of fresh cars, all driven by women, that were causing a jam at each entrance to the car wash. "Although I don't know if you need it now."

"Sorry, I didn't mean to disappear on you," I said. Had he really been calling his friends for me? "All these customers showed at once."

The wry smile again. "Eh, I get it," he said as we walked back toward his car, where Lizzy was waiting in the passenger seat.

Joe glanced at Bobby again, who had no less than five women thrusting money at him so they could go first. "Hey, do you have Columbus Day off? Maybe we can practice?"

"I do." I paused. "But I have to get a dress for my dad's wedding in the morning."

"That's okay—we can do it in the afternoon," he said. "I think you should come to my house. I have a lesson plan."

"Sure," I said. I peeked at Lizzy, but her bored expression indicated she wasn't threatened by Joe and me hanging out. Good.

"Nice wash, ladies," he called to my team. He handed me a twenty.

"I'll get your change," I said.

He shook his head. "No, keep it." He smirked. "Told you I tip." I watched him put his arm around Lizzy as he pulled away.

Tina tapped me on the shoulder. "So you've been talking to the guy from Dan's party? And didn't tell me?"

I looked at my feet. "He's been helping me with soccer," I said.

"So you're getting *private lessons* and you didn't tell me?" Tina repeated. She flicked me above the elbow.

"Ow," I said, not flicking her back, because she was right, it had been kind of shitty to keep it a secret. "I was going to. He's just a friend. So it didn't seem important."

"A guy doesn't have to be your boyfriend to be important," Tina said. "That's cool, he's helping you."

"So you agree, a guy showing you how to play a sport is a friendly thing?" It seemed weird that it hadn't even crossed Joe's mind that our friendship might put Lizzy off. I had zero interest in Joe, but was I really so lacking in the sexiness department that I didn't make her nervous at all? Or that Joe wasn't worried I would?

"If that's what you say it is, then why wouldn't it be?" Tina said. I'd been expecting to have to list the reasons why Joe wasn't right for me—too much of a flirt, a little cocky, a never-ending stream of sexy punk rock girlfriends, overpays for subpar car washes—but apparently it wasn't necessary. "Besides, if he saw the way you just ate up Bobby with your eyeballs, he knows he doesn't have a chance."

Now I flicked her.

"So that fancy footwork shit that you pulled on Marie the other day—that was him?"

"You mean the chop?" I grinned. I was getting really good at that.

Tina flicked me again. "That's for keeping your secret weapon a secret. Show me how to do that and we're even."

"Deal," I said, then pointed to a guy in a pickup truck who'd just pulled in. I grabbed a fresh rag and fluffed my hair. "Let's go make some money."

We ended up washing cars for more than two hours past the time we'd planned to be outside. I was pretty sure at least one woman slipped Bobby her number and another one had given him what looked like panties. His shirt was wet and clinging to him, and he had a red lipstick mark on his cheek from a grandma type who'd told him what a nice boy he was. When all was said and done, we had more than four hundred dollars, most of it thanks to Bobby.

But when he counted the last bill, he just said, "We did it, team! We're going to Wisconsin!"

We were cold and wet and our waterproof mascara hadn't held up, but none of it mattered as we let out a whoop so loud that passing cars honked in support.

Fourteen

I spent the day after the car wash catching up on homework and babysitting Kevin, this four-year-old who lived on Keating and always made a point of telling me that his previous babysitter had been prettier, and that was probably why she had been caught by his parents for having her boyfriend over when they weren't home. Still, Kevin was better than Randy the Terrible, and the money I earned by not entirely neglecting Kevin would help pay for some new pajamas for the trip. On the off chance Bobby saw me dressed for bed, I did not want to be wearing my holey Barraco's Pizza T-shirt and the shorts from my old gym uniform.

On Monday, in the midst of a detailed dream in which I had a yellow Gran Torino and Bobby washed it carefully while wearing a tight mechanic's jumpsuit, my mom knocked on my bedroom door. "Susan, did you forget?"

"Forget what?"

"Dresses, with Polly. I need to drop you at Donna's Bridal on my way to work," she said.

"I didn't forget, but . . . it's Columbus Day." I moaned. "He discovered a whole continent—can't I stay in bed?"

"Correction: He found a place to park his ships—people had already discovered it just fine. And you need to discover a dress." Mom came into my room and found a pair of jeans and a clean shirt, which she threw at me. "Polly's treating you, so you can at least be on time."

Mom seemed edgy in the car, and she was still wearing her jeans and a plain blue blouse. "I thought you had to work?" Normally, she wore slacks or a calf-length skirt to work, with a pair of stacked brown loafers that she got resoled once a year.

"Late start," she said. "I'll go change after I drop you off."

When she pulled up in front of Donna's, I hopped out of the car. "I bet dusty peach is going to make me look more like a moldy peach."

"Be nice," Mom said. She raised an eyebrow. "What goes around comes around."

"Not bridesmaids' dresses," I said. "They follow you to the grave." But seeing the elegant mannequins in the store's window did make me the slightest bit excited. The last time I'd gotten a fancy dress had been eighth-grade graduation, and that one had had a Peter Pan collar.

As soon as the tinkling bell chimed on the glass door, Polly rushed toward me, partially wearing a wedding dress that hadn't been fastened up the back yet. She held it against her chest with one hand as she hugged me with the other. "I hope you don't mind," she said. "I'm trying a few on early. I'm coming back with my mom tomorrow, and I want to have the choices narrowed down before she sees anything. My mother is . . . very opinionated."

"That one's nice," I said of the long-sleeved lace dress that was askew across her chest. I really couldn't tell with it only half on, but with her shiny hair and long neck, she resembled a bride on a cake topper.

"You're too sweet, but I think it will give me too much cleavage," she said, lamenting a problem I couldn't imagine having. "I'm going to try something with a higher neck." She went back to the dressing rooms, and I wandered deeper into the store, unsure what to do. I saw some dresses on a rack, but nothing that looked dusty peach.

"Can I help— Susan?" Dawn Murphy came out from the dressing room area and squinted at me. "You're not getting married, are you?"

"Uh, no. . . ." I pointed toward where Polly had gone. "I'm with Polly. You never said you had a job." It sounded like an accusation, even though I hadn't meant it to.

"Well, it's not like we're friends," she said. Dawn's words were direct, but her tone wasn't cruel. Our not-friends status was stated as a plain fact, same as if she'd told me it was Monday.

Still, it bugged me, because we should have been friends, shouldn't we? We played on the same team. Though, if I thought about it, my only real friend on the team was Tina, and if I went down the roster, most of the girls were people I just saw at soccer, not people I shared secrets with. Plus, I never really said all that much to Dawn even at practice, probably because of the baby rumors. I immediately felt like a jerk; the right thing to do would have been to ask her, but there was no good way to ask someone to confirm or deny gossip about themselves.

"I guess I mean that after tryouts, you've never missed practice to work or anything," I said.

She shrugged. "I took more weekend shifts once I figured out Bobby was serious about practice."

"Oh." I hoped Polly would emerge soon, because I was just about out of things to talk about with Dawn. "Do you like working here?"

Dawn peered around as if looking to see who was nearby. "Not really," she said. "But we get commission, and it's kind of easy to make sales since we're the only bridal shop in Powell Park."

"That's cool," I said. "I still just babysit. The kid I watched yesterday made me listen to him sing 'Bohemian Rhapsody' seven times and I still only got two bucks an hour."

Dawn laughed. "Kids are the worst."

"I know, really," I said before I caught myself. If she had a kid, that wasn't the nicest response. "Some kids are okay, though."

She crossed her arms over her chest and made a clucking sound, then turned away from me to start organizing a rack of dresses sandwiched between white jewelry cases carved with swirly designs. A prickly heat covered me. I'd totally said the wrong thing.

"I mean some kids are fun, if you get to know them . . . ," I rambled.

"If you want to know if I have a baby, you can ask me," Dawn finally said. She pushed several dresses on the rack to the side, making space, then spun around to retrieve several putrid green dresses hanging on a hook nearby and clicked their hangers onto the rack. "I know what everyone says about me."

"I didn't . . ."

She held up a hand. "I know, and I don't care," she said. "But I don't have a baby. My dad ran out on us last year. We had to go live with my aunt in Michigan while my mom figured out what to do for money. Then my dad came back, and my mom's with him again, but I'm working. My mom thinks he's sticking around this time, but I'm not going to be screwed over again by relying on him. Or her."

I wandered toward a bowl of Jordan almonds on a white desk in the middle of the store. I took a green one, turning it over in my hands instead of eating it. How did you answer that? "I didn't know," I said. "But I'm sure people would understand."

"Maybe. But I would rather people make up stories about me than know my dad's a deadbeat and my mom thinks she can't do any better," Dawn said. "Plus, the rumor only makes sense if you're a raging sexist. Like, who's the guy who knocked me up? Why didn't he get sent away? Where is he in all these stories? Oh, yeah, no one thinks about that, 'cause he's a guy."

"It's not really fair, though, to you," I said.

"I don't care. It's kind of made me think. Like, doesn't it bug you that girls are supposed to be ashamed if we have sex, unless we have plans to, like, marry the guy or something?" She made a broad gesture to the store full of white dresses. Her point struck me hard, and I realized that the rumor about Dawn had also made me assume she wasn't very smart. I was an asshole.

"I don't know if people feel that way," I said.

"They do. All that *It's the seventies! Women can do anything a man can!*" Dawn said, her tone fakely enthusiastic. "Bullshit."

"Well, we can have sex, as long as we don't enjoy it too much," I joked.

"Yeah, and as long as we're not frigid and holding out, either," Dawn said with a laugh.

"Hey, but if we have sex, we can get a boyfriend out of it," I said.

Dawn put a hand over her heart. "I'd love to score a meathead boyfriend, but I'll only want to have sex when *he* wants to. I don't want him to think I'm a slut."

I helped her clear some space on a rack for a froofy wedding dress she was trying to rehang. "Yeah, why is it that only boys can want things?"

"Oh, we can want things, as long as it's having a house and looking super pretty for our man," Dawn said. "Just ask my mom."

Maybe I wasn't the only girl who fantasized about something better than the gropey, dopey guys from Powell Park. But a bridal store was no place to compare masturbation techniques. "Well, I'm sorry I didn't ask you what really happened last year. It wasn't fair of me."

"What is fair?" Dawn pulled a few orange-looking dresses off the rack and handed them to me. "You're dusty peach, right?"

"So I'm told," I said. "Thanks." I took the armload of dresses, half dumbfounded. Maybe Dawn didn't care about the rumors, but next time I heard someone whispering about her, I could say something—"You don't know that for sure," or even, "Who cares if it's true?"

The dresses were heavy, and they lay limp across my arms like a dead body. "You found some already! You're the perfect maid of honor," Polly said, lifting the fabric of the top dress, which seemed to have four hundred skirts piled on top of each other. "Which one do you like?"

I looked down at the dusty peach pile, not sure where one dress ended and the next began. "I guess I need to see them on," I told her. "And what the other bridesmaids like."

Polly squeezed my arm affectionately. "It's your pick. I have two cousins in the wedding from out of town—Mother's orders—but I'll ship them what you choose so they can get alterations. Why don't you go to the dressing room?"

Dawn appeared at my side, taking the dresses from me. "This way, miss," she said, and smiled in a friendlier way than she ever had before. As soon as we'd stepped away from Polly, though, she relaxed. "Good luck with those," she said as she put me in a fitting room. "Taffeta can make anyone ugly."

She wasn't wrong. The first dress clung to my midsection but drooped around my boobs. "I look like what happens when summer commits suicide," I said aloud to myself, but when I came out, Polly exclaimed in delight.

"You're a vision! A harvest miracle." She came up and zipped the dress the rest of the way, and it looked slightly less bad.

I went to the mirror at the front of the store, pulling up the fabric pooled around my feet, when the door chimed again. "Susan, you left your purse in my car," I heard my mom say, and I spun around.

"You look nice," we said to each other at the same time. Only the way she said it to me was complimentary, and the way I said it to her definitely sounded surprised. My mom wasn't in her usual somewhat frumpy work clothes—she had on a straight skirt slit to just above her knee, and over it, a belted blazer and a creamy silk scarf at her neck. The color and fit worked to make her look taller, like she'd had the suit made for her. The outfit had to be new, like the black heels she wore over black pantyhose. Her hair was done and she had on red lipstick. My mom was normally a Lip Smacker person, like me.

Polly poked her head out of her dressing room, "Oh, Dierdre, you look wonderful. I love that jacket on you. Good luck with the interview!"

The interview? What interview? And why did Polly know?

"Thanks so much, Polly," Mom said. "Fingers crossed. And good luck with wedding dresses."

As Mom set my purse down on a white upholstered chair, I asked, "Were you going to tell me you had a job interview?"

"I was, but after it happened." She reached out and fixed one of the flounces around my shoulders. "I'm superstitious."

I crossed my arms over my chest, and the ruffle over my boobs instantly enveloped me to my elbows. "You told Polly. Is it good luck to tell your ex-husband's bride?"

"Susan, not now. I have to go." She leaned in to kiss my cheek. "That one's nice, but see if they have something with a simpler bodice."

She pushed out the glass door and walked down the street, looking like someone I didn't recognize.

Dawn's manager was talking to Polly about how long it would take to alter a wedding gown. Dawn, who'd been pulling more dresses from one of the racks along the wall, took down an empire-waist gown with spaghetti straps. "That must be awkward," Dawn said. "Having your mom and stepmom be friends like that."

"They're not friends," I said. "They just, like, get along." Could they be friends, though? I pictured coming home one day to Polly and Mom at the kitchen table, having coffee and talking. Talking about me, maybe. It wasn't normal, but it was abnormal in a way I couldn't exactly be mad at. It was infuriating, my parents being so reasonable. The only response they'd left me was to be agreeable, to flatten any rough edges and slip smoothly into my new role as everyone's daughter, to be dressed up and lied to and posed happily in photos. Had anyone even asked me how I felt about all this? Dad got a new wife, Mom and Polly got new friends, and I got passed around among them.

Everyone got something out of the divorce but me.

Dawn handed me the dress she was carrying. "This is pink," I said.

"It comes in dusty peach," she said, and walked me to the mirror, where I held it up against myself. "I thought the straight line would be more flattering for you, and your arms are skinny, so they'll look good in the spaghetti straps."

I tried it on, and Dawn was right. It was still a bridesmaid dress, but I looked taller because of the way the column of fabric flowed over my body.

"Thanks," I said to Dawn. "This one's actually okay."

"That's what teammates are for," Dawn said.

I sat down on the velvety cream couch in front of the mirror and picked up one of the magazines to flip through. It was *Brides*, and it was boring.

"I have a favorite, but I'll have to show my mother. She's picky," Polly was saying to the manager, then turned to me. "Susan, I saw a really pretty dress with a sweetheart neck that might be nice."

"I like this one. It comes in dusty peach," I told her, not standing up. I kept my voice flat. My pity for her was gone. Was my mom somewhere in her bridal wish book? Maybe they could go get their nails done together, so Mom would have another way to be too busy for me. I didn't have to pretend every second that everything was easy, even if my parents and Polly thought it was. At that moment, I wanted to be annoyed, and to leave. "And I have to go."

Polly must have seen the look in my eyes, or registered my irritation. "You know, you're right," she said. "Simple is best."

Fifteen

Joe lived in a two-story yellow house with red trim. It was one of the smaller ones on that block of Lynwood, but it stood out for how neat it was, with a lawn that was fading but still green even in October. It was the second time I'd thought of something of Joe's as not matching his punk persona. Though I guess the house really belonged to his parents, and I doubted they were punks.

I knocked, and a girl, maybe twelve, with Joe's same dark hair flung the door open instantly. "Joe!" she yelled, before I even introduced myself.

I heard footsteps clattering down stairs I couldn't see from the entry, and then Joe emerged from a small hallway that led to a living room with new-looking furniture and a long bookcase. "Hey, come in," he said with a wave. He had on his usual soccer clothes. "Well, come through. We're going out back."

The girl, his sister, I guessed, cleared her throat loudly. She had her hands on her hips, and though the gesture was one of annoyance with him, I could tell instantly that she liked her brother.

"Oh, this is Rachel. Rachel, this is Susan. She's a soccer player."

"Hi," I said, as Rachel made no attempt to hide that she was looking me up and down.

"Thanks for acknowledging my existence," she said in a dry but pleasant enough way. "Your shoe's untied."

"She's got to put on her cleats anyway," Joe said. He pointed at Rachel. "You're on music duty."

"Then I get to watch *Laverne and Shirley* tonight," she said, with her chin stuck out.

"But *WKRP in Cincinnati* is . . ."

Rachel glared at him.

"Fine," Joe said, and she bounced away. "Sorry, she's a pain in the ass."

"I like her," I said, tying my cleat. "How was the movie?"

"It was the same as the last five times I've seen it," he said. "Lizzy hated it. She's more into horror movies. How was the rest of the car wash?"

"We made enough for Wisconsin," I said. I tried to think of something else to ask about Lizzy, but in my head, every question sounded like I was asking about his dating life in a way that could be taken wrong.

Before I landed on the right question, Joe chucked me lightly on the shoulder. "Nice! I promise you'll learn something useful today."

He gestured for me to follow him through the house, which I did, surveying the trigonometry textbook open on the kitchen table and the notebook next to it filled with Joe's scrawl. His work looked neat and orderly, but a page he'd ripped out was covered in doodles of his band's name.

We went out a screen door to his backyard, where the grass was more trampled than in front. I saw why right away, as Joe bounded in front of a practice goal set up in front of the fence that separated his yard from the alley behind it.

"So, what's this lesson plan you have?" I asked. I hadn't expected him to start practice at his house with the same efficiency as at the park. But what did I want, a tea party first?

"You're gonna learn headers," he said. Then he looked up at the second-story window where Rachel was sitting, flipping through a magazine. "Ramones!"

"Again?" Rachel said.

"Where's your mom?" I asked. I kicked the ball to him.

"Both my folks work, so work," Joe said, kicking the ball back to me. Besides Tina, whose mom owned a salon, I didn't have many friends with two working parents, especially if they were still married. "They both do sourcing at the Merchandise Mart downtown. They commute together and everything."

I heard faint music from upstairs, bouncy and energetic. "Volume," Joe hollered, and Rachel turned it up. I liked whatever it was.

"So you're . . . babysitting?"

"Nah, Rachel can take care of herself. I just thought if you really want to learn the good stuff, you need music, and she knows how to flip a record."

"I'm doing it for *Laverne and Shirley*," she called.

Joe toed the soccer ball and flicked it to me, and I stopped it with my foot, then kicked it back toward the goal. He stretched an arm out to stop it and smirked. "Nice try."

I laughed. "What did you say I'm learning? Headers? What's that?"

Joe widened his mouth in an exaggerated shocked face. "What? Coach Hot Pants hasn't even mentioned headers?"

"Coach McMann," I corrected him, toeing the grass. "Maybe he doesn't think they're that important."

"Maybe not. They might even be idiotic, but they're fun." He tossed the ball high in the air and then, as it came down, jumped in the air and hit it using his forehead. He sent it straight at me.

I jumped out of the way.

Joe chuckled. "A natural reaction." He jogged over to the ball and picked it up, holding it under one arm. He explained that if I wanted to do a header, I needed to use the exact right part of my head. Then he came over and, like before, said "May I?" and gestured toward my forehead.

I nodded.

"I never touch anyone's hair without permission. I know how it feels," Joe explained, massaging his spikes with his free hand as he looked right into my eyes. Then he gently traced an oval that encompassed the middle of my forehead to not quite the very top of my head. I drew in a breath. My scalp tingled under his fingertips, and I remembered how much I used to love when the school nurses came around to do lice tests, flipping up sections of hair with a pencil, the featherlight touch so relaxing and thrilling at the same time. I never told anyone about that.

"This is header territory," he continued. "Face the direction you want, keep your shoulders straight, and bash the ball with this part of your skull."

He stepped away, but I could still feel where he'd drawn the oval. "Okay, how do we practice them, though?"

I barely had the words out when Joe hurled the ball toward my head. I jumped out of the way again.

"Good reflexes, bad header," he said.

"I don't get why anyone wouldn't dodge," I said.

"Because some of the best stuff in sports is doing something kind of stupid and pointless and feeling really cool that you know how," Joe said. "I mean, baseball's great, but who thought, 'Someone should throw this ball at one chick really fast and that chick can whack it with a stick as hard as she can'?"

He'd chosen women for his example, even if he called them "chicks." I buried a little smile as I thought about what a good teacher he was. He was different than Bobby, who gave motivating speeches to make us see the best in ourselves. But Joe's way of teaching—with all its rough edges—was no less inspirational. It *would* be both ridiculous and cool to learn a header.

But every time Joe tossed the ball toward my face, I lost my nerve and ducked or jumped or evaded it somehow. "The music's not helping."

"You need to let it infect you," he said as the record ended. We stood there, looking at the window, waiting for Rachel to turn it over.

"New album, Ramones, *Road to Ruin*, B side," Joe shouted at the window. No response. "Rachellllllll!"

"I was reading!" Rachel leaned out the window, holding the

page in her book with a finger.

"I'll take you to McDonald's if you shut up."

"Oh, is McDonald's punk rock now?" I asked.

"I like her," Rachel shouted. I warmed as a blush crossed over my face. Did Rachel think I was Joe's girlfriend? Hadn't she met Lizzy? Or the girl before Lizzy?

Rachel put on the new record, and soon the words *"I wanna be sedated . . ."* leaked through the window. I'd heard the song before.

As Joe lobbed another ball toward my head, I bit my lip and went for it, but only managed to swipe the ball with a piece of my hair. "Is this song meant to be about me after I have a concussion?"

"You're close, I can feel it," he said.

"Why do I even need to know this?" I said. "Am I ever going to use it?"

"It's not calculus. It's knocking a ball as hard as you can with your head. Much more useful."

Rachel leaned out the window. "You're only saying that because you can't do calculus." She grinned at me. "He did too many headers."

I liked his sister. I liked his music. I liked all of it. How easy it was, to just exist there. It felt homey, like Candace's.

But I didn't think I was going to get a header to work for me.

After a while Joe suggested a break and took three bottles of pop from the fridge, which we drank on his back steps with Rachel. The record had stopped, and we sipped in comfortable silence.

"Can I pick some music?" I asked him. "When we start again?"

"It depends on what it is. Is it a punk song?"

"Whatever. You were listening to 'All My Love' in your room two nights ago." Rachel said, and turned to me. "He learned about punk music last year from our cousin in New York and now he thinks he's better than everyone."

Joe blushed and nudged her with his elbow. "That's not true. I knew some stuff before Artie told me about it," he said. "I had to escape 'Hotel California' somehow."

"This again?" Rachel peered around him at me. "Do you want to hear my brother's thoughts on 'Hotel California'? Because he's going to share them whether you want him to or not."

I wrinkled my nose. "Does anyone think that much about 'Hotel California' anymore?"

"Joe does," Rachel said.

"Look," Joe said. "That song was supposed to be about how gross the music industry is and, like, okay, that message is kind of punk. But then they paid off like every radio station in the world to play it a million times a day."

"Change the station," I said.

"Ha!" Rachel snorted.

"I get the feeling whatever song I ask for you're just going to shoot down," I said.

"No, I'll replace it with a better song. You need enlightenment," Joe said. "Punk enlightenment."

"You're acting like some lame authority figure on music who claims to hate authority figures?" I teased.

Joe's lips smiled around the top of his soda bottle. "You've been listening," he said out the side of his mouth. "I'm getting you riled up. Perfect for headers." He put down the bottle and turned so we were facing each other. "Fine," he said. "Sell me on a song. What's going to be the soundtrack for your first header?"

I thought for a second. "'Gimme Shelter,'" I said, naming a Rolling Stones song I liked.

"Okay, but if I'm going to tell Rachel to put it on, you have to convince me. I'm missing *WKRP* for this."

He had an eager look in his eye, and I'm not going to lie, it excited me. Was this what people meant when they said someone was a good listener? "That opening part. It makes me, like, imagine I'm high up someplace, looking down on my life, and suddenly I'm some kind of god who can command everything and wipe all the dumb shit away." I'd never thought that hard about the song before, but as I explained myself, it felt accurate and true. More important, I realized I didn't care if Joe thought I sounded stupid.

He studied me then, and I wondered if I was wrong and I should have worried about sounding stupid.

What he said, though, was, "What dumb shit are you trying to wipe away?"

I couldn't say Coach McMann, and how I'd joined the team for him and how I still had dirty daydreams about him and wanted him to like me best. I didn't want to talk about Candace having a boyfriend, and how it had only added to her acting like she was a relationship expert and I was a dunce. I could have said something about the divorce and my dad's wedding, and Polly and my mom being friends, but while I think I might have actually trusted Joe to understand, I couldn't explain what I felt about it all because I didn't know. I couldn't even say that the song's effect on me was a lot like when I orgasmed, temporarily lifting the discomfort of being in my body, being a girl, being seventeen. I definitely couldn't say that.

"I dunno," I said, my grin a camouflage for my confusion. "Like, maybe what's the point of learning headers?"

Joe raised his eyebrows. "Well, okay then. Rachel! Cue up 'Gimme Shelter.' It's on *Let It Bleed*."

Rachel grabbed the soda bottles and went back inside with a smirk on her face, and Joe grabbed the ball and headed for the goal. I followed him, wondering if I *should* have told him what I'd meant by "dumb shit," and wondering why he hadn't pressed for details, either.

The opening strains of my song drifted out from the window.

I listened, satisfied as the music did drain away the stupid shit. Most of it. The tempo quickened, and out of nowhere, Joe tossed the ball at me. Without thinking, I jerked my head forward, giving the ball a meaty *thwack* and sending it right over his shoulder.

And somehow, improbably, into the goal.

Joe peeked down at the ball behind him, and then back at me as a wide grin took over his face. "Well, fuck, look at you, Pelé."

I touched my forehead, which vibrated with a pleasant sting. When I smiled, it felt like something I hadn't done in forever.

"*Now* do you get the point of headers? Ridiculous, and satisfying." He chucked me on the shoulder. "By the way, I love this song. And I get what you meant."

"Thanks," I said, believing that he did.

"That was my lesson plan. You passed. Are you hungry?"

I realized I was starving. "I could eat."

Sixteen

We decided on Jr's, because a hot dog special and a milkshake were calling my name. After I ordered, Joe said to the cashier, "I've got hers, too." He passed over a ten.

"I've got money," I said.

"You need money for your Wisconsin trip," he said. "Plus, you nailed a header. This is my way of telling you good job."

I'd never had a boy pay for anything for me. "Um, thank you?" I said.

"No biggie." He waved me off. He was definitely not trying to make a big deal out of taking me for a hot dog. This was how friends paid for hot dogs, and I was making it weird because Joe was a guy.

"How do you even make money?" I asked as we waited for our number to be called.

"Nosy, aren't you?" Joe said, but grinned. "Sometimes the band gets paid to play a party, but mostly I make cash helping out my dad on weekends—he paints houses sometimes—or at St. Mark's."

"You're not an altar boy, are you?" I said, not remotely able to picture it.

"Ha, no way," he said. "But there are a couple of nice nuns who pay me to do some odd jobs around the place."

I raised my eyebrows. "Nuns have money?"

"They don't have *priest* money," Joe said. "But a lot of them are good at poker."

"Hmm, you're full of surprises," I said. It was strange how much he was not what I'd first pegged him as, but also exactly how I expected him to be.

Joe shrugged as he went to the counter to get our order in its greasy paper sack. My stomach growled when I saw the bulging bag. "Eh, nuns have good stories," he said. "I like people with good stories." He handed me my milkshake and I took a long sip.

"Well, next time it's my treat," I said. "But thanks again."

"You're welcome again, and deal." He nodded at me. "So how do you make *your* money?"

I told him about Kevin, and Randy the Terrible. "If you know any kids who wouldn't make me certain I never, ever want to have any, please let me know."

"I'll get back to you," Joe said.

Jr's was mostly carry-out, and the few tables it had were tiny and also occupied. "Do you want to eat alfresco?" Joe asked.

"Who's Al Fresco?"

"It means eat outside," he said. He was already pushing through the glass door to the street.

"Did you learn that from the nuns?" I asked as I followed him.

"Actually, I did." He opened the passenger-side door for me and jogged to his side. "Plus, like, forty ways to cheat at cards."

We got in and he gave me the bag to hold. The aroma of the food was killing me.

"I have this weird thing where I love to hold a hot pizza box on my lap," I said. "And especially when it's cold out. It's better than a blanket."

"Well, yeah, it's pizza," Joe said. "Pizza is better than most things. But you're right, it's comforting and exciting to have something that warms you up but you can't wait to shove in your face."

"Exactly," I said.

It was a warm night, and Joe drove us to Oak Meadows, our soccer park. He pulled a blanket from his trunk and brought it to the middle of the field.

"You have a blanket in your car?" I asked. I imagined Joe taking girls for spur-of-the-moment picnics, or maybe he used it for back-seat makeout sessions on cold nights.

"I put it over my amp," he said.

"Ah. I never asked what instrument you play."

"'Play' is a strong word, but I sometimes hold a guitar and use it to make noise while I scream into a microphone."

"You're probably better than you think," I said.

"No," Joe said. "But what the Watergate Tapes lack in quality, we make up for in enthusiasm."

He laid out the food and we sat across from one another. Once the foil and waxed paper wrapper were off my first hot dog, I demolished it in seconds. Thankfully, we'd both ordered the special, which came with two. I ate the second hot dog slower, savoring every bite.

When we finished, Joe flopped onto the blanket. "Whoa, why are hot dogs so good?"

I settled down on my half of the blanket. "I don't know if *all* hot dogs are that good," I said. "Jr's is definitely better than when my mom used to cut up an Oscar Mayer and serve it to me in baked beans."

Joe sat up and looked down at me, his face stricken. "You don't like that? I loved it as a kid."

"I'd rather just have the hot dog, not, like, chunks floating in bean juices."

"When you put it that way, it does sound unappetizing," he said. "But I'd still eat it."

He lay back down and we stared at the sky a bit.

"Do you like Powell Park High?" Joe asked.

It was hard to shrug lying down. "'Like' is pushing it," I said. "I don't want to burn it down or anything. Do you like St. Mark's?"

Joe laughed. "The weird thing is, I think I do? Or I guess I like knowing it will be over someday, so I try to pay attention to it now, while it's going on."

"That makes sense," I said. "Like, I sometimes think about how I just want to be an adult already, but I don't know if the adults I know are having fun, so maybe I should make the most of high school?"

"Yeah, and making the most of it might be barely enduring all the assholes but being amused and appreciating that they're assholes we go to school with, and not assholes we have to work with yet?"

"You're a senior, right? Do you know what you're going to do when you graduate?"

"I've kind of been thinking about colleges," Joe said. He turned his head toward me, so I tilted mine toward his. His dark eyes caught some of the light from the lamps over the field. "I never used to, but it's going to be 1980, you know? It feels like the future or something, and it seems like if I can keep learning stuff, it's maybe better than getting some job that might just disappear in a year."

He seemed shy then, like he was waiting for me to tell him he wasn't nuts. "I'm not sure things will be any different in a year," I said.

"Maybe not," he said, and he was looking at my face carefully. I stared back at him. It was odd, how exciting it felt to give yourself a minute to really look at someone's face and notice all the pieces of it separately and in ways you can't when you look at the whole thing at once. Joe had a little scar on one eyebrow, a slice of white through the dark hairs. He had a small freckle just beneath his nose, and his lips curved up on one side like they were ready to grin.

"Do you think you'll go to college?" he said softly, still looking at me.

"I never thought about it either," I said. "I guess I can't see myself there. Wherever 'there' is."

"I can," he said. "I can totally picture you standing up and giving some cool speech about 'Gimme Shelter' or something."

I grinned. "I can't believe I did a header today," I said.

"I can," he said. Then he touched my chin lightly and I drew in a sharp breath. His face neared mine, and just as his lips almost covered my own, I shoved aside the bolt of excitement that had rocketed through me and pulled back.

Maybe this *was* his making-out blanket.

"Whoa, I'm not one of your girls," I said, a little sharper than I meant to. What was I supposed to say, though? Yesterday, he'd taken Lizzy to the movies. Just because he could go around making out with everyone like it was no big deal didn't mean I wanted to. Well, not that I didn't *want* to, exactly—there was no denying the surge that had shot through my body when he'd gotten close. But I could drum up that same surge thinking about the channel 5 morning weatherman *and* its sports reporter. My body wasn't a well-tuned antenna picking up one strong signal so much as a powerful radar that pulsed any time it detected someone decent in range. The only difference was Joe was one of the first guys I knew in real life—besides Bobby—to bring it on, without me having to imagine he'd been spliced with Paul Newman or something.

Joe's face was a study in mortification as he sat up. "That was stupid," he said. "I'm sorry."

He seemed to really mean it. I sat up next to him and touched his shoulder. "It's . . . it's no big deal," I said. "It's probably, like, habit for you or something."

"Yeah," he said, and his agreement confirmed what I'd already been debating about him. He wasn't any more serious about whatever girl he was out with than he was about anything else. And that was fine—we'd both be glad later that we hadn't kissed.

"Let's not be weird about it, okay?" I said.

"Definitely not," he said. "It was dumb. Seriously, I'm sorry. Won't happen again."

He stood and walked ahead of me to the car. Watching him retreat, I felt a current circuit inside me, like a Hot Wheels car making its way around a track, vibrating beneath my lips and traveling down my arms, coursing over my chest and down to my hips, then repeating. My breath caught looking at a small tear in Joe's T-shirt collar, and at his neck. I could imagine grabbing his shoulder and turning him toward me. We'd kiss up against his Nova until we couldn't breathe.

But crossing a line in my head was different from crossing it in real life. Making out with Joe when neither of us was serious about it wouldn't bring anything good, and would put an uncomfortable wedge in our friendship, like when you had something stuck in your teeth and couldn't stop running your tongue over it.

The only problem was, judging by the more or less silent car ride to my house, the uncomfortable wedge might have been there already.

Seventeen

Friday morning, I had my mom sign my permission slip for the Wisconsin trip; we'd be leaving that afternoon. "Here," she said, handing it back to me. Then she took her purse off the counter and fished two tens out of her wallet. "For emergencies, or a souvenir."

I felt bad taking the tens, but not because of the money. The permission slip was a fake. Franchesa, Arlene, and Sarah had all worried their parents wouldn't let them go with only Bobby as our chaperone, so Dana had used official school letterhead to compose a letter stating a female chaperone would be coming on the trip with us. Dana, it turned out, loved school rules, but not enough to give up the game because we didn't have enough play-ers. Even though most of our parents—Mom included—didn't necessarily care who the chaperone was, we'd all agreed to have the permission forms signed, in case somehow our moms ran into each other at the store that weekend. If our parents asked who was going, we decided we'd say Ms. Cuddle. We figured the only reason the school lacked rules for students traveling with a teacher of the opposite sex was because there'd never been a girls' team going on an overnight with a male coach before. "We really are pioneers," Wendy had said.

"Are you excited?" Mom asked me. "Your first real game." I was about to say yes when the phone rang, and Mom answered it with an enthusiastic "Hello," just as she had answered every phone call since the job interview. After a pause, though, she said, "This is Dierdre *Evans*," correcting whoever must have used her married name. Her face fell. "I'm sorry, we're not in the market for air-conditioning at this time." She put the phone back glumly.

"I am excited," I said when she hung up, but the spark of interest in her eyes was gone. "I hope we win."

"I hope so, too," she said a little flatly as she gave me a hug. She gently pulled my head into her shoulder like she had when I was little, and I squeezed her more tightly. She may have needed the hug more than I did.

The day at school passed more slowly than ever, and by last period in Kitchen Arts, Tina, Dana, and I were stir-crazy. Just not stir-crazy enough that any of us was doing a very good job actually stirring the little pots of hollandaise sauce we each had atop our burners.

"Do you think the hotel will be nice?" Dana asked us.

"It's a *motel*, so probably not that nice," Tina said.

"Is that the difference between hotels and motels? Motels are gross, hotels aren't?" I said.

"I'm sure Bobby won't have us stay anywhere gross," Tina said. Then, realizing Candace hadn't said anything in a while, she asked her, "What are you doing this weekend?"

Candace smiled. "Something with George, probably. Maybe a

movie. Some of the other football girlfriends might get together, too." She attacked her sauce furiously.

"Sounds fun," I said, even though it didn't. The football girlfriends again? It sounded so boring, like being a member of the PTA.

My weekend was going to be so much better. I kept picturing walking out onto a real field for our first game. I wouldn't have to pretend to like some football girlfriend. I'd only have to smile at some Wisconsin girl as we took the field. And then I'd kick her ass, maybe.

"It will be," Candace said tersely, without looking up from her pot. I'd known Candace for long enough to see that she was jealous. She'd acted this same prickly way when I'd first started bringing Tina around to hang out. Now Tina and I were going to Wisconsin together, something Candace and I had talked about doing after graduation. But she would have been going, too, if she hadn't quit the team.

I wanted to say something else—some comment to let her know we were still friends, even if things were different than they'd been. But I didn't know what that would be, and so at the end of class, I said to Candace, "See you on Monday."

"Yeah, have fun. I hope the motel doesn't have roaches," she said, but I knew she hoped there'd be at least a tiny one.

When three p.m. finally rolled around, we met at the side of the school near the football fields. The plan was to get to Wisconsin late afternoon so we'd be fresh for the game tomorrow morning. We had to play at eight a.m., before the Wisconsin school's football team needed the field. We couldn't get spectators to come out, even if anyone had wanted to come—they'd have to leave Powell Park at six a.m.—and we'd be home by Saturday afternoon, but it was still exciting. Everyone had a duffel bag of stuff, though Arlene Swann had a large pink suitcase instead.

"Is that thing full?" Tina asked her. "Are you planning on *staying* in Wisconsin?"

Arlene shrugged. "You never know what could happen."

Our bus—or at least what I guessed was our bus—was parked in the narrow drive where the boys' teams loaded up for games, and where their opponents were dropped off. It was a novel sensation to know we were going to be boarding a team bus. *Our* team's bus.

Some students using the side doors exited the school and blinked at us, wondering what we were waiting for. After the first few days following tryouts, most of the school had forgotten about us. Most, except the football team, who emerged from the side doors, filing past us on their way to practice.

"What's the deal? You have a game?" Keith Barnes said.

"Yeah, in Wisconsin," Arlene said proudly.

"Gross, Packer country," Keith said. "Good luck, though."

"Was Keith just semi-*nice*?" I asked Tina.

"I think so," she said.

"Do you think he respects us or something?" I asked, hitching my duffel bag farther up my shoulder.

"Nah," Tina said. "Probably it's hard for him to hump the air wearing all that football equipment."

Whatever made Keith bestow his leaden good wishes hadn't affected the rest of the team, who regarded us first with puzzlement and then open derision.

"Is it just me, or were all those girls better looking before they started playing soccer?" Teddy Childers asked a gang of younger guys trailing behind him. They all laughed like a bunch of pubescent seals.

"Hey ladies, aren't your boyfriends gonna be upset you're leaving town?" Paul Mahoney—Arlene's ex—teased, then slapped his forehead. "Duh, forgot that, no one wants to date any of you." Arlene turned away from him and gritted her teeth.

"Ha, yeah, good thing the Dyke Squad is leaving town," Teddy tacked on, half to us and half to Len Tenley, the captain of the team, who Lynn Bandis was dating.

As Len grimaced but said nothing in our defense, Marie tossed her duffel to the ground and stomped over to Teddy, who'd put on his helmet.

"Seriously?" Marie Quinn yelled into his mask. "The best you can come up with is we might rather have sex with each other than with some asshole like you? Sounds like we have good taste to me."

"You pissed her off," Paul said, slapping his buddy on the back. "She must not be getting any pussy lately. You know what that's like, though, don't you, Childers?"

"I'd rather have my vagina sewn shut than ever let one of you touch me," Dawn said, stepping in front of Marie, who Dana and Arlene had to drag away.

"He's not worth it, Marie," Dana said.

"Oh, I am, baby," Teddy called out, taking off his helmet. Then, turning on Dawn, he said, "And from what I hear, you're gonna need a lot of string."

"Like you'll ever know anything about her vagina or any other vagina, Teddy," I spat.

George emerged with Duane Harris, a sophomore who'd transferred in from the city and played varsity running back. George gave Tina and me a friendly wave, and Duane nodded and smiled. "Candace told me about the game—we hope it's a good one!"

"Thanks," I said blandly, more to Duane than to George, even though Duane hadn't said anything. Candace's boyfriend was just so earnest, and between his dopey personality and knowing his breath probably smelled like Paul Mahoney's armpit and blue cheese, I wanted to gag. He would have been less annoying if he were making piggish remarks. Everything about George irked me. He and Duane shuffled away, toward the field, but Teddy and Paul remained.

Teddy grabbed his crotch and sneered at me. "This isn't over, Klintock."

"I don't know, I bet you start and finish at about the same time," I said.

Tina said, "Tell him" under her breath and slapped me five.

At that moment, Bobby came out the side doors.

Teddy let go of his crotch, and Paul, who'd been about to say something, clamped his mouth shut. A lot of guys made fun of Bobby behind his back because he coached a girls' sport, but I noticed when they came face-to-face with him, they lost their nerve. Most of the time, they could go around believing they were better than the zitty, nasty teenage boys they were, but when Bobby showed up, his obvious superiority threw their pathecticness into sharp relief.

"Hey, gentlemen," he said. "Hope you're wishing your fellow athletes good luck?"

"Of course, Coach," Paul Mahoney said, in a fake kiss-uppy voice. "Good luck, ladies."

Coach Stevens, the massive football coach, had emerged, and he put a hand on Paul's shoulder pad. "Coach McMann, I hope you and your girls do the school proud." He sounded as fake as Paul had.

Bobby cocked his head at the burly coach. "They're not my girls. They're their own women." He smiled. He had a way of smiling that was so confident, it came off as a challenge, but not one that announced itself.

Coach Stevens emitted one of those laughs that aren't one, the kind that came out your nose. "Well, good luck," he said.

Bobby ignored him, as if the wishes meant nothing. He turned to us instead. Coach Stevens's jaw clenched, I noticed with satisfaction.

"All right, ladies, are we all accounted for?" Bobby asked, surveying all of us. "Let's get a move on."

We loaded our bags at the back and boarded the bus. The inside matched the outside, with some torn seats that had been repaired with tape. But it didn't smell bad, and that counted for something.

"Okay, I think it should take us about an hour or so. I've got directions and a triple-A map," Bobby said, standing at the front of the bus and waving the map in front of us. "Should be a straight shot, but anyone here want to navigate for me? I haven't driven a bus since I was at Southern."

"I'll do it." My hand shot up. The opportunity to spend an hour near Bobby, chatting or breathing the same air or sharing a meaningful look, wasn't one I could pass up. Besides, my fantasies had been a bit confusing since the near kiss with Joe. Maybe being close to Bobby would help put Joe out of my mind altogether. I hadn't heard from him, and even though I'd miss our lessons, I was telling myself it was a good thing. It was a little sad, but the way Joe went through girls, if I'd let myself be one, we'd have stopped talking whether we kissed that night or not.

No one else raised their hand, and it might have been my imagination, but I thought Bobby seemed happy about that.

"You always come through, don't you, Susan?" Bobby said, handing me the map and his directions, with the exit we should take in Wauwatosa circled in marker. "Just whisper in my ear if I get something wrong."

My thighs tightened as our fingers touched. I took the seat behind the driver's as everyone else dipped into seats toward the back of the bus. Tina took a seat by Wendy, Dana and Arlene paired off, and Dawn took up a whole seat with her legs stretched out. Marie and Joanie sat on seats across from one another and Marie took out nail polish and offered to paint Joanie's toenails. Lisa Orlawski—the only Lisa of the team's original three to make it this far—opened an issue of *Seventeen* and asked who wanted to take the quiz, and Sarah raised her hand to go first. Franchesa's mom had sent snacks with her, and she shared the bags of chips and cookies with everyone else.

As we pulled away from school, Bobby cocked his head back and said, "We're probably okay until the first toll, but then can you count out the change, please?" He handed me a coffee can of coins.

I took out Ms. Lopez's latest assignment, *Great Expectations*, a book I was angry at. A novel about Miss Havisham when she was young, and *her* first-person account of how she wound up living in her cobwebbed mansion with her crumbling wedding cake, would have been more interesting than whiny Pip. I read the same sentence five times without absorbing anything, then shut the book.

I took out a quarter and a nickel for the toll and held them in my hand, to be ready. Then I dropped them back in the can, not wanting to give Bobby sweaty coins.

Behind me, the team was laughing and shrieking, and when we finally hit the toll, Bobby said, "You know, I think I can manage, if you want to join the team."

I shook my head, even though he could at best see me only out of the corner of his eye. "Nah, I don't mind helping."

He beamed as I plucked out the money. "Thank you," he said.

Worth it, I thought.

I ignored the team's ruckus, enjoying memorizing the back of Bobby's head. He had a small freckle where his neck and shoulder met, like his body had designated perfect spots for a person to kiss. I began to imagine a map of freckles, like the capitals on a map. A breathy sigh escaped my mouth, as if pushed out by the warmth flooding my body.

"Are you okay?" Bobby said without turning around.

"Uh, yes, fine, groaning at my homework," I said. Dickens would stamp out any horny feelings, I figured, and I flipped through my book again, underlining random sentences for whatever paper I'd have to write. When the time came, I handed Bobby change for the second toll.

"So, you're a junior, right?" Bobby said.

"Yeah, why?"

He cocked his head slightly so that his eye caught mine. "Have you thought at all about what you'll do after you graduate?"

Working as your half-clothed assistant at Personal Best Training sounds good, I thought. "I'm not really sure yet," I said.

I thought about the conversation with Joe about college and my mom's question about where I saw myself in five years. Was it weird I didn't have a plan? I had never thought so before, but maybe my visions of the future should feature fewer nude scenes and more, like, actual grown-up stuff?

"You should really think about playing soccer in college. There are a lot of newer teams at the college level and quite a few give scholarships right now."

"Huh, I didn't know that," I said. "I'll think about it. But I'm not sure I'm good enough."

Bobby grinned. "You're getting better every day."

He turned back to the road, and I started to wonder if he'd meant what he said. Could I play in college? And did I really want to go to more school? I sort of figured I'd graduate and get a job first and then I'd take some classes if I needed them. When Joe and my mom had brought up college, I couldn't imagine it, but now that Bobby said it, I thought, *Why not me?* My grades weren't terrible, and in a lot of ways, it sounded better than a job like my mom's.

"Susan, can you see what my directions say? I think we missed the exit." Bobby's voice roused me and I realized I'd been pondering the college thing so intensely, I hadn't been paying attention.

I sat up in my seat, grabbing for the papers. "It's exit sixteen A—did we pass it?"

"Damn," Bobby said. "Yep."

"I'm so sorry, I must have dozed off," I lied.

He was guiding the bus down the next exit ramp, and he shook his head as if to say it was okay. "I know this area—I shouldn't have given you all that responsibility," he said. My heart plummeted.

He pulled into a Mobil station and stood up. "We overshot our exit just a little," he said. "We need to fill up anyway, so stretch your legs and we'll meet back on the bus in fifteen minutes."

Arlene raced for the front of the bus, shouting, "I have to pee so bad." A couple of the other girls beelined for the restroom with her while the rest of us went inside the gas station. I was starving, having missed out on Franchesa's snacks, so I bought myself some chips. When I went to the counter to pay, Dawn and Marie were ahead of me, pooling some money as the clerk rang up two bottles of peach schnapps.

"What's that for?" I said.

Marie cocked her head to one side like she was teaching a particularly clueless puppy how to pee outside. "To drink, silly."

"You can't buy that," I said, checking out the window to make sure Bobby couldn't see us from the gas pump.

"Marie and I are eighteen," Dawn told me, hitching her gym bag up on her shoulder. It made a clinking sound, and I knew there must be more booze inside. "So in Wisconsin we can. A little room party might be fun. And everyone is on board."

"Even Tina?" I said. The team must have been planning this

while I was busy not really helping Bobby. "And Dana?"

"Tina said she's in if you are," Dawn said. "And Dana came around. The uptight ones fold so easy."

I thought of Bobby's contracts at the start of the season, and almost brought them up. But Marie and Dawn closed in on me, saying, "You know we won't be stupid." There was no way everyone would follow the lead of No-Booze Susan. The better plan was to play along and then, at the party, make sure things didn't get out of hand.

"You know those football assholes would totally be throwing a party if they were here and not us," Dawn said. She gave me a meaningful look, like we were continuing our conversation from the bridal shop. "And it's not like a few drinks will hurt us."

"You have a point," I agreed. A few drinks, then I'd urge everyone to sleep.

Dawn grinned. "By the way, thanks for sticking it to Teddy for me."

"It hurt him more than it hurt me," I said.

While Dawn and I waited, Marie smiled at the cashier and said, "Nice day, isn't it?" She gave him a sexy grin and slid the money across the counter at him. He ogled her as she grabbed the bag.

Bobby was on his way inside as we left. "You made it, ladies, your first real game," he said, smiling at us as we passed each other.

"Yep, and we couldn't be in a better state," Marie said, holding up her paper bag. "Wisconsin milk!"

Eighteen

We'd only missed the motel by two exits, and since Bobby didn't request any more of my help, I took a seat near Tina and Wendy the rest of the way to Wisconsin.

"So, does his neck smell good?" Tina asked.

"Stop, I was only trying to help," I said, but I couldn't hide my smile. "And his neck smells great. He has good taste in aftershave."

"I really thought your crush would have faded by now," she said. She glanced up front at Bobby's neck, and after a few seconds of studying it, added, "But I can see how giving him up would be hard."

"Yeah, and why would I? It's not like I have a great crush alternative," I said.

"I take it that Joe guy still hasn't made a move," Tina said. I knew she'd have a field day if I mentioned the near kiss, but fortunately, Wendy saved me from answering.

"Joe who?" she said, turning around in her seat.

"The skinny dude at the car wash who came for Susan," Tina told her.

"Didn't he have a girlfriend?" Wendy said.

"He has a bunch, I think," I said. "I'm not looking to be one of many."

"He likes Susan best, though," Tina said.

"You should give him a chance." Wendy nodded.

"Trust me, it wouldn't work out," I said.

"Suit yourself," Tina said. "But I know he likes you, and he's cute. He might be worth a shot."

"I'm not taking a shot on a high school guy. I'm waiting for something better," I said. *Someone like Bobby*, I didn't say. Someone who wasn't hopping from soccer to punk bands and from girl to girl. Bobby knew what he wanted, in a way Joe and other high school boys didn't.

Tina rolled her eyes; she probably thought that I was dismissing Todd again, which was totally not my intention, and I was about to say so when the bus stopped.

"Well, who needs any of them? We're here," Wendy said, pointing at the sign for the Luna Creek Motor Lodge.

Bobby registered us as we surveyed the layout. I silently hoped Bobby's room would be so close to ours that Marie and Dawn would be too nervous to break out the booze. Soon, Bobby reboarded the bus, dangling three keys. "You've got three doubles, so split up among yourselves," he said. "Sorry you'll be sharing beds, but it's better than leaving Powell Park at five a.m., right?"

Everyone murmured agreement and filed down the steps. Once we had our bags unloaded, Bobby blew his whistle. I panicked for a second. He'd seen the schnapps. We were dead.

"Quick announcement, team," he said. I cast a glance at

Marie, who was trying to look nonchalant with the bag of booze clutched in her fist. "Meet out here in a half hour so we can get dinner."

"Dinner?" Wendy said.

"You didn't think I'd have you play your first game on empty stomachs, did you?" Bobby grinned. "There's an Italian place not too far from here, and we have money to spare from the car wash and some extra funds the school ponied up." My guilt compounded—I had a feeling this meant he was going to pay with his own money again.

"We're, like, movie stars," Joanie said. "They get everything paid for."

"We had to take some guy's dirty underwear out of his back seat for that money," Dawn reminded her. "It's not exactly the same."

"Go get settled in," Bobby said. "And then bring your appetites!"

The motel was L-shaped; our rooms were all in a row on the top level, while Bobby's was on the lower level in the other part of the L—far enough away that the party could go on, so long as we weren't too noisy. "I wonder if we'll be able to see into his window," Arlene said as she unlocked the door to the room she was sharing with Marie, Dawn, and Dana.

"He might be able to see us from his, so we better be careful," I said, and eyeballed Marie's bag.

She winked at me. "Don't worry, I know what I'm doing."

In our room, Tina was tossing her bag onto the bed. Hoping to make up for my comment about high school boys, I said, "I was thinking, you should tell Todd to come by later, for the party. He's not too far away, right?"

"I thought about it, too, but . . . you think it's okay?"

"Of course! Anyone else would."

"He works till seven," Tina said. "I'll call him from the restaurant."

The restaurant, Sal's Bella Vista, was almost a copy of Carmela's Bistro in Powell Park. Red vinyl booths, candles stuck in old Chianti bottles, and low lights. We had a big table in the back, and Bobby took a seat at the head as we all filed into chairs down either side.

It was family-style, and we decided on spaghetti, lasagna, a giant bowl of meatballs, and a salad at Bobby's suggestion. As we waited for the food, stuffing our faces with the bread the waiter kept bringing, all talking about how hungry we were, it really did seem like we were a family. We were noisy and boisterous, and the people at other booths kept turning to look at us.

When the food came, I heaped everything on my plate and passed the bowls and platters to Tina and to Wendy on either side of me. "Make sure everyone has enough," Bobby told us. "We can always order more."

Halfway through the meal, Bobby stood at his seat and raised his glass—water, though the rest of us were drinking Tab and RC Cola. He'd probably packed his wheat germ, too. "Don't worry, I'm not planning to make a big speech. All I want to say is that I'm really proud of all of you, as individuals and as the team you've become. So toast yourselves. You've earned it."

We clinked our glasses, and the convivial spirit sent a surge of affection through me. For the whole team, not just for Bobby. Maybe a well-behaved little gathering later wasn't the worst idea. We'd been working really hard—at least since the Day of Infinite Suicide Runs—and had never gotten to celebrate our progress; when would there be a better chance to do it, just us?

Back at the motel, standing with us in the parking lot, Bobby yawned and patted his entirely flat stomach. "Okay, ladies, I'm stuffed," he said. "I know I can't enforce a bedtime, but I strongly recommend you all get some sleep. We've got a six a.m. wake-up, and I know you want to play well." He gave us a fond look, like we'd already won.

"I'm so exhausted," Marie said, in front of him, stretching out her arms. "It's definitely bedtime." I would have believed her, if not for the sly sidelong look I caught her directing at me, Dawn, and Arlene.

"Me too," we all echoed. Everyone yawning and stretching and sighing in faux exhaustion at once seemed to make Bobby feel uncomfortable. He withdrew a few steps, as if fearful we'd ask to be tucked in.

"Okay, good night," Bobby said. "I'll see you all in the morning. If there's an emergency, I'm right across the motel." He left us then, and not waiting even a second after he was out of ear-shot, Dawn, standing next to Marie like her second in command, turned to the rest of the team and said, "Party in our room in twenty minutes."

"Yay!" Joanie and Lisa screeched.

"Shh." Wendy shoved them. "Are you trying to get us caught?"

"Do we have anything besides peach schnapps? I hate the stuff," said Sarah.

"We have light beer, vodka, and those cocktail cherries, because I like them," Dawn said.

"Oh my God, I love Wisconsin," Arlene said, doing a little twirl in the parking lot. Thank God Bobby was already in his room.

When we met up twenty minutes later, Dawn and Marie had the room's clock radio set to a disco station, and they poured shots into glasses they'd gathered from all our rooms. As they did, I cleared my throat. "Everyone, just don't overdo it," I said.

"We won't, silly," Arlene said, but she tossed back her shot before we even toasted and gestured to Dawn to refill it.

"*Salut*," Franchesa said. We all clinked glasses like at the restaurant. I swallowed only half of mine.

Donna Summers's "Bad Girls" came on, and Joanie grabbed a bottle of schnapps and let out a whoop.

"I'm all for enjoying yourself, but keep it down!" Marie said as she bumped hips with Franchesa, who swiveled her own. "Whoa, Franchesa, where'd those moves come from?"

I laughed to myself and watched them dance for a while, imagining what Joe would say about the choice of music. We'd argued about disco's merits, and I told him that only guys who couldn't dance didn't like it. But why was I thinking about Joe at all?

Soon, Dawn was thrusting a can of beer into my hand. "Why do you look like you're having some kind of dilemma? Schnapps isn't supposed to make you thoughtful."

"I don't know. Dumb guy stuff," I said. "How they hate disco."

"Yeah, if they can't dance," Dawn said, reading my mind, as Tina and Wendy joined our corner of the room. Tina's schnapps glass was still mostly full. At least I wouldn't have to babysit her.

Wendy flung one arm around my shoulders and the other around Tina's and said, "Do you know my dad wants to take me to Fort Lauderdale this Christmas break?" We shook our heads. Wendy's parents were going through a divorce way less reasonable than my parents' had been. "My mom was like, 'If he does that, I'm taking you to L.A. in the spring.' But all I want is for both of them to leave me alone."

"Are you drunk already?" Tina asked her, shooting a concerned look my way.

"A little," Wendy said. "I went straight for the vodka."

"I don't have much divorced-parent advice," Tina said. "Mine split when I was so young that whatever crap went down at the beginning, I don't remember. Two vacations doesn't sound terrible, though." As she spoke, I gently pried Wendy's half-full glass from her hand. She was our goalie—she couldn't get plastered.

"All I got out of my parents' divorce is a spot in my dad's wedding," I said, and sidestepped to the restroom to dump Wendy's vodka down the sink. Then I rounded the room, covertly taking drinks to dump and returning the empty glasses. If I kept dumping refills, we'd run out of booze without drinking it all.

Dana was especially tipsy. When Arlene asked her, "Why do you like Assistant Principal Lawler so much?" I took the opportunity to steal her schnapps.

Dana, who was perched on the room's tiny writing desk and

contemplating a cigarette Marie had given her, said, loud enough to hear over the rest of the party, "Because she makes her own money and gets to do what she wants."

"Yeah, as long as Principal Dollard says it's okay," Marie said, plucking the cigarette from Dana's fingertips and placing it in her own mouth.

Marie lit the end of the cigarette and puffed it once, then passed it to back Dana, who took an inhale that was comically deep and led to her sputter-coughing as "Ring My Bell" came on. "Assistant Principal Lawler will be principal someday and she knows it," Dana slurred as she tried for another inhale. She dropped the lit cigarette on her jeans, then jumped off the desk, sending the cigarette's cherry to the carpet. Marie stomped on it.

"Someday, sweetie," she said, patting Dana's shoulder.

The phone rang. "That's Todd," Tina said, springing up and gesturing for Dawn to turn down the music, which had crept to a much higher volume from where it had started. She pointed to me. "Can you check if the coast is clear?"

I pulled back the curtain to look down at the parking lot and saw no sign of activity. A light was on in Bobby's room and I took that to mean he was somewhere inside it. "We're good."

Tina told Todd and his friends they could come up. "Are you gonna go next door and get it on?" Marie asked Tina with a wink.

Tina smirked. "We'll see," she said. Then she added, "We haven't done everything yet."

This was news to me. I'd always thought the whole long-distance thing was made worth it by sex. "Really?" I said to her under my breath. "I thought you guys did. You always tease me about never really having done anything . . ."

"I play my cards close," Tina said. "And you never seemed that interested in Todd, so I never told you."

Todd and two other boys came through the door. Tina beamed and took three long steps to close the distance between her and Todd. I recognized him from a picture she'd shown me, but now his hair was longer, and reached his collar. I knew Tina's mom would hate that hair. "Hey," Tina said softly, followed by something that sounded like "honey bunny." I was used to tough Tina, and hearing her cutesy talk made me uncomfortable, like when my mom put her lace underwear in my drawer by accident.

She pulled Todd toward me. "This is Susan." Todd gave me a wide smile. It looked like he'd been given extra teeth because he took such excellent care of the ones he had. He was cuter in person and a bit taller than Tina. He gave me a huge hug. "It's cool to finally meet you," he said.

"You too," I said, and meant it. At least one of my friends had good taste in boyfriends.

"This is Jeff and Wayne," he said, pointing at his friends, who had set down six-packs of beer. They gave those sort of mock salutes guys sometimes do, and it took no time for Arlene, Lisa, and Joanie to swarm them. I saw Wayne checking out Marie, who had greeted the boys, then had resumed trying to teach Dana to smoke. Dawn was in another corner, and I overheard her telling Wendy and Sarah the truth about her absence last year, and them being indignant on her behalf. The party was seeming like a better idea every minute.

It wasn't long before Tina and Todd opened the door to our

adjoining room. She gave me a little wave. I wondered if tonight they'd seal the deal, and whether Tina would tell me if they did.

"See, I told you this would be fun," Marie said to me, coming up at my side.

"I never worried about fun," I said. "I just don't want to let Bobby down."

"We won't," Marie said. "I wouldn't have been able to sleep anyway, so at least I'll be relaxed tomorrow."

"Why'd you join, anyway?" I asked. "I know you and Lynn are close, and she quit, so . . ."

"Lynn thought Bobby was hot, so we went to tryouts. When she walked off, I stayed more because I was pissed she assumed I'd follow her," Marie said. "And then I figured out I was good at it."

"You are," I said. I thought of Candace quitting. "How are things with you and Lynn?"

"She's got Len now, and I've got this. We'll be fine." She gave me a tight-lipped smile as Wayne and Jeff came over to us with two cans of Natural Light. Wayne held one out for Marie, who took it with a smirking "thanks."

I accepted the beer from Jeff, who regarded that as an invitation to sit down. I hoped he wouldn't be another tool like Michael Webster.

"So you guys are playing in the morning?" he said.

"Yep," I said.

"Don't feel like you have to stay here talking to me if you need to get some rest," Jeff said.

I exhaled. He didn't seem like a Michael type. "Don't tell anyone, but I'm partly here to keep an eye on things," I said. "A hungover team would be bad on the field."

"How is the rest of your season going?"

"Um, we don't have much of one. This is our first and only game," I said.

Jeff held up his can to clink it with mine. It was a cheesy gesture, but I smiled and clinked anyway. "Cheers to you, then," he said. "In a way, haven't you already won?"

"What do you mean?"

"There aren't many girls' soccer teams, right? So just playing is a big deal?"

I paused. So there were guys like Michael and my dad, who laughed off our team, and guys like Joe and Bobby, who not only respected our team but believed we could win; maybe guys like Jeff were somewhere in the middle, people who thought we should be satisfied just to play.

And while I knew I'd really like to win—in the half-formed way someone who didn't know what winning felt like wanted to win—he had a point. We didn't have to be *perfect* out there.

"Yeah, kind of," I said, taking a sip of the cool beer. Jeff had one of those friendly faces, like a guy who got along with all the different crowds at school. "How long have you known Tina?"

"Since about third grade."

"What about Todd?"

"I've known him even longer. When we were in elementary school, I knew he liked Tina before he did," he said.

"Yeah, they're really committed. I honestly don't get how they do the long-distance thing."

"What do you mean?" Jeff said.

I shrugged. "I guess, like, it makes me wonder, are you really in love with each other or just your dramatic faraway love affair?" I cringed at how horrible it sounded as soon as I said it, and I wasn't sure if I meant it, or if I was annoyed that Tina had sort of scolded me for my lack of curiosity about Todd. Or if I was jealous that she was off making out with someone she really liked while I pointlessly pined for Bobby and made things awkward with Joe, the one guy whose company I enjoyed.

"I think it's cool they take a chance on each other," Jeff said, picking at the label on his beer bottle. I could tell he thought what I said was mean, too.

"Yeah, I guess it just seems like so much could go wrong," I said, hoping I sounded more gentle. "It's a lot to deal with." I didn't mention outright that Tina hid the relationship from her mom, in case Todd didn't know that. I realized if I were a better friend I would know if Todd knew that.

"I guess, if you think you found the right person, maybe it's worth it? Risking the parts that could go wrong," Jeff said, making me feel like an even bigger jerk than I already did.

"Susan, it's your turn to get ice," Arlene said, thrusting the empty bucket at me. She gave Jeff a sultry smile and squeezed between us. "I'll keep him company."

"You know what?" I said to Jeff conspiratorially. "I've got to get the ice and make sure no one is getting out of control."

He winked as I left, but he didn't seem to mind Arlene replacing me.

I took the bucket and opened the door a crack, and saw Bobby, peering out his blinds toward our rooms. Then his lights flicked off and his door started to open. I gulped, ducking back inside.

"Pipe down," I said as calmly as I could. I swatted down our light switch. "Bobby is leaving his room. I think he saw something."

"Shit," Marie hissed.

"Just be quiet, everyone," Dawn said, way too loudly.

"I've got an idea," I said. I made sure my pajamas were on straight and took a deep breath, setting the ice bucket down on the carpet before softly opening the door. I stepped onto the walkway and dashed as fast as I could toward the stairwell that Bobby would need to use to come upstairs.

My timing was perfect. I bumped directly into him.

"Susan," he said, catching me by the arms. He held me like that for a second before sort of placing me on the stair in a less-precarious position. "What are you doing up?"

I gave him the most defeated look I could, and, hoping my breath smelled like strawberry Bubble Yum and not Natural Light and schnapps, said, "I couldn't sleep and I didn't want to disturb the other girls, so I walked outside and . . . I forgot my key in the room. I'm locked out. I don't want to knock since they're sleeping, so I thought I should go to the office for a key."

As lies went, it was perfect. Where were these bullshitting abilities when I'd been struggling to write my essay on Faulkner?

"I'll help you," Bobby said, with a glance up the stairs toward the party room. Mercifully, the lights were off and I didn't hear a sound. The moon was full and our shadows blended together in front of us. Bobby gave a light laugh. "I'm sorry you can't sleep, but I'm relieved that's all it is. I thought I heard a party, but I guess I'm paranoid."

So he *had* been coming to check on us. Guilt bubbled in me and I fumbled for a way to change the subject, but he did it for me.

"Is the no-sleep thing because of the game?" he asked.

I puffed out a breath—I could see it in the chilly air—and said, "Yeah, just a little nervous." My pajamas were thin and I hugged my own shoulders as we walked.

"Don't be," he said. "It's just a game, as they say." Then he stopped walking in perfect view of our rooms. I held my breath, willing everyone to stay put until I gave the all-clear.

Bobby shook his head. "Who am I kidding, it's not just a game. Winning would be so great." He sighed. "That sounded wrong. I mean, if the team gets a win tomorrow, you'll know what it feels like. I can't explain why it's a big deal, but it's about more than a mark in the W column. You'll get to carry it around with you, always. Especially as the first girls' soccer team at our school."

I heard a noise overhead, and Bobby flinched. How easy it would be to distract him by kissing him. I was maybe almost tipsy enough to do it—I felt a little light from the half shot and half beer I'd had over the course of the party—but I wasn't crazy. He had a faraway look in his eye, and it made me want to understand what he was thinking.

"Why did you want to coach soccer, anyway?"

Bobby grinned. "When I got the teaching job, they offered me a spot as an assistant football coach. But soccer is my passion, for one, and two, this was a chance at starting something brand-new. A women's team. And, okay, I'm going to sound extremely nerdy now, but did you know that there's evidence that people played soccer in the second or third century? And not just men. Women, too. Not the game we know today, but a version of it."

"I didn't know that," I said.

"Really. And we know through history that women have done things that are thought to be only for men, but women *had* soccer way back then. They had it again in England much later, and then in 1921 the Football Association—they call it football in England—banned women from the game."

"That sucks," I said. "But . . . what does that have to do with us?"

"Everything," Bobby said. He was excited now, like a scientist in a movie who'd just made a huge discovery. It was cute. "Playing this game is for you. All of you. And I don't want to sound like I'm some hero, giving soccer back to you, but I like to think I'm an accomplice to helping you take it back."

"Well, thank you," I said. I had no idea that behind all his motivational speeches was this person so thoughtful about every aspect of the game. Dorky history and all.

"No, thank *you*," he said. "I think you have a great shot at winning tomorrow, and that's thrilling, but I'm even more excited because you all playing might mean other girls will want to play, too."

"So your speeches would be different if you'd taken the football team coaching spot?" I asked him, almost teasing, as we resumed walking in the direction of the motel office.

With an almost devilish look, he said, "I wouldn't bother as much. Especially with the guys on our team. But mostly because boys take opportunities for granted."

I thought of the party. He definitely could not find out about it. "We're going to work hard to get a win. We appreciate everything you've done for us."

"I want you to get the win for *you*," he said softly. "You need to know how good it feels." That comment sent a wave of feeling to my pelvis. But the way he said it also allowed me to *imagine* winning in a much more complete way than I'd been able to until now. A win would feel like someone had replaced my normal blood and guts with a golden inner grace, or maybe a calming pleasure, like after an orgasm. Or both. I let out a breath as he held the door to the office for me and told the manager my situation. The manager looked from Bobby to me and back to Bobby. He thought we were a couple, I realized, and blushed.

The manager slid a new key over. "Twenty bucks if we need to replace a key," he said. "So I hope you find it."

"I know where it is, just locked myself out by accident," I said, trying to cement my story.

I walked back outside, and even though I didn't hear any noise coming from the room, I knew that every second I tried to stretch out my time with Bobby was a second more when he could find out what we were really up to.

"I think I can sleep now," I told Bobby.

"Thanks for the chat, Susan," he said. "I'll make sure you get upstairs. Get some sleep."

He watched from the parking lot, so I made a show of going into my room, where Tina and Todd were waiting for me. They were fully clothed but the bed looked mussed. "Are we in trouble?" Tina asked nervously.

"I don't think so," I said. "But we should break up the party."

I split the blinds with my fingers and saw that Bobby's light was off. Tina, Todd, and I entered the party room through the adjoining door. Everyone stared at me, waiting for what I'd say.

"He didn't suspect a thing," I said, not sure if it was true but hoping I was right.

"You're the fucking best, Susan," Marie said, raising a drink. "To Susan!"

"And Tina! And her hot boyfriend!" Wendy added, definitely wasted.

As a cheer—a soft one—went up, Tina whispered to me, "Maybe everyone can have one more? This is kind of nice." I looked around at my teammates, who were waiting for my answer. The talk with Bobby had left me too excited to go right to bed. And it wasn't *that* late yet. Keeping the party going a bit longer wouldn't hurt. Bobby had coached us too well.

If winning tomorrow would feel this good, I couldn't wait.

Nineteen

Bobby knocked on all our doors at six in the morning, just like he promised.

The problem was, we were still in Marie's room. And everyone was scattered about in various states of hungover or still drunk.

"Noo," Wendy moaned from the floor as I hoisted myself up from the foot of a bed where Arlene and Dana had passed out. Tina was sleeping next to me. I nudged her and she groaned as she rolled onto her stomach. "Rise and shine."

She looked at me, one eye still closed, holding her head. "Dammit. I feel like shit and I didn't even drink that much."

There was a pause and another knock. "Are we okay in there?" Bobby called. "Are you all awake? We need to get going soon."

"Susan, can you please deal with him?" Dawn said, ambling toward the bathroom.

With my own head throbbing more than I had expected, I didn't think I could, but I'd somehow been appointed responsible for covering up our quickly multiplying infractions. "I'll try."

I went to the door with the most composure I could manage,

and I felt like I had myself together. When I pulled open the door and the glare of an October sunrise hit my eyes, though, I made a not-on-purpose creaking noise, like someone had stabbed me in the stomach with a dull knife. "We're almost ready," I mumbled, trying to keep my foul breath in my mouth. Then I burped in Bobby's face.

He stared at my eyes and I saw the awareness that I was wrecked cross his face. His eyes narrowed as he looked past me, into the room. We'd cleaned up as much as we could when we'd wound things down just before one a.m., but it must not have been good enough. Bobby cleared his throat and used his head to gesture to a spot on the floor. An empty bottle of peach schnapps was lying just outside the bathroom and in view of the door.

"The bus leaves in five minutes," he said in a tight voice. His narrowed eyes were focused on me, while my own bleary eyes could barely focus on him. "Clean up and get your uniforms on."

He hadn't yelled, but somehow it was worse. He pulled the door shut with a click. I was pretty sure that if we weren't on the bus to the game, he'd leave us in Wisconsin.

The ride was silent, no speeches or lectures. We'd rallied to get ready, but looking at my teammates slouched about the bus, I thought it was possible we'd used all our energy for the day in getting dressed.

It was my fault. For all my patrolling and discarding of drinks at the beginning of the night, I'd still missed that a few people— Wendy, Dana, Arlene—were drinking faster than I knew. Then, when I'd gotten back from talking with Bobby, I felt so confident that we'd win the next day, I figured I'd be okay to have a couple of drinks with the team. But the drunker we'd gotten, the surer we became that nothing we did could keep us from a victory, so we kept on drinking. . . . The second bottle of schnapps had helped it make sense at the time.

The excitement I'd had the night before was replaced by dread when we pulled up to the field. It was the real thing. A football field with goals positioned at either end, and with the penalty boxes drawn in white chalk around the goals. Bobby usually just marked those off with orange cones on our practice field. The grass was level, unlike at our park. Its green was sharp and stark against the cold gray of the sky, and the silver bleachers along either side were creepy, like looming metal skeletons. The hollow feeling in the pit of my stomach should have been excitement. Maybe dread was excitement's scary twin.

Bobby put the bus in park and stood next to the door, watching as we each stumbled or limped off the bus. "I am beyond disappointed. Not only because of what you did, but because you thought I would be fooled." For all the times I'd hoped he was looking pointedly at me, this time I was sure he was, and I hated it. "But maybe you have a chance, despite your efforts to blow it. This team has only ten players, and they haven't been practicing together as long as we have. I still don't know if you're in shape to win, but maybe you can prove me wrong."

He stepped off the bus and led the way to our bench, where he set down his clipboard. We knew we were all in deep shit with him, but Bobby wasn't making it obvious to the other team or the smattering of people in the stands. He ran us through some stretches and jumping jacks, and we were doing our best not to look as sloppy as we felt.

"They don't look that great," Arlene said, staring across at the other team as she clutched her side. She was right: their practice kicks were weak.

"Do you feel any better?" I asked Tina.

"I'm mostly tired," she said. "But I'm nervous." She waved to Todd, who was wearing a windbreaker and sitting high up in the stands by himself. Jeff and Wayne must have failed to make the early wake-up call to see the game.

"Maybe we'll be fine," I said. My brain seemed to be pulsing behind my eyes. "I'm going to be optimistic."

Bobby cleared his throat behind us and said, "Okay, get out there." I would have expected an inspiring speech under normal circumstances, but we were lucky he was speaking to us at all.

"Sure, Coach," I said, my voice cracking.

We soon found that a Bobby speech wouldn't have done any good. Shortly after we took the field, it was clear how tired and hungover we were. Being in the game, I couldn't see exactly how shitty we performed, but I'm sure from the vantage points of Bobby and anyone else watching, our cumulative suckage was easy to ascertain. Dawn, who was normally pretty quick, had trouble keeping up with the ball, and a Wisconsin defender stole it from her easily. With the ball in their possession, they made a pass that Marie would normally have pounced on but that instead rolled past her and put their team in scoring position against Wendy. It was only because their forward's kick was lousy that Wendy was able to save the shot.

My head was pounding, but I felt powered by the urge to fix the mistake we'd made. "Let's do whatever we can together to get a goal," I told Tina. "I can die later."

"We can try," Tina said. She didn't sound hopeful.

Wendy booted the ball downfield, and Sarah took control and managed a weak pass that I got hold of only because no one was defending me. I brought the ball toward the Wisconsin goal and a short girl charged toward me. Dana was loping, wide open, across the field. "Dana," I shouted, and kicked a pass her way.

Dana looked up, disoriented, as my pass rolled right over her foot and directly to another Wisconsin defender, who passed it to a midfielder.

"Fuck, Dana, wake up," I said.

The midfielder handily got the ball to her forward, who squared up and kicked it neatly into our goal. Wendy barely tilted toward the ball.

The Wisconsin team scored two more goals, more because we were crappy than because they were good. Marie tripped over one of the Wisconsin midfielders' feet and pounded the ground in frustration.

Somehow, Lisa and Franchesa both scored, but neither goal was pretty. The Wisconsin goalie was clearly still getting used to her gear and had simply failed to see the ball as we made terrible passes that meandered to the goal. But those two goals were both on her right side, and I thought of what Joe had said about finding a goalie's weakness. I still had hope we could pull out a win, even if it was fading fast.

At the half, Bobby told us to take advantage of our opponents' newness. "You've played harder scrimmages against each other," he said. "I don't have anything else to say." His normally energetic tone was flattened. Disappointment radiated from him.

Back on the field, nothing improved, but at least the Wisconsin girls seemed to be getting tired. Not hungover tired like us, but tired. No one scored for some time. If anything, we were competing to see who could keep the ball for the longest without mistakenly kicking it to the other team.

But then, with a few minutes to go, I had possession. The ball had come to me when a Wisconsin defender stole from Arlene but kicked it too hard, bypassing their midfielder. I'd been covering the whole field and my sides ached from running, but I took two seconds to map a path to the goal, by dribbling down the far right side of the field.

I knew my moves were clumsy and it took every ounce of focus for me to keep the ball from getting away from me. But we could still win, if I could just get near the goal.

I was closing in on the goal and uselessly sucking in air. My muscles were ragged and limp. I planted my left foot and craned my right leg back for the kick, but the same defender who'd been hounding me appeared at my side. I pulled the ball away just as she swiped at it.

Across the field, on the goalie's right, Tina lifted her hand, signaling for a pass. I had a clear enough path to her, but I wanted to fix things with Bobby. He'd put faith in me and I'd let him down. I'd full-on lied to him, right after he'd shared a piece of himself with me. A goal wouldn't get me forgiveness, but it had to be worth something.

The defender swiped at me again. I had to shoot now. Feeling like I couldn't waste any more time, I didn't bother setting my place foot and went for the shot.

As I made contact with the ball, I felt the hollowness of my kick. It was weak, and the goalie saw it coming. She easily batted it from the goal.

The game was over, and we'd lost.

We lined up to slap hands and say "Good game" to our opponents. After we finished, Dana jogged to a trash can under the bleachers, where she puked.

"God, we sucked," Marie muttered as we trudged toward our bench.

"I wanna go home," Arlene whined. She leaned on Sarah, who wasn't up to holding her. They tottered clumsily toward the bus.

"I feel like I drank a bottle of hot pee," Dawn said, kicking a clod of mud from her shoe.

"Hot pee sounds better than schnapps," Franchesa said.

"I'm gonna be sick again." Dana gagged and ran back to the trash can.

At the bench, the smile Bobby had worn exchanging post-game pleasantries with the other coach was gone. We stood in a cluster near him. We all were waiting for him to tell us how we'd wasted our one chance. But a cascade of angry words would have been better than his silent disgust as he packed up the team's gear, hefted the bag onto his shoulder, and stalked toward the bus without even telling us to follow.

We waited until he'd put some distance between us to march

behind him. None of us spoke. The only sound was our cleats crunching against the ground.

Bobby didn't look at us as we climbed the bus stairs. And he didn't ask for a navigator on the way back to Powell Park.

Twenty

When I'd finally gone to bed the night before the game, I'd been buzzed, but still with a vision, inspired by the talk with Bobby: I'd kick the perfect winning goal and my team would surround me and be cheering so loudly I wouldn't be able to hear anything beyond their voices. Then, as they parted, Bobby would be regarding me with admiration. He wouldn't pull me to him and kiss me on the mouth, but I'd know he'd thought about it. Afterward, I would come home to tell my mom that we'd won and that we should order pizza. (Drinking had made me hungry.)

There was another version where Bobby suggested we go back to the motel and he'd admit he couldn't stop thinking about me and couldn't wait any longer to be with me. That one I'd had to squelch because there'd been ten other girls in the room.

The reality was a bus ride home with a sullen Bobby at the wheel. Our hangovers had settled in on us in varying degrees, but our disappointment and shame seemed uniform and consistent, and we were silent most of the way, even when we stopped halfway home at a McDonald's. Bobby ordered a black coffee and sat at a small table by himself. Some of the team ordered fries and burgers, more to absorb the nausea than for hunger, and ate in silence. Yesterday's excitement was gone, and if we still felt like a family, it was a dysfunctional one.

I skipped the food. The idea of wolfing down grease as Bobby drank his coffee and ate granola he'd brought with him felt like yet another shameful choice in the face of his virtue. But mostly I had no appetite.

Not only had I wasted my chance for a winning game—or even a game I could say I'd tried my best to win—but I'd lied to Bobby. We all had. I knew then that it wasn't losing Bobby I cared so much about; it was that we gave up our chance to win before we even got on the field. I knew he felt this way because I felt it, too.

We made it back just before two, and as we gathered our things, Bobby said, "Practice usual time and place on Monday." His tone was cold, but a few of us glanced at each other, surprised. We were on his shit list, but he hadn't flushed us yet.

"Well, we kind of fucked that up," Tina said as we walked to her car.

"I know," I said. "He really hates us."

"He'll be fine," Tina said. "Anyway, I know we probably don't want to talk about last night, but I will say I'm glad you met Todd."

"He seems great," I said to her, thinking of what Jeff had said about their relationship. "I'm glad you guys found each other."

"Me too," Tina said. She stopped walking as if struck by something she forgot on the bus. But she turned to me instead. "You know why I didn't tell you that we haven't had sex yet?"

That was not the question I'd been expecting her to ask. "Because you feel sorry for me since my outlook for having sex is whatever they put on a weather map when there's somehow no weather at all?"

"Don't joke," Tina said. "It was a serious question. And I didn't tell you because I wanted to see if you'd ask. Like, the way I ask you about Joe, or see what you thought of Jeff last night."

"I don't know . . . ," I began, but trailed off. "Jeff was nice. We didn't talk long."

"Yeah, you didn't talk long, but he told Todd that in that time, you covered a lot of ground. Like if we're really in love, or if we just love our high-stakes secret romance. Jesus, Susan."

"I know you're in love. I think I was jealous, or felt bad because I didn't know more about you guys," I said. "But I have always wondered, how it works for you."

Tina held up a hand. "I don't mind that you've wondered. But you've never even asked *me* about that, Susan."

I didn't have any answer for that. I couldn't look her in the eyes.

"Don't take this the wrong way, but I'm not sure if you know what friendship is."

"What?" I was tired and sore, but Tina's comment sent a defensive charge through my body. "What are you even talking about? I've been friends with you since ninth grade. And Candace since kindergarten."

Tina cocked her head to the side. "And as soon as she started dating a guy you think is a dork, you started avoiding her."

"I'm not avoiding her," I said. "She's got her football girlfriends."

"I get it, and that sucks. But you're acting like a brat—like you're trying to push her away."

Tina opened the car door and got in. I wasn't sure if she wanted to give me a ride anymore, but after a moment she reached across and threw the passenger door open. "Don't be an idiot," she said. "Get in."

"It's not like Candace asks about soccer," I said. As my body hit the passenger seat, I registered again how sore I was.

"Just like you don't ask about George. Or Todd," Tina said. "Honestly, it's not that I think you're jealous. But anytime something doesn't make sense to you, you decide you just don't care about it. Being a good friend is more than just sitting at the same lunch table and going to the movies."

"I don't want to get into the Candace stuff," I said as she started the car. "But there are . . . other reasons, maybe, I don't bring up Todd."

"I'm waiting," Tina said. She loosened her grip on the gear shift.

"It's because you're my friend with such a *handle on things*," I said. "Sometimes I can't imagine you needing anything from me because you're four hundred times more together than I am."

Tina squinted at me. "Why do you think that?"

"You're looking at colleges, you have a boyfriend, and you're strong enough to deal with all the challenges with the distance and your mom, and like, you're tall, and hot, and I'm me. Like, I don't even know why you're friends with me."

"All right, I'm stopping you there before this turns into a pity party. But I'm your friend, which means I'll tell you what you need to hear, even if you don't deserve it. One, you know you're plenty hot and you could have had Jeff if you wanted him. Two, Suzie Q, everybody you know is a mess. Even me." She released the clutch and pulled out of the lot.

"If you're a mess, how come I've never once heard you grind the clutch when you drive?" It was another joke, but it got Tina to smile.

"Well, like the college thing. I want to go, don't get me wrong. I even like that my mom mails away for brochures from places I've never heard of. But that also means pressure. Like, she looks at everything I do like it might make or break my chances. Last week, I was leaving for school and she made me take my blouse off so she could iron it, like she thinks at any minute some college dean might see me and write me off because my shirt's wrinkled."

Tina laughed to herself, and I mumbled. "It's nice that she cares, though."

"Yeah, of course it is. But if she cared less, maybe I wouldn't be hiding Todd from her. Do you know that I make him lie when he calls my house? If he gets my mom or stepdad, he has to pretend to be 'Billy, Tina's lab partner,' or 'Roger,' who I'm tutoring in English. . . ."

I thought about the first time I'd met Tina's mom. Tina hadn't been nervous to introduce me at all, and her mom had invited me for dinner within the first ten minutes. I knew it was different—a friend versus a boyfriend—but still, I said, "Your mom is cool. Do you really think she'd have a problem with Todd? I mean, I know she gives money to Reagan but . . ."

With a sad laugh and a head shake, Tina cut me off, but gently.

"She wouldn't love Todd's politics, but they wouldn't be a big deal to her if they were going to lead somewhere she can imagine. All the guys my mom wants me to date? They're college-bound, goal-oriented guys with plans. The reason I love Todd is he's not those things. He's smart and he works hard, but he'd rather go pick litter out of rivers than go to college. And I can just hear my mom saying, 'What kind of life will he give you?'"

I could hear Tina's mom saying the same thing. Once she'd asked about Tonia, out in California, and when I told her my sister was a free spirit, Mrs. Tate (her second husband's last name) had looked horrified.

"You don't have to introduce him as Todd, a guy with no plans," I said. "He could just be 'my boyfriend, Todd.'"

Tina nodded. "I know. I'm a shitty girlfriend. He introduced me to his parents. He had talked me up so much that his mom and dad practically kissed the ground I walked on when they met me."

I was gaining more and more respect for Todd.

Tina drummed on the steering wheel. "I keep wishing I would wake up and just not love him anymore, so I don't have to do anything to disappoint my parents. Did you know, once I went out with one of the guys my mom invited for dinner? Just hoping that I'd like him a lot and it would mean I could break it off with Todd and date someone my parents would be thrilled with?"

"Why didn't you tell me?"

We were at a light. Tina raised her eyebrows at my question. "Would you have cared?"

"Sure," I said. Then I paused . . . "But I might have thought, 'Tina will know what to do.'"

"Yeah, right. I felt so guilty about it that last night, when I could have been making out with him, I told Todd about the date, just to see if it would make him mad."

"He still came to our game," I said. "He must not have been."

"He was glad I opened up to him," she said. "I was disgusted with myself and he got me to forgive myself, when I would have been furious if he did the same thing."

"I've never seen you furious before," I said, thinking of Tina's calm when handling the bitchy girls at our school. And even the way she was handling me, her shitty, shitty friend.

"Yeah, maybe I do hide that stuff a bit. But I don't want you to take what I *seem* like for what I am like. And when Candace quit the team—and this is stupid and kind of bitchy, but I'll tell you anyway—I thought, 'Now Susan and I will have something.' Like we'd have a thread that you and Candace didn't."

"We do. And you're not second. I've known Candace forever, and I hate that she bailed on us for some guy, but it's not like you're my backup friend or something." The words came out fast, and as I said them, I knew that I did treat Tina like my backup friend. But it was mostly because I'd had more practice with Candace. "Look, I've spent a lot of time hearing all of Candace's innermost thoughts on everything," I continued, "and maybe that's why I'm annoyed she just took George because he was the first guy who wouldn't ditch her immediately. But you're totally right about you and me. The way I've been . . . it's not how a friend should act, and I'm sorry. If you give me a chance, I promise to do better."

"Some of it's my fault, too. I don't exactly volunteer all my information," Tina said.

"You mean like Candace, and her tirade when the pep club put her on sign-making duty for the football B team?"

Tina laughed. "Yeah, like that," she said. "And maybe it's because you've been friends with Candace so long that I hate feeling worried I have to compete. Like I'll bring up some issue of mine and you won't be interested and I'll be hurt."

"I'll be interested. And I'll ask more questions," I said. I couldn't help it as my lips rose in a grin. "Like, after last night, are you still a virgin?"

Tina swatted me. "Yes. Technically, anyway. My damn confession took up the time Todd and I needed to get it all the way on."

"He's a good guy, though," I said. "That he listens."

"He really is. His friends are, too. But I still don't get why you passed Jeff to Arlene. Unless . . ." She put her finger on her chin. "It's that Joe guy, isn't it?"

"No! But something did happen," I said. Then I spilled out the whole story of the practice as his house and the almost kiss and his "habit" comment. "And I guess it was proof that he's exactly like I thought. Girls and life are a game to him. I want someone more mature, or something."

Tina gave me a knowing look. "Just admit you're holding out for Bobby."

I blushed, thinking of how cute he'd looked talking excitedly about the history of soccer.

"Not Bobby," I said. "Or maybe someday Bobby. But someone like Bobby . . . who's the whole package, inside and out."

"And in his pants?"

"Yeah, but I'm trying to be respectful after the shitty thing we did. We blew it."

"Maybe we'll get another game," Tina said. "And we can make it up to him."

"I'm so glad no one saw us play today."

"Todd did! But he loves me no matter what," she said. We pulled up to my house, and she put the car in park as she leaned her head back against the seat and looked over at me. "Anyway, I'm going to let you continue to admire how much I have my shit together on the outside, and you're going to remember that I'm a person with feelings and ask me questions so that I can lose that same shit once in a while, okay?"

I held my hand up like I was taking an oath. "I vow you can lose your shit on me anytime," I said. Then, even though I still had to read the stupid Dickens book, I added, "Do you want to come in? I can show you a picture of the dusty peach dress I'm wearing for my dad's wedding."

"After the schnapps, I don't want to think about anything peach-related for a while. No offense."

I hefted my bag off the floor of the car and put it in my lap. "I never even got to tell you about walking around the motel with Bobby last night. In my pajamas."

"Did you try out any of your *Cosmo* strategies?"

"Well, I didn't have a bra on." I thought of how easy it had been to talk to him. "We had this kind of . . . nice conversation."

"Like we're having now?"

"Yeah, except I kept wondering if he had on underwear under his track pants."

"He definitely sleeps in the nude." Tina closed her eyes, as if imagining it.

"So he was naked like two hundred feet from all of us."

We paused to think about that.

I got out and put my bag on my shoulder, then leaned into the car and said, "I'm sorry, Tina, for being a bad friend," before I walked to my door.

"I'm sorry I'm such a badass." She waited until I'd opened the door to drive away.

Inside, I unpacked my stuff from the weekend, and even though the conversation with Tina had ended well, I still felt like a crappy friend, plus a lousy person and a letdown of a soccer player. Putting my dirty uniform in the wash to Tide away all the grime of the game was like washing away all the hard work we'd done to get there. The practices and the car wash and the lessons with Joe.

What if we didn't get another chance?

The headache that had seemed to be fading when we'd finally gotten off the expressway returned with a vengeance thanks to whatever was still polluting my system. With the dull pain came a renewed sense of despondency.

I heard my mom's key in the front door and the rustle of grocery bags. Instantly, my stomach rumbled at the promise of food. Also, at the promise of Mom's attention, which might feel good after the laborious self-loathing I'd put myself through. A mother's unconditional love was supposed to make everything better, right?

I moped down to the kitchen, watching as Mom unpacked the grocery bags, taking out elbow noodles and tuna and a bunch of celery, cans of soup, and the store-brand pop that tasted like the offspring of Coke and RC (and not a child its parents were proud of).

"Hi," I said, imbuing the word with as much woe as I could.

"Hi, honey." Mom left the tuna, noodles, and celery near the stove, no doubt to remind herself to prepare another casserole for the week. I wondered what it said about us that we ate the kinds of foods you gave to people after a loved one died. I also wondered what Polly was making that weekend.

I tore open a bag of potato chips on the counter and wolfed down a fistful. "Can you get barbecue next time? Or Pringles? Remember I said I liked those?"

I wanted Mom to register my dissatisfaction, and to connect my hungry pillaging of the new food to something besides my empty stomach.

"You know I buy what's on sale," she said. "And Pringles were not."

I pulled more food from the paper bag. Bananas. Eggs. Bread that I thought was real Wonder Bread for a second but then realized was the off-brand we always got now, Wow Bread. When my parents had been married, we'd always bought Wonder Bread.

"Can we have a real dinner?" I asked her, putting away a package of hot dogs that we'd eat on folded slices of Wow Bread, since Mom didn't buy buns anymore. I peered deeper into the fridge, hoping to see a package of meat that still bled. Visions of steak, like we'd often eaten on Saturday nights with Dad, danced across my mind. But I didn't even see hamburger.

"I don't know what you mean by a 'real dinner,'" Mom said. "We can order a pizza, but that will be it on takeout food for the month."

I closed the fridge and faced her, giving her one last chance to ask how the game had gone. "There's plenty to eat, Susan," Mom said.

"Aren't you even going to ask how my game went?"

Mom's shoulders fell. "I'm sorry," she said. "I guess I'm distracted. I found out yesterday that I didn't get that job I interviewed for, and I think I was a touch overconfident that I would. How did it go, sweetie?"

She'd asked the question, finally, but she didn't care, not really. I knew I'd probably made her feel doubly bad, pointing out her failings as a mom right when she'd gotten news that she'd failed at something else.

A little part of me, though, was glad she hadn't gotten the job. No one had told her she had to do this. Was getting to manage a title company or whatever it was she wanted to do really so much more important than everything else going on? Than me? The thing that kept bothering me about my parents having a civil divorce was its unspoken rule that I act civilized about it, too. Whatever not-so-great changes it made to my life, I had to see the bigger picture. But standing there surrounded by the crappy food we had to buy because money was tight, I was tired of the big picture. I wanted a little picture with only me in it for a while.

"We lost. The game was shitty. I played shitty." I didn't give her a second to say anything before I added, "I love how you and dad getting divorced and you getting a real job means your stuff is always more important than mine. Maybe you should have stayed married. You have thinking of only yourselves in common."

Normally, I might have thought those words but not said them aloud. But I was frustrated and I wanted someone to know, even if Mom maybe didn't deserve it. I knew what was really upsetting me was Bobby's anger and my persistent headache and Tina's observations and knowing I'd blown my chance to feel special and talented this weekend. But I was hungry, in every way. Hungry for a dinner that required more than one utensil to eat, but also hungry for the kind of attention I didn't have to ask for, like when I was a kid and would find that the picture I'd colored and left lying around had somehow made it onto the fridge.

Mom didn't say anything, but she didn't take her eyes off me as she tugged one of the grocery bags across the counter. She lifted two cans of Cheez Balls, my favorite snack, out of the bag and slid them across the counter toward me. "You're right," she said. "I'm only thinking of myself. That's rich."

I opened my mouth to apologize, or maybe just to thank her for the Cheez Balls, or maybe not to say anything but to just cram some Cheez Balls in. I wanted to say I didn't mean it, and that I knew Mom was trying her best.

But I didn't.

"I wish your game had gone better. I wish my interview had gone better," Mom said. "But has it ever occurred to you how much I have to work my butt off to get something better to happen for myself? Meanwhile, they just start up a whole girls' team for you. I'll never know what that feels like." She took the receipt from the bag and put it on the kitchen table next to her textbooks and pens, then left the room.

I told myself that she didn't know anything about what I was doing. No one had paved the way for me. They'd said, "Go ahead down that road, but we can't help you if there's a boulder in the middle of it."

But this weekend, Bobby had gotten us a game—he'd moved the boulder—and the team and I had crapped in the middle of the road. The worst part was, I wanted the win now more than I had even during the game, and I couldn't go back.

I tore the lid from the can of Cheez Balls that Mom had bought, I knew, for me. That I hadn't said thank you for.

They didn't taste as good as usual, and I didn't enjoy a single one as I finished the can.

Twenty-One

The phone rang Sunday morning and I picked up expecting Polly, or Tonia, or maybe my grandma, who'd called last week and whose message I realized I'd forgotten to give Mom.

"Hey, champ, how'd it go? You up for a practice?" Joe's voice came over the receiver instead. And he sounded like nothing had ever happened between us. Technically, nothing had, but I'd resigned myself to not hearing from him again. I'd even told myself it was for the best, because the choice was kissing Joe and having things fizzle out when he started kissing someone else, or ceasing our soccer-lesson friendship because the kiss hadn't happened. Either path led to the same result, and the second version was a lot less messy.

Still, his question, asked with his usual eagerness, shot a happy jolt through my chest. Maybe there was a third path.

"If you're up for it," I said. Then, because thinking about it had called up the awkward feelings from back on the blanket, I added, "I'm sorry I reacted the way I did the other day. I mean, I still think it's better if we stay friends. But I could have handled it better." It had felt good apologizing to Tina, and bringing up the other night with Joe got it out of the way, so it wouldn't hang unspoken between us.

"No need to apologize. We did the right thing, by not . . . you know," Joe said. His voice was plain for once, like he'd peeled off the joking layer. "I'll pick you up in an hour?"

"Okay," I said, grateful that he wasn't making me explain, and that he had said "we."

Mom came into the kitchen as I hung up the phone. "Are you practicing today?" she asked. I couldn't read her tone, but she didn't sound too mad.

I nodded. "Yeah, I figure it can't hurt."

She didn't say anything else and went to pour some coffee into her Powell Park Title Co. mug.

"Mom," I began. She looked up. "I'm sorry. I know you and Dad are trying to be good parents, and you care about me and all that. I took out my disappointment about the game on you." Another apology. Normally, I said sorry automatically, for stuff that wasn't even my fault, like when someone bumped into me. The apologies I needed to make, like this one, didn't exit my mouth as easily. As my pile of sorries mounted, they made me think of the one Bobby deserved, and how it would be even more difficult to deliver.

She set down the cup, crossed the kitchen, and wrapped me in the hug I'd needed since yesterday. "It's all hard," Mom said. "I can't expect you to be perfect if I'm not. I'm glad you're practicing today."

"Me too," I said. It wasn't the ideal truce. It still nagged me that Mom thought the soccer team and my place on it had come too easily.

"I can't tell you what to do with your opportunities, but I worry that I haven't taught you how to make most of them." The hug melted some of the frost. After how I'd treated her, at least I'd be able to look my mom in the eye. "Just promise me you'll think about what you want?"

I wanted lots of things—another game, a win, a pair of Jordaches, a paper on *Great Expectations* to materialize, already written. In the big, life-changing sense, all I could think of really and certainly wanting was so cosmically huge: to meet Bobby on another plane of existence where we weren't student and coach.

But I knew Mom was talking about the big stuff I wanted in this dimension. And that seemed much harder to figure out.

"I will," I said. "Don't worry about me."

When Joe showed up, I didn't wait for him to honk, and I also didn't wait until we got to the field to tell him about the game. "We lost," I said, the second I plopped into the car. I sank into the comfortable contours of the Nova's passenger seat, checking Joe for signs that what had happened meant our friendship wasn't going to work, but he pulled away from the curb with his same loose grip on the steering wheel and I relaxed.

"And . . . ," Joe said, looking over. "I'm waiting for the part where you tell me how the team lost but *you* did something fucking amazing."

I cringed and picked at a hangnail. "I had a fucking amazing hangover," I said. "We kind of had a motel room party the night before."

"Really?" Joe said, glancing over at me. "What were you thinking?"

I banged my fist on my knee. "I don't know! I'm so stupid. I thought I could keep the team in check, but wave some peach schnapps in front of my face and apparently I become a dumb sheep."

Joe snickered. Which annoyed me, because it felt like he was stifling a giant laugh.

"It's not funny," I said. I twisted a thread from my sweatshirt around my finger so tight, the skin turned purple.

"Okay, we're not practicing today," Joe said. He turned his car away from the park and headed down Central.

"Where are we going?" I said. "I obviously need to practice."

He ignored me and pressed play on the 8-track. The Doobie Brothers came on.

"Can we please change it to the radio?" I said.

"Nope. You can punish yourself with the Doobie Brothers until we reach our destination."

"Fair." I looked out the window, trying to determine where we were headed.

Joe was singing along with the song. I cleared my throat and raised my eyebrows. "What? It gets in your head!" he said.

Five minutes later, he turned into the parking lot for Fun Time Central, a place in Elm Ridge with go-karts and mini golf.

It was a chilly, windy day and the arcade building was the only part of the place with signs of life. Joe and I went inside. "Wait here," he said, and he jogged off, leaving me in front of the Skee-Ball machines. I watched as a mom pushed out through the glass door of the arcade dragging two screaming children after her. She lit a cigarette and leaned against the building as the kids pelted one another with SweeTarts.

"Okay," he said, returning and holding out a handful of tokens. He pointed at the machines. "We're ready."

"Skee-Ball?" I said.

"Why not? You need a win, and everybody wins at Skee-Ball."

"Ugh, I hate it when you make sense," I said.

We skeed our balls in more or less companionable silence. Or silence against a backdrop of arcade machines chiming and kids screaming—what were they feeding these banshee children? But Joe was right. Skee-Ball wasn't my game, but every so often, my ball sprang past the lower tiers of points and made its way into the 50-point hole, giving me a little surge of pleasure.

Next to me, Joe seemed to be effortlessly hitting the 40s and 50s, but he wasn't talking himself up with the same bravado he did at our practices. I wondered if it was because of the other night, or because he was really trying to cheer me up so had tempered his bragging.

It took a while for our tokens to run out, and when they did, Joe ripped off his strip of winner tickets and handed them to me with a big grin.

"Prize time," he said. We walked to the wall of stuffed animals and case of trinkets, where a couple was engaged in some quality groping. The girl held a teddy bear. My stomach tensed, and I sidestepped a little farther away from Joe.

"See, it's called the Redemption Counter," Joe said, acting

like he didn't see the couple. He pointed at the sign above the prizes.

I asked the attendant for two packs of Fun Dip, some Blow Pops, and a chunky Tootsie Roll I'd give to Mom. I handed one of the Fun Dips to Joe. "And this was me redeeming myself?"

"You get it. You sure you don't go to Catholic school?"

We ripped open the Fun Dips and each wet the candy sticks to dip in the sour-sweet powder. We were headed to the car when Joe stopped, his dip stick thoughtfully to one side of his mouth, and said, "I think it's good you screwed up your first game. Now you know how much you want to play."

"Yeah, I just wish I had realized that before the schnapps."

"Well, in your next game, even if you totally fuck up and are a disaster on the field, it won't be because you decided to get drunk on peach schnapps. If you're going to get in trouble, put yourself on the line for something good."

I stuck out my tongue at him, because I couldn't think of anything else to say. After what Mom had said about going for what I want, I worried I'd never know what that was. I'd gone to tryouts because of Bobby, but I couldn't call that putting myself on the line, since I knew in the back of my mind that Bobby was a fantasy. And if I really wanted a win, why had I so expertly steered myself toward a loss?

We got into the car. As he started it, I realized I didn't want the day to end. Hanging out with Joe now that we knew what we were was even nicer than it had been before.

Joe stopped in front of my house and shut off the radio. "I'm helping my dad paint a house next weekend, but we'll pick up lessons soon. We can work on some footwork stuff or even face off a bit," he said.

"Sounds good," I said. It was a good plan, just what I wanted, but I still felt off.

"Don't worry, champ, you didn't blow your only chance." He glanced in my direction and gave me a small smile.

"But I'm still sorry I blew the first one," I said. I turned to get out of the car, but I felt a hand on my arm, and turned back toward him. He was leaning toward me, looking at me. An unbidden thought flew through my mind—how stunned Joe would be if I kissed him—but it was gone just as quickly.

"Stop being sorry," he said.

At school on Monday, I had more than one moment of thinking it would be better not to go to practice at all. I couldn't imagine what kind of speech Bobby would give us, and I also worried that, with the weekend to think about it, he'd decided to cut us all loose for so blatantly breaking the rules of his contract. Or just for being jerks.

When practice rolled around, Tina and I were the first two to arrive, and everyone else came soon thereafter. We all seemed a bit sheepish around each other, like we'd spent Saturday revealing our deepest secrets or grossest habits and now, in the daylight, were embarrassed to be around one another.

"It's so cold out, isn't it?" Marie broke the ice. She looked at me like I might be mad at her, because the party had been her idea.

"Yeah, I think I feel my leg hair growing," I said with a laugh, freeing her of blame. She smirked.

"My nips are going to slice through my shirt," Joanie said, looking down at her *Happy Days* T-shirt. "Poor Fonzie."

"Maybe we should warm up?" I suggested. "Till Bobby gets here?"

Tina said, "Good idea. Maybe stretches first? Since it's cold?"

"Can someone show me that calf stretch again?" Arlene asked.

We stretched and then did side runs, where you more or less galloped sideways. As we cut through the brisk air, Joanie called, "So much cold air just went up my cooch, my fallopians have icicles on them."

"I think I just queefed a snow cone," Lisa said.

We were holding our sides laughing when we finished. Bobby still hadn't shown, however. "Should we do laps?" I suggested, and everyone agreed. No one wanted to admit that he might not be coming. We were on our third trip around the park, all of us anxiously looking toward the curb where Bobby usually parked to see if he'd arrived yet, when his Datsun pulled up.

"I knew he wasn't ditching us," Dana said.

"You said 'He's ditching us' literally two minutes ago," Tina said.

Bobby got the equipment from his trunk and was trying for a stern expression as he approached us, but I noticed the slightest flicker of pleasure at seeing us taking initiative. When we'd run a few more laps, he blew his whistle for us to come in, and without bringing up Saturday at all, he got us started on passing drills.

I worried Bobby was quieter than usual, maybe regretting coming back, but once I had a ball between my feet, I felt content.

For the first time since Mom told me to think about what I wanted, I felt an inkling of what that might actually be. From now on, I would focus on soccer. No more drinking. No more parties. No more obsessing over Bobby. Soccer was enough.

When I got a chance to dribble swiftly toward the goal, I switched feet to pass the ball to Tina with my left instead of my right foot, and I executed the move better than I had in weeks of bumbling it. I was good at this.

We all were better than we'd been when we'd started the season, of course, but I knew in that moment that we were also truly *good*. If Bobby had shown up today expecting us to prove that—even sober—we weren't worth his coaching, we were defying his expectations.

When Bobby called an end to the drills and told us to get ready to scrimmage, I thought of what Joe had said, how I'd have another chance. I wanted a real game, but a scrimmage was something.

After ten minutes, no one had scored, but not for lack of trying. Arlene and I plowed into each other going for the ball, and I said, "Sorry." I couldn't break the habit of saying it when I ran into someone or when they ran into me.

"Don't be," she said. "It was a clean hit."

"I know, it's a reflex," I told her, then filched the ball and started kicking toward her goal.

"Hey!" Arlene said, but she didn't sound mad.

"Not sorry!" I called.

I wished I could hold on to the feeling when Bobby called us in from our scoreless scrimmage. But besides that brief look of approval he'd given when he saw us running at the beginning of practice, Bobby had shown no signs that he'd forgiven us.

Finally, after a pause that stretched on for a long time, he said, "That was a great practice." His smile suddenly appeared, the way a flower starts as a tight bud and blooms overnight. "You're looking like a real team."

Twenty-Two

The night of the Powell Park–Howard High football game, Marie invited us all to a party at her ex Jimmy Mortenson's house. He was a St. Mark's senior who was known around town because his family owned a car dealership. It had more prestige than Polly's family's car dealership in Elm Ridge, because it was bigger and advertised on channel 9. No one in Powell Park lived in mansions or anything, but the Mortensons' house was on a corner lot and larger than most, even Tina's. The basement had its own bathroom. (These were features deemed so impressive that I'd heard them talked about even though I'd never been there.)

A few of us had been nervous about attending another party after Wisconsin, but Marie assured us that it was only to blow off steam after we'd been working so hard. "We don't have a game tomorrow, and we won't get out of control," she promised.

I was still reluctant. I'd sworn off parties. But I was also really curious to see the inside of the house, and I had nothing else to do.

Powell Park lost the football game 47–23, or something like that. Some of the other girls went to the game, but I skipped, fearing some awkward introduction to Candace's football girl-friends. After the game, we met up at Wojo's, with a plan to walk over to the party. It was cold, but Marie had instructed us to wear skimpy clothes, so no one brought a jacket.

The walk from Wojo's was a few blocks, and as we got closer to Jimmy's house, it was clear a party was going on because the street was filled with parked cars, and groups of people kept turning into the Mortensons' front yard. The house was practically bursting at the seams, and shouting and music poured out of it; everyone knew cops never broke up this party. The Mortensons sold the force a lot of its Crown Victorias.

"Jimmy always makes the basement door the main entry. That's where the beer will be," Marie said. "Going through the front door is for people who don't know any better." She led us up a side path to the backyard, where a set of concrete stairs led to a door at the house's lowest level.

"How very mole people of him," Dawn said, as we waited on the steps with the other apparently in-the-know partygoers. Ahead of us in line, a group of guys wearing St. Rita's jackets checked us out.

"Stare much?" Arlene taunted them, but she looked pleased.

When the crush of people finally squeezed through, it was our turn. As we walked inside, a stocky redheaded guy in a St. Mark's jacket rammed into me with his shoulder. I opened my mouth to apologize, but then I clamped it shut. "You could say I'm sorry," I said to him instead.

"I could, but I won't," he shot back, guffawing with his friends. His face was next to mine as he spat a loogie on the sidewalk beyond me.

"Fuck that guy," Dawn said.

"I would definitely rather not," I said. "And would recommend others avoid it, too."

Jimmy was visible at the middle of the floor, holding court with a crew of girls around him. When Marie walked in, he seemed to forget the other girls as he winked at her.

"Do you still like him?" Arlene said to Marie.

"No, but I like to make him think I do," Marie said plainly. "Let's get a beer."

We made our way to the keg, weaving around people I didn't know who must have been from Howard High. Marie stopped to say hi to Lynn, who was curled in the lap of Len Tenley, consoling him by planting little kisses on his nose while she ran a hand through his blond curls. He must have been taking the loss hard. Marie had every guy's eyes on her as she bent down to whisper something to Lynn. Apparently, their friendship was in a better spot than mine and Candace's, who I was nervous to see tonight.

"Can you believe she's the same girl who I've heard growling at me when she steals the ball?" Dana said.

"Actually, yeah," I said. I'd already thought about how we each hid ferocity under aspects of our so-called girliness, whether it was overt sexiness like Marie or quiet reticence like Franchesa. "I mean, you suck up to Assistant Principal Lawler like you're Strawberry Shortcake or something, and I still have a bruise on my rib from your elbow."

As Marie passed out red cups, I glanced across the room, my eyes landing on Joe, talking to yet another new girl. I squinted at him. He hadn't said anything about going to this party. Not that he had to tell me everything he was doing—it's not like I'd mentioned the party to him—but I wasn't expecting to see him.

That's when he spotted me and grinned, and my stomach lifted. What was going on with me?

"Hooligans," Joe said in our direction as he pulled his cigarette from his mouth and stubbed it out in a nearby ashtray.

I flipped him off. Tina jabbed my shoulder with her red fingernail. "Oh, your soccer teacher boyfriend is here?"

I shook my head. "He's not my boyfriend," I said. "He's with another girl."

"That's why he's looking at you like he won a new car," Tina said.

"I doubt it," I said, and hid the smile that brought to my face. "He's waiting for us to say hi."

Our cups filled, I led Tina over. "Hey," I said. "Are we the hooligans?"

"I haven't met your friend, but you definitely fit the bill," Joe said. We held eye contact in the crowded room; my heart thudded and my mouth tingled as Joe looked at my lips a split second too long. At least I thought he did. What Tina had said had clearly infected my mind.

The girl next to him coughed lightly and he held out his hand, as if presenting her. "Oh, this is Jeannette."

"This is Tina," I told him.

He extended a hand to her. "You're one of Susan's best friends," he said matter-of-factly.

Tina offered him a big smile. "Yeah, except when she's learning extra-secret soccer skills. She shared some moves, though, so I guess I owe you a thank-you."

"Well, you're welcome," Joe said, smirking at me.

Jeannette wore a letterman's jacket from St. Ann's. "Do you play a sport?" I asked her.

She nodded and said, "Swimming, basketball, and softball. I think we might be getting soccer next year, and then I'll quit swimming. I prefer to be on land."

Joe laughed, like the remark was funnier than it was. Jeannette playing sports, and so many, made me size her up more carefully. She wasn't as pretty as Joe's first babe, or Lizzy—she looked more like a slightly taller version of me—but she struck me as more attractive than either of them because of the glint in her eye.

"Maybe we'll play you next year," I said.

Joe had turned to talk to a guy in the corner. Tina asked Jeannette, "How do you know Joe?"

Jeannette grinned. "I don't. I saw his band play in my cousin's garage, and when I saw him at this party, I had to talk to him."

Tina shot a look at me. I knew what she was thinking: Jeannette had set her sights on Joe in a big way, and she was cute. But what was I supposed to do about it? The girl knew what she wanted, and Joe and I were just friends.

"Joe's been helping me with soccer," I said, sounding more territorial than I planned to. Jeannette was about to say something when Joe cut in.

"I taught her everything I know." He pointed the edge of his cup at me and Tina. "Any news on more games?"

"No." I sighed.

Joe opened his mouth to speak, but then something over my shoulder caught his eye. I turned, and saw that the redheaded guy who'd knocked into me had just come back inside. Felt letters on the back of his jacket spelled "SOCCER."

"Fucking Ken," he said. "I knew I shouldn't have come to this party."

"*That's* Ken?" I'd been expecting someone taller, with an Olympian build.

"Who's Ken?" Tina asked us both.

"My nemesis," Joe said. His eyes were like knives. "Don't let him catch wind that you play soccer. He's exactly the kind of asshole who'd give you hell for it." He turned to Jeannette. "You wanna get some fresh air for a minute?"

Jeanette beamed like she was getting a trophy in one of the three sports she played, and his smile ticked up at the side. No wonder he consistently found new girls to hang around. Or no wonder new girls found him. I had to admit, his lips were pretty sexy, or maybe it was the readiness of his smile that did it. No doubt he was going to engage in some habitual making out with Jeannette. I had to remind myself that I'd been the one who hadn't wanted to kiss him. Still didn't.

Tina spun toward me once Joe and Jeanette were out of earshot. "So, you jealous of three-sport Jeanette?"

"No. Yes. I don't know. He's all wrong for me."

"You don't know that."

"We should probably see what everyone is doing," I said, not wanting to get into this. Tina's question and the basement's heat pressed in on me.

"Well, I see exactly what *you're* doing," Tina said as we dodged a burly Howard player with a beer in each hand. "You can't avoid this whole Joe topic forever. The guy clearly likes you."

"Yes, that's exactly why he's probably feeling up Jeannette right now," I said. "Just forget it."

Tina and I took the stairs up to the Mortensons' living room. The walls were overwhelmed with photos of the family, with shots of Jimmy and his sister lining the stairs that led to the top floor. People were smoking and talking in the kitchen, and I wrinkled my nose when I saw Dan O'Keefe with Keith Barnes and Paul Mahoney. And ugh, George. He had his hand on Candace's waist. A few girls I took to be the other football girlfriends were gathered with them all around a pretzel bowl, laughing. Candace had changed her hair. She now had bangs and had attempted to style them so they drew back from her face, but a few small hanks had fallen from the sideswept portion.

"Candace looks like she's having fun," Tina said.

"Yeah, maybe after a while you become immune to the garbage breath," I said.

"Let's go say hi." Tina took my arm and steered me through the party toward the counter.

Candace's face was flushed from whatever she was drinking, and it seemed to take her a second after seeing us to register who we were.

"Hey, Candace," Tina said.

"Hey! What are you guys doing here?" she said. "I thought you had practice!"

"At nine p.m.?" I said. "Marie brought us. She used to date Jimmy."

"I'm glad you're here," Candace said. "I never get to see you anymore."

Whose fault is that? I thought.

"You changed your hair," Tina said. "It's cute."

"Yeah, I got it like Cheryl Ladd's in *Charlie's Angels*." She pushed the wayward hairs back. "She's George's favorite."

"*You're* my favorite." He turned toward us. "Hey, Susan, Tina!"

"How's it going, George?" Tina said. I crinkled my nose. We didn't have to be nice to George. His breath was better, I noticed, but he was the same.

"We lost, but, you know, it happens. Hey, how'd your game end up going?"

Tina gave him a greatly abridged version—no mention of the party or the hangovers. As they talked, George's hand trailed down to Candace's hip, and she tucked her head near his shoulder. She whispered something to him, then detached and stepped closer to me.

"Can you believe we're finally at the Powell Park–Howard party?" she whispered excitedly. Last year, Tina and I had slept over at Candace's after the football game, contemplating crashing the party even though no one had told us about it.

"Yeah, it's cool," I said. I drank down the last of my beer and took a bottle of Miller High Life from a six-pack on the counter. I'd said I wouldn't drink much, but I needed something in my hands. Candace followed me over to the fridge, where I pulled down a Wisconsin Dells magnet with a bottle opener attached. I pried the cap from my beer and took a sip. As I swallowed it, I realized I was tipsy. I decided I'd just carry the beer until I could go home. "So, how do you console George after the team loses? Just a hand job, or do you go all the way?"

Candace's face crumpled from its bright expression, and I thought she might cry. "It's not like that, Susan," she said. "We haven't gone that far yet. Don't you think I'd tell you?"

"You didn't tell me about him in the first place. And he's giving you hickeys and letting you wear his jacket; even a weirdo like George probably knows some moves to get in a girl's pants."

Candace pushed her wayward bangs out of her eyes with a huff. "I don't know why you're being so rude, but if and when it's time for George to get in my pants, it will be my decision."

"It was a joke," I said.

Candace shook her head. "No, it wasn't. Grow up, Susan." She retreated back toward the group, leaving me standing there like a jerk.

I sulked off and sat at the top of the stairs to the second floor, a few steps above a guy who was sleeping on the staircase. I'd been there awhile when I felt a toe at my back. I craned my neck to see Marie and Lynn, arms linked and makeup fresh. "You're not wasted, Susan, are you?"

"No, just taking a break," I said.

"Come with us," Marie said. She pointed to the sleeping guy, who'd sprawled closer to my feet. "Before he's napping on your lap and you can't escape."

I stood up and smiled weakly at Marie. Lynn Bandis reached out and fixed my hair before waggling her fingers at Marie and returning to Len's lap. At the bottom of the staircase, I looked out at the living room, my eyes landing on Joe and Jeannette. His arm was tight around her waist and their bodies were pressed together as they kissed like two people trying to see how long they could go without oxygen. Maybe she could hold her breath extra long from all that swimming. He'd be on to the next girl before she came up for air, I thought, with a cruel satisfaction I wasn't proud of.

I wondered if he'd asked "May I?" before they'd started.

Marie came up behind me and followed my gaze toward Joe. "Don't stare," she said. I hadn't known I was staring.

Then she pointed toward the middle of the room, where the furniture had been pushed aside for the party. Tina, Dana, Dawn, and Wendy formed a line facing Ken, the St. Mark's goalie, and several of his teammates, clearly in some kind of confrontation.

"What the fuck?" I said, and we took a few steps closer.

"You chicks just want attention," one of Ken's teammates was saying. "And since none of you is cute enough to be a cheerleader, you had to go with soccer."

"Why does it bother you so much that we play?" Dawn said.

"Yeah, you worried we're going to win more games than you?" Tina added.

"Pff, there's a better chance I'd take one of you dogs to prom," Ken said. He laughed, and so did his teammates. The laughter was worse than the things they were saying. I could see my teammates waver. My heart ratcheted up, like someone was kicking a ball against the inside of my chest.

"We don't care what you think of us," Wendy said. "We can do whatever you can do."

Ken shook his head. "There's no fucking way."

I hated Ken, standing there all proud in his stupid jacket, like he'd appointed himself the President of Soccer, deciding who played and who didn't.

"Hey, Ken," I yelled across the party, the ball in my chest thudding harder and faster so all I could hear was my own blood. Joe, who'd pulled away from Jeannette to watch the feud, turned his head toward me.

"You talking to me?" Ken jutted out his chin. His buddies chuckled.

"Yeah, I am." I grabbed Marie's wrist and pulled her into the crowd. We needed to take up as much room as we could to make what I was about to say work.

I put my hands on my hips and stood with my legs apart, like Bobby's coach pose when he wanted us to listen. I threw my shoulders back and got as close to Ken as I could without touching him. Even though my veins felt like they were overboiled spaghetti and my legs were unsteady, I must have looked like I knew what I was doing, because he backed up the slightest bit.

I glanced toward the corner and caught Joe's eye. His hands were still at Jeannette's waist but his mouth was open in shock, like I was the shark in *Jaws*.

"So what's your point?" Ken asked.

"If you've got a problem with us, why don't we settle it on the field?" I felt fierce, saying it. Maybe girls would never feel comfortable designating a bathroom stall as unofficially conducive to masturbating, and maybe we'd never brazenly spit on the ground or grab our crotches, but it was thrilling to assert ourselves, to say loud and clear that we were competitors. It was a relief to suspend the parts of us that wanted to be liked for a while and the parts of us that apologized when we worried we wouldn't be.

"Susan," Tina hissed.

"No," Wendy grumbled.

I cocked my head back at them and, sticking out my chin, said, "What? We can play."

"She's right," Dawn said.

Marie took a step forward so she was lined up with me. "Yeah, let's play." The whole team gathered next to and behind me, all of us staring down Ken. Mousy Franchesa, uptight Dana, surly Dawn, sexpot Marie, ambitious Tina, flaky Arlene, bitchy Wendy . . . everyone, all standing with me . . . average me. We were different from each other, even in ways that might clash, but maybe that's what made us a team.

That, and the agreement that right now, we were united in one mission against this redheaded asshole, and we weren't going to be intimidated.

The boys behind Ken murmured in disbelief, a chorus of "What the fuck?" and "She's crazy."

"I'm not crazy," I said, trying to look like maybe I was. I *felt* crazy. I was barreling over some unspoken rule of how I was supposed to act and how angry I could get. Flipping Ken off was one thing, but challenging him to a game without fear or apology was another. "What do you say, fuckwads?"

Ken laughed again, but it sounded a little forced this time. "Fine," he said. "We'll play you. I just hope you can handle it. I think our balls are bigger than you're used to."

"When?" I said, ignoring his comment.

"A week from tomorrow. Our field. Nine a.m."

It was the day of the wedding, but the game would be done in time. And asking to reschedule might make him think I was afraid. "You're on," I said.

"You'll be sorry," Ken said.

"No, we won't be," I said.

None of us moved until the boys dispersed. I put my arms down so the rest of the party wouldn't see that I'd sweat through my shirt, then turned around and said, "Let's get out of here."

No one protested, and we made our way toward the door like we'd stolen something. A few girls we didn't know spoke to us as we passed.

"Good for you!"

"He's such a dick."

"I hope you kick their asses."

When we finally emerged onto the front steps, surrounded now by smokers and drunk people oblivious to what had just happened, my teammates huddled around me.

"Holy shit," Wendy said. "You're out of your mind."

"It'll be fine," I said, not feeling fine at all. "We'll make a plan."

"A plan that will get us ready to play those meatheads next week?" Joanie said.

"All we have to do is show them we're not scared," Tina said.

We were halfway down the front path when Joe burst out the front door. "Susan," he called.

I spun around and took the few steps to meet him on the walk. In a hushed tone, so my teammates couldn't hear, he said, "What are you, crazy? Challenging those guys to a game?"

I glared at him. "What, you think we can't play them?"

He put his hands up. "Hold on, Pelé, I never said that."

"Okay then," I said. "But honestly . . . yeah, I think I might be crazy."

Joe threw his head back and laughed appreciatively, loud enough for my teammates to hear. They were 100 percent all watching us but pretending not to. When he met my eyes again, he said, "Mostly, I think I'm bummed because I have to go to Rachel's dance recital that day. I'll miss the game. But what are you doing tomorrow?"

"Do you want to practice?"

"I can't—I'm helping my dad in the morning and then I've got band practice," he said. "But are you busy at night? There's an all-ages Tutu and the Pirates show at O'Banion's. In the city. Do you want to go?"

He was being so typically Joe that I had no way of knowing if he was asking me for a date or this was just hanging out.

"What about whatsherface? Jeannette?" I asked, raising an eyebrow at him. "Don't you owe her a date? At least to give her back her tonsils?"

He flipped me off. "The bassist has a guitar made of a toilet seat. It seemed more your style of outing."

Now I flipped him off.

"It's not a big deal, but if you want to go . . ." He held my gaze, waiting for an answer.

"Sure. As friends, right?" I said, casting a look at Tina.

"Yeah, of course. I'll pick you up at five."

Twenty-Three

I dreamed weird dreams. Me and Candace as little kids skipping onto a soccer field with our dolls, then Candace disappearing to be replaced by Bobby, all alone. Bobby asking me to kick him a ball that materialized in front of my feet, me kicking it as Bobby became Ken, asking, "Who the fuck do you think you are?" Ken, turning into my mom, saying, "And what do you want, anyway?" Me, surrounded by more soccer balls than I can kick, and my soccer clothes turning into a dusty peach dress. Joe, putting a hand on my shoulder and saying, "Just like that, champ, but different."

Then I woke up and lay in my bed, too tired to haul myself out and too anxious to stare at the ceiling.

Had I really told St. Mark's boys' soccer team we wanted to play them?

I shoved the covers off and got up. I was in the kitchen pouring a bowl of cereal when Mom came in, with her hair curled and a new blouse tucked into her jeans. "You look nice," I said.

"I promised the School for Starting Over group at the college I'd help run its bake sale," Mom said.

"That sounds like a waste of good hair," I said, catching myself. I was trying to tread lightly on Mom's interests. "Sorry. I really meant to say, can you bring me a cupcake?"

Mom waved me off. "No, you're right, it's going to be awful. But I'm networking. The head of the group has a contact at a different title company and might help pass on my résumé."

After our argument the previous week, things had gone back to normal, more or less, and on Sunday night we'd ordered a pizza and watched TV together. But I still felt like Mom and I were trying to be more careful around one another, and any time soccer or her job came up in conversation, it put a wave of tension in the air.

"Are you all set with your dress for the wedding?" Mom asked, changing the subject.

"As set as I'll ever be to willingly dress like produce that's been left in an attic."

"Susan, it's one day," Mom chided.

"I know, I know. I have one more fitting Monday night, and Polly will pick up the dress Wednesday. I think we have a game the morning of, but it should be fine."

Mom's eyebrows went up over the top of her coffee mug. "That's not too many things for one day, is it?"

"It'll be fine," I said, hoping I was right. It was too many things for a *year*, the more I thought about it. Not to mention, we had to prepare for the game.

Creeping in on my thoughts about Mom, the game, and the wedding was the argument with Candace. I was bothered by how I'd left things with her the night before. But as I tried to think of what I could say to her, an antsy sensation came over me and I couldn't focus. First thing was first: I had the show with Joe that night. Tutu and the Whatevers. The toilet guitar. The city, which would be exciting. Besides a school trip to the Field Museum, I hadn't been downtown in over a year, not since Candace had heard about a store on State Street that sold discount Jordache jeans. Mom had volunteered to take me, Candace, and Tina. We wandered awhile and never found the store, so Mom had taken us to the movies. We'd seen *Saturday Night Fever*, and all of us— including my mom—had fallen in love with John Travolta in it.

I pulled out clothes to see what would be good for a punk show, but nothing looked right. Even if it wasn't a date, I still wanted to look as with it as the other girls who went to the kinds of shows Joe went to. Around two, after pulling apart my dresser and trying and failing to make any progress on my *Great Expectations* paper for Ms. Lopez, I got the idea to make a shirt like the ones Joe had said he was making for his band. I set out for Sportmart.

I was headed inside the store when I saw a familiar butt. Bobby's. He was hanging one of his Personal Best flyers on a bulletin board next to the pay phones.

"Hi, Coach," I croaked out.

He turned around and, seeing me there, offered up a big smile. "Hi, Susan," he said. "What are you doing here?"

I wanted to impress him, so saying I was here to get a shirt to wreck for a punk show wasn't the right answer.

"I . . . I'm looking for gear to get better at soccer," I said, but hearing how dumb my words sounded, I added, "Last night, I sort of challenged the St. Mark's team to a game. We play a week from today."

"Wait, what?" Bobby set the stapler he was holding on top of the pay phone and let out a breath. "St. Mark's? You mean the private school?"

I nodded.

He squinted. "Are you sure the team is ready for that? They're really good."

He didn't say, "They're boys." Joe hadn't, either.

"I think we're good, too," I said. I waited for some kind of game-show buzzer to sound, signaling, "You're wrong, dumbass!" But my statement floated to Bobby, uninterrupted.

"You're right," he said. "But gear isn't what will make the difference. Training is." He used his thumb to point backward at the sign he'd just hung.

"Maybe, since I'm not going to end up buying gear, you could show me how that works?"

"I don't have a client right now," he said. "Maybe I can show you my setup and we can figure out how we're going to prepare for this game."

"That would be great," I said.

"Okay, let's go," he said. We headed out to the parking lot, and between his shorts and my track pants, people probably thought we were a couple with a devotion to physical fitness.

We got into his car, and as he started it, he turned to me and said, "You just need to promise me one thing."

Anything, I wanted to say in response to his dark, hopeful eyes. "Sure," I said instead.

"If you think the workout is helpful, tell me, because I'll fight to get the team some time in the school weight room."

"Okay," I said, flattered that he thought my input was valuable. "That's it?"

He let out a long breath. "Maybe one other thing. . . . Please keep this game quiet. It's not that I don't think you should play, but I'm a little worried that if the school gets wind of it, the administration might intervene, or it could threaten the team."

I hadn't thought of that when I'd thrown the gauntlet down with Ken.

We drove to his duplex, which was on Mansfield, as Dana Miller had told us. He hopped out of the car and opened the side door to an attached garage. As I followed him up the driveway, I tried to peer into the residence part of the duplex. Seeing Bobby's things would give me insight. Maybe there were markers that would clue me in to what kind of man Bobby was when he wasn't coaching. Or at least clues to how much sex he had. His curtains were closed, though.

The inside of the garage was brightly lit, with no dead leaves or dust or junk littered in the corners like every other garage I'd ever been in. Instead of concrete, the floor was covered in carpet remnants that were mismatched but obviously vacuumed regularly. On a shelf was a stereo and next to it a calendar with names and appointment times filled in on a few dates.

Bobby gestured grandly at the neat, piecemeal gym. "This is it. Personal Best Training," he said. "For now."

"It's nice," I said.

On the wall behind us were posters of the human body stripped of skin to show all the muscles. Bobby started to explain each muscle group, how they functioned separately and as a system, how strengthening them in a focused and safe way would enhance my game, and my whole life. I was trying to take it all in, but it was difficult to pay attention. I felt just like I had that night at the motel. It was hard not to admire Bobby even more when he talked about what he loved. He almost glowed as he told me about clients who'd never imagined the potential their bodies had. Normally, him saying something like that would make me instantly think of the potential our bodies could have together, but in his space, as he shared his excitement, I was just happy for him and wanted his business to succeed.

He clapped his hands together, knocking me out of my thoughts. "Okay, if you were a client, I'd put you on a legs program and an upper body program on alternating days, but we're going to try a few sets on a few different muscle groups," he said. "If this game is next week, I have to say, I don't think there's much we can do. It's not good to lift too frequently right before a big competition. But it'll probably give you a nice confidence boost, which never hurts."

He turned on the radio and "Hotel California" came over the speakers.

"Oh no," I said, laughing to myself.

"What's that?" Bobby asked.

"This song," I said. "It's funny that it's kind of pointing out how messed up the music industry is but it comes on the radio all the time." I was echoing Joe's diatribe, and felt shitty for stealing his thought to share with Bobby.

Bobby looked impressed at my observation, which wasn't really mine. "The boys in your class must be terrified of you," he said, and that pleased me. "Come on."

He led me to a big machine with a low chair that tilted back and faced two metal plates for your feet. A bar extended from either side. Bobby easily hefted a round fifty-pound weight and slid it onto one bar, then did the same on the other side. He sat down on the inclined chair and pushed against the metal plates with his feet, every leg muscle flexing. "This'll build your quads, a very important soccer muscle." He sat me down and used the side of his palm to gesture up and down my thigh, not touching it but so close to touching it that I clenched up, as though he could see how horny he was making me. "You want to always push from here. Not your back."

"This is a hundred pounds," I said.

"Yep, and the way you run, I'd bet you could do more, but this is a good place to start. Try it." I pushed like he showed me, and watched the weights rise up as the chair slid away from them. It wasn't as hard as I thought it'd be. Bobby still hovered right above me, staring right into my eyes. "You've got it—let's do ten more."

I got a little woozy from the intense way he was looking at me. I knew he wouldn't make a move on me or anything, but the look helped me imagine he wanted to.

I would be carried away if I kept going down this road. I asked him, "Why do you want to have a gym?"

He stepped back to look around the space. "I told you about my brothers, right? Well, that followed me to high school, and I was a second-string guy on the football team. I almost quit, I was so angry. It wasn't very attractive. I didn't quit, but I decided to learn soccer in college, to escape the whole football thing. And once I found my game, I realized it didn't matter how good or bad I was, as long as I was growing. It was about finding my personal best. I think everyone deserves that."

"So you want to inspire people?"

"That's stupid, isn't it." He looked so vulnerable, like he was sure I'd agree. But I shook my head and said, "Not at all." I wanted to hug him.

He extended a hand to help me up from the weight bench. "Thanks for that," he said. He guided me to a mat on the floor and said, "Have you ever heard of crunches?" He showed me how to lie down on the mat with my knees bent. "You lift from your shoulders up. You want to feel it here." He gestured to his abdomen.

"So you really don't think it's too crazy I challenged those guys to a game?" I asked as I tried to gracefully heave myself up from the floor. "They were making me so mad, acting like we shouldn't be playing."

"And maybe you wanted another game to make up for what happened in Wisconsin?" He didn't sound mad, more curious. Still, I blushed.

"I'm sorry for what we did," I said. "We didn't mean to get carried away."

"We won't dwell on it. But as for playing, if you shouldn't play, then no one should. We can write sports off as silly, but they're not. They enrich us on so many levels. But they should enrich all of us. Women, too," he said. "As women, it seems like you get told you should do things for other people, not for your-selves. But screw what's expected of you. Or not expected of you."

"I never thought of it that way," I said. "But I think I do now." Up until Bobby and soccer, I'd only let myself want impossible things within the confines of my own head, maybe because I assumed what was possible in reality would only disappoint me.

I must have been silent for a while, because Bobby said, "I hope that doesn't sound like I'm coaching to give you permission to play soccer. The truth is—and this is corny—that it's more like I get to be witness to you all giving yourselves permission."

"Are you a feminist?" I blurted out. Who asked a guy that? And did I even know what a feminist was? I still hadn't read more than the dirty parts of *Fear of Flying*.

"I don't know. It hardly seems like my place to decide that," he said. "I want to be a good coach and the rest is the rest."

I'd managed to control the physical response I had to Bobby, but this was new, and almost worse. I felt protective of what he had revealed, and the precious insights were more intimate than if he'd undressed for me. I wanted him to feel appreciated. "You're a great coach," I said.

He seemed caught off guard. "Thank you," he said. "I hope you feel like you can talk to me about anything."

Someone knocked twice and the door swung open. I lifted my head from the floor to see my mom's friend Jacqueline standing there, outfitted in royal blue tights and a leotard that matched her eye shadow.

"Jacqueline, hi," Bobby said. "We were just wrapping up."

Jacqueline pointed with the inside of her hand up, causing

her many bracelets to jangle. Why would someone wear jangling bracelets to work out? "This is my friend's daughter," she said, raising an eyebrow. "She's a client?"

Bobby wiped down the weight bench and looked at me. I tried to get to my feet as gracefully as possible. "Susan is on my soccer team. She's a star. We bumped into each other and we're trying to find the best way to train for a big game."

"Well, your real customer has arrived," Jacqueline said, extending an envelope that must have been filled with cash. "So we can get started." There was something in her tone and the look she gave me that made it clear I should go.

Bobby scratched the back of his neck. "For sure," he said. He looked at me. "Can you get home okay?"

"I can walk," I said.

Or run, I thought. I had to get ready for the concert.

Twenty-Four

"So here's the thing," Joe said as we took the ramp from Cicero to the Stevenson. "O'Banion's is a complete shithole."

Tina had called me just before Joe picked me up, asking if I was ready for my date, so I had to remind her I was not going on a date, even as I started to worry it was one.

Now, though, I was sure: the guy telling you that you were being taken to a shithole was proof you were *not* on a date.

"That's great—how did you know I love shitholes?"

Joe laughed. "Well, it's a great shithole and it's a lot of fun. But it's not our first stop. I figure we're going to the city, and we both more or less look presentable, so maybe we should go get food someplace decent first?"

"Sounds good," I said. "You do look presentable. Nice, even." He was wearing a Sex Pistols T-shirt and jeans with Converse high-tops, and his hair was extra spiky. He smelled like paint and soap.

"I enjoy showers too much to be a total dirtbag," he said, merging into the left lane. "You like pizza, right? Even if it's not just to hold in your lap?"

"Every year on my birthday, I ask for a pizza that's just for me instead of a cake," I told him.

"So that's a yes."

We wound up at Gino's East on Superior. I'd never been before, but you could write on the walls, which were covered in previous diners' graffiti. Joe scribbled "The Watergate Tapes" on a beam next to our table and then handed me the marker.

"I don't know what to write," I said.

"Do you think all these couples are still together?" Joe was reading our table, which had pairs like "Danny + Debbie," "Robert and Lisa Forever," and "Maxwell and Ruby" scrawled on it.

"Probably not," I said. "Actually, you gave me an idea." I added question marks next to every set of couples' names.

"Cynic," Joe said with a grin. "You probably cursed them all."

The waiter's entire presence suggested he was massively bored and thought he was too cool to be serving us. His flat tone only lifted to ask in a singsong way, "What will you two be having?" like we were a couple. I leaned away from Joe.

"I love coming to the city," Joe said as we waited for our food. "It sounds dorky, but I always feel like it kind of wakes me up that there's more to life than Powell Park."

"God, I hope there is," I said. It was a new hope, though. I'd never necessarily loved Powell Park, but I'd never felt like it was small, either, and lately, maybe since soccer, or the game in Wisconsin, I'd been thinking about traveling, and even contemplating a visit to Tonia in L.A., once I decided to forgive her. I didn't bring her up, though, not wanting to wow Joe with tales of my wild older sister that would make me seem boring by comparison.

Instead, I told Joe about the trip to the city with Mom and Tina and Candace.

"Your mom sounds cool," he said. "What's your dad like?"

"Dad-like," I said. He smiled but didn't say anything. "He's okay." I went on to talk about Mom's self-improvement and how my dad didn't seem any different, except for the new wife thing.

"I never met anyone whose parents had a peaceful divorce, though," Joe said. "So maybe he's cooler than you're giving him credit for."

"Maybe," I said, wondering if I should tell him that my dad's most prized collection was a folder of small appliance warranties. "What are your parents like?"

"Normal, nice, sometimes trying too hard to understand my music," Joe said. "They're meeting us at the show."

"Really?" I asked. I tried not to look too floored by this, but why would his parents come?

He shook his head and his smile showed all of his perfect teeth. "The expression on your face was *terrified*," he said. "Nah. They're supportive of the punk thing as long as I'm only a Powell Park punk. I think O'Banion's would worry them. Which is half the point."

Our food came and we dove in. When there was one slice left, Joe urged me to take it. I was full but it was so delicious that I did.

We took the L from the restaurant to a few blocks from O'Banion's. "So how'd you hear about the show tonight?" I asked. I never had any idea what was going on in the city.

"My cousin Artie took me here last summer," he said. "And

this is embarrassing, but honestly, I heard about the show because I keep calling the place to try to get them to give us a gig."

"I should have worn a Watergate Tapes shirt and told them you're my favorite band."

"You haven't heard us play," he said, but he smiled like he liked the idea.

O'Banion's *was* a shithole. On the outside, it was a scary shithole that looked distinctly unloved. On the inside, though, it was more of a friendly shithole. As Joe led me in, a tall black woman in green sequins and a yellow-blond wig stopped us. "Joey," she said in a deep voice. "You here for Tutu?"

"Hey, Twinkle, yeah, definitely here for Tutu," Joe said. "This is my friend Susan."

"Susan," Twinkle said, extending her hand. "You've got a cute little figure, don't you?"

". . . I don't know," I said, looking down at my T-shirt and jeans. I'd abandoned the Sportmart plan after running into Bobby. "I guess."

"You do, sweetie," she said. "Joe, be good to this one."

Being called "this one" bothered me, but Joe actually blushed as Twinkle sashayed away. "Is Twinkle a drag queen?" I asked him.

"Yeah, O'Banion's is a gay and drag bar during the day, and then it crosses over to punk at night, but some of the drag queens like punk. Twinkle is a great crowd surfer."

O'Banion's was noisy and packed and there was no stage. People just gathered on the floor in front of the band. As we walked deeper into the space, I couldn't hear Joe as well over the music, but we got closer to the band by Joe expertly weaving through the jumping crowd.

"Is that Tutu and the . . . ," I yelled over the noise, realizing I'd forgotten the band's whole name.

"The Pirates?" Joe shook his head. "No, that's a warm-up act. They're okay. From Elgin. I guess they're better than the Watergate Tapes."

Joe pursed his lips and watched the band play. He looked like he wanted to crack the code of why that band—who looked like they were in high school, too—was onstage and he wasn't. I put a hand on his shoulder. "I'm sure you'll get a show here someday."

He beamed. "I hope you're right," he said. The group finished with a clatter of instruments and noise and whoops from the crowd. "I mean, the standards are low. Plus, Ben got dumped so we have a drummer again."

Then five new guys came out, and the guy at the mic threw a roll of toilet paper at the drummer. "That's Tutu and we're the PIRATES! Let's go, Tutu!"

The band launched into a song that seemed to be called "Debbie Debbie Debbie and her Prison Baby" and was relentlessly upbeat. Joe started pogoing off the balls of his feet with the rest of the audience, and I followed his lead. Everyone more or less danced the same, and it didn't seem to matter if you knew what you were doing or not.

"Are you having fun?" Joe hollered a few songs later.

"Yeah," I shouted, and it was true. I tried to remember the last time I'd had fun like this. Maybe when Joe had taken me to Skee-Ball.

The band paused for a second and the bassist switched guitars. "That's the toilet seat bass I told you about," Joe said. "They're gonna play 'I Wanna Be a Janitor.'"

The singer grabbed a plunger that he waved around as he sang, and the crowd went even wilder. Near me, a girl stepped into a guy's cupped hands and hurled herself onto the outstretched hands of a dozen or so other audience members, who passed her along to a second group of people, who passed her on to another, until she dismounted right near the stage. I saw Twinkle go up next and make it even farther, landing right next to the singer and yelling the lyrics into the microphone.

As the crowd's frenzy grew, Joe and I were pressed tighter together. When the band launched into a song with a tempo so fast I couldn't understand a word the singer said, a tattooed man next to me jumped in the air and the contents of his beer cup went up like they'd been spouted out by a spitting cherub in a fountain. Joe grabbed my hand and pulled me out of the way before the beer could land on me. "That was close," he said.

"Thanks for saving me," I said. His fingers were wrapped around my hand and we both looked nervously at our clasped palms before he let go.

The show wrapped as abruptly as it had started—a punk thing, Joe told me—and we spilled out of the club with everyone else.

As we made our way back to the L, Joe told me that Tutu had once opened for the Ramones. "I've wanted to see them since then," he said. "So thanks for coming."

"Well . . . if we're doing each other favors," I began, grinning so Joe wouldn't think my question was too big a deal, or feel like he had to say yes, "I need a date for my dad's wedding, and I was thinking, you want to go with me?"

"Really?" Joe said.

I smiled and nodded.

"Sure," he said. "I'll even change my T-shirt."

Twenty-Five

On Sunday, while I tried to write my report on *Great Expectations* (titled "Great Disappointments"), I kept drifting into thoughts of the night in the city with Joe. It was new territory for me to have daydreams about something that had actually happened and I hadn't made up.

It wasn't one of my fantasies or anything like that. I thought about how Joe had said he was going to apply to colleges. That would probably mean no more Saturday practices or concerts if he went far away. It was another entry on the list of reasons not to let things change between us. In movies, there was always some woman waiting for a guy to come back to her, like needing a guy was the basis for her entire character. I never wanted to be that woman.

Knowing that I didn't like the idea of being left behind— by anyone—going away to college sounded more attractive. On Monday I went to see my guidance counselor, excited to hear what she'd say. My reservations about college, I realized, were partly due to my belief that it required some kind of specialness.

Specialness that I didn't have, that Powell Park didn't have. Average people belonged in average places.

But if what Bobby said was true, and colleges were seeking out girls who played soccer, then maybe that was my specialness.

Ms. Hong had just taken a sip of coffee when I dropped in on her. When she saw me, she gulped it down and put her mug on the desk abruptly. "Susan?" she said, like she thought I'd walked into the wrong office. "I'm sorry, what can I help you with?"

I'd last seen Ms. Hong during the mandatory guidance sessions we'd had freshman year, and at the time I had made every effort to say as little as possible to her. I'm sure it was clear that I wasn't thinking about my future. Or not any version of a future you could bring up with school staff.

"I was wondering if you knew anything about . . . soccer scholarships," I said. "To college. I'm on the team here."

Ms. Hong cleared her throat and I could tell she was trying not to smile. She opened her file drawer and pulled out a folder with my name on the tab. "I know you're on the team. I have to admit, I was surprised to hear it. When we talked about extracurriculars a couple years ago, you made it pretty clear that you had no interest in joining any clubs or activities. I suppose Coach McMann made the team sound . . . alluring?"

I caught her meaning easily—she was about as subtle as a chain saw. But I decided to ignore it. "At first, I thought it just seemed like something fun to do. But I've gotten pretty good. And I know that it's still a newish sport here in the States, so there might be opportunities to play at the next level."

I'd practiced that part before I came in, and Ms. Hong stared at me like I'd started performing a singing telegram.

"Well, yes, there are scholarships, and I'll happily help you," she said. "A few smaller schools would probably be willing to look at skills outside of competition, but do you know if you have any games coming up? Some schools might want to send a scout to see you play."

After Bobby's request that we keep the game quiet, I couldn't invite scouts to the St. Mark's game. Plus, it was nerve-racking enough. "Not at the moment. But I'm only a junior, so I have a little more time, right?"

Ms. Hong nodded and, opening my file, said, "You do. I'll start getting some options together for schools you might consider. And with that extra time, see what you can do about this English comp grade, okay?"

Ms. Lopez's class. I grimaced, thinking how my "Great Disappointments" paper probably wasn't going to bring up my grade. But it was only the first quarter of junior year.

"Sure," I said before taking my special-and-not-average ass back to class.

Bobby had managed to get us a half hour in the weight room right after school on Monday and announced that we'd have a long practice that afternoon. But because daylight saving time meant sunset had crept up to four thirty and the park would get too dark, we also had a new practice venue: the boys' football field. We had to wait for the boys' teams to finish, but the field had lights, so we could stay as late as we wanted.

Tuesday, it rained, hard. Bobby sought us out and told us that since we couldn't use the field, we'd meet at the Powell Park Recreation Center, which had an indoor track that surrounded an expanse of floor typically used for little boys' basketball games. The practice wasn't as strenuous as it would have been outdoors— the space was smaller—but the fact that Bobby was making sure we practiced hard leading up to the game felt like a vote of confidence. We worked on some defensive attacks and offensive feints as a team of seven-year-olds waited to play.

As we wrapped up, I saw Mrs. Ketchum, the mom of Kevin, one of my babysitting charges, watching us. She looked bewildered. As I waved to her on the way out of the rec center, she touched her own perfect curls and appeared wounded by the sight of my sweaty ponytail. She left Kevin standing there with his team and when I got up from the water fountain was hovering over me. "Susan," she asked with concern in her voice. "Is all that exertion affecting your menses?"

". . . Are you asking about my period?" The only time Mrs. Ketchum had ever been concerned about my well-being was when she hoped aloud that I'd eaten before coming over as her way of letting me know the pantry was off-limits. "My menses are fine."

"Oh," she said, loudly. "I was worried they might be . . . stunted by all that exercise. You wouldn't want to ruin your chances for children one day." She said this at the same time her darling Kevin licked a garbage can.

"My monthly is fine, too," Tina chimed in.

"I get my period like clockwork," added Dawn.

"Aunt Flow loves her visits," Joanie piped up.

"Actually, hasn't she been visiting us all at the same time every month?" Wendy said, smiling at Mrs. Ketchum, who was now looking at us all like we were a coven of witches, and not the pretty kind who did spells by twitching their cute noses.

It was like our own version of "I am Spartacus."

"I wish mine came like clockwork, but the Quinn women have always had issues," Marie said. "Since soccer, though, my cramps are way better. And my moods. You should try it!"

Mrs. Ketchum's features pinched into a disgusted expression as she hurried back to her precious Kevin. I'd probably lost that babysitting job, but I didn't care.

Two days before the game, at the end of our last scrimmage, Bobby blew his whistle.

"You look great, and I've never seen—or been on—a team that has worked this hard. But we have a problem."

Several groans and "whats?" burbled up from our huddle.

"You all like each other too much," he said.

"What?" Franchesa said. "Isn't that the point?"

Bobby nodded. "I'm glad you're all getting along," he said. "But think about the guys you'll be playing. They don't like you. I see it going one of two ways. They might come out with kid gloves and treat you like they have to go easy on you."

"Because we're girls?" Dawn Murphy said, using her shirt to rub sweat from her face.

"For better or worse, yeah," Bobby said. "But I think it's going

273

to go the other way. I think you've upset them, and I think they're going to be angry. They're going to make this game hurt. Split up. Same teams you just had. And this time, I'm going to be on defense."

We did; my side had the ball.

"If someone throws an elbow," Bobby said, lining up with the other team, "you have to dodge, or take the blow somewhere it will hurt less. If one of these guys tries to tangle your feet up, you're going to hit the dirt, and you have to roll to make sure you don't sustain an injury. I've seen you all take knocks in practice, and I've seen Marie and our defenders dish it out. But St. Mark's is going to be relentless. Let's play!"

Bobby blew the whistle. I passed the ball to Tina, who kicked it to Dana in the open field. She had Franchesa on her and kicked it back to me. I started for the goal, keeping Tina and Dana in my peripherals. As my feet pounded the crunchy turf, I heard an unfamiliar cadence next to me. Marie's steps were lighter, and Joanie's run sounded like a ticking clock. Bobby's footfalls were rhythmic, like a heartbeat. My own sped up as I could hear him breathing behind me. I picked up my pace. Bobby would appreciate me challenging him.

I was dribbling toward Wendy and the goal when he closed in on me, his leg cutting over mine for the ball. I charged forward hoping to flick the ball left to Tina. I lowered my chin as Bobby began to pivot, his elbow flying back, hard—right into my eye.

My back hit the dry grass with a thump, and I made a sound that was like a gulp in reverse. Bobby was on the ground next to me in an instant.

He pushed the rope of my ponytail out of my eye and gasped. "Oh no, I'm so sorry," he said.

I couldn't speak, with the wind still knocked out of me, but I moved my head a millimeter in each direction, as if to say, "Don't worry about it." But *I* was worried about it. I couldn't talk, and my voice and breath felt caught in my throat. I inhaled through my nose, welcoming the oxygen.

"We have to get you to the nurse," he said, helping me up. "Thank God we're on school grounds."

With his arm around my waist, he led me through the school—it was mostly empty, though the distant strains of band practice carried down from the choral room and mingled with the squeak of shoes from boys' basketball practice, which had started last week. We headed toward the nurse's office.

"Shit, she's not here this late," he said, setting me down on the vinyl bench where I'd once lain down through a bad bout of menstrual cramps. "Hold on." He rooted through the cabinet, came back to peer at me, grimaced, shut the cabinets, then opened the small icebox under the nurse's desk. He produced an ice pack, which he wrapped in a paper towel and handed to me. I pressed it to my swelling eye.

"I can't believe I did that. Are you okay? Can you talk? Do you think I should take you to the hospital?"

I stood up. He was so nervous, I couldn't help but feel worse for him than I did for myself and whatever had happened to my eye.

"I'm fine," I said, regaining my voice, or a croaking version of it. "Really. I think you should go back out there and elbow everyone as hard as you can in the eye, because then we'll all know we can take a hit. It was the right move."

Bobby laughed. A good, deep, generous laugh that warmed the drafty room. I didn't know how the first sentences I'd uttered after regaining my ability to speak were somehow the exact right thing, but I was apparently getting more comfortable around Bobby.

"Okay, let's go suggest it," Bobby said, waiting for me by the door. I liked that he said "let's." I walked out in front of him as he locked up the office. In the hall, he motioned for me to pull the ice pack away from my eye. Gingerly, I lifted it. Bobby drew a sharp breath.

"It's bad, isn't it?" I said.

"Do you want to find a mirror?" he asked.

"No, I like surprises."

He laughed again and smiled at me, with eyes that were—was his gaze wistful? Or did I want it to be? "You really are something else."

I knew it didn't mean he was falling in love with me, but I'd remember it as feeling that way.

When I emerged onto the field again, the entire team was clustered near the fence, waiting for us.

"She's not dead," Tina said, jogging out to me and throwing an arm around my shoulder. "Shit, that was scary."

"Can you talk?" Joanie asked, coming so close to my face that with my eye covered, it looked like there were two of her.

"How bad is your eye?" Dawn said. "That was a hard hit."

"Don't remind me," Bobby said.

"Did you check her vitals?" Dana asked him, ever making a checklist.

"Do you even know what that means?" Lisa teased her.

"Like, her heartbeat and like, what if she's dizzy? Are you dizzy? Could you have a concussion? Did you hit your head? What year is it? Who's president?"

"I'm not dizzy. I fell on my back. It's 1979 and Jimmy Carter is president but people say not for much longer. And thanks for asking." She was annoying, but she was thorough.

I pulled the ice pack away from my face. Everyone gasped.

"Okay, I'm canceling practice tomorrow," Bobby said. "I want you all rested for Saturday and I think I need a day to recover from that." We started to head for our jackets and bags, but he held up a finger. "But first I have an announcement."

The word "announcement" gave us all pause. Tina looked up from working out a nasty knot in her cleats. Marie stopped midway through shrugging on her jacket. A look of concern traveled from player to player, like a wordless game of telephone.

"I didn't know what was going to happen when I took on this team. I just hoped I'd be lucky enough to find some hardworking, good players," he said. Under the light, each time he exhaled it sparkled. The ice pack, which had started to soften against my face, seemed to tighten as a gust of wind slipped by. "I was more than lucky."

Was? Was he going to tell us this was it for soccer?

"And sometimes, when a great group of players is lucky

enough to find each other, they're also lucky enough to have a great leader among them. A captain. We have one, but we don't know it yet."

He looked right at me.

"I want her to know this has nothing to do with me clocking her in the eye," he continued, "and everything to do with the fact that she not only pushes herself as hard as anyone—and that's saying something—but she also wants, more than anything, to push this team to the next level."

I was as frozen as the ice pack against my face.

"Susan Klintock, if you want the job of captain, I think we'd all agree you're more than up to the task." He was looking at me like he'd gotten down on one knee to propose marriage. And I would have said yes.

"Me?" I said, my eyes widening, which just made the left one hurt again.

The team erupted into cheers.

"I'd love to," I told them.

And that's how the day I got my first black eye became the best day of my life.

Twenty-Six

My mom wasn't happy about my black eye. Which, okay, it would be a stretch to imagine anyone's mom being thrilled to see her kid come home with a puffy, purplish encroachment surrounding his or her eyeball, but my timing for a facial atrocity was also lousy.

After answering her initial questions, which were all variations on "What the hell happened?" with my answers all being a variation on "It was an accident," she rooted through the freezer to find a bag of frozen peas that she alternately pressed to my eye and removed to see if the discoloration had magically disappeared. "What are we going to do?" She huffed out a sigh.

"Hide me from polite society?" I offered.

"Very funny," she said. "We're lucky Polly's such a nice person, or she'd think we did this on purpose to ruin the wedding photos."

"I doubt she'd think *we* did this," I said, taking the peas from her as I sat at the kitchen table for a dinner of baked beans and cut-up hot dogs. I thought of Joe's fondness for the meal and decided not to be disgruntled that captains of the football team probably got celebratory steaks. But then I hadn't mentioned that I'd been given the captain spot yet.

"Well, we need to make sure Polly's not blindsided by this," Mom said, letting out a grim laugh at her unfortunate pun. "She'll be nervous enough for her big day."

I scooped six beans and one hot dog slice onto my spoon. It was a good ratio. Maybe this *wasn't* the worst meal. "Don't you think it's a little weird that you're this concerned about Polly having a nice wedding day? Shouldn't you be at least kind of amused by my wrecked face spoiling the harvest dream?"

Mom's face suggested this was *not* amusing. "What kind of hypocrite would I be if I divorced your father so I could pursue a better version of myself but spent all my time angry that he's trying to be a better version of himself?"

"Is he, though?" I asked, thinking of my dad's posture on the couch as he watched the Bears game. He didn't seem any different.

"I think he is. I just think it's more subtle." She sat down next to me and put down two glasses with two ice cubes in them, then poured a tiny bit of whiskey into each one. "That eye's going to start to hurt. This will help you sleep." We clinked glasses. I took the tiniest sip, the way she did. The only alcohol I'd drunk was stuff like beer and the schnapps at our team party, some sips of church wine with Candace, never whiskey. A radiant, warm burn bloomed under my chest, like if a Red Hots candy had exploded next to my heart.

"It's good," I said. Not the taste, but the fact that it fuzzed up my insides.

"And it's not only for the black eye," Mom said. "I owe you an apology. I shouldn't have said what I did about things being easier for you than they are for me, like I was jealous."

"It's okay," I said, surprised she was broaching this topic.

"Drink your whiskey, young lady, and let me talk."

I laughed at that, and took another small sip.

"I know, for one, that it's not easy for you—at most, it's a little less hard. And I wish it were easier. I suppose what I said came from thinking it should have never been so hard in the first place. Did you know that until a few years ago, I couldn't even apply for a credit card on my own? When your dad and I first bought this house, it needed a new washer-dryer. We looked at the catalog, we picked one," she said. Now she took a sip of her whiskey and went to retrieve a can of Cheez Balls from the counter. "Anyway, we decided I'd go to the store and open a credit card to pay for it. When I told the salesman at Sears, he laughed in my face. I needed my husband to cosign my application, like I was too dumb to understand what I was getting into. With a Sears credit card."

"And that's why you divorced dad?"

"No! He was as appalled as I was. I'd always been the one who handled the finances at home. But applying for these jobs, it just brings back all the same frustrations. It feels like all these people, they're already thinking that a man would be better at the job before they even know me."

"Why are you doing it, then?" I dipped a hand into the Cheez Balls.

"Because if I quit trying now, I'll always know it's because

I was afraid of being hurt and disappointed," Mom said. "And I know hurt and disappointment are survivable feelings."

"But what about all the time you put in?"

"It's a commitment, sure, but I'd rather risk it not working out than knowing I gave up because I was too scared." She gently pulled the bag of peas away from my eye. "It's kind of like your black eye. It looks like hell, but I bet you still want to play."

"Yeah, I do," I said. "They made me team captain tonight."

"Wow, captain," Mom said, and held her glass up. "Sounds like a toast is in order."

We clinked on it.

Friday, Mom called me in sick from school. I phoned Tina in the morning to tell her what was happening, so she wouldn't worry. "Tell everyone I'm fine. I look like Apollo Creed fucked me up, but I'm fine. I have to do last-minute wedding stuff."

Mom had had plans for a while to head out of town for the weekend, to see some friends in Michigan—her way of avoiding the wedding hubbub. I was still letting her assume the game on Saturday was against another girls' team, not St. Mark's. She had enough to worry about.

I was meeting Polly at Wieboldt's Friday afternoon to pick makeup for the wedding; then I was spending the night at their condo. I had a duffel bag with both my soccer gear and my pajamas, and Polly had my dress and wedding shoes, which I'd bring with me to the game. Tina had promised to drive me to the banquet hall where the ceremony would be; Joe was meeting me there after Rachel's recital.

When we got to Wieboldt's, Mom parked instead of dropping me off. She took a shopping bag out of the back seat and said, "I want to give something to Polly."

"You're weird, Mom," I said.

"I know." She waited for me and we walked into the store together.

Polly was waiting by the makeup counter. She wore a cream mohair sweater that girls at my school would have killed for, over matching cream pants. When her eyes landed on my eye, she put a hand to her mouth and dashed toward us. "Susan, what happened?"

"I'm so sorry," Mom apologized on my behalf. "If I'd known soccer was so rough, I'd have told her not to play right before the wedding."

Polly took my face in one of her cool hands. "You did this playing soccer? Wow. You are one tough cookie," she said. She smiled at Mom. "I can't be mad at that." She turned my face from one side to the other and I let her. Maybe it was a good thing I'd decided to be nice to her from the get-go. She was impossible to piss off.

"Well," she said, clapping her hands together. "We're in the right place. We'll get some concealer and no one will be the wiser. Did I ever tell you I used to sell Avon?"

"I bet you were the top seller," Mom said. She pulled a wrapped box from the shopping bag and extended it to Polly. "A wedding gift."

Polly flushed. She touched the bow and met Mom's eyes. "You didn't have to," she said. "This is so thoughtful."

Mom waved her off. "It's a gravy boat," she said. She reached into her bag again and this time emerged with a book, *Creative Visualization*, which I'd seen lying around our house. This copy was new. "And I wanted to give you this, too. I read it last year, and I've been telling all my friends about it."

On hearing the word "friends," a tear came to Polly's eye—also made up in shades of cream and gold. "I love it," she said, clutching the book to her chest. "Though not in my wildest imagination would I have thought my new husband's ex-wife would want to be my friend."

She hugged my mom tightly, and my mom hugged her back. "You're an amazing woman, Dierdre," Polly said.

I saw a tear slip from my mom's eye, too. "So are you," she said.

If my mom and my stepmom could get along, maybe there was hope for me and Candace. We were talking, but not really talking. She didn't know about me being team captain, and I didn't know what was going on with her and George. But maybe two women who approached how to be a woman in completely different ways didn't have to feel like threats to each other.

"Ms. Jeffries, is this the girl whose colors I'm doing?" A brisk woman in a belt that appeared to be suffocating her waist took my shoulder and turned me around, kind of roughly. She gasped. "Oh my God, her eye. How am I supposed to do colors for someone with an ugly shiner?"

Polly gave the woman a prim smile that somehow conveyed that the woman better watch it. "Well, it's a good thing she's so beautiful. Isn't it?"

It seemed clear, then, that in my parents' noncliché of a divorce situation, I could be a cliché, or I could appreciate that I'd been the one in a million picked to win the child-of-divorce lottery.

Twenty-Seven

Since my last visit, Polly had outfitted the condo's second bed-room with a new queen-sized bed for me, a small desk that looked out the window, and a poster of a Manchester United soc-cer player. "I went to the little shop in Evergreen Park that sells British imports, and that was all they had," she said. "But you can decorate however you want. Your Dad and I are hoping you might want to stay overnight more often."

"It's perfect," I said, looking forward to telling Joe about what was sort of a punk rock move on Polly's part. My dad probably hated the poster.

I was keyed up thinking about the game, but eventually the clean scent of the soft sheets lulled me to sleep, and I didn't wake up until my alarm went off at seven. I dressed in my soccer gear and took both my duffel bag and the garment bag containing my bridesmaid dress that was hanging on the closet door. I neatly put the heels and the new Estée Lauder makeup bag in with the rest of my stuff.

Polly was already up and had a breakfast of toast and eggs laid out for me. "I couldn't sleep," she said. "Is that your uniform? It's cute. Who's your game against?"

"Actually . . . St. Mark's . . . the boys' school," I said. It felt a little wrong to tell her when I hadn't told Mom, but Polly had asked outright. What if lying to a bride on her wedding day was bad luck? I explained how I'd challenged Ken.

"Wow," Polly said, nodding as she took a slow sip of her coffee. "This Ken sounds like a real jerk."

She paused, and I was so nervous she'd tell me I couldn't possibly go head-to-head with a bunch of angry boys on the day of her wedding. She put her coffee down on the counter and crossed the kitchen toward me. She took away my plate with one hand and put her other hand on my shoulder. "Sounds like you need a bigger breakfast if you're going to kick their asses."

We'd agreed to meet at the gate outside the field a half hour before the game. Everyone was even earlier than that, and everyone was nervous.

"Are you sure we should be doing this?" Dana asked me.

"We can't call it off now," I said. My captain voice was my normal voice, just louder. "They'd call us chickens." That seemed worse than anything else they'd called us.

I pushed through the gate, aware of my teammates behind me.

The stands were empty. We'd obeyed Bobby's request not to risk the game or his job by spreading the word—and really, I didn't expect people who saw us challenge St. Mark's at the party to remember it had happened or believe the game would actually occur—but I thought maybe *someone* would show. At the very least, some assholes from St. Mark's who wanted to heckle us. I wished Joe was there, but I thought it was nice that he didn't blow off his sister for me.

"There were more people at our Wisconsin game," Joanie said, squinting toward the bleachers as if she might have missed spotting a crowd.

"Next game, we'll tell everyone to come. But this is still a big deal, audience or not," Wendy said.

"Yeah, I feel . . . strong," Marie said. "Or maybe it's just that all my anger converted itself to muscles."

"Like the Hulk?" Sarah said.

"I guess, if he had to put up with more assholes," Marie said.

"Whoa," Tina said, as we stepped onto the field. St. Mark's soccer field—or pitch, as Joe would remind me—was only used for soccer, not football or anything else, and it had benefited from the expensive tuition the school charged. Even though there'd been some cold nights the last few weeks, the grass here was summer green, and the white lines on the field were crisp and new. "Did we die and go to heaven? Because I was hoping for a beach."

"Wow, what a field," Bobby said, sounding like the Country Mouse visiting the City Mouse's opulent home for the first time. "Let's go warm up."

We had no idea if there would be a place for us to change, so we'd all worn our uniforms to the field and didn't bring much extra stuff with us. My dress bag was in Tina's car for later.

A brisk wind whipped by, activating a patch of goose bumps

on my legs as I stretched. We took a lap around the field and kicked some practice passes with the bag of balls Bobby had brought. It was quarter after nine.

"Do you think they got the time wrong?" Dana asked me. "Didn't we say nine?"

"Yeah," I said, peering across the field toward the school.

"They're gonna show, right?" Dawn said. "They wanted to play us."

"Maybe their coach wouldn't let them come?" Franchesa suggested.

"I guess we have more time to warm up," I said.

We ran up and down the field, working on our passes. We lined up to take practice kicks at the goal.

But we grew more listless as it dawned on us that we'd been stood up.

"They're not coming," I said. Dawn kicked a ball, hard and off-kilter, so it landed in the empty bleachers. No one else moved for a minute, almost like we couldn't. The air had gone out of us. It was worse than heartbreak. It was insulting.

"What do you want to do, Susan?" Bobby asked me.

I took in the disappointed faces of my teammates, hating that the only option I could think of was to leave. Then a clatter rose from the equipment shed at the far end of the home bleachers.

"It's them," I said, feeling a thrill for a second. Maybe there had been a small miscommunication, but now the game would go as planned. I smiled at my team. "They're here." A happy medley of relief filled the air.

That is, until two dozen soccer players, naked except for their cleats, burst from the shed and ran toward us, whooping and hollering. They all waved something white—underwear, it looked like—over their heads.

"What the—" I started to say, as the herd barreled right through the center of the circle we'd formed. We jumped back and stumbled over one another to get away from the nude mass of boys. One of the guys—not Ken—tossed his underwear onto my shoulder, and as I tried to swat it off me, another boy squirted me with something. Liquid splattered my face and entered my stunned and open mouth. It was floral and vinegary. The acidic taste made my lips pucker. I spat at the ground.

They'd doused us all with it. By the time everyone had wiped the liquid from their skin, hair, and, in a few cases, eyes, the boys' pale naked butts were far away, headed toward the school.

"Assholes," Dawn yelled, kicking away the graying briefs that had landed on her cleats.

"Cowards!" That was Tina.

If the boys heard us, it didn't matter, because they were disappearing inside the building. The last nude boy, who I recognized as Ken, took a few steps back toward us and yelled, "Go home!"

I opened my mouth to hurl an insult at him, but I felt like I had when the wind was knocked out of me. The words were there in my throat but stuck under my rib cage. My insides felt scraped and dry, as massive tears came to my eyes. I used the back of my hand to wipe them away, hoping no one would see.

The awareness that I was utterly useless to stand up for us against a team of naked boys made me want to sit in the middle of the field and curl into a ball. Had they been watching us as we practiced and waited? Of course they had, and they'd been laughing at us. That was the worst part.

I started to run toward the door where they'd gone. "Susan, no," Bobby said, putting a hand on my shoulder.

"But those assholes," I started, and I couldn't keep the tears from falling. Bobby took one of the towels out of the equipment bag and handed it to me. I held it to my face, pressing it tight against my skin. "They can't do this," I sputtered.

I wasn't being captain-like, I knew, but fury had started to spiral inside me, twisting around hurt. I blinked away more tears that were pushing at my eyes and spat more of the vinegary taste from my mouth. It smelled like soap and salad dressing.

Joanie, whose jersey was wet in places, smelled it. "Did they . . . douche us?"

Wendy sniffed the damp ends of her hair. "This is definitely Summer's Eve."

"And the underwear . . ." Marie started to say, gingerly plucking a pair that had caught in Franchesa's ponytail. "They're dirty." She wrinkled her nose and whipped the tighty-whities away.

"Please let me go . . . do . . . something," I said to Bobby, trying to think of what, if anything, I could possibly do. My mind was blank except for seeing the naked guys running at us over and over.

As angry as I was, the tears kept reappearing. It was my fault this had happened, and as captain, I had to fix it. My stomach churned, imagining what all those boys together would say to me if I confronted them. But if I let them get away with it, I wasn't a good captain.

"Look," Bobby said to me and the rest of us. "You have every right to be angry. But sometimes we bring our best selves and it's not enough—"

Tina scowled at him. "So we're supposed to be the bigger people? After that?"

I leaned my head on her shoulder in gratitude. It was like she had read my mind. I had no interest in hearing one of Bobby's big speeches right now. He might be our coach, and under other circumstances, I would probably love hearing whatever calm, high-minded suggestion he was about to make, but today I didn't want that Bobby.

I wanted St. Mark's to pay.

"Here's what we're going to do. Or what I'm going to do," he said. "We have all the area coaches' numbers in the athletics office. Home numbers, too. I'm going to drive over right now and track their coach down."

"But we weren't even supposed to be playing this game. You'll get in trouble," I said.

"I promise, I won't." He patted my shoulder very gently. He looked from me to the team. "I still think it's great that you came ready to play. It's a shame your opponents couldn't do the same." He picked up his equipment bag and started for the gates. When we didn't follow him right away, he turned and said, "Come on, let's go. I'll handle all this, and you all can go . . ." He seemed stumped for the right word for what we might do after getting sprayed with Summer's Eve and pelted with dirty underwear. ". . . recuperate."

We looked at one another like we had no choice but to trudge behind him toward the street. When he reached his car, he said, "I'll let you know what their coach says at practice on Monday."

After he'd driven off, my teammates and I stood there, and I knew no one wanted to go home. "Should we get something to eat?" Dana suggested.

Most of us shook our heads or mumbled, "Not hungry."

"Me neither," Dana said.

"We don't have to let these guys get away with this," Tina said, directing the comment at me, as if together, we'd find the right solution.

"Are you thinking . . . revenge?" I said.

"Not Carrie-at-the-prom revenge, but yeah. Light revenge?" She tossed the idea out but seemed nervous, like she thought the team might call her crazy.

"Yes, that's exactly what we need to do," Marie said.

"Why should they get away with this?" Dawn extended a hand to Tina to slap five. "Even if Bobby gets ahold of their coach, he'll probably just laugh when he finds out what his players did."

"What do you have in mind?" Wendy said, slinging an arm over Tina's shoulder. "Because I'm in."

Ideas started to fly. "We TP their houses!" "We fuck up their cars!" "We'll break into their cafeteria and pee in their soda machine!"

"Those are all good suggestions," I said. Finally, with the team rallying around our revenge plot, my energy had started to return. "But we need a punishment that fits the crime. We need to hit them where it hurts—"

"Their dicks?" Marie said.

"For sure," Dana said. "They can put them back where they came from."

"Their moms?" Joanie said.

"No, I mean . . . never mind," Dana muttered. Tina and I traded an amused look.

"I think she's trying to say she wants them to put their dicks away forever," Dawn said.

"Screw that," Marie said. "I'd like to see them run through here when we're prepared for their dicks."

"They're more than their dicks, guys," Arlene said, like this was something she'd learned in kindergarten. "They're bad people no matter what they have between their legs."

"I think we need to settle on a plan so we can stop saying 'dick,'" Franchesa said.

"Please," Tina said.

"And we don't give their dicks any more attention," I said. "They think the world revolves around them as it is. But . . ." I pointed at the ground, where one of the pairs of underwear lay. It had a telltale butt-crack-length brown stain up the back of it. So did several of the others lying in view. "I think that even though they're assholes, they don't know how to wipe theirs."

"Disgusting!"

"Do you guys think there's sideline chalk in that shed?" I said. "Because I have an idea."

Just as I suspected, the boys had been too stupid to lock up the shed. Inside, there was white chalk and line stripers, for marking off lines on the pitch and the football field. We took everything and returned to the soccer pitch.

"We have to work fast," I said. "Who knows how long we have!"

It took us about an hour to mark the pitch. We went over every letter with a second coat of chalk, and then a third, ensuring that it wouldn't be washed away if it rained before next week. Heck, it would take hours to erase it even with firehoses.

"Is this kind of mean?" Joanie said when we were done. "Like, is it beneath us?"

"I think it's perfect," Marie said, hoisting her paintbrush in the air. "Hell hath no fury like a woman scorned, but nobody whines louder than a man whose ego has been bruised."

Once we'd put everything away, we all walked to the top of the bleachers to stare down at our work. It reminded me of what I'd told Joe about listening to "Gimme Shelter," that feeling of going up high to look at my life. In this case, though, I was looking at the St. Mark's soccer field, where we'd painted, in bright white letters:

EAT SHIT, ST. SKID-MARKS!

We'd then used a pair of pliers we found to pick up the pairs of shit-stained underwear and draped them over orange cones down the length of the field.

I laughed, imagining Ken's anger mounting in him until his skin was redder than his hair. Joe was going to declare this very punk rock.

"I wish I had a camera," Marie said.

"I know," Franchesa said. "We'll just have to remember it."

"I might block some of it out," Tina said. "But this part's

good. I can't wait until those assholes and all their friends come to school on Monday and see it."

"I still wish we'd gotten to play the game," Dawn said.

"What game?"

A male voice yelled up from below and behind us. I spun around and looked down at the ground beneath the bleachers.

Two police officers were standing there, and from the looks on their faces, they didn't think our work was as good as we did.

Twenty-Eight

After all the blood felt like it had been drained from and then returned to my body at a colder temperature, I shared a moment of "oh shit" panic with my teammates. I had to catch Dana by the arm so she didn't fall over at the top of the bleachers. The cops summoned us to join them on the ground, where we stood in front of them, not knowing what we were supposed to do next.

"That's Officer Nadler," the taller officer said, pointing at the stockier cop. "I'm Officer Dickerson."

"Nads and Dick? Haven't we dealt with enough of that?" Marie whispered to Lisa, who giggled.

"Not a very ladylike thing to say," Dickerson said, stepping up to her so his face was inches from hers.

"Who's responsible for you girls?" Nadler asked, with his hands on his hips.

No one spoke at first. Since I was the captain, I decided I should answer. "Um, we're responsible for ourselves. We're a soccer team."

Why had I said that like it was a Get Out of Jail Free card?

Dickerson stared at me like I was a talking bear, then took a step closer. He loomed over me.

"Mind telling me what a girls' soccer team is doing on a boys' field? And what this vandalism has to do with playing soccer? If that's even what you really do?"

I bit the inside of my cheek, trying to think of what to say. Everyone else had gone silent, but it was probably for the best if only one of us was doing the talking. In movies, there was always one guy who did the talking. "We do play soccer," I said, pointing at our uniforms. "And we were supposed to have a game with the boys' team here."

Officer Nadler gave one of those laughs that was more like the noise of someone clearing a booger from one nostril. "You expect us to believe that?"

"It's true," Tina said, backing me up. "They forfeited."

Dickerson shot Tina a dismissive look. "And then they left?"

Did he not know what forfeiting was? I nodded, as my knees trembled. "Yeah, and we've been working hard for this game, so I guess we were mad, Officer."

"So you wrote this trash?" Dickerson asked. He stared at the "St. Skid-Marks" message on the field as if it caused him physical pain.

I wanted to tell him what the boys had done to us first, but we had no proof, except for the tighty-whities draped around the field, but what could cops do with those? Go door to door to ask people if their sons had lost a pair of stained briefs?

"Are you not going to answer me?" Dickerson said. "Are you ashamed of yourselves? Because I sure hope you are."

I wasn't ashamed and I still thought the revenge was worth even the hassle from these cops. But I didn't want to go to jail or anything, either. "If I say yes, can we leave? It's just chalk."

"Look, little lady—though calling you a lady is a stretch, writing stuff like that—I'm not letting you girls go home until you tell me who I can call. You're lucky I'm not charging you all with vandalism." Dickerson looked like a guy who immediately settled into his easy chair when he got home and made his wife fetch him beers. He was probably looking forward to that chair too much to deal with writing up eleven girls.

"If you give us a name, we can finish up here," Nadler said.

"Bobby McMann," I said at last. "You can try the athletic office at Powell Park High." I hoped he was still there. It was better him than any of our parents.

Officer Dickerson crossed the field to use the pay phone. We watched as he spoke into the receiver, but we couldn't hear what he was saying. "He's on his way," he hollered as he hung up.

When Bobby arrived fifteen minutes later, he shot me a concerned look over Nadler's head. Then Dickerson led him around the field to read what we'd written there. It felt like it took hours for them to read four giant words.

"I see, Officer, I understand" was all we heard Bobby saying when they finally returned. They were standing to the side of us, and we all pretended to look at our feet as we eavesdropped. Bobby said, loud enough for us to hear, "Look, it's my fault. They were supposed to play a game against the boys' team here, and those boys committed a lewd, aggressive act that, if you ask me, should be punished. My team will be appropriately disciplined by me for what they've done here, but you should really talk to the St. Mark's coaches as well. I reached their athletic director, and he seemed disinclined to even entertain the idea one of his teams would do such a thing. But I saw it with my own eyes."

Nadler and Dickerson exchanged a glance, like they'd been partnered on a huge case. Nadler drew himself up and said to me, "Did they violate you girls in some way?"

"I'll fill you in, Officer." Bobby gestured for Nadler and Dickerson to come closer, and the trio retreated farther from us and spoke for a few more minutes. Both officers' faces were grave.

"Bobby's not making us out to be victims or something, is he?" Tina said.

"He'd better not be," Marie said.

"Maybe he has to, if he's cutting a deal," Joanie said. "Who cares? Better he plays the 'poor girls' card than we sit in a cell or something."

The officers left. "Mercy," Dana said. "We must not be getting arrested."

Bobby was headed back toward us. I couldn't gain anything from his expression as he read the words on the field one more time.

"You know, even if Bobby's pissed, this was fun," Wendy said. "Someday, you'll all be my bridesmaids or some shit and we'll think about this day."

"You're going to have ten bridesmaids?" Tina said. "That's not a wedding, that's a circus."

"You can all wear your uniforms," Wendy said. She playfully

punched Tina in the arm. "Anyway, I'm not going to get married. My parents made that sacred institution look pretty nasty."

"Well, if you change your mind, I'll be your bridesmaid," Tina said.

"Bridesmaid . . . ," I said, the word turning noisily in my brain, the way you cranked a penny you'd put inside a gumball machine. "Oh, fuck! My dad's wedding!"

"Girls . . . ," Bobby was saying as he got closer—he must have been about to lecture us or at least tell us what the officers had said—but when he saw my face, he stopped short. "What's happening?"

"I'm supposed to be at my dad's wedding, like, already! Oh my God, oh my God, oh my God! What am I going to do?" It wasn't only that I should have been at the banquet hall by now, it was that I was covered in weather-resistant chalk, smelled like a mixture of Summer's Eve, dirt, and sweat, and knew I wouldn't remember how to cover up my black eye the way the Estée Lauder lady had taught me. "I'm gonna be sick."

"No, you're not, you're going to be fine," Tina said. She was holding my shoulders and speaking her words slowly to calm me down. "We'll help you."

"We'll go to the high school, you can clean up in the girls' locker room, and I'll drive you to the wedding," Bobby said. "I'll explain that it's my fault you're late. Whatever you need."

Everyone looked at me with a mixture of astonishment and envy, as if Bobby's offer was some kind of proclamation of his love and devotion. And who was I kidding? It felt kind of great.

At the high school, I washed up quickly under the scorching locker room showers. As soon as I emerged, my teammates surrounded me, equipped with everything in my makeup and toiletry bags, plus some of their own add-ons.

"Who's got the hair dryer?" Tina said.

"Got it," Joanie said, holding it in the air and jogging over to stand at attention next to Tina. "And the hot rollers I keep in my locker. Every magazine says these are essential to go from day to night."

"Good, I need you first. Makeup, be ready."

"I'm on makeup," Marie said, who'd found my new makeup bag and set it on the locker room bench next to me, along with a bag of her own.

"I'll help," Arlene said. "I can do all the blending. I'm really good at that."

"Good," Tina said. "Take her from don't-mess-with-me-I'm-a-vandal to everything's-under-control-I'm-the-maid-of-honor," Tina said. She shook her head at the way Lisa rolled up a chunk of my hair. "No, don't make the curls too tight. She needs a soft wave to fall over her black eye, if we can." Finally, she looked at me. "See? You're going to be fine."

"You're going to be late for your dad," I said. Tina's dad was driving in from Wisconsin to take her to dinner downtown.

She waved me off. "He can deal with some uncomfortable time sitting at my mom's house."

"Thank you," I said and, realizing how lucky I was, added, "You're the best."

Tina shrugged. "I know."

Dana Miller tapped Tina on the shoulder, as if she were seeking an audience with me but needed Tina's approval. She extended a bottle of Chanel No. 5 toward me, cupping it in both hands like it was a delicate baby bird. "It's from Assistant Principal Lawler's desk. She lets me put some on sometimes. Do you want to use it?"

I took the bottle with a grateful nod. The glass felt thicker even than the bottle of Charlie perfume my dad had given me for Christmas, as if to prove the contents were more expensive and exclusive.

"Thanks," I said, spritzing it on, not sure if I liked the scent but touched by Dana's generosity.

Everyone worked fast, and then Tina and Dawn helped me step into my dress. Dawn used her Donna's Bridal skills to make sure everything was fastened and lying smoothly. Franchesa handed me my dyed pumps.

"Wait," Sarah said, picking at my upper arm with her fingernails. She knocked off some chalk that had congealed. "Okay, you're good."

I looked in the mirror. I was good, or at least good enough. No one was going to put me in a beauty pageant, but hopefully Polly and my dad would be so busy as the guests were arriving, they wouldn't know how close I'd come to missing their big day. And hopefully Joe wouldn't be too upset I was late once I told him the story.

"You guys are the best teammates," I told everyone, hoping the comment would cover everything, from getting me ready to painting the field to being willing to play the boys in the first place.

Bobby was waiting for me at the front of the school, pacing with his head down. When I came out, he said, "All right, your chariot awaits."

Tina whispered in my ear, "Don't do anything I wouldn't do." I tried not to let my imagination determine the details of what that could mean.

We walked to Bobby's car, and he opened the door for me so I could duck inside. "I'll keep your gym bag so you don't have to lug it with you," he said, taking it to put in his trunk.

"Are you mad . . . about earlier?" I asked as he slid into the driver's seat.

He paused for a second and squinted as if thinking about it. "You know, I shouldn't tell you this, but they deserved it."

"They really did," I said.

"Their athletic director was a real piece of work," he said. "He basically hung up on me. I should have tried the nuns."

"I have a friend there who knows the nuns," I said, wondering if Joe could pull some strings. "They do sound cool."

Bobby seemed to consider this. "Maybe. But I don't think that team respects a woman's opinion. Even a nun's. It's a shame."

"Well, then I'm extra glad we got them back," I said. "For the nuns."

Bobby put the car into gear. As he backed out, he gave me an approving look. "I can barely tell I gave you a black eye. By the way, I still feel terrible about that." he smiled. "You look really pretty."

"Thank you," I replied, the words catching on my jumping, unsteady heartbeat. He'd called me pretty, and it was like tearing wrapping paper to see the gift you'd been wanting forever.

I told him where to go: Chateau D'Amour, a big, white-pillared banquet hall on Ridgeland, not far from his apartment. When he pulled into the circular drive that led to the front steps, I saw Joe waiting for me. The spikes were gone—he'd combed his hair neatly across his forehead—and he was wearing a dark suit. He looked extremely cute. He also looked worried, but his face brightened when he saw me in the car window.

"Your date?" Bobby said.

"My friend," I said. "Joe."

Bobby hopped out on his side and opened my door, helping me emerge in the long dress. His hand, callused from all the weight lifting he did, sent a chill up my arm. I felt faint, and I unintentionally squeezed his hand as I stood up.

"Are you sure you don't want me to talk to your stepmom and dad?" he asked. "Give your cover story some help?"

I hated the question for the way it reminded me that Bobby was my coach, not some lusty suitor. "No thanks, I think I'm okay."

"Have a good time tonight," he said. "I'll see you Monday."

I made my way toward Joe, conscious that both he and Bobby were watching me. When I reached him, he said, "Wait, your coach drove you?"

"Bobby, yeah," I said, trying to act like this was no big deal, and like I wasn't still thinking about the ride. "Because I was late."

"Huh," Joe said. "So . . . the game? Tell me everything!"

I opened my mouth to answer as he started to pull open the

door for me. Then he stopped suddenly, letting go of the door to look at my face. "Wait, what happened to your eye? Did those guys . . . ?"

I shook my head at Joe's horrified expression and touched the bottom of my bruised eye. I'd thought the makeup covered it pretty well, but Joe didn't miss anything.

"No, that's from practice." The Bobby-free truth. "We didn't even play the game. They forfeited. Or, really, they showed up just to humiliate us," I said. "And then we got them back, and then the cops came. . . . It's a really long story."

Joe seemed to be having trouble deciphering what I'd said. "Wait, you didn't play? And the cops? Are you okay? Fucking Ken."

"Yep, he was definitely the leader," I said, but I was edgy about spending more time recounting the story than I already had. "I'll tell you everything. But I should find Polly. I was supposed to be here an hour ago."

"You had me nervous," Joe said. "But you look nice. Better than nice. Really pretty." He grinned as he reached for the door handle a second time. "And the shiner with the fancy dress is pretty foxy."

"Is it that obvious?"

"Only if you're really looking," he said in a low voice. I shivered a little, not sure if it was from his tone or the light breeze on my bare shoulders. But, really, the night was uncharacteristically nice for November.

He was holding the front door for me and standing very formally. We both seemed a little stilted compared to our normal selves, but maybe it was the special occasion.

"You look nice too. Handsome. I like your hair better the other way, though."

Joe self-consciously touched his head. "Yeah, well, it's a wedding."

I shook my head and smirked. "Not very punk rock of you."

"Hey, it's a way of being!"

Polly was easy to find. She was right inside the front doors, next to a tall potted plant. She had on her wedding dress and was smoking over a tall ashtray. I'd never seen her smoke before. She beamed when she saw me and quickly stubbed out her cigarette.

"You're here!" Polly reached out and smoothed my hair, very gently, like she wasn't sure she could make such a gesture.

"I'm so sorry I'm late, this is Joe," I said all in a rush.

"It's nice to meet you, Joe." She offered her hand for Joe to shake.

"Thanks for having me," he said.

"We had an issue after the game and—"

"It's okay," Polly said. "We haven't even started, and I'm out here hiding from my mother. You father's probably worried about marrying me after seeing her in action."

I'd only met Polly's mom once, in passing, at the last dress fitting. She was a small, pinched woman who had swept a finger over the boutique's jewelry case, looking for dust. When Polly emerged in her dress, looking like an angel, her mother had said that the lace bodice was "awfully sheer" and wasn't the cap sleeve inappropriate given a November wedding? The only time I'd seen Polly's cheerful personality punctured was when her mother was around.

"You don't seem to have a lot in common with her," I said. "I'm sure he's not worried."

"They say that women become their mothers, but your dad is always reassuring me that I'm my own person," she said, and I wondered who this reassuring version of my dad was. "Anyway, I'm relieved and happy to see you." She squeezed my shoulder. "And you." She smiled at Joe.

"Can we do anything to help? Like, maid of honor stuff?"

"No, everything is good as it's going to get." She sniffed the air. "I need to put on some perfume so I don't smell like the Marlboro Man during the ceremony."

She gave me a hug that caught me by surprise and I made eye contact with Joe, who grinned at me as if to say, "You've gotta go with it." I squeezed Polly back.

"All I want is for you two to have fun," she said, pulling away. "I'll see you at the ceremony."

➡➤✳◀⬅

The ceremony was, predictably, short and sweet. Or at least short. Maybe because we barely attended church services, Trinity Lutheran had sent a minister who had all the enthusiasm of the DMV employee who'd half-heartedly conducted my driver's test. But my dad looked happy, and his hazel eyes even shone with an appreciative tear when he said "I do."

As soon as he'd kissed the bride and they'd walked from the small chapel area to the reception, which was down the hall in the Sweetheart Ballroom, Dad waved me and Joe over to him and Polly. After I'd introduced Joe to my dad and it was only mildly awkward—my dad had noticed that their ties had similar patterns, and they talked about it for two full minutes—Dad turned to me.

"Thank you for being here," he said, taking me aside for a hug as Polly crouched to squeeze two of my stooped great-aunts and Joe struck up a conversation with my uncle Rich. "And for being so nice to Polly. It really means a lot to her. And me. Your mom did a great job raising you and your sister."

The invocation of my mom should have stung. It was the point when, in the standard parent-remarries part of a child-of-divorce story, I would have said, "Why didn't you stay with her?" But I *could* see the difference in my dad now, with Polly, the same way I could see a difference in my mom. It wasn't a crystal-clear one-eighty from his previous self, but he channeled something new, and more positive. As for me, it wasn't so much I was above that standard response. It was that I could see how things could be sad and happy at the same time. If life was going to present surprises, wasn't it best if you were both sad for what you lost and happy for what you gained?

"So did you," I told my dad, remembering a Father's Day when he'd taken me and my sister to a White Sox game. Almost every other dad there was with sons, leaving me to wonder what other fathers with daughters were doing that day. The team had been really bad that year, but my dad had told us about the players who would get better over the next few years. Candace's dad only ever took her brothers to baseball games.

"Let's get a beer," Dad said, and headed toward the bar, where some of the guests were waiting to congratulate him and Polly. A bartender not much older than me slid two Old Style beers over the counter, and Dad folded a five and put it in a glass filled with tips.

"Congratulations, sir," the bartender said, and my dad tipped his bottle in gratitude before handing me mine and clinking with me. Now I'd had a drink with each of my parents in the last week. It was strange, in a good way.

Polly had come into the room with her mother on her heels, and judging by Polly's rigid walk, Mrs. Jeffries hadn't let up on her nitpicking. Polly excused herself as she made her way to me and Dad and, with a grimace, said, "Apparently I've seated some cousins I barely recognize at a table that's not good enough for them."

My dad kissed her cheek and asked, "Do I need to handle something?"

Polly waved him off. "Whatever we do at this point, my mother is going to find fault, so just order me a gin and tonic."

I took a sip of the cold beer in my hand and felt like I was floating as it hit my empty stomach. The laughter and conversation in the room rolled over me in a soft wave. I caught Joe's eye and he gave me a cute grin, even though my uncle Rich's meaty hand was clutching his shoulder.

Polly and my dad pointed out my seat at the head table and Joe's at the date table right next to it, then went off to greet more of their guests. When I put the bottle down, the bartender slid a Coke across the bar with a wink. "Hope you like rum," he said.

I took a sip, noticing how the rum's warmth spread through my body differently from the burn of the whiskey I'd had with Mom.

I made my way toward Joe and tapped his shoulder. "Hey," he said. "So, your uncle Rich is . . . nice."

"You mean weird."

"Yeah, but I didn't think I should say that."

I gave him my glass. "Have some," I said and watched him sip and taste the rum in it.

He peered at me. "I like it," he said. Maybe it was the booze, but I was already feeling less formal around him.

Then, before I had time to talk myself out of it, I slipped my hand into his and said, "Let's get another one."

Joe gave me the kind of look he might have if we'd stepped outside and his beat-up Nova had been given a surprise paint job in his favorite color. "Sounds good to me," he said. We shared the second rum and Coke and were still holding hands when waiters began setting down plates at each table. I didn't know how or if I should address the hand-holding, but as I was doing it, I knew it was what I wanted to be doing.

"That's my cue to go to the head table," I said. "But save me a dance later?"

"I'm basically here to do whatever you want and eat some chicken," Joe said as we broke apart to go to our tables. His smile made me feel better than the drinks had.

As I crossed the room, someone tapped my shoulder. I spun around to see Mrs. Trillo, with Mr. Trillo standing behind her. Mrs. Trillo's enormous boobs had somehow been hoisted into a dress with spaghetti straps, and she wore a stronger perfume than her usual Jean Naté.

She drew back slightly at my black eye, and I knew I should go reapply my eye makeup. I moved my hair shield back into place. "Susan, honey, how are you doing?" She said it so gravely, you'd have thought I was at one of my parents' funerals, not a wedding.

"Things are good," I said, trying to hit the right note. If I sounded too chipper, it might seem snotty. I didn't want to seem like I didn't miss her, or Candace, because I did.

"We haven't seen you much lately," she said, looking so sad I wondered what Candace had told her. Or maybe Candace hadn't said anything and I was just missed.

"I know. Soccer and school and Candace is . . . busy," I said, assembling an awkward attempt at a sentence. "I have to get to the head table now but . . . I'll see you later."

"Bye, honey," Mrs. Trillo said, as Mr. Trillo gave me a distracted but fatherly smile.

I replayed the conversation in my head, thinking that if that was the thorniest moment at my dad's wedding, I would count myself lucky.

With dinner came wine, but I stuck to sips of the rum drink. Joe and I caught each other's eyes a few times. Maybe Tina had been right about taking a chance on him. If she hadn't been with her dad—she'd left right after she got me ready—I would have found a pay phone and called to ask what I should do. But she'd probably tell me to go with it, and given the way Joe and I couldn't stop smiling at each other . . . maybe she'd be right.

The day's collection of unforeseen events—the game that wasn't one, the reckless thrill of chalking the field, the team's rush to get me ready, Bobby's compliment, hand-holding, and now trading these looks with Joe, like we weren't just friends—put an extra sparkle on my buzz. I was happy, and it surprised me, especially when I compared the feeling to how I'd reacted when Polly first told me about the wedding. I felt important at the main table, seated next to my dad, who slung a proud arm around me every time someone came up to congratulate him. When they'd comment on what a beautiful woman I was becoming, Dad would mention how I was quite an athlete, too. He must have been a little buzzed, like me. But his pride was genuine.

I'd eaten half my chicken and a few forkfuls of vegetables and potatoes when the lights dimmed for the first dance. Polly and my dad had opted to have couples join them on the floor. Joe waited for me to finish a dance with my uncle Rich, who was my dad's best man. Then it was our turn.

We started to sway to "Just the Way You Are" by Billy Joel, and Joe put his hands on my waist. My head came up to his chin, and when he cocked his head to whisper in my ear, his breath was warm on my neck. "So is it weird, being in your dad's wedding?"

"It's not as weird as you'd think," I said. "Or maybe I'm getting used to dealing with strange circumstances."

"So now you can tell me what the strange circumstances were with St. Mark's."

"Well, I don't know how to say this, but there are dirty movie theaters downtown where I'd see fewer penises than I did today."

"Wait . . . what?"

I told him about Ken and the team's streaking, and douching, and what we'd done to the field, and how we'd gotten caught and Bobby had managed it. "I was really afraid he'd be pissed, but he actually approved of it."

"So you and him . . . talk a lot?" I could sense the bigger question—whether I had a thing for Bobby—underneath the one he'd asked. But he was the one who'd had about thirty different girlfriends since we'd met, and Bobby was just my coach.

"He's . . . a good coach," I said. "But that's it."

"Huh," Joe said. The same "huh" from outside. Then he leaned closer to me, his mouth right next to my ear, and whispered, "Do you think I need to kick Ken's ass on Monday?"

Before I could tell him I was happy with the way the team had handled it, he said, "Wait, sorry, I'm being a douche. I mean, a jerk. You already got him back."

"You don't need to defend my honor," I said in a light tone. "But if you feel like kicking Ken's ass, I'm sure he deserves it for other reasons."

"Yeah, I never told you the whole story, but he and I used to be friends."

"What?"

"He joined the team after me and he was my backup at goalie. And I guess he didn't like that, because one day he was tending goal and I was playing forward at scrimmage and he tripped me on purpose. And if you pull your foot back right when the other guy is flying, you can really fuck up their quad muscle. But he got what he wanted, and I'm better off, I think."

"You're such a good player, though," I said, and looked into his eyes so he'd know I meant it. "But . . . I guess we might not have met if you were still hanging out with him."

"Yeah, I'm better off," Joe said. He bit his lip and my heart pounded. At that moment, my entire focus was on him, with no distractions or daydreams intruding. No Paul Newman, no Han Solo. I wanted Joe to kiss me, and I felt like he wanted the same thing. I felt like if I stared at him longer, I could make it happen.

But I also liked the feeling of anticipation. I glanced away, looking around the dance floor.

"The concert the other day—why did you ask me and not Jeannette?" I asked. "Or Lizzy, or one of the other ones?"

Joe pulled back so our eyes met again. He put the tip of his tongue against his upper lip, like he was thinking of the right answer. Then a smile came over his face and, without looking away from me, he said, "I guess I can have a good time with a lot of people, but when you know the person you like hanging out with best, why waste time hanging out with people who aren't her?"

"Oh, I think I get it," I said, hiding my smile as I tested resting my head on his shoulder. I trusted that he meant what he said, and wasn't just saying it. It explained why he kept asking me to practice, and to do other things. And I liked hanging out with him, doing anything. He gave me the same feeling I'd get from holding a hot pizza box on my lap. Being with Joe was comforting and exciting at the same time. It wasn't how I felt with Bobby.

His hands ran down my back until his fingertips grazed the top of my butt. I cocked my head back to look at him and he said, "I'm sorry, is that okay?"

"Yeah," I said. "It definitely is."

I closed my eyes and enjoyed the pressure of his fingertips, and then Joe was whispering into my neck, "I'm enjoying this dance," and I could feel the light stubble where he shaved. I pressed my body closer to his. There was no space between us now. A deep sigh emerged from him, and he clutched me tighter.

"Me too," I said. "It's nice."

But it was better than nice, and way worse than nice. I felt like I couldn't get close enough to Joe. I'd worked myself into a state of horniness so thorough, I couldn't take it. My breath was coming short and shallow, and I put my lips just at the top of his collar, where it touched his skin.

I heard him take a sharp breath, and his fingers pressed into my hips. The very idea that I'd made him feel what I was feeling made me want more. Every touch felt so good, and I liked him so much.

I really liked him, and that was the strangest part of it all to me.

I put my lips near his ear and said, "Should we . . ."

Joe finished the sentence. "Get out of here?"

At the same time, with the same resolution, we both said, "YES."

Twenty-Nine

Joe had my hand and we tried not to look like we were running for our horny lives as we bolted from the ballroom.

"Should we go for a drive?" he asked. "Someplace else?"

"I shouldn't leave," I said. "But maybe we can go somewhere in the building." I saw a door and dragged him toward it. I opened it. It was a coat closet. "This okay?"

"It's great," Joe said.

I pulled him inside. I didn't wait for him to make the first move—I made it, and pushed him up against the back wall of the closet. Neither of us kissed the other one first—we were synchronized as our lips met for the first time. The kiss was an avalanche, toppling out of each of us and pulling us together, like gravity. We were kissing and pressing and panting and my shoe got stuck in a fallen hanger and I slipped so he had to catch me before I hit the floor. We laughed, giggles that collided in the dark. Then, as I righted myself, I nearly elbowed him in the face. "Watch it, killer," he said, before kissing me again, slower this time. I grabbed the back of his neck and he pressed a thumb under the narrow strap of my dress. We stumbled again, as a pair, and I had to put my hand on the wall to keep us upright.

I was only one minute in, but making out with someone I really liked—shoving old ladies' coats out of the way, fumbling around in the dark, excited and laughing as our limbs and feet and hair tangled—wasn't anything like the soft-lit love scenes I'd seen in most movies. It wasn't like sex ed, either, where every step was like the instructions to assemble furniture. It was clumsy and messy, but also perfect and better.

The strap of my dress fell down and then part of my dress, and I started to pull it up, and Joe did, too, but his fingertips on my skin felt so good that I said, "No, leave it." And my boob, not even my favorite one, was partly out. Joe trailed his hand down my collarbone and then down to my chest and when he touched me, I gasped.

I was so horny I thought I'd die. I tugged at his shirt and pulled it from his pants so I could touch his skin. We kept kissing the whole time, and as I ran my hands down his chest, I stopped at his pants and then, touching his belt, asked him, "May I?" like he'd asked me.

"Yeah," he said, his voice thick, and he still had my breast in his hand and, as his thumb rolled over my nipple, a dizzying electricity surged through me. Between my legs I had the feeling of having to pee but not having to pee. As I unzipped Joe's pants and let them drop to the floor, I hiked my dress up so that we were pressed together, underwear to underwear.

"I don't think we should . . . ," Joe started.

"We won't," I said, thinking, *We won't YET*, as I moved against him. Joe was as excited as I was, but it was more obvious on him, and the friction as our fulcrums met, coupled with the kissing—Joe touching my face, swooping his fingers lightly down my cheek and across my jaw in a way that gave me happy chills—felt sensational.

There was nothing dignified about dry humping, but I didn't feel the least bit uncomfortable doing it with Joe. He was a good guy, like Bobby. Wait . . . why was I thinking about Bobby? Oh God, why could I not think about Bobby, just a little? Bobby driving me in his car, at his office, in the health food store, at the motel in Wisconsin—Joe kissed my neck, and I ground my hips harder against him. I was so close to coming that the added pressure was all I needed to tip me past the edge.

Then I *was* coming. Pleasure rolled over me in a wave as I uttered, "Oh my God, Bobby."

Yes. I said, "Oh my God, Bobby."

Joe dropped his hands from my face and stared at me. "What did you say?"

For the first time since we got inside the closet together, I felt too naked. I stuttered useless syllables as I began to answer, but then the door flew open and a man's voice said, "It's been a while since I smoked a cigar."

My dad's voice.

The lights came on. My hands were still on Joe's hips and he was still pressed to the wall—his arms limp at his sides—but when we registered my dad, with Mr. Trillo right behind him, Joe wrenched away from me, pulled up his pants, and bolted past them.

My first thought was that I'd climaxed with a guy—a guy I

liked—for the first time, and I'd called him the wrong name. My second thought was that I might never be aroused again, after being caught by my dad and Mr. Trillo.

And I *was* caught. My dress was partway down, my hair was now a puffy mass, and one of my pumps had come off. The looks on their faces were nearly as bad as Joe's had been.

"What the hell is going on? . . . Are you . . . ? Were you?" my dad sputtered.

"Oh God," Mr. Trillo said, like he was a soldier stepping over mauled and bloody bodies.

"I'm sorry," my dad said to him. "I don't know . . ." Neither one was moving, as if they were in shock.

I turned to find Joe, to apologize, and to grab him so I could take him somewhere else to explain. But then I remembered he was gone. I pulled up my dress and scrambled past my dad and Mr. Trillo, picking up my stray shoe and taking off the other one.

I ran. Out the front door of the banquet hall, down the steps, across the circular drive where Bobby had dropped me off hours earlier. I ran to the parking lot, searching for Joe's car. Searching for Joe. Then, when I was sure he'd left, I stopped and stood there.

He would never want to speak to me again.

I looked toward the reception hall, but I couldn't go back in there. And no one was coming out for me. So I ran down Ridgeland, probably a ridiculous sight in my peach dress, and cut to a side street where I stopped to think.

I sat inside an empty bus shelter, grateful for the small mercy of a warm November night, and not knowing what to do. Mom was out of town, and Tina was with her dad. I had my teammates but I didn't know their phone numbers, or where they lived. Candace was probably with George, and I didn't want this to be the first time I spoke to her since our fight, anyway. My house was miles away. A bus stopped, but I couldn't even get on because I had no money with me.

Then I remembered: Bobby's apartment was only a few blocks from the banquet hall. It was Saturday night, and he could be out for the evening, but I'd try him first, and if he wasn't home, then I'd call Candace. There was no way I could tell him what had happened, but he could drive me home. Maybe he'd have some motivating words if I told him I felt like I'd fucked everything up. He'd said himself I could tell him anything.

I smoothed my dress and composed myself as best I could, turning down 107th Street toward Mansfield. I hated Cinderella even more now. She didn't have real problems. Who cared if the prince knew her carriage was a pumpkin and her dress was rags? He hadn't given her an orgasm as she called him by some other prince's name while her freakin' *dad* watched. I didn't even want to think about what my dad would tell Polly, and I could only hope that I hadn't ruined their day. There was probably only an hour or so of the reception left. *Pretend like nothing happened, at least until tomorrow, Dad*, I thought, hoping the message would reach him. *Say I didn't feel well, or you told me I could go for a drive with Joe.* Polly deserved that.

It was just after ten. The lights were off in Bobby's duplex, but music came from the garage and a light shone under the door—he must have been working out. I knocked once, then pushed open the unlocked door. "Hey, I hope it's okay I'm here—"

Bobby jumped away from Jacqueline, who was almost entirely nude, with her leotard pulled down to her thighs. She covered her bare breasts with her hands.

"Susan," Bobby said, fumbling to pull up his shorts. *The* shorts. The ones I thought of as *my* shorts.

Jacqueline said nothing, and when she recognized me, a faint smirk tugged her lip upward and she dropped her hands from her breasts, as if to show me what she had that I didn't. She slowly pulled up her leotard as her expression grew more satisfied, like she'd pulled up in a car I'd never be able to afford.

Now the numb shock was mine. He was having sex with Jacqueline. Of all the women he could have, he'd picked someone like her.

It took me less than a second to feel years older. All the ways I'd previously known I was young and inexperienced and naive—all the ways I'd known better, deep down, than to imagine Bobby and I could ever be something—were compressed into a single moment. The years folded in on themselves. Seeing him then, I caught up to him, felt like I was knowing and wise enough for him, finally.

And I never wanted to see him again.

For the second time that night, I ran.

Sprinted, really, my shoes abandoned, down Mansfield, turned onto 107th. I saw Bobby's car pull up at the corner and ducked into an alley. As I leaned my shoulders against cold brick, hiding, I wondered how he'd gotten rid of Jacqueline.

He got out of the car and called my name. I waited until he gave up and left, and after he did, I stood there as the air turned too cold for me to stay any longer.

I had to call Candace.

There was a convenience store, Pop In, Pop Out, a few blocks away. It was now almost eleven. Some of the store's customers were just getting their evenings going, but mine was so obviously over that I drew stares from the people milling around the beer case or in line to buy cigarettes.

The clerk looked me over and said, "You okay, honey?"

I told her I was fine, thinking she'd have to be an idiot to believe me. "I just need to use the pay phone."

She pointed me toward the back. I dialed the operator and asked to make a collect call to Candace. She was probably with George. She would tell him everything I told her the moment we hung up. Like she used to tell me.

Candace accepted the charges, and when I heard her voice, she sounded worried. "Susan, where are you?"

"Pop In, Pop Out."

I waited for her to ask more, but she didn't. She just said, "You sound awful. I'll come get you."

"What happened to you?" Candace said when she pulled up in Frank Jr.'s pickup truck. I was sitting on the bench outside the store with my arms around myself. "Why aren't you at the wedding?"

"I got caught with my date in the coat closet," I told her. "Remember that guy from Dan O'Keefe's party?"

"The spiky-hair guy? How did he end up at your dad's wedding?"

"We've been hanging out," I said, understating the truth and skipping over all the good parts, since they didn't matter now. "He was helping me with soccer. We were friends . . ."

"You never told me about him. Do you like him?"

Leave it to Candace to worry about my romantic entanglements when I looked like dusty peach roadkill. "I do. But I'll definitely never see him again." She didn't ask more, to my surprise, and I said, "Why weren't you doing something with George?"

"He was over, but I told him you needed me and he thought I should come get you by myself, so we could talk."

"Oh, sensitive," I said. And then, because I thought Candace seemed smug to announce how understanding her weird boyfriend was, I added, "Are you sure he's not just pretending to be so caring to get in your pants?"

Candace slammed on the brakes. We were close to her house. "What the fuck, Susan? Is it so impossible to believe someone really likes me?"

"No, of course not," I said, a perfunctory response. Giving thought to George Tomczak's real feelings wasn't my priority at the moment. "But do you even like him?"

"I do like him, and you'd know that if you hadn't completely ditched me for soccer," she said.

"Whatever," I told her. "You've been ditching me for guys since we hit puberty. How am I supposed to know if you actually like him, when it's always seemed you'd take anyone who'll be your boyfriend?"

"At least my love life exists in reality, unlike *some people's*," she said. "If you really did screw it up with that guy, it's probably your fault. Did you freak out when you realized you might actually be falling for a real boy instead of some made-up man creation in your head?"

"Fuck you," I said, having no other answer.

"No, fuck you," Candace said, as I got out and slammed the car door.

I walked the rest of the way home, like I should have in the first place.

Thirty

I ditched school on Monday. Mom chalked it up to my busy weekend, and the way she said it, I knew no one had told her what had really happened. "You don't have a fever," she said. "But you do look a little peaked. Too much excitement."

She was in a flurry after getting back from her trip, because she'd gotten an interview somewhere she said had a female hiring manager, which she hoped might mean a better shot at getting the job. The interview wasn't until Thursday, but she'd laid out her outfit already—the briefcase, the shoes—and while she vacuumed before leaving for work, I heard her reciting answers, or parts of them. "My strengths: staying calm, pressure, resourcefulness, attitude." I hoped more than anything she didn't have to hear about the wedding until after the interview.

Tina called and I pushed my pseudo-symptoms. "My throat really hurts," I said. "I've been throwing up." I wasn't sure those things were consistent with any particular disease, but she didn't press me. She also didn't ask about the wedding, which I thought meant maybe Candace had told her what had happened and Tina was giving me the choice to tell her. But I didn't want to. Not right then, anyway.

I still didn't go back on Tuesday. For Mom, I feigned worsening cramps and a headache. She sat with me on the couch in the morning before she left for work and we watched *Bozo's Circus Show*. Some kid cried when he missed the last bucket, and Bozo comforted him with a shoulder pat that made the kid cry harder.

After Mom had left for the day, telling me there were Lipton soup packets in the pantry and aspirin in the bathroom, I alternated the first few hours lying in my bed or on the couch, staring blankly at the ceiling or the TV, imagining what would happen if I did go back to school. I couldn't look at Bobby again, that was for sure. But I wasn't nearly as sure of anything else.

Why had I said Bobby's name in the closet? Was I really afraid of a real relationship? God, did I have any idea what I even wanted at all? Maybe I'd been fooling myself about everything, from playing soccer to thinking about college.

Tina called from a school pay phone that afternoon. I was sprawled on the floor of Mom's room, painting my toenails. I had two toes with busted purpled nails from soccer, but the three coats of red I'd used were hiding them nicely. "What's going on?" she asked. "You never miss two days in a row."

"Cramps, horrible ones," I lied.

"Mmm-hmm," she said. "And yesterday you were throwing up, with a sore throat. When do you think these cramps will subside? Everyone was looking for you at practice yesterday. Bobby seemed really concerned, too."

Telling her that I wasn't ever coming back to practice seemed like something she deserved to hear in person. And, ugh, did I have to tell the whole team, because I was the captain? The title felt like a booby prize, a concession you gave someone too stupid to realize it meant nothing, like the cases of Rice-A-Roni they gave to the loser on a game show. For a second, you thought at least you'd gotten something, until you had to lug twenty pounds of rice to the airport. If I wasn't captain, I could just stop showing up.

"I'll be back soon," I said.

I guess that wasn't enough for Tina, though, because she showed up at my house that day after practice. The doorbell rang, nearly startling me off the couch, from which I hadn't moved in several hours. I ignored it for the first buzz, but it kept ringing and ringing so I couldn't hear *Family Feud*. I dragged myself to the door, figuring that if it was someone selling something, at least the hour of boredom I'd spent curling my hair that morning could be appreciated. (I thought I looked like a brunette Judith Light on *One Life to Live*, but I might have been delusional from my TV fog.) Before I'd opened it all the way, Tina stepped inside.

"I know you're not sick," she said. She set down my equipment bag on the floor. "I told Bobby I'd give this to you. It was in his car."

"Thanks," I said, thinking maybe I'd throw it away later. Tina was studying my hair. She pointed at me like she'd figured something out. "Are you sneaking out somewhere? Candace told me you guys had a fight, and something went wrong with that Joe guy."

Wordlessly, I led her to the kitchen and she followed me. "Okay, you're starting to scare me," she said.

I opened a can of Cheez Balls, set it on the table, and got us two bottles of soda from the fridge. I sat. She sat. We each ate a Cheez Ball.

"Do you have anything else to eat? I'm starving. Practice was rough," she said. I wondered what they'd learned. Bobby had promised to work with us more on improving our fakes, which he was probably good at, because he was one.

I pulled lunch meat and cheese from the fridge and set it in front of Tina and opened my bottle of RC. "I'm done with soccer," I said finally, like I thought this would go down easier with the food. "It's stupid. We can't even get a game."

Straying from the real reason was shitty of me, but as I said it, I thought maybe it could be true. Hadn't this whole thing really only been an experiment to see what could happen with Bobby? I'd learned that. I'd screwed up a real thing with Joe for an imagined thing with Bobby.

"Bullshit," Tina said, flicking a Cheez Ball at my hair. It stuck to one of my sprayed curls. I plucked it out and ate it. "What happened at the wedding?"

"Me. I happened. I . . . called Joe 'Bobby' at the exact worst time, because I'm an *idiot*, and that didn't go over well at all."

"Poor Joe—that had to mess with his ego," Tina said. "But you can fix that, can't you?"

I shook my head. "I don't know. I haven't talked to him."

"Well, first things first. You should try," she said. "But what does it all have to do with Bobby and soccer?"

"I don't want to play for him anymore." I liked the way the words stuck in the air, their finality. I had never been sure about what I wanted, but it was nice to know what I didn't want.

"But do you want to play *soccer*?" Tina said, taking a big bite of her sandwich. I was almost jealous because the hunger after practice was so much more gratifying to satisfy than the hunger after sitting around all day and curling my hair was.

I thought about the field, and the feeling when I ran, and the surge in my chest when I managed to knee the ball—a new trick—and kick it off the top of my foot like it was something I was born doing and not something I'd only recently learned. I thought of what Joe had said about sports, how they got you to do ridiculous stuff but that was sort of the point. I sure as hell wanted to play soccer. Goddamn it. I wanted to *not* want to.

"Yeah, I wanna play. I miss you guys," I said. "But I don't want to play for him. He's . . . not who I thought he was."

"So? What does he have to do with it?" she said. There was no escaping her penetrating stare. I squirmed.

"He's the coach." I wouldn't meet her eyes as I rolled a piece of bologna and bit it.

Tina got her impatient look, like I was being intentionally dense and she was annoyed to have to exert herself to enlighten me. "I don't know what went down and you're obviously not going to tell me," she said. "But who cares if he's not who you thought he would be? I love driving, and you didn't see me not getting my license because the DMV sent me out with a tester who called me princess and asked if I knew which one was the brake. I hated that guy. I wanted to open the passenger door and push him out,

I was so angry. But I wanted to drive more. I think you like soccer enough that even if a mouthbreather like Paul Mahoney was coaching, you'd want to play."

"That happened to you at the DMV?"

"That's not the point," she said.

"I think I'd rather play for Paul Mahoney than Bobby."

"I won't even entertain that idea. I saw him reach down into his pants to adjust himself today and then put that same hand into a bag of chips." Tina winced at the memory. "But you're obviously going to be stubborn. And I mostly wanted to deliver your equipment bag as an excuse to talk about something else."

"Something else sounds great." I chided myself for not asking Tina right away what was going on with her. "What's up?"

"So you know how Todd has to be covert when he calls my house?"

I nodded.

"Well, he flubbed. He said he was Victor, my chem lab partner, but I took chemistry last year . . ."

"Uh-oh."

"Yep." Tina traced the opening of her soda bottle with her fingertip as she stared at our ugly yellow-and-brown wallpaper. "And my mom point-blank said, 'Who is this, really?' And Todd said Todd Lindholm, because he didn't want to lie anymore."

"So now what?"

"Well, now I have to be home by six thirty every night." She glanced at the clock. "And no phone until I tell my parents what's going on."

"Have you talked to Todd?"

331

She nodded. "I called him after practice, from the pay phones. And I think he doesn't understand why I won't just own up to it. I don't understand, either."

I thought of the way Tina's house was filled with photos of her, scrapbooks devoted to every certificate and achievement award she'd ever received. How her mom had even sent away for a college brochure from Oxford University in England, "just in case."

"Maybe you know that once you tell them, it'll change the story they have written for you," I said, thinking of Bobby and the story I had made up for him.

"I think I'm most scared because what if my mom is right? I want a lot of the same stuff for me that she does, and what if it turns out Todd won't fit in with my plans?"

We'd finished the Cheez Balls. I wished we hadn't. I needed one. "Maybe he won't. But so far, he does, and he supports you. Plus, you love him. Whatever you decide you want to do with your life, don't you want to do it for the real you?"

Tina wrinkled her nose at me and stared at my face with skepticism, like she was accusing it of saying the wrong thing.

"You're annoyingly right." She flicked me on the arm.

"I know." I flicked her back. Even if I wouldn't have soccer, or Joe, and might have lost Candace, I still had Tina, and being able to give her good advice made me hopeful that I wouldn't screw that up, too.

"I might have to ease my way into telling them," Tina said.

"If you don't kick the ball when you can, you'll never know if you made the shot."

"Look at you, with your soccer metaphors." Tina looked satisfied. "You'll be back on the team."

"Yeah, if Bobby's gone, I'll come back," I said.

"You better tell me if he's a serial killer."

"He's not," I said. "Take a shower before you talk to your mom. You smell."

Tina smirked. "Okay, and you enjoy your fake-ass cramps."

I thought all night about what Tina had said, but I still couldn't see the point of playing. I had existed before soccer, and I didn't need it to survive. It wasn't a boyfriend like Todd who felt like a soul mate. I'd used soccer to get close to Bobby and kept playing because I thought he saw something special in me. But he was a liar. I didn't have potential. I wasn't going to get a scholarship. There was never anything special between us, and there never would be. I hated the girl who thought that. She was stupid, and I didn't want to be reminded of her.

Still, all night I dreamed of playing.

I woke up Wednesday, the day Mom went in to work early so she could make it to her night class, wondering if I should go to school. It was also November 7, a date I remembered as Bobby's birthday from Dana's early reconnaissance on him. I wished him an awful one. Part of me wanted to go to school just so I could ignore him if I saw him.

The phone rang. I checked the clock: seven thirty. I wondered if it was Tina.

I tried to sound deathly ill when I answered. "Hello?" I croaked.

"Hello. May I speak to Susan Klintock, please?"

His voice was unmistakable. I started to hang up.

"Wait," he said. "Susan?"

"Yeah." *Whatever, Bobby,* I thought. *Did you get older and wiser today, or are you still going to fuck Jacqueline for money tonight?*

"Look . . ." I heard voices behind him, and he was almost whispering. He must have been in the athletic office already.

"I saw," I said harshly.

He ignored my remark, or maybe let it sink in. I could see him in his algebra teacher clothes, hunched toward the phone in the corner of his desk. "I know that situation was . . . strange," he said. "But the team's wondering about you. And so am I."

Hearing him still had an effect on me; the slight rumble underneath his voice, especially over the phone like this, made me shiver. I knew I could never see him again or I'd have to fight off the attraction that I wanted not to feel.

I needed to end this, cut it cleanly, the way a smoker who wanted to quit had to flush cigarettes down the toilet because she was afraid the trash can wasn't going far enough. "You can tell them that I'm done."

I hung up. I stood next to the phone, staring at it, wondering if he'd call again, wondering if I could keep my resolve. But nothing happened.

Finally, I picked it up and dialed the attendance office. I tried not to cry as I pretended to be my mom and said, "Susan Klintock won't be at school today."

Thirty-One

After the call from Bobby, I went from sad to angry to deflated. I didn't even have the energy to turn on the TV. Candace was right. I did live in a fantasy land, and I'd let it wreck my reality.

Mom called at ten. I must have sounded really bad when I answered, because the first words out of her mouth were, "Do you need me to come home?"

"No, Mom, I'm fine," I said. "Or feeling better. I'll be able to go back tomorrow." I had to. Now that I'd told Bobby I was done, I could be done. He'd tell the team and I'd go back to Regularly Scheduled Susan.

I only had a little more than a month until midterms and winter break, and then maybe I could convince my mom to let me get a GED instead of returning to Powell Park for the rest of junior and senior years. Who was I kidding, thinking college was a real possibility?

"Okay, well, I told Polly she could swing by," Mom said. "She wanted to drop off something you apparently left at the wedding."

Oh no. What could I have left at the wedding? My dignity? My father's love, or at least any chance of his approval? Joe? No, he'd left me.

I didn't want to see her, but I owed it to her to be here so she could tell me in person how awful I was. I deserved the punishment.

I got dressed, in a newish pair of jeans and an actual blouse that I ironed. I looked like someone who was capital G, capital P Going Places—that would be the title of the photo spread in *Seventeen*. But Polly would see through my lousy disguise.

When the bell rang, I went to answer it like I had no idea who I'd see on the other side. Polly wore a crisp blouse, too, pink, with fuchsia slacks. Her version of put-together so exceeded mine, it felt like a slap in the face.

"It looks like you're feeling better," Polly said in her usual voice. Her tone contained not one iota of malice. "I thought we could get a sandwich. If you're up for it. Veli's?"

My mouth watered. I hadn't had a Veli's patty melt since the summer. They were my favorite. "Okay," I said.

We got in Polly's maroon Caprice. A Road Runner air freshener dangled from the rearview. "This is a nice car," I said.

"Don't tell anyone, but it's a bit of a clunker," she said. "My dad couldn't sell it, and so it's my wedding present." She put the car in gear and pulled away from the curb, nodding her head to the Billy Joel album in the 8-track player. "I should have asked you if you wanted to drive."

"It's okay," I said, listening to the crunch of the leaves under the tires.

At Veli's we found a booth, and a waitress filled our water and took our order. Veli's rushed everyone. "I haven't been here in so long," Polly said. "I always go to the Denny's by the car lot."

"I love this place," I said. Why weren't we talking about what happened? This was worse than if she'd laid into me immediately.

The waitress brought our drinks. Polly took a sip of her iced tea before she slid a long, thin box across the table. "I forgot to give you your maid of honor gift," she said.

Did she not know what I'd done? Or maybe the gift was a dog turd she'd smushed and wrapped. I tore away the creamy paper and opened the velvet box inside.

"Oh my God," I said. It was a golden necklace with a floating heart charm. A small emerald sat just above the tip of the heart. It was like one I'd pointed out to my mom last Christmas, knowing I wouldn't get it. I loved it.

"Your mom gave me some ideas," Polly said.

I closed the box. "I can't take this," I said. "I was more like a maid of dishonor." I had to get it out in the open. Polly was taking the good stepmom thing too far.

But she just smirked knowingly. It was the first display of something bordering on sarcasm I'd ever seen from her, and I knew, almost with relief, that she was aware of what had happened, and I wouldn't have to explain it to her.

"Of course, there's a time and a place for everything . . ." She paused.

I waited, hands wrapped around my Coke, for her to say that now was the time and place where she'd loudly tell all of Veli's that I was a sex fiend who'd ruined her wedding.

"But who cares?" Polly took another prim sip of her iced tea, and then clapped her hands together to admire the bowl of chicken and rice soup the waitress set before her.

"I do," I said. "I ruined everything." My sandwich was in front of me and my stomach rumbled, but I didn't want to take a bite until Polly had realized how mad she should be.

She neatly dipped her spoon into her soup and lifted it to her mouth. "My mother told me I looked bloated, and that it doesn't matter your dad is older since I probably can't have children, because I'm so old. I'm only thirty-five. And my uncle grabbed my ass at the bar." She dipped her spoon again and swirled it around a bit. "You, on the other hand, made me feel like you're actually happy to be my stepdaughter. I'm sure it wasn't fun for you or Joe to be . . . discovered like that. But I'm not a dope. You brought an extremely cute boy to the wedding, and this may be more than I should say, but I know good chemistry when I see it."

"Saw it," I said. "That's over."

"I won't be nosy and ask for details. You can tell me if and when you want to. We were worried about you, though, leaving. Your father, too. He thought you went to find Joe, and then we couldn't find you."

I hadn't even thought of that. "I'm sorry to have made you worry."

"I should be ticked off at you, I know, but I also had this weird thought that this must be what it's like to have your own family. It's not just getting fancy photos taken for the mantel. There's all the stuff you don't commemorate, too." She sipped her tea again. "Plus, I made your dad drive by your mom's house that night to make sure you were okay. There were lights on and I saw you watching TV in your dress."

"From the street?"

Polly blushed. "No. I peeked in the window. I'll never forget creeping in the bushes on my wedding night. I assumed you didn't want company."

I gulped, touching the velvet jewelry box. The soft texture was soothing. "You did all that?"

She shrugged. "I figured it was an awkward moment for us all, but part of the growing process. I imagine it's hard to have a parent remarry."

I plunged into my sandwich, unable to wait any longer. It was perfect, melty and greasy. Once I swallowed the bite, I said, "Are you a real person? How can you be so calm about this?"

"I'm not, really. I have worried every day since we told you we were getting married that I would say the wrong thing to you, or force you to wear a dress you hate, or seem like I'm trying to take your mom's place. I'm a mess." Polly took another messless spoonful of soup. "You may think you screwed up, but all I've seen is a girl who handled her father's remarriage with nothing but grace. I appreciate that. And I adore you."

"Um, thank you," I said. I wanted to say something nice back but I was still confused.

"That wasn't too much like I was trying to be your mom, was it?" Polly said, holding her breath as she waited for my answer.

"No," I said. "It was like you."

She got up from the booth and sat down next to me. She hugged me and I hugged her back, grateful that my dad had picked this person and had once picked my mom. He had good taste, for someone with a bad haircut.

I was crying a little when we let go. "Dad hates me, though," I said. "He's never going to look at me again."

Polly waved this away. "Your dad still has some things to learn about women. And honestly, he was so shocked by the whole thing that it gave me a good opportunity to discuss female sexuality with him." She put a hand up to her mouth. "I'm sorry, that probably grossed you out."

"You owed me," I said, laughing a little. "But seriously, I do feel really bad that I left, and the whole . . . incident. I saw your wish book. Those things were not in it."

Polly laughed. "My wish book is a fantasy, Susan. There's a picture in there of a couple making their vows while they sit on white horses on a beach."

"Sounds nice. As long as you like horses."

"Sure, it sounds dreamy, and when I was younger, I did think about this big day and had so many expectations. But my real life is better, because it's *mine*. Like sitting here with you right now? I'm not going to forget this, even if the circumstances getting here aren't the kind of thing you glue into a wish book." she said. She reached across the table and put her hand over mine, and she didn't start speaking again until I looked into her eyes. "Wishes are great and fantasizing is fun, but when it comes down to it, some of the stuff we cook up in our heads probably would not be as great as we think it would. And then some stuff—like for me, having a relationship with you—might not be what we imagined, but is something so much better."

"But what about when you go for something that isn't vows on white horses, but more realistic? And maybe you get it or almost get it, but it ends up being disappointing?"

"I guess you try to not let disappointments turn you into someone who stops trying," Polly said. She sounded like my mom talking about going for the job she wanted even if it didn't work out. Maybe that was why they got along. "Or into my mother."

"It's weird that you're related to her," I said.

"Thank you for that," Polly said.

"I know you're right, but sometimes figuring out what I want in real life scares me. Like getting this necklace after wanting it so much. Now I have it and I'm afraid I could lose it someday."

"And you might, but does that mean you never want to wear it?"

I shook my head and pulled the necklace box toward me. "Can you help me put this on?"

"Of course." Polly gently lifted the necklace from its box, and I held up my hair as she looped it around my neck. Her cool fingertips fastened the clasp, and she turned me around to admire it.

I liked the weight of the necklace, and the coolness of the metal. I'd wanted it so badly last Christmas. Maybe what Polly had said wasn't *entirely* true. Some wishes did turn out exactly like you'd hoped.

Thirty-Two

I sat in front of my mirror, looking at my necklace.

Polly was right. I might never have fantasized about soccer, and I had found it only because of a crush on Bobby, who had disappointed me. But that didn't change how much I loved the game. Maybe there were pages in my mental wish book that I should tear out and other ones that I could write anew. I could make something happen, even if it was a colossal failure.

I was going to get a real game against St. Mark's.

And maybe it didn't have to be a failure. When we kicked their asses in reality, it would be better than any daydream.

When Mom got home from her night class at eight, I asked if I could borrow the car.

"You look like a new person," she said, holding out the keys. She gestured to my chest. "The necklace is pretty on you."

"Thanks for telling Polly I wanted it," I said, admiring my mom. How cool was it that she could let my dad's new wife do something nice for me without feeling threatened by it? I hugged her suddenly.

"What's this for?" she asked, hugging me back.

I shrugged. "No reason. But I have to tell you something." I'd debated whether I really wanted to say what I was about to say. But Polly knew, and Dad knew, and it seemed unfair for Mom not to know.

I told her the whole story, starting with the game, all the way up to what had happened with Joe. I even told her about how hot and heavy things had been, and how I'd called him the wrong name. My mom always tried to be open with me, and she deserved to be trusted.

She listened with the kind of diligent precision you saw from doctors on TV. It was the kind of listening you'd expect from a mom who'd once carefully explained the workings of the vagina to you.

When I was done, she inhaled one slow breath through her nose and exhaled.

"Well, it sounds like you like this boy," my mom said. "But I don't know that I have good advice for how to smooth things over with him. Except maybe being honest."

"Polly isn't mad, but I think Dad thinks I'm a deviant or something," I told her. ". . . Are you mad?"

Mom rubbed her temple, as if the answer was waiting there. "I'm not going to be upset with you for doing something utterly natural. As for your choice of venue, being caught by your father in a private moment was punishment enough. If it helps, I'm sure someday you'll be able to laugh at this."

Having my mom and Polly both react so serenely to something I'd thought was a major fuck-up felt like the kind of gift you couldn't accept, because it was so extravagant. But maybe it wasn't a gift, when someone understood you. Maybe letting someone understand you was an exchange you both got something out of.

"Can I still have the keys?" I asked her.

"Yes," she said, extending them to me again. "But fill it up. I have that interview tomorrow."

"I know," I said. "And you're going to be great." I kissed her on the cheek and charged down the steps. I was going to be great, too, but I needed a game.

Joe's car was parked out front of his house, and it felt like a good sign. I realized how badly I wanted to see him, even if I knew I couldn't expect it to go well.

I parked carefully, not wanting to screw up Mom's car before her big morning. Crossing the street, I adjusted my posture and smoothed my hair a little. I was glad I still had on my Going Places outfit. It was evening, so Joe's parents were probably home; if his mom answered, and on the chance that Joe had ever mentioned me, she'd be pleased to associate my name with this straight-backed girl with nice hair. I was past worrying about a lot of things at the moment, but I still wanted my friends' moms to like me.

I rang the bell and waited with my hands folded. It was Joe who opened the door, as a woman's voice—clearly his mom's—called from the other room, "Joe, you're staying in tonight, remember?"

He rolled his eyes. "Yeah, Ma, don't worry. It's no one." He turned back to me.

"Thanks a lot," I said.

Joe didn't laugh. "I think you have the wrong house," he said pointedly.

"I'm really sor—"

"You don't have to say you're sorry." His voice lacked its usual charged tone, and his flat stare was the opposite of welcoming. But he hadn't slammed the door in my face. That was something.

"Sometimes I don't," I said. "But to you, I do. So whether you want to hear it or not, I'm really sorry." Then, even though I didn't want to admit it, I offered a real explanation. "I did have a crush on Bobby. I think you suspected that. I . . . sort of . . . had this story in my head about him—a fantasy—and when you were making me feel so good, it surfaced. It wasn't like I'd have rather been with him. I wanted—*want*—to be with you. And I know I blew it, but you deserve to know the truth."

He didn't smile or respond, but he listened. Maybe he wasn't unserious about everything.

"If you don't like me, I understand," I continued, hoping he'd protest. He didn't. "Still, I wanted to ask if you'd help me get a rematch with St. Mark's."

"Did he want you to get the game?" I knew that by "he," Joe meant Bobby.

"This isn't about him," I said. "I don't want to see him anymore. I'm team captain and I decided."

Joe's eyes flickered, just slightly, and he caught his mouth before he grinned.

"Your graffiti went over well," he said, and I was happy that he couldn't resist paying this small compliment. "Everyone went fucking nuts on Monday."

I shrugged nonchalantly, even as the flash of the old Joe gave me a surge of hope.

"Thanks, but they owe us a game," I said. "Can you help me or not?"

Joe leaned against the doorframe, long arms, long legs, dark hair a little messy. I didn't breathe, waiting for his answer. If he said he'd help, he still liked me. If he said he wouldn't, well . . .

He finally spoke. "Look, if you want them to take you seriously, you need to get the game yourself," he said. Deep down I knew he was right. He pulled away from the door and stepped into the house. "Now I have to get back inside. *CHiPS* is on."

"You hate *CHiPS*," I reminded him.

He grinned, big, but not for me. "Sure do," he said sarcastically and shut the door.

I turned to leave, my legs weak. He hadn't wanted to help me. He didn't like me. A sob crept up my throat, but I forced it down.

I was waiting to cross the street to Mom's car when I heard Joe's door open again. I spun around, hating how hopeful I was it would be him, when it was more likely one of his parents, taking out the garbage. But there was Joe. "They had an away game tonight," he said. "They probably just got back. They'll be at Wojo's by now."

I looked him dead in the eye and, hoping my smile would communicate more than appreciation for that bit of information, said, "Thanks, Joe."

"Sure, champ." My heart fluttered, hearing him call me that. Maybe I had a chance.

I left Joe's and went straight to Wojo's before I had time to think about it. I flipped on the radio, hoping for a song that would psych me up. "Gimme Shelter" or something equally powerful. Instead, ABBA poured out, "Take a Chance on Me" filling the car with pert Swedish pop. It was not going to make me feel like someone who couldn't be trifled with, but as I started to sing along, the song wasn't important. I *was* someone who couldn't be trifled with, or streaked by, or sprayed with douche and pelted with underwear. I was also so nervous that I half hoped the team wouldn't be there when I arrived.

But as I pulled into the small parking lot next to the restaurant, I could see Ken holding court with the rest of the team at the booth with the best view of the street. Facing that way, they wouldn't see me as I came in the side door.

My hands trembled as I flipped down the car door lock and got out. I made my way into the restaurant. My mouth had gone dry at the same time a red heat rose under my hair, sending a trickle of sweat down the back of my neck. There were so many of them, and one of me. If they wanted to humiliate me, they had the numbers.

Susan, I told myself, *the last few days have been a huge mess. How bad could this be?*

Wojo's was a tiny place and it was always packed. They had a white menu board that was overwhelmed with black plastic

347

letters offering anything you could make on a grill or deep-fry, but the real draw were the seventy flavors of milkshake spelled out on a painted sign next to the register.

It was also, I now remembered, impossible to enter without someone seeing you. As soon as I walked inside, one of Ken's friends heard the door chime and swiveled his head toward me. He tapped Ken's shoulder and Ken whipped around.

"Well, if it isn't Soccer Barbie," he said as I took my first steps toward his table. He looked me up and down and then looked back at his friends. "Or really more like Soccer Skipper."

They all laughed like he was fucking Richard Pryor or something. I didn't waste an ounce of energy to flip him off or think of a response. I knew what I wanted to say, and stumbling over a witty reply wasn't going to get me there.

"Are you here for another show?" Ken said. "Because there's a strict No Shirts, No Shoes, No Service policy. But we can arrange something for another time." He patted his upper thighs.

The entire team laughed again. I wanted to leave. I couldn't breathe.

Now Ken turned in his chair and looked up at me, like I was lost. "Can't you talk? Are you here by mistake? This is a guys' soccer team. And we're not looking for cheerleaders."

"Our cheerleaders would be better looking," one of Ken's buddies said.

"She's not bad," Ken countered, and stared at my butt in a way that made me uncomfortable.

Stay focused, Susan, I reminded myself, clenching my fists at my sides. I wanted to do something cool, like put my hands on the table and loom over Ken threateningly. But with the way he kept staring at me like I was a five-foot-three Wojo's milkshake, I crossed my hands over my chest instead.

"I know why you didn't play us," I said, my voice shaking. "You were too scared."

"Yeah, right," a guy in a baseball cap by the window said.

"We just didn't want to hurt you," Ken said, almost sweetly, as he put his chin in his hand and batted his eyelashes at me. Every bone in my body wanted me to knock him down and punch him for as hard and as long as I could.

I took a step back toward him and pointed my finger in his face so fast, he flinched. Just a little, but he knew he'd done it. "Nope. You were scared," I said. "Just like you were scared Joe was better than you, so you took him out instead of trying to earn your position fair and square."

Baseball hat guy said, "What's she talking about, Ken?"

"He won't tell you," I said, as Ken squirmed. "He's a cowardly turd . . . no, less than that. He's a shit stain, just like the ones in his underwear."

Now Ken pushed up from his chair so he was standing over me. "Fuck this," he said, the smell of his onion breath curling sourly in my nose. "I don't care if we hurt you. You want a game? You're fucking on."

I smiled my best Polly smile. "Great," I said chipperly. I handed him a slip of paper I'd written out in advance with a date and time on it. "Your field again. And you'd better show up to play. Wear clean underwear this time, in case you need to go to the hospital."

I turned and walked to the door, praying they couldn't see how wobbly my legs were.

"We'll be there," Ken said to my back.

I flipped him off over my shoulder without looking back.

I didn't need to see his face. I'd wait to enjoy his expression when we beat him.

Thirty-Three

On Thursday, while she was styling her hair, I put a note in mom's briefcase wishing her luck on her interview. Then I put on my soccer jersey. It was still as sweat-stain yellow and hideous as the day I'd gotten it, but today it felt like armor. It said, "Keep away from me, because I don't care what you think."

Tina came to give me a ride and, when she saw me in my jersey, said, "I thought you were done with soccer."

"I'm done with Bobby," I told her. Then I grinned. "But I got us a rematch against St. Mark's."

Tina landed a heavy foot on the brakes, stopping way before the intersection. "Are you crazy?"

"What have we got to lose?" I asked her.

"Teeth," she said. "After the St. Skid-Marks thing, they're going to want to kill us."

"Yeah, they definitely do," I said. "But we can't let them scare us. The team needs this."

"And I'm the first one you told?" Tina looked like she would throw me out of the car if this wasn't the case.

"Yes."

"Okay then," she said with a little smile. She pulled away from the curb and continued to school. "You're getting awfully bold, Suzie Q."

"Yeah," I said. "So spill—did you talk to your mom?"

Tina nodded, never taking her eyes off the road. "I started to. She knows about Todd, and that we've been dating awhile. It wasn't pretty. She's mad I was keeping secrets. But after some fireworks, she and my stepdad said they want to meet him."

"How do you feel?"

Tina pursed her lips as we stopped at a light. "Relief that it's out in the open, and that Todd is really happy," she said. "But terrified that he's going to let it slip that he opted out of senior-year calculus to take an extra art class."

"Maybe they can meet him at the game," I said.

"Thanks for that. Now I can worry about some St. Mark's dickhead breaking my jaw instead of my mom asking Todd about his intentions."

She put the car in gear without releasing the clutch all the way, and it made a grinding sound. I gawked at her. I'd never seen her make a driving mistake, even a small one. "Don't worry about anything," I said. "We're going to be fine." I half believed myself.

I skipped homeroom—after three days out, it didn't seem to matter—and went straight to the athletic office. The nervous hitch in my step was different than it had been the night before at Wojo's. Then, I'd been afraid of how the boys would act; today, I was more afraid of how I would. I didn't want seeing Bobby again to alter my resolve.

My heart pounded in my chest so hard, it seemed to be powering me forward as I neared the door to the athletic office. The sounds of students in the hallway melted together into a pulsating drumbeat. I felt like Michael Corleone in *The Godfather*, which my dad took me to see when they brought it back in a theater. There was a part where Michael makes a promise to his family to kill a cop who allowed his dad to be shot, and he goes to a bathroom to find the gun he'll need but he's fumbling as a train rumbles by because even though he's done big things before, he knows this is the most important, biggest thing he's ever done. He knows that when he pulls the trigger and the cop dies, things will never be the same. That was me. And my pledge was to myself and my team. How Bobby saw me didn't matter anymore. Or it was a sacrifice I was willing to make.

I marched into the office, where Bobby was alone, grading algebra quizzes. He looked up with the same drop-jawed expression he'd had when I caught him with Jacqueline. Before he could speak, I said, "We have a rematch against St. Mark's. I'll tell the team at practice today."

His mouth closed and his eyes softened with concern. He was about to say something he thought was important. Some excuse, something that could smooth things over. But maybe he thought better of it, because he said, "Susan . . . we can find other games."

"The season's almost over. And I want this game. We play on November sixteenth." I turned to go.

"Here, sit down." Bobby gestured to the chair next to his desk. "I got a real chair, no bucket."

I shook my head. "I didn't come here to talk," I said. "And I'm not asking permission. I'm the captain."

He put down his red pen and turned his chair toward me. "And a good one. My favorite player, but don't tell anyone else I said that."

I didn't know if he meant it or if he was just trying to patch things up, but hearing him say the words had none of its former effect on me. I'd never really known him, not like I knew Candace, or Tina, or even Joe. Knowing someone meant understanding their flaws as well as their strengths. Bobby, who I'd only known parts of—whose blank spots I'd filled in myself—was not one of those people.

"You're too good for Jacqueline," I said.

He gathered his papers into a neat pile, grabbing the red pen and a stack of blank worksheets from his desk. The bell for first period rang. "Not good enough to refuse her money," he said, standing up. "Sometimes, we tell ourselves we have good reasons for doing the wrong thing."

"I thought you were better than that," I told him.

"All I can say is, I'm still learning, too," he said, his eyes meeting mine. "That might not be what you want to hear, but just because I talk about 'personal bests' doesn't mean I've hit mine."

"Maybe it's not about being your best all the time," I said. "Maybe it's about screwing up, and knowing that what matters about our mistakes is fixing them."

He gave me a wry smile. "You might be right," he said, not apologizing.

But then, did he really owe me an apology? He was just a man.

Everything else I'd thought of him had been my own creation.

"I can stay out of your way for a while, let you lead the team," he said. "But I hope you'll want me to be your coach again."

I let this settle. The notion that he wanted some role in my life was flattering, and I almost felt sorry for him as he stood there in his algebra teacher clothes. His collar was a little yellow. I wondered if it always had been, and I just hadn't let myself notice.

"All I want is to kick a goal so hard past Ken's face that it feels like a close shave of the beard he can't grow," I told him. "Whether you're my coach or not."

Together, we walked out into the hallway, now mostly empty except for a smattering of students late for class. "I'm your coach," he said. "All the way."

"Then it's settled," I told him.

We walked next to each other, without talking, to the end of the hall and turned separate ways when we reached the trophy case at the end.

"See you at practice," Bobby said.

"Okay," I said. Then added, "Coach."

Some habits were hard to break.

Thirty-Four

Bobby and Tina might have been on board with the St. Mark's rematch—or, first match, technically—but the team was taking some convincing. Even as we practiced longer, and were now allowed to use the football field at night when the boys were done with it, the school's attention was going to winter sports, and whatever small amount of money the school had been funneling toward us was coming in a much narrower trickle. We had started the season with nearly twenty balls and now were down to ten serviceable ones. The temporary goals we had to use on the football field needed new nets, and some of Bobby's beloved cones had been crushed to the point that they couldn't be revived. One night, the grounds crew even turned off the field lights on us midpractice.

"Do you really think this is a good idea?" Dana asked me that night as we brought equipment back inside to the athletic office. "Playing an actual game against them?"

"We know it is," I told her, trying to forget a few sloppy moments in practice when it felt like we'd gone back to the soccer know-nothings we'd been in September. "We just need to treat them like any other team."

"We've only played one other team, though." She was trying to knock out a dent in one of the remaining cones, and focusing on her task. She looked up and said, "I didn't mean that to sound snotty."

"It didn't," I said. She had a point, too. We'd played only one game in nearly three months. The team wasn't forgetting how to play; we were tired, and having no one at the school seem to give a rat's ass about us wasn't exactly a morale booster. "We need something to cheer everyone up."

"There's the pep rally," she said.

The pep rally for fall sports was the capper to the season. One last all-school assembly to give a hurrah to the fall athletes before the winter dance and the transition to winter sports. It was due to take place right before the winter dance, the day before our game.

"Perfect," I said.

While Bobby had been calling most of the shots during practice, he'd also been deferring to me to talk to the team at the end of each one. Most days I didn't know what to say, but after practice the next night, when he said, "Anything to add, Susan?" I was prepared.

"We should all wear our jerseys tomorrow for the pep rally," I said. "We deserve some school support, and we've all been working hard, so let's remind the student body that we're here and we're not going away."

"Like, and go out in front of the whole school?" Franchesa said.

"Our game's not even official," Wendy said.

"I think it's a great idea," Marie said.

"Me too," Tina seconded.

"Then it's settled," I said. "Let's get ourselves some pep."

The day of the pep rally, as seventh-period classes filed into the main gym, the girls met up near my locker so we could walk in as a team and take seats near the floor together. When we arrived, the boys' football, tennis, and cross-country teams were taking up most of the lower bleachers, and the two girls' teams that had been around longer—badminton and swimming—were positioned in the rows behind them. No space had been marked off for girls' soccer. We were standing next to the gym doors, and when Bobby arrived with the rest of the coaches, he came right over to us. If we felt ignored as soccer players, Bobby certainly wasn't as the soccer coach. Almost every set of female eyes in the gym turned toward him.

"I don't know why we don't have bleacher space," Bobby said. "I'm sure it was just an oversight."

The pep rally began with a few words from the principal, followed by a routine by the Powell Park cheerleaders that was more or less a repeat of what they'd done for the pre-homecoming pep rally, which had only been for the football team. Afterward, the coaches called their teams to the floor. The six guys on the tennis team and the twelve on cross-country drew only slightly more applause and whoops than the girls' badminton and swim teams. When football's Coach Stevens came to the floor, people stomped on the bleachers and called out "Thompson!" "Tenley!"

and "Wallinski!"—the team's senior captains. The enthusiasm was so high, I had to remind myself they were four and six on the season.

"There's no way they're putting us on after that," I said, whipping my head around at Bobby. "They forgot us!"

"What the hell?" Marie said. "This is . . ."

"Bullshit," Tina finished for her.

"I'll fix it," Bobby said. He strode to the center of the gym and whispered something to Coach Stevens, who shrugged and handed him the mic.

"Nice ass," a girl's voice called from somewhere high in the bleachers.

"I lost my G spot, can you help me find it?" someone else yelled from the other side.

Bobby ignored the catcalls and cleared his throat into the mic.

"Go back to the disco," a guy hollered.

I almost felt bad for Bobby.

"I think you've missed a team," Bobby said. "Your first Powell Park girls' soccer team came together—"

Marie snickered at that. Dawn said, "Cut it, Quinn."

"—We were still getting our bearings as the school year started, so you haven't met the fine team we've put together. These girls have been working hard all season, and I think you should all give them some Powell Park pride." Bobby then began calling each of our names.

As Dawn, Marie, Tina, and the rest of the girls jogged onto the gym floor to stand on either side of him, there wasn't loud applause, but no one was booing us, either.

"And finally, team captain Susan Klintock," he said, waving me out to join them. I jogged out and, not even thinking what I was doing, grabbed the mic from Bobby.

"Coach McMann didn't mention it, but we've been working hard and we've got a game against the St. Mark's boys' team tomorrow afternoon," I said, looking out into the sea of faces staring at us. "Five p.m., their field. I know how much Powell Park hates the St. Mark's Knights, so I hope to see you all there."

Invoking St. Mark's actually drew some louder cheers. For us. "Kick their ass," someone yelled. "St. Mark's sucks!" came another bellow. "Hell, yeah!" someone else screamed. Maybe we had support. Or maybe everyone was glad the pep rally was nearly over.

As the crowd grew rowdier, the athletic director stepped in to take the mic from me. "That game's not sanctioned," he said to me in a gruff whisper.

"You can't pretend to care now," I said, thrusting the mic back at him as we left the gym floor. As the band began to play the school song, the team converged on me in the hallway, everyone in a frenzy.

"Did you seriously invite the whole damn school to our game?" Tina said, her expression one of fear and awe.

"I think I did," I said.

"I don't know—" Bobby started, but Marie cut him off.

"You've got balls!" she said.

"Who needs balls when you've got a giant vagina?" Franchesa said, then frowned. "That came out weird."

The pep rally broke up, and the double doors on either side of

360

us burst open. Students poured out and some of them said nice things, like "You guys are pretty badass!" "I'll be there tomorrow!" and "Crush 'em!" The captain of the boys' cross-country team, John Patel—we'd met once in the weight room—even stopped and said, "Good luck tomorrow. We'll try to be there after our practice." He extended his hand for me to shake. "Guys' cross-country doesn't exactly get much respect. I think it's the lack of testosterone-fueled violence. So I know where you're coming from."

I gratefully took his hand. "Thanks," I said. "We'll be at your next meet, too."

As he departed, the team stood in a circle, looking at each other, and the charge between us was palpable. But as people dispersed and the hallway grew more silent, it really sank in. I'd invited the whole school to watch us play.

"What do we do now?" Wendy said. "What if they all show up?" I couldn't tell if she was excited about the prospect or dreading it.

"What if we lose?" Dana asked, as if this possibility only now crossed her mind. A loss, and my fear that we'd suffer one, had made sleeping hard for me.

"We give it our best," I said, at the same time Bobby did. He gave me a faint smile and I returned it.

We split up, Bobby telling us all that he wanted us to rest that night before our game. Tina and I made our way toward my locker. We'd gotten in the habit of going to her house or mine to do homework before returning to school to practice, and I figured tonight we could just hang out.

I saw Candace at the end of the hall, closing her locker. She wasn't with anyone, and a feeling of affection washed over me. Why had I been so horrible? Of course George really liked her. I'd known it all along—it was obvious even back on Lasagna Night. But fear of losing Candace for good when she found someone who liked her had made me treat George terribly.

"Candace," I called. She glanced up from her book bag and started to lift her hand in a wave, then brought it down like she'd remembered she should be mad at me. I closed the distance and started to talk before she could walk away. "I'm so sorry," I said, leaping into the apology with the same quickness I'd dismissed George. "You were right about everything. I suck at reality. I never commit to anything, and I was acting like you shouldn't, either. But I think it's great that you found someone who makes you happy, and you went for it."

Candace was an easy crier, and she started to now. When she cried, her face contorted itself into a mask of agony. Once after we watched *The Way We Were* and she couldn't stop crying, she'd caught her face in the mirror and had spent the rest of the night practicing crying prettier in case she ever had to sob in public. She was making no attempt to pretty-cry now, and tears streamed down her face, leaving trails of black mascara across her splotchy cheeks.

"But you were right, too," Candace said. "I do ditch you for boys. I take you for granted. And you, too, Tina."

I turned to see Tina behind me. "Well, we can all do better," I said.

"I think we're doing pretty good lately," Tina said.

Squeezing Candace, I said, "And George is pretty nice, and his breath did get better, so good work."

Candace smiled. "Yeah, it was touch-and-go there for a while, but it's amazing how fast a guy will start using Listerine if you tell him it turns you on."

"If Garbage Breath George can have a minty mouth, maybe we can beat St. Mark's," I said.

Tina nudged me with her elbow. "That's gonna take a lot more than mouthwash, Suzie Q."

Thirty-Five

The morning of the game, I woke up with a crick in my neck. I'd spent part of the night on the phone with Candace, bending my neck to hold the receiver between my ear and my shoulder. Despite the pain, I felt lighter, now that we knew everything about each other again.

Mom had heard from the female hiring manager—she'd left for her regular job early today so that she could take a train into the city later for the interview. I'd heard her rushing around but couldn't force myself out of bed, where, in a half-sleep state, I was envisioning what I felt would be a win that evening.

I'd told her about the game, but I still wrote her a note to remind her, in case she forgot and came home from the interview and had time to get over to the field.

I packed my jersey and cleats and socks with solemnity, placing each item in my duffel bag carefully, like I was going off to war and the things I brought could mean a difference between life or death. In a way, they could. My entire life felt tied up in this game. Whereas before, I would have wanted to play well to prove something: to show my father that he'd been wrong to act like soccer was silly; to show Candace that I was good and make her regret quitting the team; to prove to all my classmates who made fun of the soccer team, as if we didn't deserve their respect or even acknowledgment, that we were worth their attention. All my visions of victory included their amazed expressions, their admiration or awe. And they all included Bobby, as if my playing well could make anything possible between us.

My new vision was of me and my team, dirt-covered and tired but victorious. I was happy to imagine the awed faces of a crowd, but I didn't care what that crowd thought. We were free from the judgment of an audience wondering if we should be playing soccer in the first place, if we were allowed, if it was good for us. It only mattered that *we* knew it was good.

I zipped my duffel and went downstairs to wait for Tina to pick me up. When I hopped into her passenger seat, double-checking my bag, Tina said, "I don't think I'm going to be able to think straight at school today."

"I know—I wish we could just play now," I said. "I feel ready, but also like I might puke."

"Yeah, it's sort of unreal," Tina said. "So you and Candace are okay now?"

I nodded, choosing my words carefully. Tina and I had become closer these last few weeks, and while it didn't mean she replaced Candace, it also didn't mean that I wanted her to feel like she was second best. "Yeah, I think we both let the fact that she has a boyfriend come between us."

"I get it," Tina said. "On your side and on her side, too. There's nothing wrong with being excited about a boyfriend."

We stopped as a little girl crossed the street near the elementary school, skipping like she didn't give a shit about anything. I envied her. "Yeah," I said. "I think one of the best parts of soccer has been that we don't talk about boyfriends. Or that it gives us more to talk about than *just* boyfriends. The world is a big place. It's going to be 1980!"

Tina laughed. "Well, that makes this next thing I'm gonna say kind of weird," she said.

"What?" I asked.

"Todd decided to ditch school for the game. He's coming down," Tina said. "And afterward, I'm going to introduce him to my parents."

"Wow, that's big," I said. "Are you nervous?"

"Right now, no," she said. "But I know when I do it, I'm going to want to piss myself."

I chucked her on the arm. "We can piss ourselves together."

"I appreciate the offer, but let's both try to hold it," she said. "I'm hoping that when we destroy those guys, maybe my mom asking Todd, 'Why don't you tell me more about yourself?' won't feel as scary."

The rest of the team was equally keyed up. Wendy said her dad had offered to buy her a car if she didn't play in the game. "I'm turning down a car for this," she said. "But my mom said he never keeps his promises anyway. And she told me I can get a perm if I play."

At lunch, Dana Miller ran up to our table and said, "We have a bus! We have a bus!"

"What?" Tina looked at her. "Slow down. What do you mean, a bus?"

Dana took a deep breath and let it slowly. "I overheard Assistant Principal Lawler tell someone there was a bus budget overage from a cross-country meet that got canceled, and I asked if she could reallocate it to us!"

George, who was sitting with Candace at our table today—he and Candace had decided to alternate whether they sat with us or his friends—held up his blessedly plain turkey sandwich in victory.

"Way to go!" George said to Dana. "You guys deserve it."

I smiled at George, even if I wanted to roll my eyes. Then I dropped my half-finished sloppy joe back onto my plate.

"I'm sorry," she said. "Is that stepping on your authority as captain?"

"No fucking way," I said. "We have a bus! Good work!" I stood up and hugged Dana, who looked more surprised by my hug than I had been to hear a sophomore use the word "reallocate."

"And we didn't have to wash any cars to get it!" Franchesa said, pumping her fist.

Candace stole one of George's fries and said, "We can't wait to see you guys."

"Maybe you can join back up next year?" Tina offered.

"I was thinking about badminton," Candace said. Then she whispered to Tina and me, "I need something that requires slightly less boob taping."

As the day went on, the rest of the team found out about the bus. Dawn in particular was really enthused by the development.

"Is it true we have a bus?" she asked me when our paths crossed after fifth period. When I said it was, she grinned. "There's going to be a scout from the college where my aunt works in Wisconsin," she said. "The bus makes the team look a lot more established."

"A scout?"

"Yeah, for a small college with a soccer team," she said. "I mean, it probably won't lead to anything, but if I can get any money for college, it would be huge. It's the only way I'm going to get out of here."

"Do you think they'll be watching all of us?" I said, thinking it couldn't hurt to get a scout interested in me early.

"I don't see how they couldn't," Dawn said. "So look alive."

I was pretty sure I could do that.

We gathered at the front of the school to meet our bus. Bobby did a head count, then said to all of us, "You look ready." He'd been somewhat short on his speeches lately, and we also hadn't needed them as much. But then he said, to all of us, "Whatever happens, this is your team. I got to witness it, but all of this was all of you."

I hated him the slightest iota less with each passing day.

Since the pep rally, people had been promising to come to the game, but I hadn't really believed many of them until we got off the bus at St. Mark's and saw the stands were full. Or at least full enough to fill the rows about halfway up. John and the cross-country guys were actually there, and so were some of the people who'd praised us in the hallway.

Candace had shown up with George, Duane Harris, and, improbably, Keith Barnes. George held up a homemade sign with a big foot on it that read "OUR GOAL? STOMP ON ST. MARK'S!" It was extremely corny and very George, but I couldn't help smiling.

My huge grin faded when my eyes landed on Polly and Dad in the front row. Dad pretended to be setting his watch, but Polly waved. As I passed, Polly leaned forward, exaggeratedly mouthing, *He's fine*. For all I knew, "he's fine" might only have meant that he was sitting in the stands at my soccer game and somehow not having an anger-based heart attack, not that he approved of what he was seeing, or of what he had seen at his wedding.

"Holy shit," Tina said. "I can't believe there are so many people. Now, whatever happens, people are going to *remember*." She waved at her parents then leaned closer to me. "Todd is sitting kitty corner from them. Oh my God, I hope he doesn't say anything during the game."

Todd had a sign that read "POWELL PARK . . . GO, FIGHT, WIN!" and he held it up and waved it side to side until Tina smiled at him.

On the other side, St. Mark's had its own crowd, mostly other boys from the school. Their signs weren't as friendly. "CHICKS SHOULD BE IN THE KITCHEN, NOT KICKIN" was about as clever as they got. I didn't see Joe, though. I'd half hoped he'd make a punk rock gesture and sit on our side of the bleachers, but he wasn't even on his school's side. At least if today sucked, he wouldn't see it, I tried to tell myself. But I knew that I wanted him to see the game, good or bad.

St. Mark's was warming up, making kicks that sounded like someone pounding bloody chunks of meat. Ken caught my eye across the field and flipped me off.

I was about to lift my finger to return the gesture when Bobby stepped in front of me. "You're better than that. Flip them off by winning." His jaw was stern and tight. I knew it was probably risky for him to let us play a boys' team in front of all these people, and I wondered what it could cost him to be as serious about this game as we were. I appreciated him for it, in spite of myself.

I dropped my arm to my side. "Should I lead warm-ups, or do you want to?"

"You can handle it." He looked past me toward the boys' side of the field, as if to catalog their abilities. He didn't say anything to indicate that the boys were far better than the Wisconsin team who'd beaten us, or that I'd made a mistake in getting us into this game. Both thoughts had crossed my mind, but I was still riding along on the wave of improbability that I'd gotten the rematch in the first place. I truly thought we had a chance.

With everyone watching, I called the team together, sensing my dad's eyes on me as the rest of the girls followed me onto the pitch. I started warm-ups, feeling like how well I guided the team through stretches, practice kicks, and jumping jacks would be what put me in my dad's good graces again. We jogged around the perimeter, but I could sense everyone was distracted.

As we gathered near our bench just before the game was to start, the ref called over Bobby and the St. Mark's coach—a tall, reedy man with a long face and skin so wind reddened, it matched his St. Mark's jacket. "Are we sure we want to do this?" the ref said, with a thick Chicago accent.

He clearly meant the whole game, not the coin flip.

The St. Mark's coach shrugged, as if the ref was asking him if he liked the weather we'd been having. "It's really up to him," he said. "I don't know if his team is ready for my boys."

"My team is ready," Bobby said calmly. "We're surprised you showed up in uniform this time," he added.

The other coach flinched. Bobby winked at us.

"Here goes nothing," I said.

"Or everything," Dana added.

"We might not win, but we won't have our asses handed to us," I said, hoping I was right.

When it was time for kickoff, we charged onto the field like we had nothing to fear.

"Let's fucking go," Wendy muttered under her breath as she strode onto the field and pulled on her goalie gloves.

We didn't crush them. We were entirely outmatched. I would have rather been handed my actual ass than endure the trouncing we got, starting from the ref's first whistle.

St. Mark's won the coin toss and got to start the game with the kickoff. When their forward stepped into the circle and made a kick that seemed almost aimed for Dawn, I think we all felt like our first goal was going to be easy. But as Dawn brought the ball toward the goal where Ken was stationed, St. Mark's largest defender zeroed in on her, ripping the ball away and almost toppling Dawn. He sent the ball hurtling in the direction of one of their forwards, who took control and easily wove through our defenders before he gave the ball a solid kick. It rocketed toward the goal and was headed right for Wendy's face. She lost her balance trying to deflect it, and was left sprawled on her butt less than one minute into the game. St. Mark's got the goal.

"They meant to do that," I huffed to Tina as we ran back to the middle of the field. Sarah kicked off and Franchesa at forward had it, glancing at me to signal that she was going to pass it. I moved into position, clocking Franchesa's progress as she evaded St. Mark's players. *Screw them*, I thought. They'd practiced for that humiliating goal, but we wouldn't let the rest be so easy.

But as Franchesa got closer, weaving expertly around her opponent, another defender approached on her opposite side and rammed her shoulder. Franchesa's foot rolled over the top of the ball, and she slid twelve feet across the field. A St. Mark's midfielder got possession, not even waiting to see if she stood up. In the stands, Franchesa's brothers were on their feet—their shoulders together formed one broad set—as if they intended to storm the field, but Franchesa, wobbling slightly, managed to stand.

"We have to get meaner," Marie huffed. "I want us to have the ball. Be ready." On their next possession, as a lanky forward moved closer to scoring position, Marie, Dawn, and Sarah made a *V* and closed in on him. The guy twisted his body toward the goal as if aiming for it, but then, with a swiping kick, sent the ball sideways toward another forward. Marie, who'd been closest to him, took a hit to her shoulder and flew backward to the ground, landing awkwardly on her wrist. Even from across the field, I could hear as she let out a high wheezing noise, and I knew she was hurt.

A few of us kept after the boys' team, but two others and I

circled Marie to see if she was okay. "You should take yourself out," I told her as she held her wrist tenderly.

She grimaced, flicked her head like she was trying to dodge an annoying fly. "Just a bruise," she said. "Let's get them."

But that's when the ref blew his whistle, calling a penalty on the play and awarding St. Mark's a free kick on our goal, claiming Marie charged the St. Mark's jerk. There'd been no penalty kick when Franchesa was sent flying.

"I should say something," I huffed.

"No, don't," Tina said. "At least we get a minute to breathe."

They didn't make a goal on the free kick, but they got possession quickly and scored right after it.

It went on like that, almost as if St. Mark's had planned to give us hope on each possession, only to take the hope away. Worse, they were playing pretty rough, and the ref wasn't calling them for anything, like he believed he'd shown us mercy at the coin toss and now wanted to make us beg to quit. I got a free kick when a St. Mark's defender openly pushed me right next to their goal. But that was more humiliating than anything else, because I had to look right into Ken's smug face as he blocked it.

It went on like that for the entire first half, which finally ended with a score of 17–0.

As we limped off the field to go to the locker room, our fans, if we could call them that, were silent in the bleachers. They pitied us, or maybe feared for our lives. Polly and Dad were the only people who looked directly at me, but I was so embarrassed, I turned away.

Thirty-Six

Bobby didn't say anything except to tell us we'd be going to the women's lounge at St. Mark's, where nuns took their breaks between classes. Since it was a boys' school, there was no girls' locker room, and the only reason we even had this space was that one of the nuns had insisted to Bobby that we be afforded the same hospitality as a boys' team. As we made our way into the school, I hoped that they had also prayed for us, even though I normally didn't buy into that kind of thing.

We followed a nun who introduced herself as Sister Anthony down the hall. She was as tall as the St. Mark's coach, with an equally long face, and I wondered if they were related. She wore a men's-style suit with her nun headpiece, so that from the back she looked like the Grim Reaper if he stuck around and changed for your funeral. The thoughts of death felt appropriate at that moment.

The hallways smelled like a mix of church and boy: incense and dust plus BO and fried food. Our feet squeaked against the clean linoleum.

I thought of things to say. Captain-y things. But if I pointed out the few good moves we'd made in the first half (and to call them good would be a stretch), it would sound hollow and phony.

Dawn punched one of the lockers as she passed it. "Fuck, we shouldn't be out there."

"Get some water," Dana urged her as they passed a fountain.

"I need hemlock, not water," Dawn snarled.

Sister Anthony opened a dark wood door and flipped on the light switch. We followed her into the lounge, a wood-paneled room with some old furniture and a noisy fridge running in one corner.

"There's some water," she said. "If anyone needs a bandage, there's a kit." She gestured to a first-aid box on the wall. Then she retreated to a corner of the room and fired up a cigarette. There were ashtrays stuffed with cigarette butts scattered everywhere. Nuns liked Marlboros, apparently. I suspected Sister Anthony was one of the nuns Joe liked.

We fell onto the couches and chairs, all of them overstuffed, comfortable traps. Maybe Sister Anthony just wanted us to fall asleep here.

Bobby stood at the center of us and walked the circle, peering at Marie's wrist, which she shielded with her other hand, and Franchesa's scuffed-up legs. He was silent amid our groans and sighs, as if trying to interpret what they meant.

"You've done a great job," he finally said. "You might not see it that way, but you've challenged every possession, and you've kept up with them every step of the way." He looked from girl to girl. "I don't know if I've ever seen a team work so hard on the field," he added. "You should be proud."

His remarks were the kind of thing I had debated saying, but if I'd said them, they wouldn't have been in past tense. I leaned forward in my seat, hanging on his every word, but not in the way I used to. It sounded like he was giving us a pep talk so that we'd be okay with bailing on the second half.

And I was right.

"I think you've really proven yourselves today, but there's no harm in letting this game go."

I almost jumped from my seat. "What is this? A funeral? We're not dead yet," I said, facing off with Bobby. I gestured to my teammates, who did, admittedly, look a touch dead.

Bobby's jaw clenched. "Susan, you might want to go back out there, but what about your team?" Looking right at me, and only me, he added, "There will be other games."

"I don't think we'll feel like we gave it our personal best if we quit now," I said, like I was explaining a simple concept to a stubborn child. I looked around the room to see if someone, anyone, was on my side.

Dana Miller was the first to speak, and I braced myself. But she just said, "Susan's right. We have to finish this game." She came and stood next to me.

"We can finish," Tina said, also rising. "It will be ugly, but we'll survive."

"Yeah, I don't want to give them the satisfaction," Marie said, and joined us. She didn't give any sense she was in pain, but I saw her touch her hurt wrist as if checking to make sure it was intact.

Slowly, the rest of the team got up and stood next to us.

Bobby's eyes were still on me, his expression fretful. He looked around the room, waiting for someone to take his side, but the only one left was Sister Anthony, whose face was now hidden behind a paperback mystery novel.

Maybe it was being surrounded by so much holy stuff, but realizing that Bobby not only had flaws but also fears was an epiphany. Then and there, I forgave him entirely for not being who I'd wanted him to be. He was my coach, and he could get things wrong.

When it was clear we wouldn't back down, I could almost see an idea form in his head as he nodded to himself. "Okay, your captain has spoken," he said. "You've all spoken. But I'm not sending you back out there without a path to victory. So here's the deal: We just need one goal. If you can score one goal, that's a win, as far as I'm concerned."

With the way the first half had gone, I didn't know if we could get even one goal, but he was right. A single point on Ken would feel more like the ending we needed than playing the entire rest of the game only to come up with nothing.

"That's fair. We accept," I said to him. I said it to the real him, the worried, unsure one, and I felt less worried and more sure than I ever had. "One goal."

I held my hand out flat, and waited while my teammates piled their hands on top of it. "On the count of three, Powell Park Pirates," I said.

Bobby added his hand to the pile, and I counted, smiling at him.

"Powell Park Pirates," we said in unison, and with that, half-time was over.

We made our way toward the door, if not restored, then at least united. We were still battered and bruised, but we were standing. "Think we can do it?" Wendy whispered to Dawn.

"Stranger things have happened," Dawn replied. "We're here, aren't we?"

Franchesa, Lisa, and Sarah made the sign of the cross as they passed by a painting of the Virgin Mary over the light switch. I was the last one out. In the corner, Sister Anthony looked at me over the top of her book and winked.

I winked back.

One goal.

Thirty-Seven

Our fans cheered for us as we returned to the field. They must have been expecting us to quit, too. Feeling freer than I had in a while, I offered a smile to Polly and Dad, who both smiled back. Dad's was a little faint, but there was approval in it. I would take what I could get.

By far the most satisfying thing was seeing the looks on the faces of the St. Mark's boys. Given how stunned they were, you'd have thought we'd already scored that goal.

We had the ball to start the half—but we didn't hang on to it long. St. Mark's racked up three more points without even seeming to try. On the last of those goals, Marie was knocked to the ground as she came shoulder to shoulder with their biggest midfielder. I helped her up and saw that her wrist was swollen and looked worse than before. "You can't keep playing like this," I told her.

"I don't want to fuck you guys over," she said, then winced and grabbed her wrist.

"You haven't at all," I said. "You need to take yourself out."

"I know," Marie said, almost crying. "Just get the goal, please."

"We will," I said under my breath as she made her way to the sidelines. The score was 21–0 and we were down to ten players on the field—with no defender as good as Marie. There were twenty minutes left. At the rate the boys were going, they were going to end up with forty goals.

"How are we going to do this, again?" Tina muttered, as we watched Sarah and Arlene try to keep up with the tall blond forward who passed the ball neatly to St. Mark's striker. Without Marie, Sarah and Arlene were even more outmatched. The striker lined up a perfect kick deep into the corner of the goal. Wendy sent her body parallel to the ground to grab it, but the low, fast shot sliced past her gloves.

"Kick off to me," I told Joanie on the next possession. I didn't know what I could do that would make any difference, but as Joanie's kick soared toward my head, I nailed it with my forehead—maybe because I wished Joe was there, or maybe just to show St. Mark's I could—and sent it flying across the field, near one of the St. Mark's defenders. It was a flub. I'd wanted to send it toward Dana, who was wide open. I sprinted after my wrongly placed header, reaching it as it dropped, and before the St. Mark's defender realized it, I'd hurtled the ball right to him. I chopped the ball with the outside of my foot and pushed it away from him, adrenaline coursing through me as I drove toward the scoring box.

Then a solid mass hit me in the back and I flew forward in the same direction as the ball, my chin skidding along the grass, my arms stretched in front of me, like I was body surfing across the pitch.

"Oh my God," I heard someone gasp, my face still pressed to the ground. A patch of grass was in my mouth. Hands turned me over and I blinked up into my mom's face. She was wearing her best suit, crouching in the grass over me. Her briefcase lay across the field like she'd abandoned it there.

"You came," I croaked, spitting out lawn.

She wiped a small tear from her eye and sucked in a breath as if to fight back more tears. "Of course I came," she said. "I had to see you play."

"Thanks, Mom," I said. "How did the interview go?"

"I got the job," she said, her hand still on my face.

"You wanted it so much," I said. I didn't want to get up; it was so nice to lie on the grass with my mom taking care of me.

Then the ref was hovering over my mom's shoulder.

"Ma'am, ma'am, I can't have you on the field," he said. "Is the player hurt?"

"The player is my daughter," Mom said, not taking her eyes off me. Bobby was on the field behind her and waved the ref off.

He crouched behind Mom. "Is she okay?"

She ran a hand along my chin and said, "She's okay." I nodded in weak affirmation of this. Everything hurt. But I was okay.

Mom helped me up, her heels sinking deeper into the grass as she ignored the ref's growing impatience. A cheer rose up from our stands, I guessed because I'd survived. Or maybe for Mom's surefootedness wearing three-inch pumps on the grass. She squeezed my arm. "I'm so proud of you," she said.

"I'm so proud of *you*," I said.

She nodded like she knew and pointed toward St. Mark's goal. "Now go get 'em."

Bobby gave me a quick look, as if to confirm I could still play, and when I nodded, he jogged ahead of Mom, retrieving her briefcase and handing it to her. She made her way to a seat near Dad and Polly. Polly clutched Dad's arm, but Dad was the one with the worried expression. His shoulders were up near his ears as he leaned toward the field.

Then Mom said something to Dad, and he looked at me and smiled. No, he beamed. He was proud, too.

So was I. My parents, all three of them, together like that sent a warmth through me that I was 85 percent sure was not internal bleeding.

As I limp-jogged down toward our goal to help bolster our defense against what was sure to be another St. Mark's goal, I let my eyes graze the bleachers, which had filled up even more. I saw Joe's little sister, Rachel, wearing a homemade shirt that, even from the field, I could see read "Wipe Out St. Skidmarks! (Someone Needs To!)" Next to her, Joe was wearing the same shirt. Of course he had come up with the best slogan. He caught my eye and grinned. I managed to smirk back at him, like seeing him was no big deal and hadn't made my heart drum "He's here, he's here" as if gearing up to lead a parade in Joe's honor.

With twelve minutes left to play, St. Mark's had already slaughtered us so badly that people in our stands were now cheering for us regardless of what was happening. Our improbable survival was as good as a victory. The St. Mark's fans continued to shout in support of their team, too, as if they wouldn't be satisfied until the boys had left our bodies on the field. To them, I guessed, it didn't matter if the matchup was unfair; they wanted us punished for even wanting to play in the first place.

We had the ball again, and Tina brought it down the field, looking at me so I'd know she was sending it my way. She drilled it toward me and I began to dribble toward Ken, who, in this second half, had assumed an almost casual position in the goal, like he didn't think us scoring was even a remote threat.

I was slowed down from my fall and, in my peripheral vision, saw two defenders coming up on me. Dana was open, and I flicked a somewhat weak pass around my defender that miraculously rolled to Dana's toes. She took it to the top of the box, and their defenders put their attention toward her. Dana pulled back for the kick. My stomach tightened as I neared her, hopeful. Please, let her get our goal, I thought.

But she froze. She caught my eye and looked—for the first time in her studious life—like she didn't have an answer. I stepped toward her and planted my left foot between the ball and the defender. "I'm sorry," Dana said.

"Don't be," I told her. I used the inside of my right foot to send the ball sideways over Dana's foot, like we were one person or I was doing a two-player chop. I almost wished I could have watched it from the stands, and I heard Joe yell, "Fuck yeah, champ!"

I feinted back behind Dana and cut between her and another defender, who fell backward, as I took the ball. I dodged another big guy and was inside the scoring box.

I was in front of the goal. Ken was crouched, arms out, and took a step toward me.

"Go ahead, try me," Ken said. "You'll wish you gave up already."

He wanted to scare me, but it wasn't going to work. My mind was racing, but it was what Joe had said that popped into my brain.

Find his weakness.

With my left foot planted next to the ball, I pulled back and hammered a direct kick. At Ken's balls.

Ken spewed out an involuntary and high-pitched keening sound as the ball hit him between his thighs with a loud *SLAP*. But it didn't go in the goal. Instead, it bounced off Ken's crotch and came sailing at my head. With Ken still bent over, I neatly headed the ball into the corner of the goal.

Into. The. Corner. Of. The. Goal.

Off my head. I shot a look at Joe; he and Rachel were jumping up and down wildly.

"Holy shit!" I screamed, forgetting we were playing in front of a crowd of parents at a Catholic school.

Behind me, my teammates had burst into frenzied cheers, and even though we still had seven minutes to play, everyone poured onto the field, surrounding me and screaming.

"You did it!" Tina said.

"We did it!" I said, hugging her.

"We won!" Joanie yelled.

"Did they just say they won?" I heard a St. Mark's defender ask one of their forwards.

"I think they did," the forward said.

Dana threw herself at me and I grabbed her under the shoulders and tried to lift her, even though she was much taller than me and it was virtually impossible.

"I'm sorry I froze out there," she said. "I can't believe you kicked it at his balls."

"It was a good play," I told her. "I mean, I think we could work on it a bit."

Bobby was making his way through the rest of our players, giving hugs and praise to each girl as he went. And then he was hugging me. We were at the center of the team and the world fell away and his arms were around me and he said, "I know amazing potential when I see it."

His arms were strong and his voice was low and meaningful and I couldn't hate him if I wanted to. I wouldn't have felt as good as I did at that moment if it hadn't been for him. If, back in September, I hadn't been as horny as I was and he hadn't been as hot, this team playing this game and having this moment right now would not exist.

I'd like to say that scoring that goal and the surge of pride and camaraderie it inspired had also elevated me to a new level of consciousness, one where desire to reach ever higher accomplishments and serve my team in new ways somehow usurped my desire to get off, or to imagine undressing Bobby. But in fact, in the crush of people, I thought how easy it would be to grab his butt, how satisfying it would be to feel it in my hands just this once. But I savored the daydream and then placed myself back in reality. Maybe his butt, like Bobby himself, was better to enjoy in my head.

"How do you feel?" Bobby asked me, holding me at arm's length.

Like I'm still thinking about how hot you are, I thought. *Like I'm so happy I got that goal, but I'm even happier I get to share it with the team, and Tina and Candace and Polly and my mom and dad. Like I plan to be horny and daydream a lot of the time but also like I want to commit to my real life more than my fantasy one. Like my mom was right, and hurt and disappointment are survivable, and risking them only makes winning feel fucking amazing—orgasmic, even. Like I wonder what Joe's doing later. Like I'm really grateful guys like you and him exist, if only to help cancel out some Kens.*

I didn't say any of that. Instead I smiled and said, "I'm thinking that I can't wait for next season."

Bobby beamed. "I was hoping you'd say that."

Thirty-Eight

Once the team finally calmed down, we realized that everyone in the stands and all of St. Mark's team were waiting on us, entirely befuddled by our celebration. The score was 24–1, and there was still time left on the clock.

But we'd made our decision at halftime, and once we had the goal, we walked off the field.

Most of us, anyway. Ken limped away from the goal, eyes shooting daggers at me. I smiled and shrugged, like "What can you do?" For once, he had nothing to say.

Mom, Polly, and Dad rushed from the bleachers to entrench me in a group hug, and it was Dad who spoke first. "Man, you're tough," he said. "That's my girl."

"I might cry," Polly said. "Watching you girls out there was the most amazing thing I've ever seen. Don't you think, Dierdre?"

Mom nodded. "I can't wait for the next game."

Someone tapped me on the shoulder and I turned to see Candace. "You were great," she said, hugging me.

"That was amazing," George said. "It was way better than any of our football games."

"Thanks for saying that, George," I said. I smiled gratefully at him, and Candace squeezed his arm and mine.

"Come Sunday for Lasagna Night, okay?" Candace said. "Tell Tina."

"Okay," I said. "Thanks for being here."

"I wouldn't miss it," Candace said.

My own family started to talk about dinner—Polly wanted to celebrate my goal and Mom's job. Dad said I should get to pick where we went after how hard I'd played, and they began again to recount highlights from the game. I let their talk about how great the team was and how great I was wash over me, and a few feet away, I saw Tina being hugged by her parents as, on the edge of her circle, Todd took a tentative step toward her. She stretched out her hand and took his. She peered at me over her shoulder and raised an eyebrow, as if to say, "I'm so nervous."

I gave her a thumbs-up. She was brave. I made the signal with my hand to indicate she should call me later and she nodded. I couldn't hear what anyone was saying, but from Tina's mom's open expression, I thought Tina and Todd were going to be okay.

Wendy's face was covered in dirt, but I could see her beaming as both her parents hugged her. Clearly, they at least agreed on how proud they were of her.

Dawn was talking to a man with a clipboard—the scout?— and she had the expression of a lottery winner who couldn't believe her luck. She pointed at me and mouthed, *You're next*, and my heart flipped.

Franchesa's brothers were carrying her on their shoulders and only put her down so that she could accept congratulations from a few of the girls on the badminton team, who'd shown up to watch. Lynn Bandis was tenderly examining Marie's wrist, as Len Tenley stood to one side, perhaps realizing that he was being ignored by both girls. Marie beamed at me.

"So what's it going to be, Susan?" my dad asked.

"Pizza?" I suggested, and saying the name of a food out loud made my stomach growl.

People were leaving the field in groups. Dana, who was talking to the cross-country captain, called to me, "Are you taking the bus back?"

I shook my head. "I think I'm going home with my family."

"Got it," she said. "See you on Monday. Captain."

Walking toward the chain-link gate that separated the field from the school grounds were Joe and his sister. "Can you give me one minute?" I asked my family. Not waiting for an answer, I jogged toward Joe.

"Hey." I tapped him on the shoulder. He and Rachel spun around.

"Susan, you were way cool out there," Rachel said. She was looking at me so worshipfully, I almost forgot why I'd come over.

"I love your shirt," I said to her.

"Thanks. Joe's idea," she said. "I'll wait in the car," she added with a knowing smirk. Joe handed her the keys, then turned to me.

"I didn't see you at first," I said.

Joe shrugged and glanced down at his feet almost like he was shy. Shy was not a quality I associated with him. "We wouldn't miss it," he said, and then, lifting his head so he looked right into my eyes. "And I heard you told off Ken in front of the whole team. About that . . . thing he did. Thanks for that."

I smiled. "It was no big deal," I said. "He deserved it." Where were my funny comments and replies? Had I sweated out the amusing portion of my personality? The blood was pumping in my veins harder than it had during the game. I'd always been at ease around Joe before, and I'd been putting off thinking about him—or him and me—until after this game was over. But now I knew something for sure. I really liked him. I wanted to see what could happen between us, even if I was a little scared.

"So, um, I wanted to ask you something," he said.

"Sure," I said.

I was not sure. I braced myself for a question about the night at the wedding. I thought I'd covered that when I went to his house. He grinned, though, and his mischievous smile put me at ease.

"Why did you go for the direct kick on Ken? Not that I didn't enjoy it."

I gave him a long, appreciative look. God, he was cute. Like, ridiculously cute to the point where I couldn't believe I hadn't filled my skull with thoughts of him from the first second I met him. "Someone really smart told me to go for a goalie's weak spot, and since he's a huge dick, I figured it was his balls."

Joe laughed, his grateful, unrestrained laugh. "Solid thinking, Pelé," he said. He cocked his head to the side and pointed to my shoulder. "You've got some dirt . . ." He lightly brushed a clump of grass off my jersey, and his touch warmed me like a torch that fired from my belly out.

"Thanks," I said.

"So if you're still up for a practice sometime, you can call me. Or whatever."

I wanted the whatever. I wanted to tell him I wished I'd done things differently, and that he never had to worry about Bobby. I wanted to ask him to play Skee-Ball and eat at Jr's and go to concerts in the city and talk about wild things and regular things. I wanted to know if he would ever forgive me. I wanted to know if I still had a chance.

Instead, I asked myself what I'd do if this was a daydream, or a fantasy, and I knew that I'd ask the one question that would get me all the answers I needed at once. Joe was looking at me with his head tilted and his eyes intent, like he was ready to be asked.

I grinned and met his eyes, and, focused entirely on him, said, "May I?"

His expression changed, as if trying to figure out what I meant. When his eyes lit up with recognition, I grabbed his shoulders and kissed him.

He wrapped his arms around my waist, and even though my jersey was sweaty and covered in dirt, he pulled me closer as the kiss went on and on. My daydreams, always at the edges of my mind, were entirely crowded out by this excellent new reality.

"So that's a yes on practice?" Joe said, pulling back ever so slightly and speaking the question into my ear.

It was November 16, 1979, but unlike the day Bobby McMann

showed up at school, there wasn't a single moment when everything changed all at once, that wave rolling over. And maybe there hadn't been one on that day, either.

"What do you think?" I grinned and kissed Joe again. My daydreaming hadn't been pointless. But fantasizing was like trying to play soccer without any goals—you were just running back and forth, putting nothing on the line. Taking the kick made things real, even if you missed. But when you made it, there was no better feeling.

Life was full of possibilities. I was full of amazing potential.

And for the time being, and thanks in part to Bobby McMann, I had achieved my personal best.

I couldn't wait for my next one.

Acknowledgments

I can say that this book is so much better because it's not just mine. Getting a book out into the world is a team sport, as if dozens of people are keeping a cantaloupe in the air while corunning a marathon and also applying liquid eyeliner to the cantaloupe. (Though this, honestly, would go better than all my attempts to apply liquid eyeliner to my eye.) So, now that we've gone the distance and our cantaloupe looks really seductive, here are the people I need to thank:

First, I'm so grateful to everyone at Balzer + Bray who, like Bobby, saw Susan's amazing potential. I especially need to thank Jordan Brown, who connected with Susan's voice right away, and whose thorough and thoughtful editing made me eager to dive back into this book each day. I owe a huge thanks also to Tiara Kittrell, who offered essential notes and suggestions throughout this process. Thank you in a big way to Alessandra Balzer, Donna Bray, and Suzanne Murphy, for taking a chance on this book, plus dozens of others I adore. Jenna Stempel-Lobell and Alison Donalty have been tireless in giving this book its delectable '70s design. Ebony LaDelle, Shannon Cox, and Sam Benson, thank you for the proverbial pep rally you've shown this book. Finally, I'm in awe of the fine-toothed comb Renée Cafiero ran over this text, and Mark Rifkin is likewise due thanks for his help in that arena. (For real, if not for Renée, this book would feature historically inaccurate high fives, which weren't an officially named gesture until a wee bit later in sports history. Look it up. It's nuts.)

I've had the pleasure of working with Alloy several times now, and at risk of sounding too earnest, you guys just get me. Josh Bank, our detailed conversations about what makes Bobby Bobby definitely belong in some kind of spiral notebook that we pass back and forth between classes and take great pains to protect from authority figures. Sara Shandler, I remember distinctly talking to you after you read early pages of this book and how much your calling me your favorite dirty writer buoyed me. I want the words "Sara Shandler's favorite dirty writer" on my tombstone.

And Viana Siniscalchi, where to start? Thank you for all the phone calls, emails, pep talks, and brilliant suggestions, not to mention assuring me I wasn't too bonkers and weird to exist when I most likely was. Also, that we traded stories of our own inappropriate crushes in working on this means we basically made a blood pact. Your secret is safe with me, forever.

Also, many modern-day high fives to the rest of the Alloy huddle: Joelle Hobeika (who's always been an awesome teammate), Romy Golan, and Matt Bloomgarden.

I also must thank Mary McCoy and Katie Schwartz for

reading and talking about this book with me in its early stages, and cheering me on.

And the perennial thank-you crew:

To my dad, Bill. I might be your baby girl, but I'm so glad you always treated me like the badass you know I am. Not to mention that you read early pages of this book and didn't flinch at the content but told me to pull no punches. I know a lot of daughters whose dads could never be so cool. I love you, Dad.

To my mom, Debra, who I wish was here to read this. She let me read whatever I wanted, which went a long way toward making me a writer, and, like Susan's mom, always offered me a sounding board to be frank, even if I didn't always take it. I wish I had more often. I miss you and love you so much.

To my sons, Nate and Clark, who I love beyond measure and imagination. Nate, your capacity for creating is an inspiration. Seeing you declare yourself an artist has made me more confident in declaring myself a writer. Clark, I'm so proud of you for countless reasons, which makes me feel that much more lucky when you say are proud of me. I'm not speaking solely as your mom when I say your thoughtfulness and heart astound me.

To my husband, Steve Stanis, who for some reason has believed in me from the get-go and somehow continues to have faith in me and my work even when he sees me at my worst moments. The life I'm so grateful for wouldn't be the same without you. You are my personal best.